GW01336250

RECKONING

BOOK THREE OF KIRA'S STORY

By Rebel Miller

Rebel
MILLER BOOKS

Copyright © 2017 by Monifa Miller

Rebel Miller Books

All rights reserved. No part of this publication may be reproduced, distributed, or transmitted in any form or by any means, including photocopying, recording, or other electronic or mechanical methods, without the prior written permission of the publisher, except in the case of brief quotations embodied in critical reviews and certain other noncommercial uses permitted by copyright law.

This is a work of fiction. Names, characters, businesses, places, events and incidents are either the products of the author's imagination or used in a fictitious manner. Any resemblance to actual persons, living or dead, or actual events is purely coincidental.

Editor: Stephanie Fysh

Cover design: Russell Morgan at www.goodsandcargo.com

For mature audiences

ROMANCE, SCIENCE-FICTION, NEW ADULT

ISBN 978-0-9947702-2-6 (EPUB)

ISBN 978-0-9947702-5-7 (PRINT)

To the inspiring readers and authors I've met along the way

Thank You!

Thank you for reading Reckoning, the final book in Kira's trilogy. Look out for details at the end of this book about my upcoming releases and to connect with me on [Facebook,](Facebook) Twitter and Instagram - I'd love to hear from you!

Sincerely, Rebel

Books by Rebel Miller

The Realm Series — Kira's Trilogy

Awakening

Promising

Reckoning

The Realm

Locations of Significance

Prospect Eight (P8)

Helios — site of rebel activity and where Kira was taken after abduction

Merit — Kira's hometown and where the P8 Judiciary is located

Argon Four (A4)

Virtue — city where Liandra Ambassador's residence is located

Dignitas One (D1)

Capita — center of Realm governance and law and location of Gannon's primary residence

Hale Three (H3)

Tork — town where Gannon's father, Marcus Consul, was killed

Septima Two (S2)

Arc station — where the Corona and Kira were nearly killed in a rebel attack

Part I

CHAPTER 1

It's just all getting to be too fucking much.

I slumped down on the edge of my bed then choked out a laugh. Gods, who was I kidding? My life had become *too fucking much* a long time ago.

I shoved my fingers into my hair and stared down at the leather trim of my skirt. I must have been a glutton for punishment, or maybe it was for abject fear, because only the gods knew why I had decided to go to the Judiciary. I had dressed over an hour earlier with every intention of heading to work that day, determined not to let Gabriel and Maxim's threats affect me, but just before I stepped out of my bedroom, a wave of anxiety had washed over. Maybe going into work was a poorly thought-out idea.

No doubt, Tai would wholeheartedly agree.

Dropping my hands to my lap, I frowned at the memory of my heated argument with Tai.

After throwing down the gauntlet about my unresolved feelings for Gannon and shortly after Rhoan had arrived, he had exited my apartment. Considering how angry Tai had been, the last thing I had expected was a message from him later that night.

Stay home until we come up with a plan.

I had stared at the glowing text on my bedroom monitor, worrying my bottom lip with the edge of my teeth. Tai was right. The best thing was for me to stay home, to avoid being accosted by Maxim, Gabriel or one of their thugs again, but I couldn't help it — my thoughts went immediately to the Judiciary and the responsibilities waiting for me there.

I inched closer to the monitor and tapped out my response on the screen.

I have to go to the Judiciary.

His reply was quick:

STAY. HOME.

My shoulders fell at Tai's uncompromising, yet expected, response.

Tai had once said I never listened to him. Any pushback now would only prove that, but then, wasn't *he* the one who had always been so adamant about me not drawing attention to myself? After the role I had played supporting the special committee on exploration, it would be nothing short of suspicious for me to have simply fallen off the edge of the Realm.

Justification intact, I replied:

There's still so much to do. People will wonder where I am. It just wouldn't be like me.

A full minute passed during which I almost gave in. Finally, he responded.

Avoid your usual path and regular schedule.

Even in written words, Tai's disapproval had been clear.

All Above, that seemed like *months* ago, not just two *days!*

I started at a sharp knock on my bedroom door, looked toward the sound then sighed. Why Rhoan even bothered to knock escaped me. I dragged myself to my feet and approached the door. My brother had a code for all the doors in our apartment. If he wanted to interrogate me *yet again* about my whereabouts before the weekend, all he needed to do was disengage the lock.

Gannon and Tai had been adamant that I not tell anyone about what had happened to me, that I let them come up with a plan to locate and capture Maxim and Gabriel. They understandably believed they had enough resources at their disposal to handle the two dissidents without further incriminating my family in rebel activity. So when my brother had returned home, frantic from searching the streets of Merit for me, Tai had proven why as a protector he had earned the great respect of his peers. Without missing a beat, he had informed Rhoan that I had been in a minor accident, one that had damaged both my comm and tablet beyond repair. Unhurt, I had apparently gone to visit my best friend, Sela, and since I was without my devices, had been inaccessible to anyone's calls and messages. Tai had been so convincing, even *I* had almost believed him.

Rhoan, on the other hand, didn't buy a word of it.

Tai was persuasive, but Rhoan had known me for all twenty-one years of my life. This was the same man who had figured out that our parents were in a multiple relationship *long* before I had even considered a career at the Judiciary. So, in the end, the result of Tai's well-delivered fabrication was relentless rounds of questioning by my brother.

After a fortifying breath, I disengaged the door and opened it. Not finding Rhoan, I followed the sound of the monitor into our sitting area, where my brother now stood, dressed for work, watching the floor-to-ceiling screen. The volume on the device was low, but from the images of the Corona — the Realm's sovereign leader — and other members of Realm Council, I guessed Rhoan was watching a newsfeed reporting on the upcoming meeting to review the special committee's recommendation.

I must have made a sound because Rhoan said over his shoulder, eyes focused on the screen, "A package came for you."

My eyebrows rose. I had expected an inquisition, not a *delivery*. I stepped farther into the room, glancing about. A sleek black box sat in the middle of the couch. I went to it then recoiled. Who had sent me a package? Anyone who would want to deliver something to me would have given me notice. Wouldn't they?

My hands started to shake. *My gods, is this it?*

I had not heard from Gabriel or Maxim since they had threatened to reveal the truth about my family's dissident activities. I had wondered how and when they would contact me for the high-level information they had demanded. Perhaps this package was how.

"Who —" I cleared my throat. It had suddenly become parched. "Who's it from?"

"There isn't a name on it," Rhoan mumbled, eyes still focused on the monitor. "But if the words 'Official Parcel of the Realm Protectorate' plastered on the underside are any indication, it's probably from Tai."

Thank gods.

I blew out a breath at the same time my brother turned to face me. He must have caught my reaction, because his eyes narrowed, a suspicion I had been victim to over the last two days clear in his light green eyes.

I smiled tightly and picked up the package, ignoring my brother's intent observation. Perhaps I could make it back to my room before he started in on me again.

"So …" Rhoan began, calling out behind me, "tell me again what happened the other night?"

Shit. I cringed, turning to face him with the box cradled in my arms. "I told you what happened," I said, shoulders stiff.

Rhoan crossed his arms and pinned me with a glare. "Actually, *Tai* told me what happened," he said. "I haven't heard *you* explain anything yet."

Irritation frayed my already ragged nerves. "Where in the worlds did you *think* I was, Rhoan?"

His eyebrows raised. "To be honest," he said, "I thought you may have lost your mind and run off with our soon-to-be high chancellor."

I frowned, arms tightening around the box until its sides folded in. "I told you," I said. "That's over."

Rhoan considered me quietly, disbelief in his eyes. I lifted my chin, refusing to allow him to see just how much it hurt for me to say that Gannon and I were no longer involved. Finally, my brother thinned his lips and turned to collect his jacket from the back of one of our armchairs.

"I saw this report earlier," he muttered, shrugging into his coat and jutting his chin toward the monitor. "This Liandra Ambassador's something else, huh?"

Liandra? I stepped closer to the screen, beside my brother, holding the box to my chest. Though her petite build was gaunt and the red of her hair dull, Liandra's presence managed to fill the screen. *Why in the worlds are they reporting on her?*

Liandra Ambassador was someone who should be begging to be listened to — not receiving airtime on any of the Realm's communications streams. In addition to having been charged with engaging in exploration, an activity banned by Realm Council, Liandra and her late father had been accused of coordinating an attack on Septima, one that had almost killed the Corona and *had* killed many others.

All Above. Had they discovered that she and Maxim had been involved prior to Argon's expulsion? Had they learned that *she* was his motivation to destroy the Realm?

I glanced up at Rhoan. "I thought she was in holding, on Dignitas," I prompted him, hoping he had answers to my unspoken questions.

"She is," he said, studying Liandra's image on the monitor. "Apparently, she sent a video message to the Corona, calling the sovereign a hypocrite who's unfit to rule and warning of further unrest if she doesn't accept Argon back into the Realm."

My eyes widened at Liandra's audacity. She was challenging our sovereign leader in the most public and combative of ways. But truly, I couldn't blame her. I would be just as fierce in my demands if I were in her position. The Corona had condemned Argon for an act that the Realm had been secretly been carrying out for years! But something didn't make sense. If Liandra was in holding, she shouldn't have been permitted to communicate with anyone, much less be able to broadcast her anger across the Realm via newsfeed.

"How did her message get out to the public?" I asked.

"That's what everyone's been trying to figure out," Rhoan mumbled.

A clip of Liandra's video looped onscreen. Rhoan turned up the volume, but in truth he didn't have to. Every part of Liandra's body conveyed her contempt, her body bristling as she spoke. In a strident voice that belied her fragile appearance, she vented her frustration with the system, condemned the Corona for her decision and demanded exemption for her and the citizens of Argon.

Eyes glittering, Liandra ended her message by citing the Realm's motto, "Strength, Resolve, Adherence." Since leadership considered Liandra and her late father to be the exact *opposite* of the virtues our system upheld, one could only take her reference to them as a diplomatic version of "fuck you."

Rhoan chuckled under his breath. "Good for her," he said.

I swung my gaze to him, struck by the odd note in his voice. While Rhoan was no fan of leadership, even *he* must understand Liandra's approach as reckless and futile. As far as I could tell, our sovereign leader was not one to be threatened into action.

Rhoan's eyes skimmed Liandra's image one last time before suddenly focusing on me. He cleared his throat and stepped away from the screen. "I'll be at Beth's tonight," he said, turning on his heel and walking to the apartment door.

Relief hit me like a wave. I could use the time without him hovering over me to get my thoughts in line. "You've been spending a lot of time with her," I said, trailing behind him, eager to help him out the door.

He snorted. "To hear Beth tell it," he muttered, "I've been ignoring her."

I smiled at that. Rhoan's past girlfriends tended to want to be the sole focus of his attention, and Beth, it seemed, was no different.

Suddenly, Rhoan stopped and turned to me. An unexpected look of unease flickered across his face.

My smile fell as I tightened my hold on the box. "What?"

He shot a glance somewhere off to my side before coming back to me. "Look, I've been thinking," he began. "I've known Tai for a long time. He's done a lot for our family. The truth is he's a good guy." My brother rolled back his shoulders and nodded decisively. "So, I approve."

I blinked. "Approve of *what* exactly?"

He made a face, appearing pained. "Of you and …" He scowled, but pressed on with what looked like an incredible amount of effort. "Of you and *him*."

I stared at my brother, jaw slack. Rhoan and Tai had been on rocky terms since Rhoan had learned about Tai's feelings for me. Even though the two had seemed to be mending fences over the last few weeks, Rhoan's out-of-the-blue endorsement of his on again, off again best friend still came as a complete surprise … and a confirmation of my brother's supreme obnoxiousness.

May the gods help Beth. My brother is so bloody full of himself sometimes.

I rolled my eyes. "Thank you for your approval," I muttered before stalking away, targeting my room. "Now *all* is right in my worlds."

"Hey, it took a lot for me to say that," he called out. The indignation was so clear in his voice, it stopped me in my tracks.

"Yes. I know," I said, turning and resting the box at my hip. "A few of your hairs actually went *gray* as you said it."

Rhoan frowned, joining me by the door to my bedroom. "Tai's not a person who shows a lot of emotion, but when he couldn't find you the other night, the man was out of his mind," he said. "I haven't seen anyone that frantic since Ma, Da and Khelan found out you were on the arc craft the rebels attacked on Septima."

I lost my starch. *Really?* When I had returned home after Maxim and Gabriel's abduction, Tai had been there, waiting for me in my apartment. He had certainly appeared worried, but *frantic?* I tried to remember, but I had to be honest with myself: I had been too focused on one goal to fully notice his concern. The first thing I had wanted to do was contact Gannon to let him know I was all right. In hindsight, I supposed *that* could have waited the few moments it would have taken me to tell Tai what had happened to me.

My gods, no wonder he was so angry with me.

Rhoan leaned against the doorframe with a sigh, studying me. "I don't know why Tai's willing to cover for where you were the other night, but I know that whatever the reason, it's probably a good one," he said, shrugging one shoulder. "He wouldn't do anything to hurt you. What more could I want for you than someone like that?"

Words failed me. I didn't know what would come of my relationship with Tai, if I could actually call what was between the two of us a *relationship*, but knowing that my brother had gotten over his contempt for Tai and would accept him if I did lifted my mood considerably for the first time in days.

I smiled and leaned into my brother for a quick embrace. "Thank you," I whispered, emotion making my voice shake. "You don't know how much that means to me."

He returned the hug then added as we pulled away, "The truth is you could do a *whole* lot worse."

And just like that my brother turned into an asshole all over again.

I scowled, which only resulted in Rhoan bestowing me with one of his annoying smirks. With a wink, he sauntered off and out the front door, leaving me blessedly alone in the apartment.

Thank gods.

The contents of the box jostled when I sat down on my bed. I slid a finger under the lid, breaking the tight seal and peered inside. My lips parted as I took in the most sophisticated technology I had ever seen.

A comm, tablet and ... I picked up a small plastic packet that rested on top of the two gleaming devices.

What in the worlds is this?

Inside the clear pouch was a simple silver chain link bracelet that glinted in the morning light coming through my windows. I raised a brow. Tai was many things, but the type of man who gave a woman jewelry after an argument he was not. Plus, *he* was the one angry with *me* — not the other way around. He had no reason to send me an olive branch.

Frowning, I returned the packet to the box and ran my fingers over the glossy screen of the tablet before taking it out. The device was so light, I almost lost hold of it, expecting more weight. When I held it up, the light from the window filtered through it. I gasped: the device was entirely transparent. A smile growing on my lips, I searched for the button that would make it flexible enough for me to roll it up, into the portable scroll-like form that other tablets could assume. When I found a clear tab, I pressed it and marveled at how the device went from hard as a board to slack in the blink of an eye.

After a moment more of inspection, I tucked the scroll back into the box and quickly picked up the comm, eager to inspect it too. Rather than being black plastic and metal parts like the one I used to wear, the device was entirely transparent like the tablet. Tiny, almost nonexistent clasps fastened the see-through straps of the comm to its screen. Suddenly, a soft amber hue bloomed across the device's screen and a familiar call code displayed.

Tai.

I searched the device for some way to activate it. Finally, I tapped the side like I would have my old comm.

"Good." Tai's deep voice filled the room. "You got the delivery."

I looked over the contents of the box. "I did. Thank you, but why?" I said. "I could have gotten new devices on my own."

"The ones I sent you are Protectorate-grade," he said. "The newest and most secure models."

Of course they are. Tai would have considered nothing less.

"I understand the comm and tablet," I said, my sight landing on the small clear packet. "But why the bracelet?"

It took a second before he replied. "It's not a bracelet," he said. "It's a tracking device."

I must have heard wrong. "W-what? Why?"

"Maxim destroyed your communications devices," he said. "This way I'll have some way of locating you if something happens to you again."

A chill ran up my spine as I glanced at what no longer looked like an innocent piece of jewelry. I hadn't seriously considered that Maxim would attempt to abduct me again. Why would he? He was smart enough to know that now that I was on alert, he no longer had the benefit of surprise.

"Even if Maxim or one of his thugs don't try to abduct you," Tai continued as though reading my thoughts, "someone has to contact you at some point to tell you what files they want and when they want to retrieve them."

I closed my eyelids shut at his logic. *Damn it. I didn't think of that.*

"The comm's highly secure," he pressed on, "so we'll be able to speak freely when using it. There's an activation code for the tablet somewhere inside the box. I've already activated the bracelet."

I opened my eyelids and stared down at the tracking device. "All right," I said. "I'll enter the code and put the bracelet on right after our call."

He grunted his approval. "I managed to gather some information about Gabriel and Maxim," he said. "We'll need to meet to go over it all."

I perked up. "Does that mean you and Gannon have come up with a plan?"

He hesitated. "I think so," he said. "But I need to look into another lead my contact in Helios shared with me. I'll contact you when we're ready to meet."

I exhaled a deep breath, relieved. Maybe this ordeal would be over soon.

I sat there, staring at my shiny new comm, wondering what to say next. Usually when Tai called we spoke somewhat freely, ending up more often than not in a heated argument, but this time around he was as quiet as he was cool. My heart squeezed as I came to realize what he was doing. He was building a wall between us, in his usual self-defensive way.

Gods, I hate this.

"Tai," I began, wrapping my fingers around the comm, holding it tight. "About the other night with Gannon. I —"

"I believe we have more important things to discuss," he said. "Don't you?"

I paused, cheeks burning at the way he cut me off. I wanted to talk things through, smooth the awkwardness between us, but he was right: we needed to deal with Gabriel and Maxim before getting into this. And truthfully, what was I going to say? That I didn't know what to do about my feelings for Gannon? Tai had already *told* me what to do. He had told me that I needed to make a decision. And who could blame him? My mess of conflicting emotions would have tested the most patient of men. In fact, they had! Tai had been nothing but understanding as I tried to get passed my feelings for Gannon and get him out of both my heart and life.

My shoulders slumped. But *had* I tried to get Gannon out of my life? Truly?

On a number of occasions, I had found myself back in Gannon's arms. Hallowed Halls, after barely noticing Tai's concern for me after my abduction, I had taken back Gannon's promise ring, right in front of him! Tai should have written me off at that point. But he hadn't. Even while filled with frustration and anger, he had still found the motivation to help my family and me.

I exhaled deeply, overcome by the tide of emotion that had been building inside me over the last few days, weeks, *months*.

"Thank you," I said in a quiet voice, tears stinging the backs of my eyes.

Tai released a heavy, almost beleaguered sigh. "For what, Kira?"

"For setting aside your differences with Gannon to help us — *me*." I released a sad laugh. "Once again."

His reply was long in coming. So long, I began to fear our connection had been lost.

"Protecting you is just common ground," he said finally in a clipped voice. "Don't make too much of it." Then the amber color on the comm faded, the screen going clear as he ended our call.

* * *

"So, were you abducted by aliens or something?"

I startled, knocking over the framed photo of my family that sat on my desk. I righted the picture with an unsteady hand and glanced up just as Asher strode into my office, a tablet under his arm and a broad grin etched onto his face.

"I beg your pardon?"

"Just before the weekend," he explained before falling into the stainless steel chair on the other side of my desk. He hooked an ankle over a knee. "You were supposed to meet up with me and a few of your fellow Prospect Eight Judiciary subordinates at Drunk Dominion."

Shit. I had forgotten about that.

I searched my mind for an excuse. Telling Asher the true reason for missing the after-work gathering would only embroil him in my problems. I didn't want that.

"I'm sorry," I said, shaking my head. "I don't know what to say. It slipped my mind."

Asher shrugged. "No worries," he said, unrolling his tablet on his lap. "You were missed at Drunk, though. Everyone wanted the lowdown after the special committee's approval of the recommendation."

I cocked my head in question. "They could have asked *you*." Asher was at the meeting too, after all.

He leveled me with a look, snorting. "They wanted to hear it from *the* one and only Kira Metallurgist." When I stared at him, baffled, he added, "*You're* the one all over the newsfeed."

My stomach hollowed out. *Oh right. That.*

He grinned, oblivious to my distress. "You should be heading to Mila right now demanding she erect a building with your name on it based on the Realm Anarchist's articles *alone*," he stated with a glimmer of awe in his eyes.

I stole a look at my monitor. I had been perusing one of said articles just a few minutes before receiving Asher had arrived. The one currently displayed on my screen had the headline "Kira Metallurgist: The Voice of the Subordinate Caste."

I stifled a groan. Whoever this *Realm Anarchist* was, he was having a field day drumming up a fervor since my remarks at the last special committee meeting. Like with most of his articles, he had published an accompanying poll, which showed I had heavy support from my caste. Actually, "heavy support" was an understatement. Based on the results, should I decide to petition for the right for subordinates to paint all Judiciary buildings across the Realm a spectacularly horrific shade of orange, I would have a few million citizens standing blindly by my side.

That kind of support was the last thing I needed. These overblown articles would do *nothing* to dispel Gabriel's belief that I had become a citizen of some influence, a person with access to whatever confidential information he and Maxim needed.

With a sigh I tapped at the screen, switching it from the newsfeed to the Judiciary's dashboard.

"Holy shit," Asher said. "Does that thing beam you into another dimension?"

I followed his line of sight to my wrist, where my new comm's smooth surface reflected the bright lights of my office.

I smiled and gestured for him to give me his wrist. "I wouldn't be surprised if it did just that," I muttered, tapping my comm against his own to transfer my new contact information.

It occurred to me then that I needed to share my new call code with my family and friends. On top of everything going on in my life, my best friend, Sela, was due to deliver her first child very soon. Her impending delivery was the one shining light in the middle of all my personal turmoil. I wouldn't want to miss her call when she went into labor. Bearing that in mind, I made a mental note to send a message to her, my parents, my brother and a few other contacts before the end of the day.

Asher leaned back in his chair. "So, why didn't you show up?" he asked.

I blinked. "Where?"

He laughed. "At Drunk," he said, and I caught up. "I sent you a couple messages but didn't get a response."

Damn it. Were we still on that line of conversation?

I winced and dropped my gaze to my desk, searching for an excuse. I hated to lie to Asher. He had become more than a colleague to me. He had proven to be a friend I could entrust with any secret. In addition to knowing about my relationship with Gannon, he also knew about the Realm's secret history in exploration and had kept it all close to his chest, never telling anyone. Asher was someone I could confide in, but this was one thing I couldn't share with him. The repercussions of him knowing about Gabriel's and Maxim's connections to me were just too dangerous for him.

Asher's chair creaked, and I looked up to find him leaning toward me, a knowing look in his eyes.

"Ah, *that's* why you ducked out," he said, eyebrows rising above the rims of his glasses. He then lowered his voice despite the privacy of our surroundings. "I thought we agreed that wallowing in misery alone over things not working out between you and the chancellor wasn't an option."

I blinked, recalling when he tried to coax me into joining him and my colleagues at Drunk Dominion. Asher had made an incorrect assumption that now conveniently provided me with an excuse.

I wrestled with my guilt and said, "Something like that."

He sent me a look of empathy that made me glance away. My eye caught on a notification that must have just appeared on my monitor. I tapped at the screen, opening the message from Mila.

> **P8 Date Stamp: 07.21.2558**
> **P8 Time Stamp: 10h 20m 36s**
>
> **Kira,**
>
> **I'll be on Prospect Eight tomorrow. I need to speak with you first thing.**

M.

Office of Mila Minister of Prospect Seven (Interim Minister of Prospect Eight)
Origin: P7(3): Solaris

My superior's message was to the point, just like her, so the brevity of it didn't take me aback. It was her urgency that made me pause.

"Let me guess," Asher said, drawing my attention. "Mila?"

I nodded. "She wants — rather, *needs* — to meet with me."

He grinned. "Hey, maybe you're gonna get your building after all," Asher quipped, and swiped through his tablet.

I snorted. A building in my honor was *definitely* not in my future. She must want to discuss Realm Council's review of the special committee's recommendation ... but then why wouldn't she ask Asher to meet with her too? *Both* of us had worked on the project.

I tapped at the message again, closing it, and the screen faded to black. It relit a second later with the Judiciary dashboard. Color-coded messages from citizens from various branches across the Realm rolled up the screen. Normally I would have eagerly tapped away at each one, sifting through them, making notes and planning tasks for the day. In stark contrast, since I had arrived at work that morning, the number of messages had been steadily racking up, beckoning me to open them with little success.

Asher continued reading his tablet. Meanwhile, I frowned at the screen. I had to get it together. Despite having some vengeful elite and his sidekick senator on my trail, I needed to *focus*. I had been appointed to the position of director mere *weeks* ago. On top of everything that was on the line, I couldn't lose my rank too!

Mentally, I ran through my conversation with Tai. He had said that he and supposedly Gannon too had learned a lot about Gabriel and Maxim. Tai was a highly regarded protector, for the gods' sake, and Gannon soon to be the high chancellor of the Realm. If the two of them couldn't come up with a plan to stop Gabriel and Maxim, then no one would. And the truth was there was nothing I could do until the three of us met. In the meantime, I couldn't — *wouldn't* — let those two assholes bully me into a corner, making me cower and wonder what they would do next.

Decision made, I drew my chair up closer to my desk and opened another message on the screen. The most productive use of my time would be to prepare for whatever Mila planned to throw my way at our meeting tomorrow morning.

Asher popped up from his seat. "I see some wind has caught your sail," he said, rolling up his device.

I glanced up, and he sent me a wink. It dawned on me then that he had stopped by my office simply to find out how I was. I smiled. "Thank you for checking in on me."

Asher grinned. "No problem," he said with a shrug. "I just wanted to be sure you hadn't fallen victim to some sort of foul play over the last few days."

My smile slipped. "O-of course not," I said. "It was just a case of a broken heart."

He frowned, a wealth of compassion returning to his face. "Hey, don't worry about that, all right?" he said soothingly. "I have a feeling it'll all work out."

* * *

I made it. Thank gods.

I leaned back against the front door of my apartment and released a tight chestful of air. My journey home had taken me more than an hour that evening, but it couldn't be helped. I had agreed to stay off my usual path and schedule, and so I had. I had no intention of reneging on my promise to Tai. I was lucky enough as it was that he hadn't put me under house arrest.

I hung my jacket in the closet by the front door and wandered into my bedroom just as Gannon's name flashed across my monitor, accompanied by its cheerful jingle. Without a moment's hesitation, I voice-activated his call.

The dimness of my room lifted as the monitor filled with a view into Gannon's office, the wall of glass lining one side of the room clearly visible.

"So, you went to the Judiciary," Gannon said from somewhere off-screen before his tall uniform-clad figure stepped into view. My heart fluttered foolishly as his light blue eyes roved over whatever he could see of me.

I frowned at his question — no, *statement*. Then it occurred to me: Gannon, like Tai, probably would have preferred it if I continued to stay at home, hiding in my apartment for days on end. Well, I had the same news for him that I had for Tai.

"I refuse to let Gabriel and Maxim intimidate me," I said, bracing myself for his argumentative response. "I have work to do at the Judiciary, and I won't let them stop me from doing it."

Gannon arched a brow. "I wouldn't have expected anything else," he said. "I just wish I had known your plans so I could have made arrangements for you sooner."

My eyebrows rose as I lowered myself onto the edge of my bed. "*Arrangements?*"

He nodded and crossed his arms. "I've assigned Jonah to protect you until further notice."

My eyes widened. "What?" A tracking device *and* a protector? Hallowed Halls! By the time Gannon and Tai were done with me, I would have more protection than the Corona herself! "Why?"

He cocked his head, eyeing me as though I had lost hold on reality. "I understand your desire to make a stand in the face of adversity," he drawled, "but I'm not going to allow you travel the Realm *unprotected* while two self-professed renegades threaten your life."

My gods. "They won't *kill* me," I said. They had threatened to reveal the truth about my family's dissident activities, not take me out. That wouldn't make sense. "They need me for information."

"Gabriel and Maxim are both laws unto themselves," Gannon said with a deep scowl. "Who knows what they'll do next?"

I took in his mutinous expression, a look now very familiar to me. Gannon was determined and absolute in all ways, so I shouldn't have been surprised to see those traits emerge once again when it came to my welfare. He had become fixated on protecting me after his father was killed in the rebel attack on Hale Three. I should have anticipated that Gabriel and Maxim's threats would only ramp up his determination to keep me safe. I truly didn't want to fight him on this, but the vision of his straitlaced protector standing vigilant in my surroundings, everywhere I went, put me on edge.

"How am I supposed to explain Jonah's presence to my friends and family?" I asked.

Gannon gave me a mulish look. "Jonah's been trained to work under the radar," he said. "You'll hardly know he's there."

That wasn't the problem. I had no doubt Jonah would be textbook, the perfect protector, when it came to guarding me. Surely, only an ordinance by the gods themselves would stop him from carrying out Gannon's order to keep me alive. I just struggled with the idea of having so many people — well meaning or not — monitoring me like some sort of felon when *Gabriel and Maxim* were the rebels, not *me*.

I shook my head. "Isn't the bracelet enough?"

Gannon drew back. "*Bracelet?*"

I frowned at the surprise in his voice. "Tai sent me a new comm and tablet, as well as this tracking device." I held up my wrist to show him the deceptively innocent piece of jewelry. "I thought you knew."

Gannon lifted his chin. "Tai may have mentioned it," he murmured, eyes narrowing. "It's not a bad idea, but I'd prefer preventing anything from happening to you in the *first* place rather than have to track you down *after* something did."

I expelled a heavy breath. Once again, sound logic was outweighing my right to privacy and independence.

I relented. "All right."

"Good," he said then glanced behind him, through the glass wall. A mature man in a Senate uniform — Arthur, I thought his name was —nodded to him before walking away.

"Do you have to go?" I asked.

Gannon turned to me. "Soon, but I need to tell you something first." He paused, studying me. "The Corona asked to meet me this morning. Realm Council will be reviewing the special committee's recommendation at their meeting next week."

I drew back, stunned. *Next week?* I had expected it to take a few weeks, if not months, before leadership considered the recommendation.

"Why so soon?" I asked.

"As usual, our sovereign is focused on keeping things moving despite the factions running rampant throughout our system," he said. "She sees it as a show of defiance, the Realm's unwillingness to acquiesce."

Yes, that sounded just like her. The Corona hadn't even wanted to slow down after the rebel attack had nearly killed her on Septima Two *or* the one that had led to the death of Gannon's father on Hale Three. It was hard to imagine her backing down now.

"I see."

He inhaled deeply, the corners of his mouth turning down. "I've asked the Corona to appoint me as high chancellor at that meeting," he said. "I'd rather avoid the pomp and ceremony of this appointment and keep this whole thing low-key."

I read the grim lines that grooved his eyes. Of course he wouldn't want to make a big show of his appointment. *No one* would want to celebrate a position that had only become available as a result of a father's death. My heart squeezed.

"I'll be there to see your appointment then," I said with a smile, hoping the fact would lift his mood the way it was doing my own. As support to the special committee, Rhoan and I would be in attendance at the Realm Council meeting, and I looked forward to it now even more.

A small smile softened his face as he stepped closer to the screen. "That's not all," he said, holding my gaze. "Discussing my appointment wasn't the only reason she summoned me. The Corona filled me in on her plans to make the subordinate representative position on Realm Council permanent."

I sat up straight with a gasp. The Corona had told me about the position the last time she had met with me, but I hadn't expected her to speak with Gannon about it. By doing so, she was pretty much confirming the role.

"Do you still question her motives?" I asked. Gannon's reaction after I had told him about the Corona's plans was dubious at best.

He snorted. "As always," he replied. "But now that I've heard a bit more about what she has in mind … I don't think it's such a bad idea."

I frowned at his about-face and waited for him to continue with an explanation, but he simply studied me, with an expression of deep contemplation.

How odd, I thought. It wasn't Gannon's style to be so vague. "So, what did she have to say about the position?" I asked to prompt him. "What would this person be expected to do exactly?"

He considered that. "Among many other things," he said, "act as a liaison between the Subordinate and upper castes. The idea is for this person to not only voice the opinions of subordinates but influence policy too."

I smiled. Rhoan would be pleased. He had been the subordinate representative on the special committee who had influenced their decision to recommend lifting the ban on exploration to Realm Council.

"I can't wait to tell my brother," I said, imagining how shocked Rhoan would be. He had started out thinking he would only be a token on the special committee, that no one would take him seriously, but now he would see that he had been wrong. He had made a lasting impression on leadership, one that led to the establishment of a permanent position on Realm Council!

Gannon hesitated. "I wouldn't tell your brother yet," he said, and I frowned.

"Why not?"

He hesitated then said, "You know how fickle the Corona can be. Wait until she makes the announcement about the position."

I didn't like the idea, but it made sense. During my various interactions with our sovereign I had learned she moved in mysterious ways. Bearing that in mind, I really shouldn't get Rhoan's hopes up without having the position announced by the Corona herself.

"You're right," I said, slumping. "Plus, we have more urgent things to focus on now anyway." Gabriel and Maxim loomed, ever present, in the background of my thoughts.

Gannon stepped toward the screen, and so closer to me. "We're going to stop them," he vowed, not needing or wanting to call the names of who he was referring to. "I won't let them hurt you and take away everything you've worked hard for. Do you understand?"

I nodded, compelled to by the determination in his voice.

"After that," he began with the same conviction, "you and I will be together."

I stilled, heart flipping over by surprise and a sudden surge of longing. "We *can't* be together," I said. "You know that!"

Gannon looked me over, eyes narrowing. "And yet you took back my ring."

And there it was, the unavoidable truth.

I forced myself not to react even as the challenging look in his gaze threatened to gut me.

What Gannon and I had was over. I had been the one to leave him because the risks of us being together were too high. Not only were we from different castes, but he was about to become *high chancellor*. If anyone found out about his relationship with me, a subordinate who had ties to rebels, his future would be ruined. I couldn't have allowed that, so here we were: apart, but not quite.

I pressed my lips together. The resentment of the restrictions between our castes that I had buried somewhere deep inside came to the surface, nearly suffocating me. Nevertheless, I needed to draw the lines between Gannon and me again, no matter how blurred they had become.

"You caught me off-guard," I tried with an unsteady lift of my chin. "I didn't have a choice."

A flicker of something close to disappointment shadowed his eyes, making their blue appear almost gray. "You had a choice, Kira," he stated. "You've *always* had a choice."

I swallowed around my guilt then said, "And my choice is Tai," I said, reminding him of the white lie I had told him to keep him at bay.

"So you've said," he replied with a mocking shake of his head.

I clenched my fists, frustration making me grind my teeth. Didn't he understand that the stakes were too high for both of us? "What do you want from me, Gannon?"

"I want you to face the inevitable," he replied promptly, bracing his hands in front of the monitor, on the table or desk on which his monitor must have been resting.

I searched his face, trying to keep it together, wondering when he would understand. "We were never *inevitable*," I said on a shaky breath. "We were in *denial*."

He drew back, the color of his eyes darkening to a shade I had never before seen. "I suppose only time will tell then," he said evenly. "Won't it."

CHAPTER 2

Under the radar, my ass.

I stepped under the awning that swept across my apartment building's entryway the following morning and eyed the protector Gannon had saddled me with. It would have been difficult to miss the man. Jonah stood stern-faced by the curb, in front of a hover that glistened in the light morning rain. Gannon's eye-catching vehicle would have been enough to draw anyone's attention on its own, but Jonah's stoic and uncompromising stance just made it worse.

I sighed as a passerby shot an anxious look at Jonah then hurried away. It didn't make sense bemoaning his presence now. I had agreed to have Jonah watch over me, and so he would. With a shake of my head, I pulled the hood of my light wool jacket up over my hair and strode over to him.

Jonah tapped a small panel on the side of the hover. "Subordinate Metallurgist," he said, greeting me as the vehicle's door slid open.

I gave him a tight smile in response and ducked my head as I slipped into the vehicle. As Jonah made his way around to the driver's seat, I imagined what was going through his head. He was probably checking off the multitude of more important things he could be doing, none of which involved chauffeuring me — the woman who, in his mind, was probably nothing more than his superior's latest fling.

I frowned, slumping back against my seat. No, *latest fling* wasn't fair to Gannon or me. It was too flighty a term. We had meant much more to each other than that. I just didn't want to think too hard on that fact.

My comm vibrated just as Jonah started to navigate the hover up and away from my apartment building. I checked it to find a message from Ma.

Can you come by the house tonight?

I frowned, wondering at the urgency. *Tonight?* Had she heard from Uncle Paol? My family and I hadn't heard from my uncle since he had run off to exact revenge for the death of his wife, my aunt Marah, leaving his daughter, Adria, in our care. Perhaps the reason for Ma's sudden need to see me was to share news regarding his whereabouts.

Should I bring Rhoan?

I imagined her laughing when she replied:

Oh no — there's no need for a family meeting! I just found a few gifts for Sela hidden away in my closet. I want you to give them to her.

I scrunched my nose. Sela's baby welcoming had been *weeks* ago. Why would Ma still have gifts for her? Though now that I thought about it, Ma had been in her element leading up to the event, buying up gifts as though the forthcoming child were my own. I supposed it would have been more confounding if Ma *didn't* still have packages stashed somewhere in our family home.

I shook my head and responded.

All right. I'll pick them up on my way home from work.

Of course, that was, if my *bodyguard* approved of such an excursion. I sighed and peered out the window.

The early signs of squall season were visible in the darkening sky and in the growing puddles on the streets of Merit. The hour was early, but the stormy weather made it look much later in the day. Usually, this was my favorite time of year, because it signaled a coming change, a fresh and renewed landscape, encouraging Prospect citizens to endure the harshness of the season just a little while more. But now, looking out the window and struggling not to succumb to the troubles hanging over my head, I had a hard time summoning any appreciation for the promise in the shifting climate.

Gradually, the Judiciary's building came into view, and Jonah navigated the hover toward it. The moment we landed I reached for the door, eager to allow the protector to be off and on his way. I frowned when Jonah exited the vehicle at the same time I did and came around to stand by my door. I stepped onto the curb and squinted up at him against the rain.

"Is anything wrong?" I asked.

"I'll be waiting in the lobby until you're ready to leave," he said, gesturing toward the bustling entrance to the Judiciary.

I balked. Gannon hadn't said *anything* about Jonah staying with me! "I don't think that'll be necessary," I said. "I'll be in the Judiciary, a *government building*, all day." Surveillance cameras and high-level security abounded.

"Those were my orders," Jonah said simply then gestured to my comm. I held up my wrist and he tapped my device with his own. My comm glimmered with its amber hue as it stored his contact information. "You should message or call me if you need anything or need to leave the building."

Well, then. It seemed I had no say in the matter. After giving Jonah a weak smile, I joined the stream of people entering the Judiciary.

"Kira!"

I stopped and turned to find a tall young man waving at me from across the marble-tiled lobby. His red hair was damp from rain and stuck up in every direction around the crown of his head.

I groaned. Heath Manipulator-of-Truth Reporter was the last person I wanted to speak to, but it seemed I didn't have a choice. He made his way over to me, weaving through the crowd with his familiar shuffle.

When Rhoan had introduced me to Beth weeks ago, she had told me that her brother Heath was on his way up, just like me. It had been a compliment at the time, but now, having been the focus of Heath's journalistic attentions, I would have rather been likened to a snake in the grass than him.

"Do you have a minute?" he asked with a wide smile.

I thinned my lips. "Actually, I don't." I turned to head for the bank of elevators then added, "I have a meeting with my superior."

He followed me, keeping up with my pace. "I promise," he said. "This won't take long."

I stopped and pushed the hood off my head before leveling him with a look. "I'm not doing any more interviews with you, Heath." After the way he had misquoted me, I wouldn't be doing him any favors again.

His dark blue eyes went wide. "You've made that very clear." He held up his hands as though fending me off. "It's just that my articles covering the special committee meetings went over so well that my superior assigned me to cover Realm Council's review of your recommendation."

"You mean the *special committee's* recommendation."

"One and the same." He grinned. "If Realm Council approves it, then I'm supposed to write a story on how exploration will be implemented across the system. My superior says after this, I could gain rank!"

I sniffed, hiking the strap of my bag up higher on my shoulder. "I'm glad having such a casual relationship with the truth has been working out for you."

His face fell. "I'm going about this all wrong," he said. "I owe you an apology."

Well, this was a surprise! Ever since Heath's fabricated story had nearly gotten me in trouble with Mila, he had shown no remorse for his actions. In fact, he had seemed downright smug about the whole thing, as though he had been doing me good. I crossed my arms, waiting to see where this led.

Heath shoved his hands in his pockets. "I should have apologized long ago about the story I wrote about you," he said with a frown. "Please. Accept my apology now."

I *had* to give it to him: he appeared sincere. Then again, his apology seemed fueled more by his ambition than any sense of moral integrity.

I stifled a groan. I didn't have time for this. I had a meeting to get to! "What do you want, Heath?"

He swept back a chunk of damp hair from his forehead. "Well," he began, his expression hopeful, "having you quoted in my articles … that would be a *really* big boost."

I stared at him. He must have been hard of hearing. He could wrap it up anyway he wanted to — interview or quote. I had no intention of helping him out the way I had in the past. I made a beeline for an elevator that had just opened up.

"Wait!" Heath stepped in front of me, blocking my path. "I promise it won't take up too much of your time. I would just need to meet with you every now and then."

I looked him over, taking in his remorseful expression, and cringed. *Maybe I'm being too harsh.* It wasn't as though any of his actions had resulted in my demotion or affected my role on the special committee. And Heath *was* Beth's brother. It would do no good to Rhoan to have his sister on the outs with his girlfriend's sibling.

I poked him in his spindly arm. "Just tell the truth, Heath," I warned. "That way, you and I shouldn't have any more problems."

His eyes lit up. "Will do," he vowed. "I promise. You won't regret this!"

I pursed my lips, watching as he hurried off. I'd better not regret it. I had more urgent matters to attend to, which reminded me ... *Where in the worlds is Jonah?*

I searched the lobby, hunting for the protector when my line of sight fell on a heavy-built man in a dark, thick coat with his head bowed.

My pulse lurched, body seizing up as it went on high alert. My eyes widened as he strode toward me with purpose. A moment later, a middle-aged subordinate woman rushed up beside him laughing. As they passed me by, the man I had mistaken for one of Maxim's thugs wrapped an arm around her shoulders with an open and friendly smile.

I exhaled a ragged breath at the same moment Jonah stepped in front of me.

"What happened?"

I started at his brusque tone.

"N-nothing." I swallowed, placing a palm to my chest and kneading the knot of fear away that had lodged there. Unfortunately, I couldn't help the slight shake in my hands. "I'm fine."

Jonah appeared doubtful and turned to scan the expanse of the lobby. It dawned on me that though I hadn't known where the protector had been, he had been focused on me the entire time.

Jonah faced me, jaw firm, a few moments later. "I'll accompany you to your floor," he said, dipping his head to another elevator that had become available. "Let's go."

As I followed him inside, I sent him an apologetic smile, cursing myself for my paranoia. Maybe having Jonah nearby wasn't such a bad idea after all.

Reckoning

* * *

"Everything used to be so much fucking simpler before Argon's expulsion," Mila muttered, glaring at her screen. The scent of *hurim* tea greeted me where I stood, waiting, just inside Mila's office door.

"Should I come back at another time?" I asked as Erik, the Judiciary's recently hired receptionist, rushed in with a small potted plant in hand. He set the bright orange miniature shrub on her desk then hurried out as quickly as he had come in.

Mila's scowl contorted the smooth lines of her face. "No," she said, still glowering at her monitor. "This is one meeting I can't defer. Sit down."

With a nod, I did as commanded before unrolling my tablet onto my lap. When my gaze landed on the plant on her desk. I smiled, recognizing it as a *Gallah* plant, a common housewarming gift. Hope filled me.

Mila had come to Prospect Eight only to fill in the position of minister until an election was held. While some people at the Judiciary would describe her as combative and crude, I preferred "headstrong" and "plainspoken." But no matter what anyone thought of Mila, everyone had great respect for her and, like them, I would be sad to see her go.

"Are you planning to stay on Prospect Eight, after all?" I asked, hoping she'd say yes.

Mila sent me with a look that would level most protectors. "Despite the efforts of everyone in this Judiciary to make this office my home," she drawled, gesturing to the plant, "no. I don't plan to make your world my permanent residence."

I digested that with a frown. I would have enjoyed a longer time supporting her.

Mila braced a hand against the edge of her desk and sat back. "I want to speak with you about something that came out of my meeting with the Corona yesterday," she said. "Realm Council will be reviewing it at a meeting next week."

Huh. Apparently, our sovereign had been making the rounds over the last few days. Gannon had been right: the Corona was focused on keeping things moving. Well, so was I.

I sat up. "Is there anything I can help you with?"

"As a matter of fact, there is," Mila said promptly, as though she'd been waiting for that very question.

I gripped my tablet, eager to hear what she had to say.

"You brought up something interesting at the last special committee meeting," she said, brown eyes boring into my own. "You said that someone from the Judiciary's Office of Exploration should advise Realm Council on how to properly implement exploration across our system."

She didn't need me to, but I nodded in response, encouraging her to continue.

Mila folded her arms on the desk. "By the time Realm Council approves our recommendation, I'd like to have that advisor in place, ready to start, right out the gate."

I sensed where this was going. "You want me to pull together a briefing package with all the relevant laws for the advisor," I stated.

She nodded. "I figure you may as well since I'm appointing you to the role."

I froze. "To the role of what?"

She gave me an indulgent smile. "Advisor to Realm Council."

My eyes widened. *What?* "M-me?" I choked out. *What about Rhoan?* In addition to being the sub rep on the special committee, my brother was a regional councillor who had *years* of experience on me. "Wouldn't Rhoan be better suited for a role like this?"

Mila shrugged and picked up her tea. "I considered your brother," she said, glancing into the mug. "But Rhoan's superior wants him back working on a number of other projects that have been neglected because of his involvement in the special committee process. Plus the advisor will need to interact often with reporters. From what I remember, the media seemed to rub Rhoan the wrong way."

That didn't sit well with me. Yes, Rhoan hadn't taken well to being the subject of rabid media, but the role of advisor would be one he would want. Wouldn't it? He had worked hard on this project, just as hard as me.

Mila sighed, looking me over. "If it makes you feel any better," she said, "I'm going to ask Rhoan's superior to allow your brother to attend Realm Council's meeting next week. He deserves to be there when they review the recommendation he worked on. But after that, his time on this project is done."

I expelled a heavy breath. Mila had clearly made up her mind. A wave of anxiety rolled over me as I realized the significance of the role she was offering me. I would have to have been a *fool* to pass on something like this.

The wheels of my brain started to spin. "All right," I said slowly. "To prepare, I'll need to consult with citizens in the Office of Enforcement of Fair Practice." They would be able to help me advise on the laws that would form a basis for exploration.

Mila grinned. "I couldn't agree more," she replied, sitting back and placing her mug on the table with a clunk. "Which is why I asked Erik to arrange for a group of directors to meet with you the day after Realm Council meeting."

I stared at her, dumbfounded. It seemed my agreement to the position had been a given in Mila's mind.

"They're all very accomplished," she continued, "but wet enough behind the ears that they'll be eager about this whole process."

Wet behind the ears? I balked. *I* was wet behind the ears!

"Don't worry," she said, no doubt reading my expression. "You won't be alone. I plan on sitting in on most of your meetings."

Well, *that* did nothing but ratchet up my anxiety even more. The notion of managing a group of senior subordinates on my *own* was nerve-racking enough as it was. The fact that I would have to do it under the watch of my *superior* only filled me up with dread. Dear gods, I'd be lucky if I didn't succumb to another one of my panic attacks before the end of the anxiety-inducing process!

"So, this is how it's going to go," Mila said, adjusting the lapels of her Senate jacket. "We're going to haul our asses to Dignitas for Realm Council's review of our recommendation, then return to Prospect to start getting you prepared for your new role." She studied me. "I believe this is going to be good experience for you."

I nodded, rolling up my tablet with unsteady hands. "Thank you, Mila."

Her expression became grave as her eyes narrowed. "Kira," she said, leaning forward, "you *do* realize that as advisor you'll be reporting *directly* to Gannon Consul, don't you?"

I forced myself not to flinch. "Y-yes," I said, even though I hadn't actually processed that yet. "I do."

She raised a brow. "Will that be a problem?"

I hesitated, wondering why she thought it could be. I had suspected some time ago that Mila knew about my relationship with Gannon, but she had never spoken to me about it, at least not directly. The furthest she had gone in mentioning it was to give me a word of caution after witnessing a tense interaction between Gannon, Tai and me. Regardless, no matter what she assumed about my personal life, I would challenge her or anyone else to find fault in my work. I had always given the Judiciary my best.

I lifted my chin. "Of course not," I said, pleased at the confident tone of my voice.

Mila studied me. "You've been working on some very important projects here at the Judiciary," she said. "People are starting to take notice. I wouldn't want anything to come between you and your success."

Where was this coming from? And what was she getting at? Then it dawned on me. *Damn the Realm Anarchist and his overblown articles!*

"I know the media has a fixation on me," I said, clutching my tablet tight, "but I can assure you, Mila, it *won't* be a problem."

"It's not just the media who've taken notice," she said. "Leadership as well."

That stopped me short. *They have?*

She tilted her head. "I want to help you succeed, Kira," she continued, "but I have to know what you want."

I slumped, confused. What *did* I want? It should have been an easy question to answer, but I had never actually been asked that question, much less considered it.

I had always dreamed of working in the Prospect Eight Judiciary, but my motivation had been based primarily on the desire to follow in Khelan's footsteps. Now, months after I had first stepped foot into the building, it was safe to say that the Judiciary had become more than just a place where I worked. It was a place where I had become more than I'd thought myself to be, where I made a difference in some way.

That was it!

I met Mila's gaze with a smile. "I want to uphold the law, to advance my dominion, our *entire* system."

"Why?"

My smile slipped. "Because … it's the right thing to do." Wasn't that obvious?

Mila thinned her lips. "That's not good enough," she said, easing back into her chair. "At some point, you're going to have to come up with a better motivation. I think you're going to need it."

* * *

And *why*, pray tell, are you surprised?

I frowned at Asher's message, baffled that he didn't share my dismay. Shifting into a better position on the couch in the sitting area at my parents' home, I entered my reply:

I only *suggested* that Realm Council *appoint* an advisor. Who would have thought Mila would give the role to *me?!*

Asher's reply was quick:

Only *everyone* at the Judiciary.

And a second later, he added:

And I mean EVERYONE.

I rolled my eyes. He was exaggerating. Yes, I had been working on the project since the very start, but I could think of at least a dozen other people from across the Realm, in *addition* to Rhoan, who could have been considered for the position ahead of me.

Guess it's a good thing you haven't changed your caste name yet …

I smiled. Asher knew as well as I did that citizens didn't change surnames for appointments to temporary positions.

Do you need any help?

I laughed out loud at Asher's absurdity. He had been a great support to me throughout the special committee process. I wasn't about to let him go.

If you think I plan on doing this without you, you've lost your mind!

Asher must have been laughing as he replied:

As always, I'm at your service.

I grinned, breathing a little easier as I responded.

> **Better be. Meet me in my office tomorrow afternoon.**

Footsteps scuffled the floor on the other side of the room, making me glance up. I found Da walking into the sitting area.

"When was the last time you had a panic attack?" he asked.

I blinked, his out-of-the-blue question briefly fogging my mind. "A few months ago, I think. Why?"

He sat down in an armchair to my left, in front of the fireplace, with a twinkle in his green eyes. "Maybe you outgrew them."

I scoffed. "I don't think that's possible."

He shrugged, his grin reminding me of my brother's. "Well, you grew *into* them," he said. "I don't see why you couldn't grow *out* of them too."

I chuckled at his logic. It was *so* like him. He always had a simple response to the most complex of life's problems.

When I had told Jonah that I needed to stop by my parents' home after work, I had expected him to argue against it, but the protector had surprised me by simply asking me for the directions. He had said he would take me anywhere I wanted to, so as long it was safe. Less than thirty minutes later, Jonah had delivered me to the front step of my parents' house before disappearing just like he had done at the Judiciary…, which meant that he was probably waiting on me, at the ready, somewhere close by.

"That's quite the comm," Da said, glancing down at my wrist. He leaned forward and took my hand, flipping it over to see the underside of my shiny new device. I smiled. He was a metalworker by trade — it wasn't a surprise that he was attracted to the comm's sleek design.

He raised his gaze to mine. "Impressive." He sat back, running a hand along his jaw. "I've never seen anything quite like it. Where did you get it?"

"Tai gave it to me," I said. There was no point in hiding the fact. It was the *reason* Tai had given to me that I had to keep under wraps.

Da's brows climbed his forehead. "So your Ma was right," he said. "Things *are* going on between you and Tai."

Oh no. Not this again.

I had assumed Khelan had corrected Ma's belief that Tai and I were romantically involved, but it seemed there was no convincing her otherwise. I frowned. If only I could have convinced Gannon of my relationship with Tai as easily I had inadvertently convinced Ma!

I glanced away, uncomfortable with the direction of our conversation. I needed to change the subject, and quick.

I had arrived at my parents' home expecting to find Ma with an armload of gifts for Sela only to hear from Da that she and Khelan had taken my cousin out on an errand. I had assumed they would be making only a quick trip since Ma was expecting me, but I had been there for over two hours with no word of her returning soon. I had used the time while I waited to tell Da about my new position, anxious to hear what he thought Rhoan would say about me being given the role instead of him, but my anxiety had been for nothing. Da had simply said, "I wouldn't be worried about Rhoan. I have a feeling your brother is meant for less ... *diplomatic* paths."

Shadows had started shifting on the walls an hour ago. It really was getting late. I imagined Jonah was outside, itching to be on our way and get me home safe and sound, but I didn't want to leave without seeing my cousin. I hadn't seen little Adria since after Ma told her that her mother had passed away. I couldn't imagine how abandoned the child must be feeling. She needed to have as much family as she could close by. The thought that her father was out there somewhere, conspiring with rebels instead of consoling his daughter, irritated me to no end.

I frowned. "Have you heard from Uncle Paol?" I asked, but I probably could have guessed the answer. If my uncle had contacted my parents, one of them would have already told Rhoan and me about it.

Da grimaced and ran his hands down his thighs, pushing himself to his feet. "Unfortunately, no," he said, walking to the window, where he pulled back the curtain to look outside. He too was probably wondering what was keeping Ma and Khelan so long.

I shook my head. "I just don't understand."

Da glanced at me over his shoulder. "What?"

"Uncle Paol," I explained. "How can he just ... *abandon* his daughter, not making any attempt to contact her or at the least find out how she is?"

Da released the drapery and it fell back in place. "Leaving her with us is the only way to keep Addy safe."

That was a poor excuse. "I'm sure Aunt Marah would have preferred him to be *with* his child," I said. "Not out there somewhere, seeking vengeance for her death."

Da ran a hand through his brown hair, ruffling the gray strands that glinted around his temples. He walked back to the chair and sat down heavily. "Love makes people do very unusual things."

I had nothing to say to that. Well, what *could* I have said? I had pined away for one man for years and was now willing to risk my reputation for another — all in the name of love. My own parents had put a lot on the line for that very emotion.

After telling me that I was Khelan's biological daughter, my parents had explained how they had come to be in a multiple relationship. It had been a heartrending tale. While multiples were commonplace in the Realm, they weren't widely accepted in Septima, Ma's native dominion, or by her family. For that reason and the fact that Khelan had given up his status as a senator so he could be with Ma — a citizen from a lower restricted caste — my parents had hidden the truth about their relationship from everyone, including Rhoan and me. They didn't want us to suffer any negative consequences should their secret come out.

I studied Da, wondering for the first time about his feelings about all of this. Whereas Khelan was hot-tempered and opinionated, Da was much more even-keeled. It made me wonder how he had managed Khelan all this time. Considering their very different personalities, it must have been frustrating at times for him to be in a multiple like the one he had found himself in.

"Do you ever resent him?" I asked, taken aback like Da seemed to be, by my own abrupt question.

"Who?"

I shifted on the couch and lowered my feet to the floor. "Khelan."

He drew back. "Why in the *worlds* would you ask such a thing?"

I shrugged, playing with a button on the sleeve of my dress. "Because you told me once that things had been tense between you and Khelan when he first became part of your relationship with Ma." My parents had admitted me that very thing after telling me who my birth father was.

Da's brows knitted. "Well, we do well enough now."

I searched his face. "But you and Khelan have such different personalities," I pressed. "I just don't understand how you make it work."

He sniffed. "It's really quite simple," he said. "We make it *work* because we love your mother."

"That's it?" That was all it took? Love?

He studied me. "Why are you looking for some lingering animosity between Khelan and me?"

I blinked. "I-I'm not," I said, wondering why I had opened my mouth, what I was trying to get at. I shook my head. "Never mind. I'm sorry." I fell back against the chair.

Da considered me for a long moment then sighed. "I should be the one apologizing," he said. "The three of us all lied to you about who Khelan was to you your entire life. Of *course* you have questions."

My eyes widened at that. This was the first time *any* of my parents had called their deception exactly what it had been — a lie.

Da leaned forward, resting his elbows on his knees. "There's something I've wanted to get off my chest for a while," he said, looking at me with an earnest gaze. "Do you remember when we all went to Realm Exhibition for the first time?"

I drew back. How could I not? Though it had happened five years ago, I would never forget the eye-opening experience. "Khelan took Rhoan and me on an arc trip to Argon Four."

"That's right." Da nodded with a shadow of a smile. "For you, it was adventure, but for Khelan, well, it was a chance to share a part of him that he hadn't been able to."

I smiled, recalling how Khelan had been almost as excited as me.

"It meant the worlds to him to be able to show you where he came from," Da said. "But after that trip, Khelan wasn't himself. He was filled with a lot of anger. For a long while, he kept himself apart from your mother."

I stared at him, frozen by surprise. This was news to me. I had been over the moon for *weeks* after that trip, thrilled by everything I had seen. I had simply assumed Khelan had been the same.

"Why was he angry?" Had Khelan resented *Ma* instead of *Da*?

Da shook his head, lips thinned. "He was angry because of the system and its leadership's restrictions on our castes," he said. "He was angry because he had to choose between the life he had on Argon and his love for your mother, you and Rhoan. I've given up being the only one your mother loves, but Khelan's given up his entire life to be a father to you." His eyes became somber with meaning. "I accept Khelan, *get along* with him, because of how much he loves his family and how much he makes you happy."

I looked at him with watery eyes, speechless.

He reached over to take my hand, his own gaze glistening. "I want you to know how sorry I am for everything," he said. "For lying to you, for hurting you. You have to understand we only wanted to protect you."

I nodded, swallowing. "I do," I said, and in that moment, I *did* understand. It hurt me to admit it but, all things considered, my parents loved me. They had truly done the best they could have to keep our family together.

When I sniffled, Da came over to join me on the couch. He wrapped an arm around my shoulders and hugged me firmly into his side. For a few moments, we sat together, leaning against each other, failing to hold back our tears.

Da's body shook. I drew back, stricken that he had become so overcome, only to find him laughing.

"Why did your mother ask you to stop by?" he asked.

I blinked. "She said she wanted to give me some gifts for Sela she found around the house."

Da chuckled, shaking his head. "She already delivered those packages to Lilian — just this morning, as a matter of fact."

That didn't make sense. Why would Ma have asked me to come by if she had already given the gifts to Sela's mother?

He smiled down at me, giving my arm a tight squeeze. "Your mother's been telling me to stop moping around, worrying about my relationship with you. She's been telling me to just talk things out with you, but I couldn't bring myself to do it," he said. "I was too nervous about how to get everything all out."

Wait a minute. "She *planned* this?"

"I believe so," he said with a grin. "Your mother can be very crafty when she has a goal in mind."

No kidding. She had used reverse psychology on me in the past to encourage a relationship between Tai and me. I shook my head at her latest cunning maneuver.

"So …" Da said, giving me a sheepish grin. "How'd I do?"

My heart squeezed at the insecure note to his voice. "Let's just say," I said with a smile, "I think Ma will be very pleased."

CHAPTER 3

The following day, Asher and I walked out of the Judiciary boardroom and into the busy work area.

"Did you know Mila was almost in the Protectorate?"

I stumbled, nearly tripping over my two feet at Asher's question. I stopped then pivoted to face him, hand at my hip. "I beg your pardon?"

His brown eyes sparkled. "I thought that would get your attention."

What was he talking about? "Mila's a *senator*," I spelled out unnecessarily. "She can't enlist in the Protectorate, and why would she?" Becoming a protector would mean a demotion in her rank.

He grinned and leaned in. "I didn't say she *enlisted*," he said in a conspiratorial voice. "She just enrolled in the training program."

I frowned. "To what end?"

Asher stepped passed me and bumped my shoulder with his own, encouraging me to follow him. "Word is," he said, "she wanted to find out, first hand, what the big deal is about Protectorate training. Apparently, it wasn't at all it was cracked up to be, because right after she passed first-level evaluations with flying colors, she left the program and accepted her appointment as minister."

I absorbed that. All right. I supposed I could imagine Mila putting herself in such a challenging situation just for the fun of it, but the truth of it warranted some verification. "How do you know all this?"

"Ana told me."

I gaped, almost tripping again. "Ana *Director?*" I would never have suspected the quiet woman Gabriel had once chosen instead of me to support him to be the Judiciary's office gossip.

Asher winked at me. "The very one," he replied. "She told me the other night, while we were waiting for you at Drunk."

Huh. Who knew?

I shook my head, turning toward my office. At the end of hall, Erik appeared and was making his way up with a package in hand.

"Mila's not the *only* minister with an interesting past," Asher said.

I shot him a raised brow. "Who else?"

"Gabriel."

My blood went cold as I staggered to a stop again. "Gabriel?" I whispered. "What about him?" Had someone found out about Gabriel's support of the factions?

"Ana says Gabriel only gained status as a senator because his mother was raped by a member of the caste," Asher said, turning to me. "His mother was so grief-stricken and resentful after finding out she was pregnant that she wasn't able to care for him. After Gabriel was born, she sent him to live with her estranged family, and hasn't seen him since."

Asher shook his head ruefully. "No one thought Gabriel would amount to much, but he did. Well … until he was dismissed from the Judiciary."

Because of me. Fuck.

Just one more hour. I exhaled a deep breath, hoping I could last that long.

Tai had messaged me just before my morning meeting with Asher telling me to meet him at Gannon's residence right after work, which could only mean one thing — that he and Gannon had come up with a plan. *Thank the gods.* I didn't know how long I could go through the motions while Gabriel and Maxim were somewhere out there plotting against me. And now, with me preparing to become advisor to Realm Council, putting on a show of normalcy was only going to become more difficult.

"Hey, I have to go," Asher said, checking his comm. "I'm supposed to do an orientation with the new clerk. I'll have that background information on the advisory group members for you first thing tomorrow morning."

I nodded absentmindedly as he jogged off, crossing paths with Erik, who met me by my office door. He smiled and, with a flourish, handed me a thick plastic folder.

"Mila asked me to give you a copy of Realm Law on Enforcement of Fair Practice, section two eighteen," he said.

My eyebrows drew together as I took the docket. I had referred to this specific law during the special committee meeting, so it was one of the documents on my list to read it through, but I had assumed I would need to get digital copies. The Judiciary maintained strict rules around who could access official print files.

"I didn't think anyone was permitted to get print copies of official records," I said.

Erik's gray eyes sparkled. "Mila's made a special exception for you," he said. "You'll probably want a lot of records over the next few weeks, so just let me know what you need."

Oh. With rank came access — even for lowly subordinates like me. I probably should have been impressed by the fact; instead it unsettled me. This *special exception* only supported Gabriel's belief that I had the necessary opportunity to get any classified information he needed. My shoulders wilted.

"Thank you," I murmured, wrapping my arms around the file. "Is there anything else?"

Erik's cheeks mottled with bright splotches of red. "Just one other thing," he said. "I want you to know that everyone in the Judiciary's rooting for you. Well, the *subordinates* are." He laughed. "When you start working with Realm Council, it'll be history in the making!"

Good grief. History in the making! The nerves I had only just managed to quell came bubbling back up to the surface.

"There have been advisors to Realm Council before," I said, cheeks warming.

"But not in support of exploration," he said, eyes wide.

I blew out a short laugh at his zeal and the sheer irony of it all. All Above, if the advisory group knew just how mired in dissidence I was, they probably wouldn't view me as any better than Liandra Ambassador!

"Some of the subordinates were betting on who would be appointed," Erik confided with a grin. "But I figured you were a shoe-in. I mean, you're the one who's been working on exploration this whole time! There's just no one else better qualified!"

I swallowed. "I see." I struggled to stay steady under the weight of his high expectations. "Thank you for the support, Erik."

He returned my uneasy smile with a blinding one of his own before walking off back down the hall, where he started up an animated conversation with another subordinate.

With a frown, I entered my office, wondering what Gannon and Tai — the only two people in the Realm who had knew the full extent of my troubles — would have to say about my new role. I imagined Tai with a scowl on his face, anxious as usual about yet another boost to my already very public status. Meanwhile, Gannon would probably get excited on my behalf, encouraging me to view it as some strategic career opportunity. *But to what end?* Mila's question about what I wanted and my motivation floated through my mind, but I'd have to think of an answer to that some other time; I had enough on my plate as it was.

Sighing, I placed the docket on my desk, and my gaze fell to a neatly folded sheet of paper laying on its surface.

That's odd.

I had cleared my desk before heading out to meet with Asher, expecting that I would leave the Judiciary soon. I picked up the paper and unfolded the typed note.

> *My dearest Metallurgist,*
> *I thoroughly enjoyed our chance meeting the other day. How fortunate it is that we now have another opportunity to work together!*
> *I trust you've had enough time to consider my proposal and are now eager to comply with my request. I look forward to discussing it in great detail a week from today, at 18h 00m 00s, at Merit's central arc station.*
> *Until then,*
> *Your mentor and leader of the Quad*

My hands shook so hard, the paper fluttered. Only *one* person called me Metallurgist — *Gabriel!* But how had he managed to get into the Judiciary, much less my *office*, to leave this note? Someone *must* have seen him. A name popped into my head.

Erik! Maybe he knew who left the letter, or at least witnessed who did.

After tapping out a message to alert Jonah, I hurried out of my office, note in hand, to track down Erik. I found him easily, the top of his blond head weaving through the aisles between the cubicles and out of the main work area.

"Erik!" I called out sharply, startling a couple subordinates as I rushed to meet him just inside the reception area.

He turned around, a baffled smile on his face. "Do you need another file?" he asked when I stood in front of him.

I shook my head and held up the sheet of paper. The note trembled in my grip. "Do you know who left this on my desk?"

He knitted his blond brows. "No," he said, eyeing the sheet warily. "What is it?"

Damn it. I lowered my hand and searched his face. "Did you see anyone go into my office then?" I pressed, dismissing his question with one of my own.

He blinked. "I didn't see anyone go in, but …" A shadow of doubt flitted across his face.

I stepped up to him, scared and anxious at the same time to hear what he had to say. "Tell me."

"I saw someone come *out* of your office," he said. "Just before you showed up. I had gone looking for you earlier to give you the docket, but you weren't there."

Oh gods, no. "Who was it?"

"I don't know," he said with an apologetic shrug. "I knew you had a meeting with Asher. I just assumed he had been part of it."

I gripped Erik's wrist, and his eyes widened. "What did he look like?" I demanded.

He took a moment to give my question some thought. "Dark brown hair, medium build … *maybe* green eyes." He shrugged. "I can't be sure, but he was a subordinate."

Which meant the person had been wearing all black. Aside from the build, Erik's description didn't match Gabriel *or* Maxim, but then *they* wouldn't come to do their dirty work themselves. Would they? They would probably send one of their goons.

Erik shifted on his feet. "If you let me go now," he said, looking pointedly at his arm, "I just may be able to save it."

I followed his line of sight and found his limb still in my vise-like grip. "Oh," I said, stepping back at once and releasing him. "I-I'm sorry."

He eyed me for a second then gave me an awkward nod. He went to his desk just as the elevators opened and Jonah strode in. The protector assessed Erik with a cool once-over before his gaze homed in on me.

"What happened?" he demanded, approaching me at a clip.

I handed him the note, ignoring the curious glances from Erik and a few other citizens milling about.

As Jonah read, hard lines formed around his mouth, edging out the usual impassivity on his face. He lifted his gaze to mine.

"The chancellor should be at his residence by now," he said flatly. "Let's go."

* * *

I read Gabriel's note a fourth time as Jonah navigated the hover out of Merit's city center and toward Gannon's residence.

Chance meeting ... another opportunity to work together ... mentor?

Who the fuck did Gabriel think he was?

The murderer wasn't only *threatening* me, he was *taunting* me — treating my emotions and life like some toy to be played with. I stared at the letter through a red haze and latched onto my rising rage. It was better to give in to *that* than to my underlying despair.

I crushed the note in my fist and glanced at Jonah's face in the rearview mirror. He didn't appear to be in any better mood than me. His expression was becoming stormier the closer we got to Gannon's townhome. *What did Gannon say to him?* While we had returned to my office to collect my jacket and coat, Jonah had spoken with Gannon, telling him what had happened and that we were about to be on our way. Since then, the protector's disposition had been devolving at a rapid pace.

I peered through the raindrops that clung to the hover's window. The city buildings had given way to rows of gray-stone townhouses. One stood out among the rest. It occurred to me that I hadn't been to Gannon's residence for a long a time — since I had left him, in fact. I breathed through the pang of familiar heartache. How would I manage being there, with him, in a space where memories of our time together, both bitter and sweet, still hung in the air?

I bit my lip, cursing myself. I needed to set those emotions aside, maintain the distance I put between us and focus on the here and now — not on some fantasy that would never come to pass.

Ping.

I stuffed the now wrinkled note into my bag then checked Gannon's message.

Where are you?

I took another glance out the window. Jonah was navigating the hover into a spot on the ground.

I'm outside.

As if on cue, the front door opened and Gannon stepped out onto the small porch, squinting against the rain with his hands on his hips. After exiting the vehicle, I rushed up the narrow pathway, ahead of Jonah, telling myself it was because I wanted to get out of the rain and figure out what to do about Gabriel's note — nothing else. But when I reached him, all my shored-up resolve to maintain the distance between us crumbled, overpowered by an unexpected swell of fear about Gabriel's threats mixed with nostalgia from being here with Gannon again.

Gannon watched me as I went to him on unsteady legs then took me in his arms, rubbing a palm up my back, holding me against him as I tried to hide my tears between the folds of his shirt. I hadn't realized just how shattered my nerves had become after all that had happened — was *still* happening — to me.

After a lengthy moment, Gannon gripped my upper arms and pulled away to look me over. I swallowed, pulling myself together. He must have been satisfied by what he saw, because he nodded.

"Come on," he said, tucking me under his arm. "Let's go inside."

Only when Gannon cut a cool look over my head did I remember Jonah. I glanced over my shoulder at the protector as Gannon led us inside the house and into the sitting area. Jonah hung back, however, by the entryway, while Gannon helped me out of my coat and tossed it on the couch.

"Where's the note?" he asked me with a grim set to his mouth.

I pulled the wretched thing from my bag and handed it to him. After a quick read, Gannon addressed Jonah. "How did this happen?" he snapped.

The protector stiffened then stepped into the room. After a moment's hesitation, he said, "I'm not certain, Chancellor."

I frowned, looking between the two men. *What's going on?* Realization came.

"It's not his fault," I said to Gannon, searching his face. "How could Jonah have known that Gabriel or *whoever* it was he sent would have been able to get into the Judiciary?"

"It's his job to know," Gannon replied, sliding a challenging look at me. "What's the point of him being a *protector* if he can't *protect*?"

I crossed my arms at the stubborn set to his mouth. It really was no use arguing with him when he was like this. I sent Jonah a look of sympathy, which the protector either chose to ignore or was too focused on his superior's displeasure to notice.

Gannon held the note out to Jonah. "Give this to Talib and ask him to check the surveillance cameras throughout the Judiciary," he ordered. "He might find something that will help in our investigation."

Jonah squared his shoulders and accepted the letter. "Yes, Chancellor," he said before walking out of the room with a renewed sense of purpose.

"Tai should be here soon," Gannon said, dragging a hand through his hair as he walked to the other side of the room. He picked up a tablet from the antique desk, which held an organized assortment boxes and sheaves of paper. "He told me he has some new information to share, but I may as well bring you up to date until he gets here."

I nodded, eager to hear what they had learned.

Gannon returned to me, tapping the device's screen. "Gabriel and Maxim have made quite a few friends over the last few weeks." He handed me the tablet.

As I took it, a chart filled the screen, divided into four sections containing with Maxim's and Gabriel's names those of two other citizens.

"What is this?" I asked, studying the quadrant.

"Each citizen represents one of our four castes," Gannon explained, moving his finger from one section to the other as he spoke. "Subordinate, Protectorate, Senate and Elite. Maxim's the elite and Gabriel's the senator. They recently partnered with other two members — a subordinate and a protector. Together, the four of them have been busy forming a more organized and widespread group than we first thought."

Four of them. "The Quad," I said, my gaze snapping up to Gannon's. "*This* is why Gabriel signed off the note as its leader. This is what he's talking about."

Gannon thinned his lips. "Seems so, but he's only *one* of its leaders," he told me. "And this *Quad* of theirs has a growing army of followers."

He swiped the screen, switching the quadrant out for another, much larger one.

"From the information we've dug up so far," he said, "there are nearly a thousand citizens from each of the castes who've pledged allegiance to the group. The Quad is more than just some pillaging faction."

My jaw went slack as I looked at row upon row of names. "My gods," I breathed, "what are they trying to achieve?"

I understood that Maxim wanted vengeance for Liandra's expulsion and so would be motivated go to such lengths, but Gabriel? By his own admission, he had no interest in the rebels' cause.

"A new Realm order," Gannon replied, taking the tablet from my unsteady hands. He rolled the device up and tossed it onto the couch with a twist of disgust on his lips. "At least that's what we assume. Gabriel and Maxim know there's no coming back after everything they've done. We figure they want to reset the system, with themselves positioned on top."

That made sense. Gabriel had alluded to being power-hungry when he had threatened me in Helios. I held a breath.

"But if they're *this* organized," I said, thinking it through, "they must have access to *any* information they want. They don't truly *need* me, do they?" Hope filled me. Maybe now that Gabriel had his band of delinquents, he would leave me alone.

Gannon shook his head, folding his arms. "The citizens on this list are on the fringe of society," he said. "Either they have a bone to pick with someone or someone has one to pick with them. In many cases, they're felons with nothing to lose in signing on with a group that promises to improve their standing, no matter how it comes about." His blue eyes dimmed. "The point is, citizens like this, they won't have access to the type of information Gabriel or Maxim would want."

My shoulders dipped. "So I'm still on their Most Wanted list."

A scowl was Gannon's only response.

My earlier anger returned full force. I clenched my fists, turning away. Gods help me, but I wished Tai had *murdered* Gabriel Minister instead of merely beaten him into a pulp the way he had on my behalf so many months ago. Since then, Gabriel had been determined to take me down the way he believed I had done to him. I breathed deeply, trying to slow my pulse.

Gannon took my hand, pulling me to him. "Listen to me." He rested a hand at my jaw, forcing me to look at him. "Tai and I have come up with a lot about what Gabriel and Maxim have been up to in only a couple days. It's only a matter of time before we close in on them."

Gods, I hoped so. "I don't know how much more I can take," I said on a ragged breath, peering up at him.

He frowned, his eyes roaming my face.

A buzz at the front door broke through the silence between us, and Jonah suddenly appeared.

"That's probably the commander," Gannon said to the protector, releasing me. "Let him in."

Jonah stepped out, and a few moments later, Tai entered.

Tai scanned the area in that watchful way of his before his eyes met mine. I managed to hold myself back from throwing myself at him in the same shameless way I had done with Gannon, but maybe I should have. Perhaps it would have warmed up his cool disposition, one that matched his distant tone during our last conversation.

Tai held my gaze, appearing briefly indecisive before looking to Gannon. "Did you bring her up to speed?"

Gannon gave him a sharp nod. "I did." He glanced at me. "But there's been a development."

When Tai's focus returned to me, I inhaled deeply and said, "It's Gabriel. He contacted me."

Tai took a step forward then stopped abruptly, glancing me over as though looking for signs of injury or distress. "How? When?"

I sighed. "This afternoon." I walked over to the couch. "He or someone who works with him left a note for me in my office."

Gannon beckoned Jonah over from where he waited at the threshold. The protector took the cue and handed Gabriel's letter to Tai.

"The *Quad*," Tai spat, after reading it. "What does he think this is? Some fucking game?"

"That he does," I mumbled, sitting down heavily. "And I'm the chess piece he's playing with." I wrapped my arms around my waist, peering up at them.

Gannon and Tai exchanged a look. After Jonah took the note back from Tai, Gannon dismissed the protector then said, "You told me you had new information to share."

Tai nodded. "Since Helios is a rebel stronghold that's been showing a lot of activity, I positioned someone there, undercover, to see if we could find out what Maxim and Gabriel have been up to," he said, his gaze hardening. "My source learned what's been keeping Maxim busy — *aside* from plotting takeovers, that is. He's been in regular contact with Liandra Ambassador."

Gannon shook his head. "That's not possible," he said. "Liandra's in holding on Dignitas. Since the factions started popping up all over the place, security there has been elevated to the highest level. It's a fortress. You know as well as I do, *nothing* can get in or out of the city without the Protectorate's knowledge, much less communication between a dissident and an exiled leader."

"And yet," Tai drawled, crossing his arms, "a video message from Liandra blasting the Corona found its way into the hands of the media."

Gannon's mouth tightened.

Meanwhile, I stared at Tai. "You think *Maxim* did that?"

Tai shrugged. "Not him exactly," he said, "but maybe some rogue protector. Possibly one of their newly minted Quad members could be acting as their go-between."

Having seen that long list of Quad members, I had to admit that that was a *definite* possibility.

Tai's mouth fell into a grim line. "There's more."

I tensed, wondering how much worse things could get. "What?"

He ambled over and lowered himself to the couch, beside me. "It's about Paol."

I gasped, eyes wide. "My gods. Is he all right?"

Tai winced. "He's fine," he said, taking my hand, calming me. "My source spotted an unfamiliar face around Helios. After a little legwork, she discovered the person's name was Paol Auditor. As soon as I received the report, I planned on going there to confirm it for myself, but by the time I made arrangements, my source told me Paol had already left. No one's seen him since."

I closed my eyelids, wrapping my fingers around his. *Where in the Realm is he going? What's he up to? And why, damn it, isn't he giving all this up to be with Addy?*

My eyelids flew open. "Maybe he's decided to separate from the rebels once and for all," I said, unable to keep the thread of hope from weaving through my voice.

Tai released a heavy sigh. "I would like to believe that," he said, running the pad of his thumb across my knuckles. "But, Kira, even if Paol decides to give up on helping the factions, he *will* be detained by the Protectorate if he returns to Merit."

Meaning my uncle could possibly never see his daughter again. *No.* I groaned, squeezing Tai's hand tight, praying he was wrong. There must be some way he could get out of this mess!

My gaze rose to Gannon's, searching for some hopeful remark, but he remained silent. Something about the quiet, contemplative look on his face compelled me to ease my hand out from under Tai's.

I gritted my teeth and stood up. "We have to *do* something," I said, pacing the short distance between the two men. "What's the plan?"

Tai was the one to reply. "I was planning on going to Helios to work with my contact to befriend some of the recent Quad recruits, see if either any of them could be threatened into selling Gabriel or Maxim out," he said, running a hand along his jaw, "but the note you received today presents a better opportunity."

"How?" I asked.

"Because *now* we know where he'll be and when," Gannon murmured, considering Tai.

"That's right," Tai said, rising to his feet. "This way, Gabriel comes to *us* instead of us going to *him*."

Gannon nodded. "It's a good idea."

"All right then," I said, straightening my shoulders, gathering up my courage. "I'll go to meet Gabriel at the arc station just like the note says." It would be the most frightening thing I had ever done in my life, but gods help me, if it helped protect my family then I would do it.

The two men's gazes fell on me.

"I'm glad you've managed to maintain your sense of humor throughout all this," Gannon bit out while Tai glowered.

I stiffened. "You just said the plan was a good one, that Gabriel's note tells us where he'll be and when," I said, wondering why they weren't taking me seriously. "*I* should be the one to lure him in."

"Kira," Tai said with a patience I didn't know he had. "You're not going off on your own to face Gabriel and his Quad of Fucking Vengeance."

I made a face. *On my own?* What did I look like, a fool? "You would come with me," I said. "And Jonah would too."

Tai cocked his head, looking to Gannon. "Why Jonah?" he asked.

Gannon crossed his arms. "I assigned him to Kira," he said. "He's been by her side for the past two days."

Tai scoffed — nearly laughed, really. "Much good *that* did."

Gannon met his response with narrowed eyes. "Your *high-tech* tracking device did little better."

Tai curled his lip and I groaned. Hallowed Halls, I needed a *plan*, not some ... *pissing* match over which man protected me better!

"Do either of you have another idea?" I demanded. "If *I* don't go, who will?"

Tai drew himself up. "Me."

I stilled, but Gannon didn't miss a beat. "A *much* better idea," he drawled, resting his hands on his hips.

I chewed on my bottom lip. It actually *was* a better idea. Tai was a protector, after all, and would be much better prepared to confront Gabriel than me. But still my heart sped up with worry.

"You shouldn't go alone," I said. "Suppose he brings one of his thugs?"

"I'll bring a handpicked group of protectors with me," Tai replied, tossing a glance to Gannon. "Once we capture Gabriel and cross-examine him for answers, it won't be long before we find Maxim."

Gannon nodded. "Then we can stop the two of them once and for all."

CHAPTER 4

"Is it possible to outgrow panic attacks?" I asked as I walked into Sela's office, days later.

She blinked, turning to me with a hand on her hip. "Not that I've read." She shrugged. "But then I suppose anything's possible."

I smiled, imagining Da's reply when I told him what my best friend, the medical professional, said.

My mood had lifted since I'd spoken with Gannon and Tai, so much so that I had been able to be more focused at work over the last week than I had ever been. And it was a good thing, too. I would be heading off to Dignitas the following day to attend the Realm Council meeting and then, when I returned, would lead the advisory group. Even though Asher had helped prepare me as best as he could, I still found it hard to think about the advisory group without experiencing a tight knot of anxiety in the middle of my chest.

Thank gods, Rhoan's willing to help!

The night before, I had told my brother about my upcoming appointment with a wince, still worried he would be upset I had been selected for the role and not him. But my concern had been misplaced, just as Da has suggested. Rhoan had simply sent me a cheeky grin and said, "Better you than me."

Sela crossed the small distance in the room to stand in front of me. "Are you mad at me?" she asked with a frown.

I drew back, shocked by her question. "About what?"

She shrugged. "I haven't heard from you since my baby welcoming," she said, gray eyes wide. "I figured you were still upset about me bringing up Gannon in front of Nara."

I blinked. I hadn't wanted Nara to know about my relationship with Gannon, fearing that it would harm our friendship, but given everything that had happened to me since then, Sela's remark alluding to Gannon had been the *furthest* thing from my mind. Certainly, I had been a little put out that Sela had spoken so casually, but it wasn't as if she'd mentioned Gannon by *name*.

I sighed. "I'm not mad," I said, sitting down on a stool and hooking a boot heel over its rung. "I've just been … preoccupied."

Sela's frown remained. "With what?" she asked. "I thought the special committee process was over."

I averted my eyes, wondering how to reply. As much as I wanted to unload my worries on my best friend, I had no intention of doing that. Dear gods, she'd be frantic with worry and would want to raise every alarm. I couldn't risk that — not when she was so close to delivering her first child.

I sat up, remembering why I was visiting her — a convenient distraction from the direction of our conversation. "Mila's going to appoint me as advisor to Realm Council," I said, smiling, anticipating her surprise.

Sela snorted. "Of course she is," she said. "Who *else* would she choose?"

I shook my head, staring at her as she walked to her desk. Truly, I didn't deserve such loyal friends — like Asher, Sela couldn't see past her belief in me to acknowledge the line of other, more qualified citizens across the Realm who could have easily taken my place.

Sela turned to me, eyes narrowed. "Wait a minute," she said. "If you're going to be the advisor, then you're going to be in regular contact with Gannon."

"That's right."

She cocked her head. "How are you going to handle that?"

Mila had asked me a similar question, as though I'd let my feeling for Gannon impact my work. It seemed Sela's belief in me only went so far.

I thinned my lips. "I'll manage," I said. "As I always do."

Sela nodded slowly then folded her arms above her pregnant belly. "And how are things between you and Tai?"

I recalled the remote look in Tai's eyes when he had arrived at Gannon's house. "Business as usual," I said with a shrug. "We had an argument. Again."

Her eyebrows raised. "The last time we spoke you said Tai committed to fighting *for* you — not *with* you," she said. "What happened?"

What *hadn't* happened?

I shifted on my seat. I really didn't want to get all riled up again about my fight with Tai. "Let's just say I may have pushed him too far."

She studied me for a long moment, eyes boring into mine. "You're not still thinking about being with both men, are you?"

I gaped at her. "I never was!"

She snorted. "I distinctly remember you, Kira Metallurgist, saying to me — and I quote — 'I wish I didn't have to choose, that I could be with *both of them.*'"

My shoulders drooped. *Oh right, that.* "I might have considered it in a moment of weakness," I mumbled, "but I've returned to my senses."

"Kira …" Sela's voice was filled with warning.

I stiffened. "Even if intercaste restrictions were out of the picture, the last thing I would want is to handle those two men." *Does she really want to argue about this all over again?* "You said it yourself — there's no way they could see eye to eye."

"I just know how determined you are, Kira," she said, searching my face. "When you really want something, you go for it, and you usually get it. You love *both* Gannon and Tai, so I can't see you simply giving either of them up."

I glared at her, resenting her incredibly faulty logic. "Might I remind you," I said, "that I've *already* given Gannon up."

"And yet you haven't committed to Tai," she said with a knowing look in her eyes. "Why?"

I froze, the question like a cold splash of reality. After I'd pined for Tai since the age of sixteen, anyone would have expected me to have done just that — commit to him. Tai had finally told me he loved me, that he was done pushing me away. He'd been pretty much mine for the taking. But instead of taking what I had always wanted with both hands, I had held back, leaving him as confused and frustrated as me.

I looked at Sela helplessly. "I don't know why."

She sighed, coming close to me. "Well, I do," she said. "It's because committing to *Tai* means ending any chance you have to be with *Gannon*."

My sight went blurry with a rush of tears. *This* was why Sela was my closest friend. She knew me inside out and made me confront the truth, no matter how much it hurt, as long as it was for my own good.

I sniffled as tears of frustration rolled down my cheers, and Sela pulled me in for a hug. I tried to fit myself around her belly, but it was no use. I gave up with a blubbery chuckle, and she embraced me from the side with a laugh.

"Thanks gods I'm having this baby soon!" she cried. "I don't think I can get any bigger!"

The gentle rustle of clothing caught my attention. I pulled away and turned to find Margot, Sela's assistant, by the door.

"I'm sorry to bother you," Margot said to me, hands fluttering at her waist, "but I'm wondering just how long that forbidding young protector you came with will be here. He's making the patients in the waiting room — um, how should I put this? *Nervous.*"

Shit. I gasped, swiping away my tears as I stood up. I had forgotten about Jonah!

Since the cool dressing down he had received from Gannon, Jonah had been making his presence felt. When I had told him that I wanted to visit Sela, he had muttered something about her clinic being an "unfamiliar site" and a "potential threat." Apparently, my best friend's clinic warranted a higher level of surveillance: after we had arrived at the clinic, he had positioned himself by the front door instead of vanishing into thin air as he usually did.

Sela's eyebrows raised. "*Tai's* here?"

"No," I hedged, gathering my belongings. "It's someone else."

Sela looked at me expectantly, silently asking for explanation. Luckily, I was prepared for that question and had come up with an excuse on the way to her clinic.

"It's because of the media." I hiked my bag up onto my shoulders, forcing myself to hold her gaze evenly. "With all the attention I'm getting lately, Mila said it would be wise for me to have protection."

A crease of concern formed between Sela's brows as she went to her office door. Margot moved out of the way so she could peer into the waiting room, where Jonah stood. "Should I be worried?" she asked, looking back at me, mouth turned down.

"Oh no," I rushed out. "He's just a preventative measure."

She considered that for a moment. "I hope so," she said, frown deepening. "I'd hate to learn anything happened to you."

I gave her what I hoped was a reassuring smile. "You and me both."

* * *

"*Metas al Corpo Meridius.*"

I blinked, dragging my gaze from the bustling hall and to the tall female protector standing in front of me. "I beg your pardon."

The woman lifted a brow. "'Welcome to Realm Council,'" she said, this time in Samaric, my dominion's official language instead of Gildish, that of Dignitas.

I winced. "I'm sorry," I mumbled, heat crawling up my neck. "There's a lot to see."

She motioned toward my wrist and I presented my comm, allowing her to scan it with her own. "I take it this is your first time to Capita," she said, flipping her gaze up to mine.

"My first time to *Dignitas*," I corrected her.

She glanced at her device then nodded as though my reply checked out. "Yes, well, it can all be very overwhelming," she said then waved me on.

"Overwhelming" is an understatement.

I entered the sprawling rotunda of the Realm Council building, looking around, trying to keep the awe from my face.

My Primary Academy education and the newsfeeds had done me a great disservice. The building where the highest level of our governance and law conducted their affairs was more spectacular than had ever been described or displayed. It was a gleaming coliseum-like edifice of glass walls and steel beams filled with breathtaking works of art and an intimidating amount of advanced technology. Overhead, a glass ceiling glimmered with a projected map of the Realm. The diagram switched between images of our orbiting worlds and a view of the bright blue sky beyond. Around me were soaring murals of life-like paintings of current and past leadership as well as landscapes unique to each of our dominions.

But the most staggering feature of the space was below my feet. I stopped to stare down at a floor made entirely of glass or some other transparent material that allowed me to see right through to the floor below. That level too teemed with citizens from every walk of life.

My heart fluttered wildly against my ribs as I continued walking through the stream of citizens flowing around me. Who would have thought that I, Kira Metallurgist, would be attending a Realm Council meeting! I only wished Asher could have been there to experience this all with me.

I frowned. Asher deserved to be here in this crowd, witnessing history, as much I did, but Gannon hadn't been exaggerating when he said Capita was a fortress. When I had asked Mila the day before whether Asher could come with me to the Realm Council meeting, she had refused, saying that she wouldn't be able to obtain authorization for him. According to the Protectorate, Asher was my support, and so, "nonessential." I had taken umbrage at that. Little did they know how helpful to me he had been during the special committee process, the *very same* process that had led to Realm Council reviewing our recommendation that day!

My eyes caught on a gold-plated sign with the words "Corridor of Dominions" etched onto it. That was where Mila told me to meet her. I hastened my step toward the corridor, at the same time pointedly ignoring the curious glances of a group of senators and subordinates nearby.

I had been receiving odd stares like that since arriving in Capita — or maybe it was that I only noticed the stares more here, outside of Merit and my own world. Either way, they were starting to unnerve me. At first, I had assumed the looks were because of Jonah, a protector, who had escorted me into the building, but after he had disappeared, the frequency of the inquiring glances had only increased. Only then did it occur to me that people were probably recognizing me from the newsfeed.

"There you are."

I turned at the sound of Mila's strident voice rising above the hum of the space. I straightened as she cut through crowd and stopped in front of me, a severe scowl on her face.

I cocked my head with a frown. "Is everything all right?"

"Depends what you consider *all right*," she muttered, pursing her lips. "I just enjoyed the *displeasure* of being interviewed by the most persistent reporter I've ever met."

I peered around her shoulder and noticed a familiar tall, red-headed male standing in the middle of a group of people. "You wouldn't happen to be talking about *Heath Reporter*, would you?" I asked, glancing at her with a raised brow.

Mila sniffed. "So, you *too* have made his acquaintance."

I nodded then smothered a laugh at the painful expression on Mila's face. She hated the media as much as my brother did, so I could only imagine how difficult it must have been for her to endure a conversation with someone like Heath.

Mila glanced about, gesturing toward a hall on her left. "We're meeting in the main assembly room in the Dignitas Corridor," she said. "Walk with me."

I followed her, quickly matching her pace.

"After the meeting," she added, "I want to debrief with you and Rhoan."

I made a mental note to tell him when he arrived. My brother had opted to travel to Dignitas on his own rather than with me. And that was fine with me — I didn't know how in the worlds I would have explained having Jonah as my private escort.

"Where would you like to meet?" I asked as we neared a throng of citizens and members of the media huddled in front of a pair of large gold-plated doors.

"I've booked a small antechamber in the Septima Corridor, on the other side of the building," she said. "Room forty-eight. Meet me there half an hour after the meeting."

I nodded, and two senators opened the doors and allowed us to enter the assembly room. As Mila walked off toward the front of the space, I tried not to appear too stunned by its size and gravity.

The massive theater-style room was bright, shiny and intimidating. Its beams were steel, but it was decorated with burnished gold tapestries that hung from the ceiling against deep purple walls and pooled on the marble-tiled floors. The seal and motto of the Realm had been embroidered onto each shimmering bolt of fabric. Together with the skylight, the luxuriant drapery lightened a room that would otherwise have been weighed down by its dark wood furnishings and more than four hundred years of history.

I swallowed, searching for Rhoan. I spotted him sitting upstairs, in the mezzanine, and steadied my breath as I walked up to meet him. After sliding into the seat next to his, I whispered, "Mila wants to meet us after the meeting."

He nodded and handed me a palm-sized packet. I immediately recognized the small silver devices inside. I had used similar translation earbuds at Primary Academy during guest lectures by professors visiting from other worlds. I smiled my thanks to Rhoan since, like all of Realm Council meetings, this one would be held in Gildish.

I inserted the buds, and a moment later a hush of silent anticipation fell over the room as leadership entered, one by one. The Corona came in first. In accordance with protocol, she wore a black, purple-trimmed Elite uniform, but in deference to the significance of the day's meeting, she had also donned her ceremonial gold, silver and diamond bird's nest headdress. Argon's representation was noticeably absent as the ambassadors from Dignitas, Hale, Septima and Prospect followed her in. Next, the high marshal, leader of the Protectorate, walked in, and then Gannon, appearing focused and authoritative in his crisp formal Senate uniform.

I exhaled a ragged breath at the sight of him and wilted in my seat. *Hallowed Halls, when will this end?!*

How long would it be before I could be near Gannon, just *see* him, and not experience this sharp pang of longing? Sela had seen right through me, and now the truth was clear as day: I wasn't willing to give Gannon Consul up. I couldn't. I had tried to, but it didn't work. I just couldn't *will* myself away. Halls, any time we were in the same space I found myself in his arms, drawn to him by some involuntary force.

But what did that mean? Was I *truly* considering going back to him?

My gods, that would mean having an ongoing illicit affair with the Realm's *high chancellor*. And wouldn't that put his rank in jeopardy? I had left Gannon to *protect* his future, to ensure he took his rightful place. He was meant to be where he was now, the leader of his caste and second in power only to the Corona. I couldn't be the reason all of that was taken away.

And then there was Tai.

What would a relationship with Gannon mean for him and me? I couldn't let Tai go any sooner than I could Gannon. I had loved Tai for so long that my love for him had become a part of me.

I stifled a sigh and tried to focus on the proceedings. My being here, at a Realm Council, was a once-in-a-lifetime opportunity. Sifting and sorting through my love life right now wasn't the best use of my time.

As the Realm Councillors settled into their seats behind a curved glass table on the stage, the Corona approached the center of the platform, holding a small gold and purple box. A podium rose from the floor in front of her, and she placed the box on it before addressing the room.

"Today's Realm Council meeting has special significance," she said, brown eyes drifting across the faces of her enthralled citizens. "In addition to starting the review of the special committee's unprecedented recommendation for regulated exploration, I will be making an appointment that I had hoped to carry out under much happier circumstances."

I looked to Gannon, and found him sitting very still, his unwavering focus on the Corona. I expelled a heavy breath and returned my own focus to the sovereign as she continued.

"A few short months ago, we lost a great leader." She lifted her chin. "High Chancellor Marcus Consul was a man worthy of the admiration and respect he held among his peers, and indeed, across the Realm. It would take a citizen with a great strength of character and mind to fill the gap in leadership he has left behind. It is fortunate for the Realm, then, and a testament to Marcus Consul's legacy as a leader and a father, that his son has proven himself to be more than qualified for the position."

A murmur of excitement flitted across the room. A few members of the media, seated behind a section reserved for ministers, started to fiddle with their various recording devices.

"Chancellor Gannon Consul," the Corona said, "is a leader who, at a time of tremendous upheaval and great personal loss, dedicated himself to the advancement of the Realm. In leading countless initiatives, including the special committee on exploration, he has proven to be a citizen of high moral character, fortitude and integrity. Therefore, I stand here today, honored and proud to be appointing him to the position of high chancellor of the Realm."

The room erupted into applause and a few hearty cheers. Meanwhile, my heart soared.

Gannon stood up, straightening his jacket. As he strode to meet the Corona by the podium, he darted a searching look around the room. When his gaze lifted to the mezzanine, I held my breath, imagining foolishly, *hopefully*, that he was searching for me. When his gaze returned to the Corona, she removed an item from the small box on the podium. It was after she pinned the glittering object to his lapel that I realized it was an official badge marking Gannon's position as high chancellor.

Gannon accepted the honor with a tight nod, and the Corona gestured to the podium, stepping back so that he could address the room. When he cleared his throat, the chatter quieted down.

"Many of you knew my father as an uncompromising but fair leader," he began, eyes drifting across the audience. "But as our sovereign stated, Marcus Consul was more than simply a leader: he was my father, a mentor to me in all ways. Like the children of many great men and women, I too struggled at times with the idea of following in the footsteps of my father — as though I could do such a thing. His legacy is as palpable in this room today as his presence was when he was alive." He paused, exhaling a deep breath within the quietness of the room. "My father once told me that being a leader simply means being responsible for your decisions by owning your failures and being generous with your successes. I stand here today ready and willing to take on this great responsibility, to lead the Senate caste and to drive the greater advancement of the Realm."

The audience burst out into another round of applause that made my chest swell with pride. Gannon acknowledged the ovation with an ambivalent expression that warmed when he focused on two people seated in the front row, to his left. I leaned forward to take a closer look at the pair and recognized, from their profiles, Gannon's mother and his older sister, Gillian. They stared up at Gannon, smiling with pride shining on their faces. Tears sprung to my eyes.

Despite the tense interaction between Gillian and me when we had first met, I couldn't help but share in the bittersweet joy that she must have been feeling, seeing her brother take on the role he was born to fill. I couldn't fault her for trying to warn Gannon away from me. She had only been trying to protect her brother's future, the same as I wanted to.

The Corona approached the podium, but Gannon raised a hand, stopping her with a respectful nod. She stepped back, confusion flickering so quickly across her face that if I hadn't been familiar with her usual expressions by now, I wouldn't have noticed it.

"I'd like to make one final remark," he said, bracing his hands on the sides of the podium. "As high chancellor, my first mandate is to restore peace and stability to our system. Too many of our citizens have been hurt or killed at the hands of factions. My family is just but one of many who have been impacted by the selfish lawlessness of the rebels." Gannon's eyes had been touching upon the faces of everyone in the room as he spoke, but when his gaze lifted to the mezzanine again, this time I knew without a doubt that he was looking at me. "I vow on the legacy of my father to ferret out those who seek to manipulate the Realm and its citizens for their own selfish interests — no matter what their caste, rank or position. I promise you this."

I fought to keep it together. While his resolute remarks were directed to every citizen in the Realm, I couldn't miss the meaning behind his words that was intended for me.

He returned to his seat amidst the silence of the room.

The Corona cleared her throat, considering Gannon with a wary eye, and returned to the podium. "Thank you, High Chancellor," she began. "I believe we all appreciate your commitment and determination to not let rogue citizens destroy everything the Realm has built." She drew herself up and looked to the audience. "Before we begin our review, I'd like to take a moment to make another announcement."

Another announcement? Neither Gannon or Mila had mentioned anything about this. I frowned, glancing at Rhoan for answers, but he shrugged imperceptibly, appearing as baffled as me.

"It hasn't escaped my notice or the rest of leadership's that the efficiency of the special committee was a result of the strong direction of our newly appointed high chancellor *as well as* the inclusion of a new contributor during discussions."

I cocked my head, leaning forward, interested in where this was going.

"Over the years," she continued, "the Subordinate caste has asked for an opportunity to sit at a higher level of government. For a number of reasons — some valid, others inexcusable —— the caste's calls were not heard. But times have changed. When the Realm must be unified in the face of dissension, *every* voice must be heard, and more importantly, listened to."

My breath caught. Hallowed Halls, this was it! The stars were coming into alignment! She was going to announce the new subordinate position on Realm Council!

I checked Gannon, trying to read his expression, but couldn't. He was focused solely on the Corona once again.

"Realm Council says it prides itself on being open to diverse opinions." She paused to survey the room. Her pale blond hair glimmered under the light. "I've decided, with the support of leadership, to put words into action." She paused, eyes skimming at a steady pace around the room. "I'm pleased to announce that I will be establishing a permanent position on Realm Council for a citizen from the Subordinate caste."

A chorus of gasps preceded the rising volume of chatter. The media had been relatively quiet up to that point, but the second the Corona made that announcement, they buzzed like a dozen kicked beehives.

I pressed my lips together to contain my excitement and looked at Rhoan to gauge his reaction. My brother stared at our sovereign, eyebrows raised, utter surprise written all over his face. Despite his disdain for the special committee process and delight over not being selected as advisor, he *must* be able to appreciate just how significant a position like this would be!

The Corona raised a hand, and the room quieted at once. "The subordinate will be a liaison between the Subordinate caste and Realm Council, representing the caste in all matters related to governance and law," she said. "The first appointment will be of a citizen who has proven to be knowledgeable, influential and inspirational to most, if not all, subordinates. You'll hear more about this position in the coming months. In the meantime, we have much work to do."

With that, she turned the meeting over to Gannon, who introduced the recommendation on exploration with a summary of the special committee's discussions. He was, as usual, eloquent and firm in his remarks, but to my surprise, I listened with half an ear, too excited by the Corona's announcement to fall into my usual romantic musings about him. By the time I looked around, the meeting had ended as quickly as it had started.

I removed my earbuds and stood up as the audience started to disperse. "What do you think?" I asked Rhoan, anxious to hear his reaction.

My brother rose to his feet with a frown. "About what?"

I balked. *About what?* Hadn't Rhoan been sitting right beside me, in the same meeting? "The subordinate position on Realm Council," I clarified with an impatient note, then lowered my voice. "I think the Corona's going to appoint you!"

Rhoan scoffed. "Gods help me, I hope not."

My mouth fell open. My brother was taking his distaste for leadership and the media to an irrational level. "Don't you understand what this position means?" I demanded. "*You're* the one always talking about how unjust it is that subordinates don't have a voice on Realm Council. Well, here's our chance!"

"I'd rather spend my time listening to the concerns of our caste and being accessible to them," he said, shoving his hands into his pockets with a frown. "Not playing politics and turning into the very thing I resent."

I stared at him, aghast. "If you become a Realm Councillor, you can *do* something about our caste's concerns, not just *listen* to them," I insisted. "You can't effect any meaningful change looking in from the outside." Didn't he understand?

Rhoan thinned his lips and glanced to the front of the room. The Corona was still there, speaking with other leadership in hushed tones.

"Look," Rhoan said, running a hand through his curly hair, focused on me now. "Even if I *wanted* the role, the Corona's not going to give it to me."

I rocked back. "Why in the worlds not? You were the *first ever* sub rep on the —"

He held up a hand, stopping the case I was about to make. "The Corona has clearly already decided who she wants for the position," he said. "If she were going to appoint me, she would have contacted me already, ahead of time, to feel me out and see whether I would be a good fit before making a public announcement."

What was he talking about? The Corona *definitely* knew who she wanted, and it *had* to be him. Who else could it possibly be?

"You're wrong," I stated.

My brother shrugged, crossed his arms and began surveying the room — a clear sign that, as far as he was concerned, our conversation was over.

I ground my teeth, but stopped fuming when my comm pinged. I checked the device.

Meet me.

My pulse lurched at Gannon's abrupt message. Did he have an update about the Quad? Maybe Tai's plan wasn't going to work out after all. I typed in a response at once.

Is it about the plan?

Even though my comm was secure, I didn't want to risk getting more specific than that.

No. I want to show you something.

I frowned, lifting my head to search for him. I found Gannon standing by the podium, gazing up at me. Someone called his name, and his focus shifted to his sister, who was approaching him, arms outstretched. He smiled before embracing her and his mother too.

I chewed on my bottom lip as they spoke, wondering whether I should go to him. Being with Gannon in some private space he had probably reserved for us to speak in would do nothing to maintain the distance I had been trying to keep between us. Although giving him up was something I now realized I wasn't willing or able to do, I still needed to think things through, get my head straight, figure out how I could make a relationship like ours work if I truly wanted it to. The fact of the matter was that Gannon was the high chancellor of the Realm. Now more than ever, there seemed to be insurmountable hurdles to us being together.

With that in mind, I replied:

I can't. I have a meeting with Mila.

I chanced a glance at Gannon, waiting on his reply. He was now escorting his family to the doors. After another round of hugs, his mother and sister exited the assembly room. After checking his comm, he tapped at his device.

It won't take long. Jonah will meet you in the rotunda and take you to me.

"Where are we supposed to meet Mila?" Rhoan asked, startling me.

I blinked up into my brother's face, forcing my brain to recall. "Septima Corridor," I said after a moment. "Room forty-eight."

He nodded. "You ready to go?"

I hesitated, trying to make up my mind, then said, "Do you mind if I meet you there?" I could find out what Gannon wanted to show me then hurry back to meet him and Mila with time to spare.

A curious glint came to Rhoan's eyes. He slanted a look the front of the room, which was now empty save for a few senators milling about. Gannon was nowhere in sight, but I could almost see the wheels of my brother's mind turning. Rhoan was no fool. No doubt he was putting two and two together, and knew the reason I wanted him to go on ahead of me.

I stood there, tense but resigned, waiting on him to call me out, demand that I stay away from Gannon or, at the very least, give me a look of unbridled disapproval.

Instead, Rhoan simply shook his head, sighed heavily and said, "It's your life, Kira. Do whatever you want."

CHAPTER 5

Where are we going?

Jonah led me through the crowded hallway of the Dignitas Corridor and into a section of the Realm Council building that was decidedly less busy than the space we had just left. The only citizens in the area were a wall of protectors standing on guard by a bank of elevators. When Jonah acknowledged one of them with a curt nod, the other man stepped aside, allowing Jonah to press a button that glowed a bright green when he touched it.

He urged me to enter the elevator ahead of him, then waved his comm in front of a panel before entering a lengthy code. The panel up with the words *Top Elevation — The Office of the High Chancellor of the Realm.*

That was Gannon's *office!*

My lips parted, and as the doors closed and the cab started to ascend, I took hold of the railing behind me. Why in the Realm would Gannon want to meet me *there?* I had expected him to want to meet at some out-of-the-way, hidden location, not a place filled with his peers! We were supposed to be *hiding* our connection to each other, not *flaunting* it!

I took a steadying breath, putting my trust in the fact that Gannon must have known what he was about, and a moment later followed Jonah out of the elevator and into a well-appointed reception area. It, like the rest of Realm Council building, was an architectural triumph of glass and steel filled with dark woods and gleaming technology.

A mature senator with an efficient air stepped out from behind a broad antique-looking desk in the middle of the room.

"Welcome, Subordinate Metallurgist," she said, approaching us.

I fought back my surprise that the woman knew my name. Not only had Gannon made arrangements to meet me here, but he had notified his support as well!

"Thank you," I said, fiddling with the strap of my bag.

She smiled pleasantly. "I'll take her from here," she said to Jonah, who replied with a curt nod before the senator motioned toward a set of doors.

I followed her into a work area whose lay out was similar to the one in my Judiciary except it had to be three times as large. The space was filled with cubicles, desks and what looked to be hundreds of the Realm's finest. Citizens walked about on gleaming white marble with the same sense of competence and efficiency as the senator I trailed after.

I avoided stares as we passed, wondering with each step at Gannon's wisdom in asking to meet me here. Thankfully, the senator soon turned a corner, leading me away from prying eyes, and stopped in front of a massive frosted glass wall. The door in the middle of it had Gannon's name and new title etched into it.

"Please go in," she said after disengaging the door.

I smiled my thanks to her then stepped into a room flooded with sunlight. As the door closed behind me, I found Gannon standing by a sitting area consisting of four leather armchairs grouped together.

"I wasn't sure you would come." He had removed his jacket, and his arms were folded across his charcoal-colored shirt.

I breathed in the sight of him before saying, "I'm not sure I *should* have come." I gestured to the passersby on the other side of the glass wall. "Won't my meeting you here raise a lot of questions?"

He shrugged. "You've been working on the special committee, which I led, for weeks," he said, walking toward me. "For all they know, you're here for work. And since you're going to be an advisor to Realm Council in a short while, it would only make sense that you'd be meeting with me."

My eyebrows rose. "You heard?" I had yet to tell Gannon or Tai about my new position, the more urgent matters between us having put it to the back of my mind.

He nodded, blue eyes warm, standing in front of me now. "Mila told me," he said. "Congratulations. It'll be good experience for you."

Huh. "Mila said the same thing."

He smiled, looking down at me. "I'm sure she did."

My cheeks warmed at the pride in his face, a similar expression to the one he had worn after I had told him about my appointment as director so many weeks ago. But at *that* time, I had been spread out beneath him after making love … just before he gave me the promise ring.

I stopped that line of thought its tracks and averted my eyes, searching for something less threatening to my willpower to focus on. I stepped around him, looking about.

The limited views into Gannon's office I had managed to capture via monitor over the past few months had failed to give me a true sense of the size and impact of the room. The office was so large it must have run the entire width of the building. My gaze skimmed the plush seating and sleek, minimalist furnishings. Opposite the glass wall that I had just entered through, a floor-to-ceiling window overlooked the far reaches of the city.

My body hummed with delight and curiosity. I had never been in a space that was entirely *him*, that reflected a side of him that didn't revolve around me or my tumultuous life.

I sensed Gannon's eyes on me as I walked to the wall of digital photography behind his desk. Gannon's photos weren't of distant landscapes or some abstract subject matter. They were of his family. I smiled, watching as some of the images faded and switched out to display others of his father, his mother, his sister and her family, each of them at various ages and different settings.

Intrigued, I touched the edge of a photo at my eye level. It became fluid, displaying a brief silent video of his five-year-old niece. She was sitting at the bottom of a staircase, giggling so hard that she fell onto her side, laughing as she then rolled onto her back. My smile grew. She reminded me of Addy. Both little girls had blond hair, blue eyes and what looked to be a similar free spirit.

Would Gannon and I have children with blue eyes like his or brown like mine?

Alarmed by the direction of my thoughts, I turned away from the wall, finding Gannon still considering me.

I cleared my throat, skin warming under the intensity of his gaze. "You have a beautiful family," I managed.

"Thank you. I know."

I snorted, and he smirked. People didn't call Gannon Consul "arrogant" without reason.

Shaking my head, my gaze fell to a small box wrapped in gold foil sitting in the middle of his desk. The note on top of it was written in a sloping, elegant scrawl.

To my darling Jamie. Your father would be so proud.

"It's a gift from my mother," Gannon explained, and I glanced up. "She bronzed the badge my father received when he was appointed high chancellor."

I smiled at the thoughtfulness of the gift even as my eyebrows drew together. "Jamie?"

"It stands for James, my middle name," he said, folding his arms. "Long story, but my mother refuses to call me anything else."

My smile widened. "Gannon James Consul." I liked it.

Gannon tilted his head. "What's *your* middle name?"

I fidgeted with a clasp of my comm, suddenly shy. "Grace," I said. "After my great-grandmother, on my mother's side."

His mouth curved up. "Kira Grace Metallurgist." He emphasized each syllable, holding my gaze. "So beautiful it rolls off the tongue."

Especially off yours.

I winced at yet another errant thought and glanced away. *Get it together, damn it!* Sighing, I rested my bag on the desk before walking to the window to catch my breath.

Capita's mountains and lakes, which I had been treated to briefly as I had entered the city by hover, stretched out far and wide in front of me. The late-afternoon sunlight reflected off the surrounding buildings in a sparkling multicolored display.

"How far do you live from here?" I asked, eyes still on the view.

Gannon joined me by the window, his arm brushing mine. He pointed to a building in the near distance, its towering height making it easy to pick out. "It takes me twenty minutes to walk here."

I scoffed. "You *walk* here?" Then, just to be smart, I glanced him over from the corner of my eye and said, "With all the attention you must attract, I figured you'd have Talib chauffeuring you around, door to door, *by hover.*"

He sent me a withering look that made me laugh.

I looked through the window again, a smile still on my face. A row of glimmering hovers droned by, and on the streets below, people bustled about, taking care of the business of life. Capita was similar to Merit, yet at the same time so different. While Merit had its own electric energy, Capita seemed somehow more charged. I suspected it had to do with the fact that it was the center of Realm governance and law.

"I like it here," I decided.

Gannon hummed. "I thought you would."

I looked up at him, catching the knowing quality of his voice. He was studying me, and my heart palpitated at the easy familiarity between us. It had been so long since we had been like this, since we *could* have been. With the troubles between and around us, we hadn't had a chance.

Gannon's eyes went dark, and my body did the impossible of simultaneously softening and tightening up, readying myself for him. I reached for him but he grimaced suddenly, stepping away as he rubbed a hand around his nape. "I didn't ask you to come here so I could seduce you, Kira," he said.

I froze, flushed with embarrassment. "Of course not," I mumbled, dropping my hand, and blurted out, "Then why did you want to meet me?"

He expelled a deep breath. "I wanted you to see where I am pretty much every hour of the day when I'm in Capita," he said, holding my gaze. "When I'm not with you."

Oh.

I looked around his office again with new eyes. When I had first met Gannon, I had learned very quickly that he was a private person, that he didn't let people in easily. And now here he was, inviting me into another part of his life. I couldn't help but be moved.

As I surveyed the space, two senators strode by in the hallway on the other side of the glass wall. One of them was a tall and slender dark-skinned woman with a purposeful gait. She wasn't Mila, but her similarity to my superior was enough to remind me of my meeting with her and Rhoan.

I gasped. "I have to go," I said, apology in my voice.

He hesitated then said, "All right."

He was giving me leave, but my feet remained firmly planted.

Gannon cocked his head. "What is it?"

"Nothing." *So why am I just standing here?*

Gannon's eyes roved my face before narrowing slightly. "You don't want to go, do you."

"No." *But I should.*

Gannon's gaze was piercing as he stepped forward, back into my space. "What do you want?"

To be with you — so much it hurts.

I squeezed my eyelids shut, cursing myself. I shouldn't have come. Facing the fact that I didn't want to give Gannon up had weakened my resolve. Gods, what did I *want?* I wanted to be with *him!* But I couldn't tell him that because I needed to think things through. At this point, my being with him was just a fairy tale, a dream that was fast becoming a nightmare.

I opened my eyelids, shaking my head, unable to speak.

Gannon stepped closer to me still, his chest skimming my breasts. "What do you want, Kira?" he repeated, his gaze never wavering from my own.

I stared up at him, the yearning expanding within me nearly suffocating. I licked my lips and his eyes fell to my mouth, giving me an idea … a way to show him what I couldn't yet put into words.

I shot a quick look at the hallway again. "Can people can see us from outside?" The glass wall was frosted on the other side, I thought, but still, I had to be sure.

Gannon considered me a moment then shook his head. "That glass is one-way," he said, "and so is the window."

Thank gods.

I rose onto my toes and reached for him again, gripping his shoulders to bring him close. Gannon's lips parted the moment they met mine, and his scent filled my senses. I tasted on his tongue the same pent-up hunger, desire and love I had banked away every single day since I had given him up. Gods, how had I made it so long without this, without the taste, touch and feel of him?

"*Lahra.*" He breathed his endearment for me between my lips, winding his arms around my waist before deepening our kiss.

I sighed, leaning into him. The desperation ratcheting up between us reminded me of him between my thighs, pumping into me with languid strokes or driving into me hard with harsh deep thrusts.

I gasped for air. "Gannon," I whimpered, plunging my fingers into his hair, as his mouth slid from my mouth to neck.

"Please," he said, kissing the space just below my ear, "tell me this means what I think it does."

I hummed, eyelids closed, lost in a haze as he slid a hand between my thighs. The dampness there, where he rubbed against my sex through the thin fabric of my pants, made me inhale sharply. He groaned and captured my lips, pouring himself into our kiss. I fought against the need to breathe and snaked my arms around his shoulders to mold myself against him as he moved his hand from my throbbing core to join his other hand at my back. Soon the two of us were panting, the hunger for more than heated kisses and scorching touches becoming too much to resist.

He broke away, eyes hooded, searching my face. "Before we go any further, *tell me*," he demanded.

I frowned, brain cloudy with desire. "Tell you what?" I asked, but I wasn't truly interested. I leaned up and pressed my lips against his, not wanting to lose the taste of him in my mouth.

He indulged me, but a second later he tangled his fingers into my hair then yanked, tilting my head back so I was forced to look up at him.

"Kira, I'll fuck you here and now if that's what you want," he demanded, eyes glittering bright, "but not before you tell me what this means."

I gasped, the fog lifting from my mind. *What this means?* Cold, harsh reality washed over me. He wanted to know if *this*, me kissing him, giving myself over to him, meant I would finally be with him.

Holy shit. What am I doing?

I had thrown myself at him, thinking only of myself, of how much I wanted him, *needed* him, knowing full well that our relationship wasn't possible. I was acting like some sort of pricktease!

It took everything I had, but I backed away, gently extricating myself from Gannon's hold.

"This just means I can't keep my hands off you," I whispered, trying to avoid his gaze, but I couldn't miss the disappointment in his eyes. "Nothing else."

His nostrils flared. "Why?"

I went to stand beside his desk, putting much-needed distance between us. *Do I really have to spell it out?* "There's just too much working against us."

He scowled. "Everything doesn't have to be *perfect* in a relationship for it to work."

I tensed. "I know that." My very own parents had proven it! "But that doesn't change the fact that I'm with Tai."

Gannon rubbed a spot on the bridge of his nose. "For the love of gods, Kira, will you *please* stop bringing up Tai," he implored. "You're *not* with him and you *never* will be."

I balked. "*What?*"

"Everything about Tai makes sense," he said, holding my gaze. "Holy gods, if I were *either* of your fathers, the man would be at the top of *my* 'ideal partners for my daughter' list. But you don't want Tai the way you want *me*."

I stared at him, speechless — *clueless*, really, as to what to say. So I went with what I knew with as much certainty as the fact he was purposely trying to rile me up.

"I love Tai," I said.

There. That should shut him up.

Gannon barked out a laugh. "Come now," he said, crossing his arms. "Are you *in* love with Tai? Or do you just love him? Because I don't think you know the difference."

I gritted my teeth, clenching my fists to stop from slapping him in the face. "I know my own mind, Gannon Consul," I hissed.

We glowered at each other, the air charged no longer by our need for each other but by the wall of frustration building between us.

Gannon spun on his heel with a curse and stalked away. He dragged a hand through his hair, pacing, seemingly at war with himself as I looked on, uncertain what to do. Gods, I wanted to go to him, tell him the truth, what I had been denying him for so many weeks — that I *loved* him just as much as I did Tai — but I couldn't. My resentment and anger at the worlds made my hands shake.

"All right," Gannon spat out, pivoting to face me. "Ask him."

I blinked, wondering what I had missed. "Ask who what?"

Gannon drew himself up, appearing to brace himself for some unappealing task. "I love you, and despite your unwillingness to admit it, I *know* you love me." He expelled a harsh breath. "And then there's Tai. The solution to this bloody predicament has been dangling in front of us this entire time."

It has? "I don't understand."

He glanced away briefly before meeting my gaze, his eyes hard. "Ask Tai whether he'll agree to be in a multiple relationship with you and me."

I had to hold onto the edge of his desk to keep from falling to the floor. My gods, I considered asking Gannon to repeat himself, but it would have been a complete waste of time. He stood in front of me, gaze unwavering, expression resolute.

Words escaped me.

Gannon watched me quietly. "Isn't that what you want, Kira?" he asked. "To be with both of us?"

Well, yes. No. I shook my head. *What?*

I turned away and thrust my fingers into my hair, dislodging some of the pins that had been anchoring my hair. I had thought about being with both men but had tossed the idea aside, not thinking for a *moment* that either of them would consider it. But here Gannon was now, opening the door to a place I hadn't ever thought to approach, much less go through. Why was he doing this? And how would it even solve the most fundamental problem between us?

I spun around. "You can't be involved with someone from a restricted caste," I said. "As high chancellor, now more than ever, you have to adhere to Realm rules. You'd be demoted if they found out about us being together."

Gannon thinned his lips. "That was before I became privy to all Realm's secrets," he said. "I know too much now for leadership to dismiss me over something probably more than half of them have already done, or *are* doing."

I absorbed that and a flicker of hope came to life. *Is he right?* Maybe, but our sovereign was unpredictable at best. "I can't imagine the Corona or *anyone* in leadership simply overlooking our relationship," I argued.

He moved toward me. "I'm not saying that we would be blatant with our relationship," he said, taking my hand. "We'd be careful and discreet, like we have been up until now."

I searched his face. He sounded so perfectly logical, as though it could truly work, but it couldn't. Could it? My gods, just *thinking* about the logistics of trying to keep a relationship like ours a secret was staggering.

Even as doubt assailed me, my heart ached at the realization of just how far Gannon was willing to go to be with me. He was offering to not only be in an illicit relationship with me, but to include *Tai*, a man he merely tolerated, if it meant he could be with me. Hallowed Halls, if I hadn't known Gannon loved me before, it was as undeniable now. How could I *not* give him the three words I had held back from him? How could I not tell him I loved him too?

"Gannon," I breathed, raising my free hand to his jaw with tears in my eyes. "I lov— "

He flinched, wincing as though scalded by my touch. "Good gods, Kira," he said, glaring at me. "Don't tell me that. Not *now*."

I blinked back tears as my body sagged. My sense of timing couldn't have been worse. Did I really believe that *now* — after Gannon had offered to include Tai in our relationship — that *this* was the right time to tell him I loved him? Telling Gannon right then, after denying him for so long, would only suggest that my love for him depended upon my being with Tai too. And *that* wasn't anywhere close to the truth.

"I'm so sorry," I whispered, my insides twisting. *How could I be so foolish?* "I-I just don't know what to do."

Gannon studied me, a conflicting mix of emotions swirling in his eyes. "Why don't you talk to Tai," he said evenly. "Then we'll take it from there."

CHAPTER 6

"I spoke too soon, didn't I?"

I stopped rummaging through my bedroom drawers long enough to find Ma standing by my door. "About what?" I asked, turning to face her.

She walked in and released a worldsweary sigh. "Tai," she said, sitting on the edge of my bed and crossing her legs. "You and he *aren't* involved, are you."

I rolled my eyes. Good grief, *this* again? Having to manage my mother, a woman hell-bent on getting me partnered, married or *both*, was the absolute *last* thing I needed! At least it seemed our conversation *this* time would revolve around the correct assumption.

"So Da got through to you," I said, folding my arms.

She nodded before making a face. "But I don't understand," she said. "You and Tai have feelings for each other. It's so obvious when I see the two of you together."

My gaze wandered away from hers then settled on the floor. "We do," I admitted. "I just need to figure things out."

Like whether I want to be in a multiple relationship like the one you have.

I grimaced, turning my back to hide the flush that was sure to be on my face.

Even hours after returning to Prospect Eight, I still grappled with what Gannon had said — no, what he had *offered*. My gods, a multiple, with Gannon and Tai! I hadn't thought it even possible. Less than a week ago I had been trying to decide between *two* men; now I wondered whether I could actually *have* both.

Ma sighed, a very beleaguered sound. "I should have held back how much I approved of Tai for you," she mumbled. "Otherwise, we would be planning a partnering ceremony for the two of you right now."

I rolled my eyes, resuming my hunt for a lapse kit. Good gods! You would've thought I'd just announced I was moving to the farthest world in our system!

When I had returned home from Dignitas that evening, I had been looking forward to burrowing deep under my bedcovers to get over a combination of jet lag and off-kilter emotions, but no such luck. Only minutes after walking through the front door, my parents and Adria had dropped by for an impromptu celebration of my recent appointment and to hear about Rhoan and my trip to Realm Council. By the frown on my brother's face when he had arrived at our apartment later, it was clear he was in no better mood than me to entertain our well-intentioned family.

I slammed the drawer shut, coming up empty, and leaned a hip against my chest of drawers. I would have to find some other blasted other way to get to sleep. Then the answer came to me. *Solumen!* Weeks earlier, when I had consumed an excessive amount of the herbal relaxant, it had knocked me out cold. This time around, I would take care to drink a less liberal amount — I needed to be on my toes the following day for my advisory group meeting.

I pushed away from the furniture and made for the door, focused on the bottle of *solumen* I kept in the kitchen.

"So who were you talking about?" Ma asked.

I drew up at the threshold, turning around with a frown. "When?"

"Just before Sela's baby welcoming," she said, rearranging the pillows on my bed, not meeting my eyes. "You asked me to tell you how I knew I wanted to be with Khelan before proceeding to confess that you had fallen in love."

Thank gods for the doorframe. I grabbed hold of it to keep myself upright. "N-no, I didn't."

She looked at me now, a carefully blank look on her face. "Of course you did."

I did? I wouldn't have said anything like that. *Would I?*

Halls, I really couldn't be sure. I had been in such an emotional state after my epiphany about the depth of my feelings for Gannon, it was quite possible something had slipped out.

I shook my head. "I'm certain I didn't say I was in *love*." I couldn't have. My brain couldn't have been so addled that I would have given away *that* much.

"Well, not in so many words," she said with a smile. "But I'll never forget the way your eyes lit up as you said how incredibly smart, supremely confident and sinfully gorgeous this man was."

My face fell as the memory of our mother–daughter heart-to-heart flooded my mind. Damn it! I should have expected the woman to commit my *every* word to memory!

Ma looked at me expectantly, arching a brow. I had to give her *something*. Her expression was the one she used when as a child I was caught fibbing to cover up a wrong and she was determined to uncover the truth. Clearly, my mother was *not* going to let this go.

"It's someone I met at the Judiciary," I said. "Just after I started work."

A smile came to Ma's lips, but she quickly stifled it, dropping her gaze as she straightened the folds of her jade green skirt. "Is he a protector as well?"

I had to admire her attempt at nonchalance. "No."

She smiled then. "Ah, a subordinate then," she concluded with a satisfied nod.

I swallowed and darted a look out the door, hoping that by some divine intervention Adria would make a distracting appearance.

"And what does he do?"

I tensed, then, for some ungodly reason, said, "He works at the Dignitas One Judiciary." I bit down on my tongue, cursing myself.

"In Capita," she stated, eyes lighting up. "He must have a very high rank."

I nearly laughed. *That he does.* "Yes."

"What's his name?"

Oh, good lords. I ran a hand through my hair then called out the first name that came to mind. "James." *Shit. Could I have dug a deeper hole?*

Ma's smile widened. "And when will we meet *James?*"

Let's see ... Oh, how about never?

I chewed on my bottom lip as my mother blinked up at me, undiluted hope brimming in her brown eyes.

Maybe I should just confide in her, hear what she had to say. My mother was in love, had a long-lasting relationship with a senator too. If I were to take Gannon's offer seriously and have anything remotely meaningful with both him and Tai, I couldn't hide our relationship from my family. At least, not forever. We were close-knit; my parents and brother knew me too well for it to remain a secret.

Then again, Gannon said we would be careful and discreet like we had been in the past. My mother had done it, had managed to hide her relationship with Khelan from me and most everyone else, but *I* would be involved with Gannon Consul, *high chancellor of the Realm,* not some random senator from parts unknown.

My heart dipped. No. I couldn't tell her. It was a bad idea. I needed to wrap my head around all that being in a multiple like that would entail and, more importantly, find out if Tai would even be *open* to something like this.

"Gan— I mean *James* — is very busy, as you can imagine," I said, forcing apology into my voice. "I don't know when he'll be on Prospect Eight next."

The light in Ma's eyes dimmed. "I see."

I shifted on my feet while she continued considering me. Ma tilted her head, running a finger along her jaw, in that way of hers that told me the wheels of her mind were turning, and fast.

"So, tell me if I have this right," she said slowly, narrowing her eyes. "You're trying to figure things out with Tai while being in love with someone else?"

"Yes," I said, relieved that she was getting the point without me having to get into the details.

"So, you want them both?"

I expelled a breath. "Something like that."

Ma nodded, but gratefully appeared mollified. Unfortunately, my relief had a short life.

"Well, there's only one answer to that," she exclaimed, eyes lit up once again. "You should be with *both* men!"

Holy gods. This can't be happening. I closed my eyes briefly against the terrible irony. "What?" I breathed.

"Don't you see?" She beamed under the brilliance of her misguided solution. "It makes perfect sense!"

The way her eyes twinkled, I hazarded a guess that she was, at that very moment, envisioning me giving her two grandchildren, each with physical traits distinct from the other.

I groaned, shaking my head. "It's not that simple."

She drew back, a lift to her chin. "Don't they want to be involved with you?" Apparently, Ma didn't like the idea of anyone not wanting to be with her daughter. I smiled at that.

"Yes, they do," I said soothingly, "but it just wouldn't work." At least, I didn't *think* it would.

"Why not?"

I shrugged, wrapping my sweater around me, tight. "It's complicated."

"Ha," Ma scoffed with a wave of her hand. "*Everything* at your age is complicated."

Recalling my myriad of problems, I truly couldn't have agreed more.

* * *

"Is Mila on her way?" I asked Asher the moment he walked into the boardroom the following day.

Asher's customary smile slipped as the door slid shut behind him. "I thought you knew," he said, meeting me at one end of the large oval table in the center of the room. "She said she was going to be late, that she needed to greet someone at the arc station before joining."

She did?

I had met with Mila just an hour earlier to run through the final agenda for the advisory group meeting, and she hadn't said a word about being late. I frowned. Then again, my mind had been split between how I would lead the meeting and what Tai was up to.

Throughout the night, I had been assaulted by nightmares that played out every possible way Tai's plans to confront Gabriel could go awry. My earlier confidence in our idea was starting to shake. Thankfully, I wouldn't have to wait too much longer to find out whether it would work. I had found a message from Tai on my comm when I had woken that morning stating that everything was in place. He would be heading out with his team later this day to ambush Gabriel at the assigned time and location, and would contact me when it was all over.

I pulled at my bottom lip with my teeth. Gods, he had made it sound so simple! I could only hope it would be. If I knew anything about Gabriel Minister, it was how cunning the man was.

Asher looked me over the rim of his glasses. "You all right?"

I straightened my back. "I'm fine," I said quickly, smoothing down the curls of my hair. I needed to get my act together. Starting off my first advisory group meeting on the wrong foot was *not* an option.

"Hey, don't be nervous," he said, correctly reading my thoughts. "You've handled Mila and whole bunch of leadership. You can *totally* handle four directors."

Gods, I hope so. I expelled a deep breath, trying to snap out of it. I just needed to focus and forget everything else ... *at least* until the end of the meeting.

"Thanks, Asher," I said, smiling, grateful as usual to have him by my side.

"And if you get nervous," he said, straightening the narrow bit of black fabric around his neck, "just think about how good I clean up in this tie."

I laughed, just as I imagined he had expected me to, and rolled my eyes at the wink he followed up with.

The door slid open and in walked a group of subordinates — two women and two men.

Asher and I jumped into action. For the next few minutes, we carried out introductions and confirmed everyone had received the briefing packages that Asher had sent out on my behalf. By the time we were done, Mila still hadn't arrived.

As everyone took their seats, I fiddled with a button on the sleeve of my jacket, surveying the group, wondering what to do.

Should I start the meeting without Mila or wait?

When the directors met my searching gaze with an expectant one of their own, I drew in a deep breath and sat down in my chair.

"I guess we should get started," I said, then consulted my tablet unnecessarily. Staring blindly at the device, I wracked my brain for some witty remark, some clever way to open the floor. Finally, I gave up and lifted my head, glancing around the room.

"Thank you all for coming today," I began. "I appreciate your willingness to be a part of the first ever advisory group on exploration."

Wyatt, a ruddy-faced man from Hale, snorted, drawing everyone's attention. He leaned back in his seat, hooking an ankle over his knee.

"Forgive me," he said. "It's just that your assumption that we had a *choice* in being here struck me as incredibly funny."

I stiffened within the silence that followed his remark.

When I had gone over the background information Asher had compiled for me about the advisory group members, I had been especially impressed by Wyatt Director's experience. He was accomplished, having over a decade of experience on special committees and in supporting leadership across his dominion. It was easy to see why Mila had selected him to be in the advisory group. He had the knowledge I needed, but that fact hadn't prevented the wave of anxiety that had washed over me when I realized who Wyatt reported to.

Xavier Minister, Wyatt's superior, had been a spoke in the wheels during the special committee process, creating challenges I had absolutely no desire to revisit during my advisory group meetings. Unfortunately, taking in Wyatt's insolent demeanor now, it seemed that history could repeat itself.

I glanced at Asher, seeking some inspiration out of the awkward situation, but someone else spoke up.

"None of us had a *choice* whether to be here or not," Elias, a striking young man with a serious face from Prospect, commented. "We were assigned to this committee by our superiors, and we all know choice doesn't factor much for them. We all have a job to do, so I suggest we get on with it and help Kira in any way we can."

Gods bless him. I had seen Elias around the Judiciary from time to time, usually when he was speaking with Mila or on his way to the top floor, where he worked. He and I never had a need to cross paths, but it was good to have a familiar face on board as well as his full support, so I sent him a smile, filled with appreciation.

"Ignore my colleague," Kate, a woman from Dignitas, said. She eyed Wyatt with mischief in her moss green eyes. "I've had the … *pleasure* of working with Wyatt before, and let's just say, the reason he's on this committee is his strong work ethic — not his *sparkling* personality."

Everyone chuckled, breaking the tension in the room. Wyatt, however, also leveled a mild look at Kate before sliding low in his chair. She laughed easily, seeming to be used to such exchanges with him.

"I, for one, am *thrilled* to be here," said the woman to Kate's right. Lenore, from Septima, a mature woman with a braided coronet of salt and pepper hair, smiled across the table at me. Her hands fluttered on the table in front of her. "I can't imagine a better way to end my career than working on such a landmark project!"

I smiled, buoyed now by the group's excitement. Well, by *most* of the group's excitement. Wyatt sat quietly with a tolerant look on his face that appeared incredibly painful for any human being to bear.

After tossing a relieved look at Asher, who sent me a wink of encouragement, I drew back my shoulders.

"As you know, today will be the first in a series of meetings," I said. "With your support, should Realm Council approve the special committee's recommendation, I'll advise Realm Council on effective policies for safe and effective exploration across our worlds."

I paused, glancing about the table to confirm everyone was following along. Kate, Elias and Lenore were focused on me, while Wyatt appeared enthralled by the information on his tablet.

"I'd like to start by discussing what is sure to be Realm Council's greatest concern and priority: our system's ability to protect its citizens against unexpected dangers like that which occurred on the Old World."

Lenore clutched a hand her chest. "We just *can't* let the massacre on Septima One happen again," she breathed. "I can't fathom the idea of losing so many lives!"

Wyatt raised his head, sending me a cool look. "Which is why we should keep our noses *here*, in the Realm, where they belong," he added. "Not in the Outer Realm, where rogue worlds can annihilate our citizens *en masse*."

I frowned as everyone in the group began to speak at once, discussing the pros and cons of Realm exploration, which was an utter waste of time. Leadership had already deliberated those very issues at length.

Elias gestured to me, capturing my attention. "We should prepare a preliminary report that outlines the advantages and disadvantages of possible safety measures."

I nodded. "Thank you," I said, appreciating his attempt to redirect the conversation back to the matter at hand. "A document like that would be a helpful starting point for discussions at Realm Council."

Kate leaned forward, resting her forearms on either side of her tablet. "Will we be required to attend Realm Council meetings?"

I opened my mouth, but Lenore jumped in before I could speak. "Oh, I hope so," she gushed.

I indulged the awe in her eyes with a smile. "Unfortunately, only direct supports are authorized to attend Realm Council meetings."

Lenore sighed. "Oh well, it's probably a good thing," she said with a self-deprecating smile, then laughed, looking at me. "I'd probably just embarrass myself in front of the high chancellor. Truly, I don't know how you managed to maintain your professionalism around that gorgeous young man."

I flushed right down to my toes. *Professionalism! If she only knew!*

I shot a look at Asher out of the corner of my eye, but he was preoccupied, trying to survive a coughing fit ... or was it *laughter* he was trying to cover up? Probably. He had a tendency to succumb to such fits at the most *suspicious* of times.

"Will we be required to speak to the media?" Kate asked, cutting into my thoughts.

"No, not at all," I said quickly, latching onto the change of subject like a drowning woman within reach of a boat.

Wyatt eyed me, leaning in. "But *you* regularly speak to the media, don't you?"

I cocked my head, noting his tone. "I *did*, yes, during the special committee process."

He raised a brow. "Should we expect you to be speaking on behalf of *this* group?"

"Of course not." What was he getting at? "I don't have authorization to speak on behalf of this group, or any other, for that matter."

Wyatt smirked. "So you no longer speak on behalf the *Subordinate caste?*"

I frowned as the gazes of the rest of the directors fixed on me, keen interest shining in their eyes, then I stilled, realizing the reason for Wyatt's odd line of questioning.

My reputation had preceded me. If they had paid *any* attention to the newsfeed over the last few months, they had probably come to believe me some outspoken subordinate with little regard for Realm governance and law — or worse, an unqualified citizen who had only been appointed to this position because of her status as a media darling.

My heart sank.

A moment later, the door to the boardroom slid open and Mila strode in. Her presence alone would have been enough to make everyone straighten in their seats, but the group came to their feet when Aresh Ambassador, leader of our dominion, walked in right behind her.

"I apologize for being late," Mila said, directing her superior to a chair on the other side of the table, directly across from me. "Don't let us interrupt."

I shot a look to my right, and could tell by Asher's uncertain expression that he too was wondering why the ambassador was there.

"I should be the one apologizing," the ambassador said, adjusting his jacket as he lowered himself into his seat before looking directly at me. "I asked to join the meeting at the last minute. I hope you don't mind."

Mind? I had already been fretting over the fact that Mila would be overseeing me as I led the meeting. Now I had to worry over the *ambassador*, too!

"Of course I don't mind," I lied, and the smile in his gray eyes had a knowing quality, as though he perceived the truth.

When Mila sat down to his right, the ambassador sat back and said, "Please. Carry on."

I swallowed then looked to the directors and Asher, who were still on their feet. "Everyone, please have a seat." After everyone was seated, I said, "Let's start with a quick review of article two hundred and eighteen and then return to our discussion on safety measures."

I glanced at Mila, checking in, and she nodded. I took that to mean I was on the right track. At least, I hoped so.

***

"It just doesn't make sense," I said to Asher as we walked into the eatery on the ground floor of the Judiciary. "Why would Mila bring the *ambassador* to the advisory group meeting?"

Asher wove through the crowd, leading the way. "Probably to test you out," he called out over his shoulder.

Test me out? I stepped around a subordinate, trying to catch up. Mila had given me the role of advisor, which meant I had *already* proven myself. Didn't it?

Frowning, I followed Asher to a table at the back. "Testing me for what?" I asked.

Asher faced me, shaking his head. "For such a smart woman," he said, "you really have a startling lack of awareness about what's going on around you." He drew out a chair and sat down.

I rolled my eyes, sinking into my own seat. "Then *do* indulge my ignorance and lay it all out for me."

He planted his elbows on the table and looked me directly in the eye. "The Corona is going to appoint you to the subordinate position on Realm Council."

After a beat of dumbfounded silence, I laughed, my voice carrying above the din of the noisy space. "Did I ever tell you how much I missed you on Dignitas?" I said, sobering with a smile. "I really could've used your humor."

When Asher didn't join in, my smile wobbled. *Wait a minute.* "You're not joking?"

He shook his head. "Nope."

I blinked a couple time then said, "Asher, I *cannot* represent the Subordinate caste."

He frowned. "Why not?"

I balked at his continued lunacy then recovered. *All right, let me spell it out.*

I shifted forward in my seat while holding his gaze. "I just started at the Judiciary less than a year ago," I said, holding up a hand and starting to tick off each completely rational reason on my fingers. "I'm only twenty-one years old. The first time I've been to our system's capital, much less to a *Realm Council* meeting, was yesterday and that was merely to watch. On top of all that …" I cringed.

On top of all that … I'm the illegitimate daughter of a senator in hiding with an uncle who's off somewhere consorting with rebels. Oh, and how could I forget? Our former minister — the asshole otherwise known as Gabriel — well, he's hell-bent on ruining my life by revealing everything about my family and the fact that I had an affair with the high chancellor.

Asher stared at me, blinking. "On top of all that … what?"

I dropped my hand to the table. There was no need to share all of *that* with Asher. "I think I've said enough to make my point."

Asher didn't appear to agree. "Your age and experience don't mean that much," he said. "The Corona was twenty-two when she was appointed sovereign. Most of leadership thought she was in over her head."

True. "But there are hundreds, if not *thousands*, of qualified subordinates who would be a better choice than me."

Asher snorted. "Thousands?" He laughed. "Name one."

Well, *that* was easy. "Rhoan."

He cocked his head, thinking. "I kinda was under the impression your brother wouldn't be interested in a position like that."

Rhoan wasn't, but that was beside the point. This was a once-in-a-lifetime opportunity. He'd be a fool to give it up. "He'll come around," I said.

Asher gave his glasses a nudge up his nose and folded his arms on the table. "Who else?"

I pursed my lips, glowering at him. *Why is he pressing me on this?*

"All right," I said. "What about Taran Adjudicator." He was a high-ranking subordinate from our very own Judiciary, but there were even more qualified citizens from other divisions, across the Realm. "And then there's Jonas Barrister from Septima and Lauren Litigator from Dignitas. Take your pick."

Asher conceded with a short nod. "I'm sure any one of them could do the job well enough," he said. "But they don't have your reputation *or* level of influence. Just look at your following."

I rolled my eyes. Oh yes, that incredibly *undaunted* following of mine that led the advisory group to believe I was unqualified to lead them. Speaking of which ... "The Corona could very well appoint any of the directors on the advisory group to Realm Council," I said.

Asher shook his head. "No one would listen to any of them the way they would you," he said.

"Were you and I at the same meeting today?" I balked. "I was hardly able to wrangle *four* subordinates into focusing on the project they were assigned to. How in the worlds do you think I could get our *entire caste* to take direction from me?"

Asher inched closer in his seat, leaning toward me. Truly, if he'd come any closer, he'd have been in my lap.

"Read the newsfeed, Kira," he said. "Our caste is *already* taking direction from you."

I stared at him, dumbstruck that he and I could have become such good friends without me knowing he suffered from madness.

"I think you've been reading too many tabloids," I said.

Asher considered me for a long moment then gave up with a shrug. "You'll figure it out." He tapped a panel in the center of the table with his comm to beckon a server.

Meanwhile, I stared at the top of his bald head as he considered the menu.

Asher was out of his mind. Wasn't he? But then, suppose he was right? Halls, I couldn't even wrap my head around that! I had graduated from the Academy with a simple desire to follow in Khelan's footsteps. The idea of representing my caste in any way, much less on Realm Council, had *never* entered my mind. It was just too much to come to grips with. In fact — I cringed — it was downright *ludicrous*.

Who do I think I am? To be appointed to a position like that I needed to earn the respect of my caste. No matter what Asher said, despite all the media attention as I had attracted, I had only become a spectacle as a result, some sort of *celebrity*. The comments from the advisory group were proof enough of that.

With a sigh, I dismissed Asher and his wild ambitions for me. A second later, my gaze fell on a subordinate sitting at a table a short distance away. His head of dark brown hair was bowed, focused on his menu, so I couldn't see his face. Nevertheless, something about him seemed familiar.

"Are you ready to order?"

I glanced up and found a server looking between Asher and me with a polite smile.

Asher and I spent the next hour discussing plans for the next advisory group meeting over lunch. By the time we were done, my head was swimming with a lengthy list of things to do.

"I'll meet you upstairs," Asher said as we walked out of the eatery and into the lobby. "I offered to meet Maralis at Prospect Council building to show her around."

I frowned. "Maralis?"

He gestured toward the doors at the front of the building where a petite young woman with a halo of pink hair and an infectious smile was waving madly at us. "The new clerk," he explained, beaming at me.

Huh. I raised a brow. "I didn't know that giving personal tours of the Judiciary was part of your job."

Asher shrugged. "What can I say?" he said, a twinkle in his eye, as he started to back away. "She's good people."

I smiled as he traversed the lobby toward Maralis with a bounce in his step.

Interesting. Asher had me pegged. I wasn't one for office gossip, but *this* was one development I *definitely* planned on keeping an eye on.

Moments later, I approached the elevators, my thoughts running this way and that until they collided with the matter I had temporarily shoved to the back of my mind. I checked my comm as I entered the elevator. Tai should be heading out to confront Gabriel soon. I shuddered at the thought.

As the doors closed behind me, I turned around then startled. Reflected in the mirrored elevator wall was the same subordinate man from the eatery. He stood behind me, just off to my right, so I had a full view of him now. When he smiled, my breath caught in my throat as recognition flooded my brain and my blood went cold.

No. It couldn't be! I spun around, jaw going slack as I looked Gabriel over, trying to understand.

"Your eyes aren't playing tricks on you, Metallurgist," he said with a smirk, looking me over in turn.

Instead of blue, his hair was brown, and his eyes were green instead of gray. Even his complexion appeared a shade darker than his usual olive tone. But it *was* him. His build and the bone structure of his face remained the same. Then it dawned on me: *optics.* Gabriel's regular use of the cosmetic-changing technology was as much a part of him as his malicious streak. They were the only way he could have managed such a transformation. My pulse raced.

All Above, was *this* how he had managed to get into my office to leave the note? I had figured Gabriel would have had one of his goons do his dirty work, but I could have been wrong. The man stood there, in front of me, in the middle of the Judiciary at the height of the work day. He could have just as brazenly entered the building in his current disguise.

Fear coursing through me, I lunged for the elevator panel, searching for a button that would stop the elevator and let me out, but Gabriel grasped my arm and bent it into an awkward position around my back. I cried out at the knifing pain that ran up my limb.

"I would prefer to keep things civilized," he said, his fingers digging sharply into my flesh. "Please refrain from doing anything that would force me to be otherwise."

Gabriel released me with a shove, and I staggered into a corner with a whimper before kneading my throbbing arm.

He stilled, considering me, as though watching for any sudden movements, then pressed the button I hadn't been able to locate in my rising panic. When the elevator slid to a stop but remained closed, another course of escape leapt to mind.

Jonah! He *had* to be somewhere nearby! I began tapping at my comm with a shaking hand.

"Go ahead," Gabriel drawled, and I faltered, glancing up. "Jonah, that protector of yours, won't be able to help you here."

I lowered my arm, trying to comprehend what he had just said. Gabriel had revealed to me in Helios that he had been keeping tabs on me somehow, but I hadn't realized until now just how *closely* had was doing it. Halls, he knew I had a protector *and* his name too!

I pressed my back against the cold wall of the elevator. "I thought we were supposed to meet me at the arc station," I said. "Why are you here?"

Gabriel tutted with a sad shake of his head. "Did you really think I would tell you *where* I was going to be and *when?*" he said. "I suspect the moment I would have set foot on that station platform, your cavalry would have arrived."

I squeezed my eyelids shut, wishing I had listened to my gut feelings. My earlier loss in confidence in our plan hadn't been misplaced.

"So tell me," he said, crossing his arms with a sly grin. "Whose plans to capture me have I thwarted? Our new high chancellor's or Tai Commander's?" He snorted. "Truth be told, no matter how much I follow your movements, it's terribly difficult to tell which one you're fucking."

I glowered at him, unwilling to be baited. "What do you want, Gabriel?" I spat.

A hard glint came to his eyes. "I can see you're no longer in a mood for polite conversation," he said, taking a step toward me. "So let's get down to business before young Jonah figures out his charge is missing."

I inched back as best I could in the limited space, bracing myself.

He drew up his shoulders. "In short order, the Corona will be meeting with Liandra Ambassador, the Realm's favorite dissident," he said. "After Liandra's recent public outburst, more than likely our sovereign has plans to threaten the woman into silence. Nevertheless, I need you to access some important information for prior to that meeting."

I narrowed my eyes on him. "How do you know the Corona's travel plans?" Did he have someone monitoring her moves like he did me?

Gabriel smirked. "The thorn in our sovereign's side also happens to be Maxim's sole obsession," he said. "Liandra told him, and he, of course, told me."

So Maxim and Liandra *were* in regular communication. Tai had been right. But considering the high security around Liandra, how were they managing it?

"Does Maxim have someone working for him on Dignitas?" I asked, eyeing him, hoping Gabriel would reveal something that would help us catch the rebel elite. "Is that how Liandra's getting the information to him?"

"Come now," Gabriel said with a frown so deep I would have believed I had disappointed him in some way. "Do you really expect me to tell you that?"

I glared at him, and his laughter sounded sharp and loud within the small confines of the elevator.

"You seem to have a lot of people giving you information," I said with a curl to my lip. "Why don't you ask one of your *hundreds* of Quad members to assist you?"

Gabriel raised a brow. "So you've done your homework," he said. "Tell me. Why should I risk any members of the Quad being found out when I already have you, ready and willing, to help so that your secrets don't come out?"

Why indeed? My shoulders fell.

Gabriel reached inside his jacket pocket and brought out a slip of paper and a slim circular metal storage device. When he held them both out to me, I hesitated, noticing the paper had a line of text typed onto it: P8J-12-029.

"That's an authorization code for records at level twelve," I said, looking at him now.

"Sharp as always, Metallurgist," he drawled. "I want you to use this code to access two dockets within the database: one named Arc Meridius, the other Zenith."

I was already shaking my head. "I'm not permitted to access records at that level." No one except leadership was. "I would need an issuer ID from a minister or someone in a higher rank to go along with such a file request."

"Then use your superior's ID," he said smoothly. "No one will ask any questions."

He couldn't be serious! Using an issuer ID under false pretenses was a *felony*. If I was discovered, I'd be lucky if I didn't get detained.

"I won't do it," I said firmly, shoving his hand, the one still holding the paper and device, away. "I can't."

Gabriel curled his fingers around the items and loomed over me, menacing. "Either you transfer the files to this chip yourself or I approach Asher Analyst to do it instead," he said, eyes glittering. "It's your choice."

I slumped against the wall. *No. Not Asher.* I didn't want him anywhere near any of this, and Gabriel knew it, so the choices he offered up could be taken as nothing less than a well-aimed threat. My stomach turned on itself. I stared up at Gabriel, wondering what to do. Dear gods, what was in these files that he would risk coming here himself? Curiosity slowly smothered my fear and fueled my logic.

Perhaps I *should* try to access the files. Not to give them to Gabriel, of course, but to find out what was in them. Maybe the information would lead to a way to stopping not only Gabriel, but Maxim and the entire Quad.

I took the paper and storage device with an unsteady hand.

Gabriel grinned. "I thought so," he said, stepping back before leaning over to press the same button on the elevator panel. My already unsettled stomach flipped over as the elevator started to descend. "I'll expect both dockets in short order."

"But how? Where?" I spluttered then froze. "Will you be coming back to meet me?" My breath shook at the thought.

Gabriel chuckled as the elevator slowed to the ground floor once again. "Don't worry, Metallurgist," he said, apparently reading the distress in my voice correctly. "You won't be seeing me again. Next time, I'll send a much friendlier face."

CHAPTER 7

"Don't go to the arc station!" I blurted out as soon as Tai picked up my call. The door to my office slid closed behind me as I walked to my desk.

"Why?" he demanded.

"Gabriel," I replied, gripping with a shaking hand the paper and storage device Gabriel had given me. "He was *here*, at the Judiciary."

Tai spoke, his voice muffled, to someone on his side of the call. "I'll be there in fifteen minutes," he said to me before ending the call.

I blew out a chestful of air before sinking into my chair.

Fifteen minutes. That wasn't very long. Thanks gods. And by then, maybe Jonah would have come up with something.

After Gabriel had exited the elevator, I had wasted little time in contacting Jonah. The protector had run into the lobby only moments after I had called him, but it was too late. Gabriel had already melded into the crowded lobby and headed out onto the busy streets, probably disappearing without a trace. Nevertheless, Jonah had ordered me up to my office to wait for him there while he searched the area.

I shook my head. "It's no use," I had told him. "Gabriel's probably already in a hover heading back to gods know where. There's nothing you can do."

"Unfortunately," Jonah had said through thinned lips, every line of his body rigid and tense, "the high chancellor won't see it that way."

My gaze lowered now to my hands, or, more specifically, to the tracking device, and I frowned at the irony. There Gannon and Tai were, drowning me in security, and Gabriel had *still* been able to get close to me — on *two* occasions, no less!

My hands shook with rage. *How much fucking longer am I going to have to endure this?!* We *had* to figure out a way to stop Gabriel! Or rather, *I* had to.

I glowered now through the opaque glass of my office door. Tai and Gannon had learned a lot about Gabriel and Maxim were up to and had put a plan in action, but Gabriel had been anticipating our every move all along. *This—* the code Gabriel had given me — was my chance to help. I just needed to find out what was in the dockets without incriminating myself.

The blurry silhouette of a slim, blond-haired figure strolled passed my door. I sat up, spotting the solution to my dilemma.

Erik had told me to contact him if I needed any other records. Of course, he had probably meant records I was authorized to access, but this was the only way for me to access the files with no one the wiser. Erik wouldn't question my requests for files at level twelve. As far as he would be concerned, I was doing research for the advisory group. Moreover, I didn't plan on actually *obtaining* the files. I just wanted to know what their contents were.

But then maybe there was another way to go about it. Gannon could access the dockets, couldn't he? Or maybe Tai? But I just didn't like either idea. So far I had been reliant on them to help me get out of this mess with Gabriel and Maxim, but this was *my* problem, and on top of that we had had little luck going through any of their routes.

Decision made, I stood up and hurried out of the room. I called out to Erik before he could turn the corner at the end of the hallway.

He drew up with a jolt, the tablet he was holding under his arm nearly falling to the floor. He turned to me with a wary look in his eye. And for good reason. The last time we had spoken, I had pretty much accosted him in a manner only little better than Gabriel had just done me.

I gave Erik what I hoped was my most friendly and open smile. "Would you please access a file for me?"

He hesitated before walking toward me. "Certainly," he said and started to unroll his scroll.

I stole a look down the empty hall. "It's really more than a *file*," I said when he stood in front of me. "It's two *dockets*."

"All right," he said, his fingers flying across the device's screen. "What's the authorization code?"

"P8J-12-029," I said quickly, having memorized the number and docket names by heart.

Erik's fingers froze, his eyes shifting to me. "Level *twelve?*"

I stiffened. "Th-that's right," I said, striving to maintain a calm façade. "I don't need copies. I just want to know the type of information they contain."

His blond brows furrowed. "I won't be able to access anything at that level without an issuer ID," he said. "Is it Mila's?"

I swallowed. "Yes."

Erik considered me for a long, torturous moment then resumed typing. "Which dockets are you interested in?" he asked, studying the screen.

I inched closer to him, peering over the lip of his tablet. "Arc Meridius and Zenith."

He swiped down the screen then looked at me after a slight pause. "The Arc docket contains itineraries and logistics for leadership travel across the Realm," he said. "It's very detailed."

Details about leadership travel? Why?

The muffled sound of chatter filtered up the hallway as two women entered it. *Shit.* I was running out of time.

"And the Zenith docket," I urged Erik. "What's in there?"

Once again, Erik began tapping at his scroll's screen. "Same issuer ID, right?" he asked, still focused on his device.

"Yes," I replied quickly and jumped when my comm chimed. One glance at it confirmed that Tai had arrived and was waiting for me downstairs, in the lobby.

"Huh. That's strange," Erik said, and my attention snapped back to him. He was making a face at his tablet.

"What's wrong?"

"There's a Zenith docket, but there aren't any files assigned to it," he said then gazed at me with a frown. "Are you sure you have the right authorization code?"

I opened my mouth, about to say yes, but then closed it just as fast. Had Gabriel sent me on some sort of fool's errand? Was this a trick? My mind swirled with possibilities, trying to grasp what this meant.

I held Erik's quizzical gaze. "Forgive me," I said, edging around him, anxious to get to Tai and figure this all out. "Maybe I *do* need another code for that docket. Let me confirm with Mila and get back to you. All right?"

Erik nodded, a deep frown marring his face.

I sent him a wobbly smile then left him standing, staring after me, by my office door.

***

When I exited the elevator minutes later, Tai was standing in the middle of the Judiciary's lobby, glowering at Jonah. Tai had one hand clenched in a fist while he jabbed a finger in the younger protector's face.

Oh no. This isn't going to be good.

I hurried over and reached them just in time to hear Tai say through clenched teeth, "And where the fuck were you in all this?"

Jonah stiffened, holding Tai's gaze. "Patrolling the area nearby, Commander," he said, a miserable look on his face. "Subordinate Metallurgist was inaccessible to me at the time."

I had to give Jonah credit — he didn't flinch the way I would have under Tai's furious gaze.

I moved closer to Tai. "It's true," I said, hoping he wouldn't make a big deal over this. "I was in the elevator. He couldn't have reached me even if he had known where I was."

Tai swept a belligerent look over me, the lines around his mouth tightening before returning to Jonah. "Subordinate Metallurgist is coming with me," he said, wrapping his fingers around my elbow and tugging.

I frowned as Tai turned me toward the door, but not before I caught the look of alarm sliding through Jonah's eyes.

"The high chancellor won't appreciate this change in plans," Jonah called out, behind us now, as Tai led me away.

Tai grunted. "You can tell *the high chancellor* to take it up with me," he tossed over his shoulder as we left the building and went out, into the damp squall-season air.

I ground my teeth as we sidestepped a puddle. "I really don't think that was necessary," I muttered under my breath. I understood he was worried about me, but that type of high-handedness was truly a bit too much.

Tai sent me a quelling look then released my arm when we reached the massive vehicle idling by the curb. With a sigh, I slid into his hover and waited as he rounded the transport to get into the driver's seat. Only when Tai had navigated the hover up and into a glide did he speak again.

"Tell me what happened," he demanded.

From the little I had overheard of his conversation with Jonah, I figured Tai was already aware that Gabriel had hijacked the elevator I was in to threaten me again, so I got straight to what he needed to know.

"Gabriel never planned on going to the arc station," I began then told him how, after holding me hostage in the elevator, Gabriel had confirmed Tai's suspicion that Maxim and Liandra had been in contact and told me what information he was looking for. By the time I finished, Tai's muscles were bunched around his neck as tightly as he was gripping the steering wheel.

"Asshole," he spat out.

"I couldn't agree more," I murmured, staring blindly at the flashing lights on the hover's dashboard.

Tai blew out a breath. "You said he wants the Arc Meridius and Zenith dockets." He shot a look at me, asking for confirmation. When I nodded, he glared through the windshield. "Give me the authorization code. I'll see if I can access the dockets to see what's inside. Maybe something there that'll reveal where Gabriel and Maxim are or what they're up to."

I shifted in my seat to face him, encouraged that he was thinking along the same lines I had been. "I *already* know what's in the dockets," I said carefully. "Well, one of them, that is."

Tai looked at me sharply. "What do you mean you *know* what's in the dockets?"

I hesitated at his tone. "I asked Erik, our receptionist, to access them for me."

His face fell. "Do you have any idea what would happen to you if anyone found out you tried to access level-twelve files?"

I stared at Tai, aghast. I had assumed we were on the same page. "Weren't you about to do the very same thing?" I countered.

Tai shook his head, an act full of utter disbelief. "You're talking to someone who once erased all reference to you in the media, Kira," he said. "I think I know a thing or two about how to cover my tracks."

I wilted, taking that in, but couldn't give up defending myself. "Erik's authorized to access any and every file in the database," I argued. "No one will think anything of him making that kind of request. Plus I didn't obtain print or digital copies. Nothing can be traced back to me."

Tai tightened his hold on the steering wheel, staring through the windshield and the now drizzling rain. "Be that as it may," he said, "I wish you'd have more confidence in me."

I drew back in my seat. "What are you talking about?" I had nothing *but* confidence in him.

He sighed. "Did it ever occur to you that I didn't *expect* Gabriel to show up at the arc station?" he asked, sliding a questioning look at me. "That I had some *alternate* plan?"

My eyes widened. *He did?* "You did?"

Tai focused on the view outside again, navigating through the other hovers passing by. "Believe it or not," he drawled, "this isn't the *first* mission I've ever led."

"But then why ..." I searched his profile, hurt that he had chosen to keep the *entire* plan from me. "Why didn't you tell me?"

"Because I didn't want you acting strangely," he said with a sigh. "It would only make Gabriel, Maxim or whoever the fuck else is tracking you more suspicious." He looked at me from the corner of his eye. "You were already nervous about the plan working. Giving you something else to worry about wouldn't have helped anything."

I supposed that made sense, but his rational justification kept my back up.

The buzzing sound of Tai's comm filled the cab.

Tai glanced down at his device. "It's Gannon," he stated, and my eyebrows shot up.

I shouldn't have been surprised by the call. Of *course*, Jonah would have reported in with Gannon, but I had been expecting him to wait at *least* until the blasted sun rose on Dignitas One! I sagged, anticipating the foul mood Gannon was sure to be in.

He activated the call and drawled, "I take it you no longer think having a protector assigned to Kira to be the more clever idea."

"Just tell me what happened," Gannon bit out, ignoring Tai's dig.

I jumped in, quickly bringing Gannon up to speed while glossing over how I had come to know what was in the dockets as Tai looked on. Tai quirked his brow at me, apparently fully aware of what I was about.

"Zenith," Gannon murmured as though to himself.

"*And* Arc Meridius," I noted then looked to Tai. "Why would the Quad want information about leadership travel?"

The hover dipped as Tai made a sudden turn. "You said Gabriel knows about the Corona's upcoming meeting with Liandra," he said. "He must want the Arc docket for information about which arc craft the Corona will be on and when."

I held my breath. "So, they can try to stop them from meeting?"

Tai frowned, flicking a grim look my way. "No," he said. "To *attack* the craft. If the Quad kills the Corona, they'll tip power toward themselves and have the upper hand in taking over the Realm."

"A new Realm order," I whispered, recalling what Gannon had assumed about the Quad's ultimate plans.

The three of us were quiet as we absorbed that. Finally, Gannon spoke.

"We have to inform the authorities," he said tightly, shaking me to the core.

Gannon and Tai had been completely against involving the authorities when I had suggested it immediately following my abduction. The fact that Gannon was willing to do so now only confirmed how dire things were fast becoming.

"I won't let anyone else die or get hurt if there's anything I can do to prevent it," Gannon said.

Tai nodded. "I'll issue a request to my superior to increase the Corona's security."

"Issue it directly to the high marshal instead," Gannon ordered. "Tell him the high chancellor approved your request. Things will move a lot faster that way."

Tai hesitated then said, "All right."

Meanwhile, I searched my brain for some way to help. "What about the surveillance cameras?" I asked.

Gannon had wanted his protectors to check them after Gabriel had left the note in my office. Maybe they had come across some information that could give us some clues.

"Talib didn't find anything," Gannon replied. "And checking the cameras won't be of any help to us now. We know for a fact that Gabriel was there. The question is where he went."

I held back my frustration and sent a searching look to Tai.

"Well then we have to use the only lead we have," he said. "We need to access the Zenith docket to find out what's inside."

I shook my head, about to tell him not to bother, that the docket didn't contain any files, but Gannon replied instead.

"Files are no longer maintained in the Zenith docket," he announced. "I had the high marshal transfer the records to a higher-level location within the database just before I became high chancellor."

He did?

Tai's eyebrows raised. "Why would you do that?"

"It was a matter of Realm security."

I exchanged a look with Tai. "So you know what Zenith contains, then," I concluded.

After a pause, Gannon said, "I do."

I waited for him to fill in the blanks, but Tai was less patient than me.

"Holy fuck, man!" he blurted out. "What's in the bloody docket?"

Gannon exhaled an aggravated breath. "It has to do with the special committee," he said. "I can't say any more than that — no matter how secure this line is supposed to be."

I frowned. Why would Zenith, a docket protected by some unknown *higher-level* security, contain information related to the special committee on exploration? Realm Council had already started reviewing our recommendation. All related documents should now be available at level one, for general access, as was required by law.

I checked in with Tai, finding a deep crease between his brows. It seemed he too found Gannon's reply wanting, warranting more questions, but we didn't get a chance to voice any them.

"Let me know when the security request goes through," Gannon said, cutting through the silence between us. A muffled sound in his background indicated he was now on the move. "I've assigned Talib to be with you from here on out."

It took me a second to realize Gannon was now talking to me and, more importantly, *what* he was talking about.

I squeezed my eyelids shut, clenching my teeth. If he was assigning Talib to me, it could only mean one thing. "Gannon, *please* don't tell me you dismissed Jonah."

"I should have," he replied with a disheartening promptness, "but I didn't. He'll be doing administrative work until further notice."

I groaned. To a protector like Jonah — *any* protector, for that matter — such a punishment would be *worse* than dismissal!

I looked to Tai, hoping for some show of support for his fellow protector, but I shouldn't have bothered. Tai held a perfectly satisfied expression on his face that revealed he was, for once, in complete agreement with Gannon.

Ha! Would wonders never cease!

I slunk back into my seat, peering through the rain as the two of them spoke about keeping each other up to date and putting all manner of thing in place to keep me safe — or at the very least, to *feel* safe.

Truly, if they only set their egos aside for a moment they would realize just how *much* they had in common: me.

I cringed at the ill-timed thought. *Now* was definitely not the time to be wondering about what my future held with either man or both. A crack of lightning lit up the view, and I leaned forward, noticing a familiar landscape, but not the one I had been expecting. A sinking sensation spread through my gut.

I turned to Tai as soon as he signed off on the call. "Where are we going?" I asked. "I thought you were taking me home."

Tai kept his eyes focused through the windshield. "Change of plans," he said. "It's time we tell your family about everything that's been going on."

It took me a few tries before I could get my mouth to work. "Weren't *you* the one who said that we shouldn't involve my family?" I said. "That you and Gannon should handle Gabriel and Maxim *alone?*"

"I also didn't want to tell the authorities," he admitted. "But *that* was before I knew about they were planning an attack on the Realm sovereign. Now that I'll have the high marshal's help, I can better protect you, but Gabriel and Maxim's band of disgruntled citizens is growing every day. At some point the media's going to pick up on the Protectorate's interest in the Quad and possibly your connection to it."

Tai was making sense, but also like we had run out of options, that there was no hope. "So that's it," I said, staring at him, falling apart inside. "We just … *give up*."

Tai's gaze hardened. "We're not *giving up*," he said, jaw firm. "I *will* stop them, Kira, but I can't promise it'll be before Gabriel throws you to the wolves, exposing everything about you and your family. *You* need to be the one to tell your family what's going on — not some fucked-up Quad member or the newsfeed."

I buried my face between my palms. *Oh gods.* Everything he was saying was logical, but I just couldn't accept it. How could I? I had hidden so much from my family, including the fact that I had been in contact with Maxim, the very person who had led our family astray in the beginning.

Hallowed Halls, but Khelan's going to murder me.

Could I be any more of a hypocrite? I had condemned Khelan for deepening our family's connection to rebels and then, there I was, firmly connected to not one but *two* leaders of the strongest faction in the Realm. My stomach turned at my family's response, yet I *had* to tell them. I had no choice. Tai was right. It was best they heard the truth from me and no one else.

My hands fell to my lap. "All right," I said, heart thumping in my throat. "We'll tell them."

Tai began to nod then caught himself. He spent the next few minutes navigating the hover into a space in front of my parent's house before facing me and holding my gaze firmly.

"You *do* realize what I mean when I said we need to tell your family *everything*," he said. "Don't you."

I blinked, staring at him. Of course I did. I understood the consequences. My parents were going to be angry. *Who am I kidding? They're going to be positively livid!* Still, I had to confess. It was going to be incredibly difficult to face their anger, *Khelan's* in particular, but telling them about Gabriel and Maxim would be *nothing* compared to telling them about my relationship with Gann—.

I gasped. "No." The word shot right out of my mouth.

Tai's eyes darkened. "Kira …"

"No!" I said so loudly this time, my voice drowned out the underlying hum of the hover.

His mouth narrowed into a hard line. "One secret leads to the other," he stated calmly, but I could tell by the way his nostrils flared that he was anything but calm. "How do you plan on telling your family about Gabriel's and Maxim's threats while leaving your relationship with Gannon out?"

That stumped me for a moment, but I rallied, pulling the reason right out of the air. "Maxim's motivation is to avenge Liandra, and Gabriel's motivation is to take me down because he thinks I've ruined his life," I hurried to explain. "All my family needs to know is that the two of them joined forced to form the Quad and are bribing me for information. Gannon doesn't have to come up. He doesn't factor."

Tai looked at me as though I were showing the early signs of madness. "Of *course* he factors!" he shouted, making me jump. "Gabriel and Maxim are threatening to expose your relationship with *the Realm high chancellor*. They're leveraging that *and* your family's dissidence to get what they want!"

I turned away from him. I didn't want to hear it. "Gabriel knows I couldn't care less if he reveals my relationship with Gannon." I had told the asshole so myself after being abducted and taken to Helios. "It's my *family* he'll use to get back at me — not *Gannon*."

"Gabriel doesn't give a flying fuck about your family, Kira." Tai enunciated each word so clearly, I could very nearly see the letters written in the air. "This is all about *you*. That fucker attempted to kill Gannon just to get back at *you*. Gabriel knows the best way to hurt you, other than through your family, is by putting your affair with Gannon on the line. He's not going to just toss that kind of leverage away."

I collapsed into my seat under the weight of that reality and ground my teeth. I wanted to scream, pull my hair out, do *something*, but nothing I could do would make what Tai was saying any less true.

Maybe I should listen to Tai. He only had my best interest at heart, but … no, I couldn't do it. I just couldn't tell my family about my relationship with Gannon. On top of everything else I was planning to tell them, this would be too much for them to take.

I took a bracing breath and glanced over at Tai. He sat, staring at me with a determined set to his jaw and a cool look in his eyes.

"Well?"

I sighed. "All right," I said. "We'll tell my family."

The tension in Tai's expression, and he shifted in his seat, about to open his door.

"But *not* about Gannon," I rushed out then winced as Tai cursed under his breath before turning back to me.

I met his gaze steadily. "I won't tell my parents about Gannon. Not unless we have to."

* * *

"Rhoan and Khelan are here," Ma announced as she entered the sitting area. Behind her, Da followed, sending Tai and me a worried look.

Both Da and Ma had been giving us fretful glances since we had arrived at my parents' home and told them we needed to speak with the entire family at once. I supposed it was a fair reaction. The last time, too, that Tai had been there, he had called for a family meeting. Then, the purpose had been to try to convince Khelan to break ties with Maxim. Our gathering had ended on a positive note, with all of us hoping that Maxim was no longer part of our lives.

I wilted, wondering how in the Realm I was going to break it to them that not only was Maxim *still* a part our lives, but so was an entire rebel group!

When Khelan and my brother walked through the front door, I sat down in the armchair closest to the fireplace, gaze wandering over to Tai. He stood, arms crossed, on the other side of the room, facing me. He sent me a small nod of encouragement, but the kindness did nothing to soothe my nerves.

Just then Khelan hurried into the sitting area, face still flush from the cool, outside air. "We got here as fast as we could," he said, looking around the room. "Is everyone all right?"

"As far as we know," Da said, shifting his gaze to Tai and then to me.

Tai frowned, and I fidgeted, anxious for my brother to enter the room so Tai and I could get on with what was sure to be a tense conversation.

After kissing Ma on the cheek, Rhoan greeted Da with a nod before taking a seat in the armchair, across from me. He looked between Tai and me, a crease between his brows. "So, what's going on?" he asked, resting his elbows in his knees.

That was our cue. Everyone was here. Thankfully, my little cousin was taking a nap, sound asleep in my old bedroom. I wouldn't be able to get through my confession if I had to worry about her overhearing a discussion that might require bringing up her father's name.

I glanced at Tai, wondering where to start. As usual, Tai believed in cutting to the chase.

"Maxim," he stated simply, a grim look on his face. "He's back in the picture."

It was a breathless moment before anyone said anything. Then, Khelan moved toward Tai, closing the space between them, to meet him eye to eye.

"Are you accusing me of still supporting Maxim Noble?" he demanded, his body bristling with indignation. "Because I can assure you I no longer have *any* connection to the man and have no intention of helping him again."

Tai held up his hands as though to fend him off. "I believe you," he said. "I'm fully aware you haven't been in contact with Maxim. Plus, he wants nothing to do with you."

Khelan lost his starch, appearing mollified, though bewildered as well. He searched Tai's face. "Then why is he 'back in the picture'?" he asked, tension making his body rigid. "What does he want?"

It would have been so much easier to let Tai continue, to explain on my behalf, but he had been doing that for *months* now. I couldn't let him step in for me this time. Not again.

I stood up. "Information, as usual," I said, gaining everyone's attention. "But this time from *me*."

I took advantage of the stunned silence that followed to fill in the blanks.

"Maxim accosted me outside the Judiciary," I said, moving to stand beside Tai. "He demanded that I help him get information in exchange for keeping quiet about our family's support of the rebels and about Khelan's former status as a senator."

Khelan went white as a sheet while Da, Ma and Rhoan stared at me, aghast.

"When did this happen?" Da demanded, taking hold of Ma's hand.

I swallowed. "A few weeks ago."

"A few *weeks* ago!" Khelan barked. "And you're only telling us this now!"

I grimaced at the fear and anger punctuating his words.

"That was because of me," Tai inserted, coming closer to me. "I told her not to tell you." He rested a hand at my back, and I leaned into it, seeking strength from his support.

Rhoan surged to his feet. "Wait a minute," he said, eyes glittering as he approached Tai. "This happened the night you and I were out, searching for Kira hours on end, didn't it. *That's* when Maxim approached her?"

I stilled as my parents swung puzzled looks between Rhoan, Tai and me.

"That's right," I said, wrapping my arms around my waists. "He forced me to go to Helios, where he's set up a base."

My mother gasped as Khelan and Da cursed.

Disbelief made my brother's green eyes bright, and he got into Tai's face. "When I returned to the apartment you came up with some bullshit story to explain where she'd been," he said. "Why the fuck didn't you tell me what was going on?"

Tai's hand stiffened at my back. "You couldn't have helped," he said. "If I had told you, you would have gone to the authorities. At the time, I believed the best thing was for me to take care of this through my own means and keep the circle of people who knew about this tight." He focused on Khelan now. "And to be honest, I couldn't be sure you wouldn't try to hunt Maxim down to offer yourself up in exchange for Kira. I couldn't risk you getting wrapped up with the factions all over again."

Khelan paled, appearing to shrink in front of my very eyes, but Rhoan pressed on. "I would have kept this to myself," he countered. "I could have been trusted."

I shook my head, stepping between them. "We know," I said, hoping to calm him down. "It's why we're coming to you all now. Because things are only going to get worse."

Da came to his feet slowly, Ma's hand slipping from his. "What do you mean by 'things are only going to get worse'?" he asked. "What's happened?"

"Maxim's aligned with someone who wants more than just information," I said. "He's paired up with Gabriel Minister."

Rhoan frowned so deep, his brows met. "What does *he* have to do with all this?"

I clasped my hand together tightly then drew in a wobbly breath. "When I joined the Judiciary," I said, "Gabriel was encouraging, someone I thought would be like a mentor to me. He seemed to appreciate my work, at first, but then his opinion started to change. He took my efforts to support him and any success I had achieved as a threat, some sign that I was trying to take his place somehow. He became so vindictive and bitter that he …" I pressed the crescents of my nails into my palms, trying to stave off tears as I remembered what Gabriel had done.

My family stared at me, seeming to be holding their breaths, both afraid and anxious to hear what I was about to say.

Tai smoothed his hand up my back. When I glanced up at him, I found worry lines around his eyes and mouth.

"Do you want me to tell them?" he asked in a voice so low that only I could possibly hear.

My heart squeezed.

As usual, Tai, my protector in all ways, was at the ready, willing to step in so I didn't have to endure any pain. I wanted to wrap my arms around him, bury my face in his chest and cry everything away, but that wouldn't have worked. It wouldn't make any of my problems go away.

Ma came to her feet, eyes glistening. She held herself rigidly as though bracing herself. "Did he …," she whispered. Her lips trembled as she took a deep breath. "Did he *hurt* you?"

My eyes went wide, instantly understanding what she was asking, why she thought I was unable to go on.

"No," I said quickly. "Not *that* way." I went to her to take her shaking hands in mine. From the way her shoulders drooped, it was clear she was relieved to learn that I hadn't been raped or tortured in some deviant way. "He struck me and made threats. *Nothing* else."

Ma gasped, and a second later, I found myself wrapped in her embrace. Tears pricked the back of my eyes as I allowed her to soothe me only the way she could. Over her shoulder, I caught the way the lines of my brother's face were twisting, contorting with rage.

"Why the fuck haven't you killed these assholes yet?" he blasted, hands on his hips, eyes focused in Tai's direction.

Ma flinched at the vehemence in my brother's tone the same way I did. I pulled out of her arms, at the ready to defend Tai, but found him staring my brother down.

"Trust me," Tai said with a curl to his lip and a tic at his jaw. "When I get hold of them, I look forward to doing exactly that."

Rhoan ground his teeth, appearing only marginally satisfied with Tai's response. Then again, I suspected nothing short of Gabriel or Maxim's death would have appeased my brother.

Khelan's body went limp as he swept a look between Ma and me. "My gods," he breathed, eyes going bleak as he swiped a hand through his hair. "This is all my fault. If I hadn't offered to help Maxim in the first place, he wouldn't have even *considered* contacting you. Gabriel wouldn't be threatening you, *us*, now."

Ma's face lost color as Da came up and drew her into his side.

"No," I said firmly, flat-out refusing his ownership of guilt. "The blame rests with Gabriel and Maxim."

Tai nodded. "This is bigger than coming after Kira to spite you, Khelan," he confirmed. "It's why we're telling you this now. Maxim and Gabriel have created a wide-scale operation whose sole goal is to take down the Realm. We suspect the information they want from Kira is to help them accomplish it by planning an attack on leadership. I have to escalate this matter to the high marshal." He glanced at me. "We wanted you to know just in case Maxim and Gabriel act on their threats."

My family sank into their thoughts, faces drawn and stricken.

Finally, Ma shook her head, searching my face, wonder and hurt in her eye. "What else have you been keeping from us?" she breathed. "What *else* do we need to know?"

My breath caught and I wet my lips, stealing a look at Tai. He raised a brow, awaiting my response like everyone else.

So far, I had managed to tell my family what they needed to know without calling Gannon's name, just as I had hoped. I had no urgent reason to tell them about my relationship with him, so I ignored the knot in my gut and pulled my gaze from Tai to focus on Ma.

"No," I said. "There's nothing else."

My brother startled me when he scoffed. "This has been an evening for truths, Kira," he said, sending me a pointed look. "Are you sure you don't have *something* else to say?"

I glowered at him, not missing his implication. I had figured *Tai* would be the one putting pressure on me to confess my relationship with Gannon, but there Rhoan was, doing it instead.

"No," I said, defiantly this time, holding his gaze. "I have *nothing* else to say."

Rhoan shook his head as though disappointed, his mouth tightening as he turned away. "I need to talk to you," he tossed at Tai before stalking out of the room and in the direction of Da's study. "Privately."

Tai's eyebrows rose. Nevertheless, a moment later, after a questioning glance at me, he followed my brother. I stared after them, a thread of unease winding its way through me.

"I hope James is worthy of standing beside a man like Tai," Ma said, drawing my attention to her.

James? I managed to catch myself before asking who *James* was. "What do you mean?"

Ma considered me, a contemplative look of wonder on her face. "Tai could have easily turned our family in to the authorities, on many an occasion," she said. "Instead, no matter what we've thrown his way, he's been steadfast in protecting us, or rather, protecting *you*."

I wrapped my arms around my waist, uncertain what to say. Tai had told me that he loved me, but his demonstration of his love yet again humbled me. There just weren't enough words to describe how incredibly moved I was by his unwavering selflessness.

Ma gave my upper arm a gentle squeeze before walking over to Khelan and Da, who stood speaking in hushed tones on the other side of the room. Khelan caught Ma's hand as she passed him, drawing her to his side. He pressed a kiss against her temple before releasing her, allowing her to go to Da.

Gannon's words drifted through my mind. *Why don't you talk to Tai ... then we'll take it from there.*

Could it really be so simple?

I hugged my waist tight, watching my parents and wondering maybe, just *maybe*, I could really have both men. Tai loved me without a doubt, as I did him, so maybe, just *maybe*, there really was a chance. My life was a shit storm of complications right now, but I needed to get answers, solve at least *one* of the problems that had been tormenting me. I couldn't wait any longer, going back and forth in my mind, *wondering* what Tai would want. It was time to find out.

CHAPTER 8

"Would you please take me home?" I asked.

Tai walked past where I sat in the sitting area and headed to the front door. He grabbed his coat off a hook by the closet then flicked a look at me. "I figured you'd want to stay here," he said, shrugging into the garment. "At least until Rhoan was ready to go."

I toyed with the edge of my sleeve. "He said something about having a drink with Khelan and Da," I said, "so I figure he's going to be here for a while."

Tai worked the buttons of his coat with a frown. "You shouldn't be at home alone right now," he said before lowering his hands to his hips. "I'll contact Talib. He can stay with you and keep watch until Rhoan returns to your apartment."

No, that wouldn't work. I came to my feet. "Could I stay at your place instead?" I blurted out, and when Tai's eyebrows raised, added, "That is, I mean, until Rhoan return gets home." I shrugged, striving for nonchalance.

"All right," he said, still appearing mildly baffled. Suddenly, his face cleared. "That's probably a better idea anyway. There's something we have to talk about."

Oh. "There is?" I had already told him everything I had learned about what had happened with Gabriel. What else was there left for me to say? "What?"

Tai eyed the hallway through which my family's voices floated out. "It's better we talk at my apartment."

Understanding that he didn't want our conversation to be overheard, I grabbed my belongings and headed to the kitchen to tell my family goodbye.

Usually when I left my parents' house, there was quite a bit of fanfare, culminating in a cheerful chorus of hugs and kisses. That evening, however, my parents' embraces and farewells were tempered by worry, fear and an unnecessary amount of guilt brimming in their eyes. It was a wonder they allowed me to leave the house. I suspected it had to do with Tai telling them about what he, as well as Gannon, had done to protect me — tracking device, protector and all.

Half an hour later, Tai led me into his apartment. It was dark and cool as though no one had been there for a while. When he voice-activated the lights in his sitting area, my nerves were only slightly soothed by the familiar sight of dark wood furniture, overgrown plants and his impressive library of books that lined the walls on shelves.

"Drink?" Tai asked, walking ahead of me to his kitchen.

"No, thank you," I said, dropping my coat and bag by the front door before following him.

On the trip to his apartment in his hover, I hadn't spoken a word. I had been so caught up in my thoughts, trying to drum up some courage, that Tai had asked me three times if I was all right. He had probably been wondering if my run-in with Gabriel had left me traumatized, but that wasn't it. I had been trying to find a way to bring up Gannon's proposition without leaving him more frustrated with me than he already was.

Halls! What did I plan on saying? *Tai, I was thinking ... Are you interested in sharing me with another man?* I couldn't just come out of the blue with something like that!

I sighed and stepped into the kitchen where I found Tai staring into his cooler, one hand braced against its door. He glanced up at me. "Hungry?"

I shook my head. Butterflies had already filled my belly.

He shut the cooler. "Thank gods for that," he said. "I haven't been here for a couple weeks. I doubt I have anything worth consuming."

I sent him a tight smile, leaning against the doorframe. He looked me over then came to stand in front of me, and I tilted my head back to maintain our eye contact.

"That could have gone a whole lot worse," he said, peering down at me.

I stared, mesmerized by the smattering of freckles on the bridge of his nose, then understanding dawned. *My family.*

I cleared my throat. "Yes," I said, shifting so I could now press my back flush against the wall. "A big part of me expected my parents to disown me."

Tai smirked. "They wouldn't do that."

I smiled, not bothering to argue the point because, well, he was right.

We considered each other, both of us with small smiles of relief on our faces. After a few long moments, Tai raised a hand to touch a curl resting on the side of my face and smooth it behind my ear with his thumb. His smile melted away, transforming into something less amiable, more sensual, decidedly more ... *hot*. My pulse raced at the flash of hunger and longing that came to his eyes.

This was it. My opportunity to ask the question that had been burning a hole in the back of my head, but I hesitated, unable to get any words out. Asking Tai to be in a multiple had seemed such a simple notion back at my family home, but now that the moment was upon me, it couldn't have been more difficult. I pressed my mouth into a line, frustrated with myself.

Tai's gaze roamed my face. "What is it?"

"I …" Damn it. I needed to say something! But what? *How?* Since I couldn't just blurt it out, I had to ease Tai into the idea. I needed to let him know that being in a multiple like the one I was proposing wasn't so farfetched. I took a deep breath. "My mother knows I'm in love with you and Gannon."

Tai rocked back on his heels. "What?!"

I cringed. "I mean, she knows I'm in love with you and *someone else*, but not who exactly."

He looked me over. "How?"

A nervous laugh bubbled up as heat spread from my neck to my cheeks. "She figured it our herself," I said, staring at the gold badge on the left lapel of his jacket. "She put the pieces together after I asked her for advice, some time ago."

Tai cocked a brow. "Advice about *what?*"

"About being in love with two men." I chanced a glance at him, searching for a sign of encouragement. Unfortunately, none was there.

"I see," he said slowly, raising his chin. "And what did she have to say?"

That I should be with both you and Gannon.

I sagged against the wall. This was a bad idea. Did I *really* think Tai would welcome the idea of being in a multiple with me simply because *my mother said so?*

I glanced away briefly, shaking my head. "Never mind," I muttered then changed the subject. "You said we needed to talk. About what?"

Tai's stance went from guarded to dismal in a matter of seconds. "I owe you an apology," he said with a heavy sigh. "I shouldn't have made demands on you the way I did. Holy shit. You had just been *kidnapped*, could have been killed, and instead of being focused on Gabriel and Maxim I tried to force you make a decision between Gannon and me."

I blinked up at him, stunned. *That's* what he wanted to talk about! "My gods," I choked out. "You don't need to apologize for that!"

"Yes, I do," he said so dismally I almost apologized to *him*. I mean, truly, *I* was the one with the dissidents nipping at my heels, the one bringing pandemonium to his life.

"I'm *glad* you forced me, Tai," I said, holding his gaze. "I *needed* that push or else I probably would have never made up my mind."

That caught his attention. "Made up your mind." His eyes went wide as they searched my face. "What do you mean?"

And here it was again, *another* chance to ask Tai about being in a multiple, but I just couldn't string the right words together. He had regretted trying to force me to decide between Gannon and him, but it was clear from the taut, hard lines of his body as he awaited my reply that, despite his apology, Tai was very eager to hear what I had to say. The realization dawned on me as I stared up at him that, all the while I had been trying to sort my feelings out, he had probably been wondering about the reason for my delay, what it meant, whether I cared for him as much as I had said I did. Well, that was where I would start — by clearing up any doubt he held.

I moved away from the wall, so we were now only a breath away from each other. "I love you, Tai," I said, taking his hand. "I want to be with you. I always have wanted to and always will."

Tai winced, stepping back, pulling his hand out of my own. "You don't have to do this now, Kira," he said before running his fingers through his hair. "This isn't the time. I just wanted to apologize. We need to figure out this shit with the Quad, not make any decisions about us."

"Time's not going to change anything," I promised, moving into his space again. "I know what I want."

A flicker of hope darted through his eyes. "Are you sure?"

Sure?

Guilt knifed through me — gutted me, really. The only other time I had seen such uncertainty in Tai had been just before he had told me he loved me. He had been concerned his feelings wouldn't have been reciprocated. I had hesitated in telling him I loved him then, mind and heart filled with agony after having just left Gannon, but this time I had no intention of holding back.

I reached up and cupped his face, pulling him down, toward me. "I'm *so* sorry for making you doubt for a second that I didn't love you," I said, emotion making my voice shake. "I've been yours for five years! I have never loved — *will* never love — anyone the way I love you. My gods, how could I *not* want to be with you!"

He stared at me, his hazel eyes dark, fathomless. Seconds passed while the uncertainty on his face slipped away. "All right," he said simply, in a voice so quiet if I hadn't been a breath away from him, I wouldn't have heard. But I did, and my heart soared.

I smiled, gasping with relief and elation as tears pooled in the corners of my eyes. Not wanting to give him a chance to think up some other, probably justifiable reason to doubt me or push me away, I pressed my lips against his.

I kissed him with everything I had, apologizing through the meeting of our lips for my delay, for not committing to him as quickly as I should have, for putting our love for each other on the line. For the first time since Tai had told me he had feelings for me, I kissed him without hesitation, pouring my love into the act to erase any and all uncertainty about my love for him.

Tai's hands found my waist and I sighed, allowing him to pull me flush against him with a gentle tug. I enjoyed the way the warmth of his body spread into my own as he smoothed his palms up my back. I arched into him, tangling my fingers with the short strands of his hair at the back of his neck, and coaxed his mouth open by running my tongue along the seam of his lips. He made a deep-throated sound that ignited my skin and made my sex swell, ache and throb. Tasting him this way, being in his arms, was like getting over homesickness, returning to a place I had been away from for far too long.

Tai murmured something against my lips, but I was too busy making love to his mouth to hear anything he said. I deepened our kiss, rolling up higher up onto my toes, as the thick cords of his muscles rippled beneath my hands and arms. He could have told me to take the next flight to our nearest moon, and I wouldn't have cared so long as it meant he would be inside me soon.

The curve of his lips broke our kiss as he pulled back, grinning down at me. "We should go the bedroom."

I smiled. Oh yes! "Good idea."

He chuckled, the sound reverberating low in his chest. "Hold on." He bent his knees and gripped the back of my thighs, lifting me up in one move. With a gasp, I wrapped my legs around his waist, fingers digging into his shoulders to keep hold.

Tai seemed to have the layout of his apartment committed to memory, and it was a good thing for both us because as soon as he started walking I recaptured his mouth, kissing him as he went to his room.

Tai's bedroom was as just as dark and cool as the rest of his apartment, but the temperature didn't bother me. The heat engulfing my body was enough to keep me warm. It was only when Tai dipped, lowering my feet to the floor that I realized that we had stopped moving. I blinked into the dimness of the room, thankful for the sliver of light coming in through the door, from his sitting area. It was enough for to see the outline of his body in front of me. Inhaling a deep breath, I slid my hands between the open folds of his jacket at his chest and pushed the garment up and off his shoulders before sliding it down his arms. The dark shirt he was wearing underneath was thin, but even in the faint, flickering light I could make out the hills and valleys of his chest.

I stood staring at him for a while, taking in how strong and beautiful he was, moved by how fortunate I was to have him in my life, not just as a lover but as a friend, someone I had been able to count on time and time again. I couldn't believe how foolish I had been, thinking I could possibly live without him, could make a choice that didn't involve him too.

I swallowed, remembering the reason I no longer had to make a choice. I had come to ask him to be in a multiple with Gannon and me, and I would — *after* I showed him just how much I loved him.

Tai touched my cheek with the backs of fingers, and I lifted my gaze to his. "You all right?"

"Yes," I said, flushing, pressing my face against his touch. "I was just thinking how much I love you."

His responding smile was a broad, satisfied curve of his mouth. "Do you want the lights on?" he asked, watching me, or at least what he could see of me.

I shook my head. I liked the idea of making love with him with mostly my senses of taste and touch to guide me. The thought spurred me into action.

What in the worlds am I waiting for?

I tackled my pants, starting to unbuckle the buttons and belt. When Tai simply stood there, studying me, I smirked. "This works a lot better if you take off your clothes," I teased, shucking my shoes.

He laughed, and I joined in as he started shedding his clothing as quickly as me.

By the time we were both undressed, our clothes were strewn all over the floor. I grinned, tossing my blouse somewhere behind me and stepping over my pants to get to him. It was a good thing it was dimly lit inside Tai's room so he couldn't see the mess we had made because he'd probably be very disturbed by it. His apartment was usually as orderly as everything else in his life. Well, that is, until I came along.

Tai took my hip and dragged me against him. He devoured my mouth, stroking every space inside it with his tongue. When he pulled back and began nudging, pushing me onto the bed, I allowed it and fell back, laughing as my head hit the pillows. But instead of waiting for him to climb atop me, I rolled onto my side and cradled my head with one hand while patting the bed with the other.

"Lay down, Commander," I ordered with a sly grin. "I have plans for you."

A slow smile came to Tai's mouth before, without a word, he did as he was told. In the dim light, I made out the expectant look in his eyes as he lowered himself to the bed.

My eyebrows rose at that. I had expected him to resist or put me in my place somehow. Maybe put up a bit of an argument like he usually did, telling me that *he* would be the one to set the pace. Halls, had I told Gannon to do that, he would have laughed and flat-out refused!

My breath caught at my train of thought. There I was, once again, laying with Tai, naked and needy, thinking of Gannon. Doing the same thing I had done after Tai and I had first made love. I steeled myself for the onslaught of guilt and its usual companions — confusion, frustration, worry. Shockingly, none of them arrived.

I smiled, exhaling a long breath as my gaze swept over the silhouette of Tai's glorious body. He laid, sprawled along my side, dipping the bed with his weight so much that I had to lean back to keep from rolling onto him, which actually a good idea, but I wanted a minute of simply enjoying the sight of him, of touching him, just being with him like this for a little while longer.

The narrow beam of light coming in from the sitting area skimmed along the hard, muscled lines of his body and fast-stiffening cock. Perhaps I should have had Tai turn the lights after all. It truly was a shame not to see a physique as beautiful as his as clearly as I wanted to. My smile grew as my gaze wandered over to the edge of the temporary tattoo on his chest. I leaned over so I could see both Tai's face and his optic better.

"It's fading," I murmured, caressing the swirling, intricate design of the artwork with my fingertips.

His brows knitted, watching my hand move across his skin. "Yes, I meant to make it permanent," he said, a flutter of confusion darting across his face, "but it kept slipping my mind."

That had to be a first. I couldn't remember a time when Tai forgot anything.

"*Tolo caro pa nu rai*," I said, pronouncing the words in his tattoo the way he had instructed me to.

His full lips curved into a smile. "That's right."

Ha! And he thinks I never listen to him. I gave him a cheeky grin. "'Everything I do is for my queen,'" I translated, earning yet another impressed look for my excellent memory.

I made lazy circles around the tattoo. "I don't know that our sovereign deserves such dedication." I knew for a *fact* the woman didn't, but then that was neither here nor there, at least not in that moment.

Tai took on a contemplative look, and after a moment, he pointed to a section of the writing, closest to his heart. "These first two letters here," he said. "R-A. They mean 'queen.'"

I hummed, smiling. "I probably should've figured that out," I said, with a rueful shake of my head. "Those letters translate to 'queen' in my name too."

He chuckled. "Yes, Kira," he said. "I know."

I wrinkled my nose. Of *course* he knew. Tai knew more languages than I could count. Plus, everything he did was purposeful, and with deliberate intent. He had probably gone through every known translation of *queen* before deciding on this very one. Having a tattoo whether permanent or not would be meaningful to him … which made the fact that the optic was for the Corona a very strange act indeed.

My lips parted as the truth dawned on me. "This isn't a dedication to the Corona," I whispered, fingers stilling. "This is to *me*."

Tai snorted. "Holy shit, I literally had to spell it out for you," he said, and I scowled.

"You told me everyone in the Protectorate has a similar tattoo," I argued.

"I lied," he said with a laugh. "Did you really think I would get a tattoo for the *Corona?*"

I thinned my lips at the mirth on his face. "Your loyalty does run deep, Tai."

"Not *that* deep." He laughed.

I glared at him. *I'll show him deep.* With a quick push, I eased up, off my side. When I straddled his pelvis, Tai stopped laughing at once, as I had expected him to. Grinning, I placed a hand on either side of his head and hovered above him. My sex throbbed as his cock strained, swelled, extending just below me.

My gods, it was heady. The thought that I had this big, strong and incredible man responding to me so urgently sent a thrilling tingle up my spine. Even with only a pale flicker of light, I could see the desire he had for me in the way his eyes hooded and his muscles flexed with barely restrained need. I smiled, holding his gaze, then reached down with one hand between us to take him. Easing down onto his cock, I sighed as he stretched into me. A rumble low and deep in Tai's chest escaped his lips as he sank his fingers into my hips, holding me in place. He rocked his pelvis up but I stopped him, sitting back to hold his wrists. This time I wanted to set the pace. I gasped at the way the change in my position pushed him deeper, up inside me.

When I caught my breath, I said, "Don't move," and then, not wanting him to be tempted to take control again, placed his hands above his head. My eyes widened when he inhaled sharply.

I froze, looming over him. "Did I hurt you?" I asked, but even as I did, I couldn't imagine having done anything to cause him pain.

His throat moved as he swallowed. "No."

He seemed sure, but still I studied him, wondering at his response. "Keep your hands here," I said. "I want to do this my way."

His body went slack even as his pulse jackhammered beneath my fingers, making my eyebrows climb. *What's this?* I searched Tai's face, rising excitement making my sex tighten around his cock.

Eyeing him, I ran one hand down his arm to his shoulder to just under his jaw where I gently curved my fingers around his neck. Tai's heartbeat throbbed heavily beneath my palm. When I tightened my hold, his lips parted and he let out a ragged pant that sounded like my name.

My gods, he's getting off on this!

Acting on pure instinct, I leaned down and pressed my lips close to his ear. "I'm going to fuck you, Tai," I said, making him grunt as his cock flex hard inside me.

"Fuck, Kira," he ground out. "Move, damn it." He lifted his hips, trying to get me to comply.

I stared down at him, marveling that he hadn't simply taken me by the hair yet. Gannon would have. I grinned.

"What are you smiling about?" he demanded, bucking up under me.

I laughed and kissed him soundly on the lips. "I love you," I said, unable to help myself.

Tai paused, the desperation in his moves lessening before a smile crept across his face. He shifted and then, in one move, released the wrist I was still holding from my grip so easily he made a mockery of any control I had believed I held over him. He pulled me down to him, crushing my breasts against his chest, and kissed me until we were both breathless and writhing with pent-up need.

I pulled away, gasping for air and shoving my hair away from my face. He smiled up at me as I placed my palms on his chest and started to ride him, slow and steady. He met my smooth moves with powerful thrusts of his own, his hands roving my body, exploring me as though for the first time. When he skimmed my breasts, my nipples became so hard, they burned at his slightest touch.

It didn't take long for Tai's caresses to become more urgent and demanding. His hands found my waist, pulling me down onto him as he rammed into me so hard and fast, I struggled to keep pace. But I did, panting and grinding down on his cock, seeking the same release he sought between my thighs. The only sound in the room was of ours sighs and groans and his cock, slick and pumping in and out of my sex.

Soon sweat drenched his brow even as cool drafts of air skimmed my back. I rode him as hard as he would let me, not stopping or pausing even for a second when his searching fingers dug into my flesh. I gasped, relishing the pinch of pain that nipped my skin and skittered up my spine. Only when my arms started to tremble, and give way from exertion, did I falter in keeping our pace. Tai pulled me down to meet his lips with one hand at the back of my head. We devoured each other's mouths as our bodies drove us toward ecstasy that was just out of reach.

Holy gods, I needed release.

"Please," I whimpered against his lips, my muscles tightening so much I feared one of them would snap. He needed to give me some sign he was ready, that he wanted me to come, because I couldn't be sure that I would otherwise.

Finally, his thrusts became more erratic, less steady in their power. I exhaled, licking the taste of him from my lips after he moved his mouth to my neck and groaned out my name with a violent release. I took that as my cue and followed him into an orgasm that left a buzz in my eardrums and spread a hum throughout my limbs.

After a languid, delicious moment of post-orgasmic bliss, I pushed up onto my elbows and smiled down at him, watching the dim light shift in his eyes.

"I think I've figured you out," I announced as his cock softened inside me. "You aren't sexually dominant."

Tai groaned and flung an arm over his eyes. "Give it up, Kira," he said with a sigh. "I like to fuck. *You*, in particular. That's it."

I laughed, not surprised by his reaction. He hadn't been too interested in participating in my type of sex psychoanalysis the first time I had brought it up either, but I persisted nevertheless.

"Bear with me," I said. "You *loved* it when I was in the one calling the shots just a while ago."

"Of course I did," he said with a snort. "Who wouldn't?"

Huh. Maybe Tai, my brave and accomplished warrior, had a few lessons to learn yet. "Not everyone likes to give up control during sex."

He lifted his arm from across his eyes to glare me into silence. I smirked and rested my chin on my forearms, which I had now folded on his chest. Whether he was sexually dominant or submissive made no difference to me, just as long as I had him.

"I missed you," I said, staring into his eyes.

He expelled a deep breath. "Me too."

I smiled, but he didn't join in. Instead, he studied me, a dispirited look on his face.

"I was going out of my fucking mind, you know," he said. "After seeing Gannon give you that ring, I didn't know what to expect, what decision you'd make."

My smile weakened, just a bit, as I wet my lips.

He touched my cheek. "You had me by the balls," he said with a rueful grin. "You could have asked me for anything, and I would have given it to you if it meant you being with me."

I searched his face. "Really?"

"Of course," he vowed.

The hope that had been flickering like a weak flame before grew stronger now. *Why don't you talk to Tai ... then we'll take it from there.*

I swallowed. "So, would you ..." Emotion clogged my throat.

"Would I what?" he asked. When I continued staring at him, Tai frowned. "Tell me, baby."

His endearment, one I hadn't heard from him in so long, gave me greater courage. I pushed up onto my elbows, so I could look him directly in his eyes and took a breath. "Would you be willing to be in a multiple with Gannon and me?"

Seconds passed as Tai stared up at me. The yawning silence compelled me to explain myself.

"I love you *and* Gannon," I gushed. "I can't *choose*. You both mean too much to me."

I couldn't tell if Tai was breathing, he was so completely still. My arms shook under the weight of my body and my rising dread.

"I've thought a lot about this," I confessed, wishing his expression hadn't gone so blank. "I can't be without either of you. I don't want to."

Tai's lips parted, but he took a moment to form his words. "You said you never loved anyone the way you love me," he said carefully. "That you never will."

My heart dipped at the frost in his voice. "I haven't," I insisted. "And I won't. What I feel for each of you it ... It just can't be compared."

Another beat of silence then every muscle in Tai's body seized up at once. He shoved himself up, making me topple off him and onto my side.

Prickles of worry ran around my neck as he turned his back to me and placed his feet on the floor with two heavy thumps.

Oh no.

I scrabbled over to him and encircled his waist with my arms, pressing my chest and cheek against his back. His body was hard as stone. "Say something," I implored. "Please."

His heart beat a loudly against my ear, but he remained silent.

Fear swallowed me whole. "Tai?"

After a heaving breath, he stood up, forcing my arms to fall away from him. I watched with a sinking heart as he voice-activated the lights and reached for his pants, shoving one leg then the other into them with harsh, jerking movements, his back still turned to me.

"I don't know what's worse," he muttered. "That you're manipulative or that you're spoiled."

I crawled off the bed, dragging the sheet with me. "What are you talking about?" I asked, wrapping the linen around my chest as securely as I could so it wouldn't end up falling to the ground.

He swung around to me, half-dressed now. "Your mother put this in your head, didn't she," he demanded, eyes glinting and hard.

I gasped. "W-what?" I spluttered.

"When you asked for her advice," he continued, glaring at me. "Your mother said you, your anonymous love interest and I should be in a multiple."

Oh gods. "W-why would you think that?" How did he know?

"Because she *had* to," he spat with a curl to his lip. "That's the *only* advice that would be given by a woman who's living a life you seem to want to live."

I wrung an edge of the bedsheet into a tight knot. "She might have said something like that," I allowed even though he was off the mark. "But I'm not asking you to be in a multiple because of her."

Tai grabbed up his shirt. "You're lying."

I flinched, eyes narrowing. He had called me manipulative, spoiled and now a liar all within the last minute! I clenched my fists and swore to all seventeen of the Realm's gods that I would slap the condescension right out of him if he insulted me again.

"I've been *nothing* but entirely honest with you," I forced out between tight lips, bearing down on him.

"Really?" He raised a brow, stuffing his arms into his shirt. "Then tell me. How was your time on Dignitas?"

Dignitas? What the fuck did *Dignitas* have to do with anything! "Don't give me riddles, Tai," I spat. "What are you getting at?"

He crossed his arms, leaving his shirt unbuttoned. "I heard you attended a meeting in Capita, and I'm not talking about Realm Council's."

I cocked my head. "Are you talking about my meeting with Mila?" *But how could he know about that and, more importantly, why would he care?*

"Not *that* one," he said, nostrils flaring.

I combed through my memory. The only other "meeting" I'd had was with Gannon. I gasped. *That* was the meeting he was referring to!

But how did he know? I glanced down at my wrist where the tracking device dangled. *I'm such a naive fool!*

"I thought you were only going to use this if something happened to me," I seethed, glaring at him now. "Not to *spy* on me!"

"I didn't spy on you," he said, looking at me impassively. "I didn't have to."

I searched his face, looking for a clue. "So how do you know?" I asked, but the pieces had already started coming together. "Rhoan."

That's what my brother had wanted to talk to Tai about privately, back at my parents' house. Rhoan had appeared suspicious when I had told him I'd catch up with him after Realm Council. *My life to live, huh?* My brother hadn't only signed off on Tai for me, he was trying to make him my keeper as well!

I planted my hands on my hips, distaste making me sweep a hostile look over Tai. "It's good to know you and my *big brother* are back to being the best of friends."

Tai scowled. "Your *big brother* told *me* because he's worried about *you*," he snapped, punctuating the last word with a finger pointed my way.

I sniffed. "*That* and because he wants us to be together." *Gods, what an about-face!*

Uncertainty skipped across Tai's features even as the flush of anger rode high on his cheeks. "Don't *you* want us to be together?"

My mouth fell open. He couldn't be serious! "For the love of gods, YES!" I yelled, throwing my arms in the air. "Haven't you heard a word I've said?"

His eyes narrowed. "Oh, believe me," he muttered, doing up his shirt and searching the room for something else. "I've heard *everything* and more."

Gods, I wanted to punch him. "What the fuck does *that* mean?" I demanded, but he ignored me. Choosing, instead, to pick up his shoes and sit down to put them on.

"Answer me!" I shouted, glowering at the crown of his stubborn head.

He lunged to his feet. "It means I thought you were choosing *me!*" he shouted, looming over me, fists clenched. "Not some *package* deal. I'm not going to allow you to butter me up with sex so you can get what you want just for some fucking kicks!"

I saw red. With both hands, I shoved him in the chest and savored the satisfaction of him staggering back. "Is *that* what you think this is?" I hissed. "That I'm trying to *manipulate* you into agreeing to some childish game? How can you think that! My gods, my heart's on my sleeve. We're asking you to be in a relationship I never imagined possible!"

Tai's eyes clouded over. "*We*," he said, frowning. "You've already spoken to *Gannon* about this?"

I shrank at the incredulous look on his face, hesitant now. "It was his idea."

He snorted. "Now I *know* you're lying," he muttered, turning away.

No, no, no. I grabbed the back of his shirt, panicking, the promise I had made to the gods about punishing him for calling me names going right out the window. "Tai." I swallowed back a sob. "I promise you, it's the *truth*."

I must have been convincing despite the unsteadiness in my voice, because he turned to face me with a slightly dazed expression. He shook it off then pointed to my clothes. "Get dressed," he ordered. "Your brother should be at your apartment by now. I'm taking you home."

My face crumbled as I grabbed his wrist, holding his hand to my chest. "I'm standing here in front of you, baring my soul, asking — no, *begging* — you to be with me." Dear gods, I had never begged for anything or *anyone* in my entire fucking life! "I want us to be together. Don't you?"

"Yes, I do," he said, anger making his moves stiff as he shook off my hold. "I want to be with you entirely. Completely. Not *sharing* you with another man who, according to a Realm protocol more than four hundred years old, is not permitted to be with you!"

My hands trembled as I searched his face, looking for a crack in the wall of his anger, some way to get through to him. "My parents made it work," I said, desperate, almost drowning now in despair. "We could too."

Tai clenched his jaw so hard it had to hurt. "Is that really what you want, Kira?" he asked. "The life your parents have?"

Tears slid between my lips, and I licked them away. My parents had love, but they had had to hide it, keep it safe by keeping a part of themselves from everyone we knew. *Of course* I didn't want what my parents had — not exactly. I wanted more, better, but I just couldn't see any other way to be with the two men I loved.

"Just ... *think* about it," I begged. "For me. *Please.*"

Tai studied me, hurt, anger and frustration churning in his eyes. With a twist to his lips, he bent down to scoop up my clothes before tossing them to me. I caught them reflexively against my chest with a gasp.

"Let's go," he bit out then stalked out through his bedroom door.

CHAPTER 9

"Do you know anything about Petra Minister?"

I dragged my gaze from the untouched coffee in my mug and focused on Asher. He sat on the other side of my desk, looking at me with an expectant waggle of his brows. "I beg your pardon?" I asked.

He gestured to the tablet resting on his lap. "Mila sent a message to us saying she's been asked to meet with her," he said. "Something about having to vet potential candidates for the election of our next minister."

"She did?"

Asher nodded. "Yep," he said. "Mila says she can't make the advisory group meeting tomorrow because of it."

I frowned, shaking my head to try to clear it. I vaguely recalled skimming through a message related to that on my dashboard, but I had dismissed it, not interested in reading about the wheels in motion to remove my superior from Prospect Eight and replace her with Gannon's former girlfriend — no, his partner, lover … whatever the blast she was. At that point, my brain had been, and still was, too crammed in its attempt to keep my head above water at work as every other aspect of my life sank into a bottomless pit.

After Tai had essentially kicked me out of his apartment, he wasted little time dropping me off at mine. The moment I passed through my front door I sailed into my brother's room, glad to find him lounging there, so I could light into him. I railed at him, cursing him out for reporting my activities to Tai. My tongue-lashing was an exercise in futility. Rhoan's complete lack of remorse just ended up making me storm off into my bedroom, vowing with every fiber of my raging being to find somewhere the fuck else to live.

Now I shoved my mug of coffee aside and ground the heels of my palms into my eye sockets.

Gods, I should just go home.

The thought filled me with dismay. I couldn't remember a time I wanted to be *away* from the Judiciary, but I guessed there was always a time for firsts. Since arriving at work, I hadn't gotten anything done. If Asher hadn't stopped by to run over last-minute details for the advisory group meeting, I still would have been staring into my mug, mind running rampant between all things related to Gannon, Tai and, of course, the Quad.

I sighed, plunking my hands on my desk and studied as Asher read his scroll. *Maybe it's a good thing Mila won't be at tomorrow's meeting.* I wanted, *needed*, to find a way to manage the group on my own. This was my chance to assert myself. How exactly I planned to *do* that, though, I couldn't be sure.

Rhoan.

Hadn't my brother offered to help me with the advisory group any way he could? After the way he had stuck his nose where it hadn't belonged, the loose-lipped ass *owed* his help to me, and a whole lot more.

"Looks like I'm not the *only* one with big plans for you," Asher said, glancing at me with a grin. When I cocked my head in question, he swiped and tapped his tablet before gesturing to my monitor. "Check your screen."

I did, and amidst a circus of fluorescent graphics and glowing text was an article by the Realm Anarchist with a headline that read: *Kira Metallurgist — Is She Truly the Best Choice for Realm Council?*

My eyes widened. *Shit.*

Bracing myself, I skimmed through the article, expecting some overdone story like so many he had written about me before, but soon found my neck muscles loosening.

The Anarchist's article was *nothing* like any he had published in the past. It was a fair and balanced overview of not only me, but a handful of other subordinates from across the Realm who he believed suitable for the landmark position on Realm Council. He gave an overview of our qualifications, including education and various projects at the Judiciary, but it couldn't be denied that the Anarchist favored me over the rest. He only stopped short of giving me an all-out glowing endorsement because he wanted to preserve his "journalistic integrity by conducting a more thorough investigation of all candidates."

I balked. *Journalistic integrity?!* Those were two words I would *never* have used in connection to the Realm Anarchist!

"Don't look so mortified," Asher said, taking in my expression with a snort. "This is a good thing."

"How?"

Asher folded his arms. "I told you you're the logical choice for Realm Council," he said. "This proves it. What the Realm Anarchist says, goes. According to this, you pretty much have him on your side, so you can bet you have the support of everyone in the Subordinate caste, too."

I raised a brow. "I'm sure Wyatt would have something to say about that," I muttered recalling the peevish advisory group member. I had no doubt the rabble-rouser had some clout, but taking the Realm Anarchist's article as a sign that *everyone* would be in support of my appointment was pushing it.

"All right," Asher caved with a grin. "*Most* of our caste, but you have to admit that I wasn't wrong. You actually have a chance at being appointed."

I sighed, resting on my folded arms on the desk. "Support from our caste is one thing, Asher," I said, "but it all comes down to the Corona in the end. She's the one who'll make the decision." And to be honest, my record of interactions with her left much to be desired. The woman seemed to tolerate me only so she could torment me with her unique form of verbal abuse.

Asher considered that then asked, "And if the Corona decides to appoint you, what would you do?"

I'd take it on the spot.

I jerked in my chair, shocked by how suddenly and easily the thought had flown into my mind.

Asher looked me over, a smirk spreading across his face. "You want that position, don't you," he told me. "I can see it in your eyes."

My gaze slid from Asher's as heat warmed my neck. I stared at the article glowing on my screen. I had assumed no one would take me seriously for such a position, but I had also never envisioned the Realm Anarchist seeing me as anything more than gossip fodder. Maybe Asher was on to something. Maybe I had more respect among my caste than I had realized.

A notification from Erik popped up my dashboard, diverting my thoughts.

Heath Reporter is here to see you.

I groaned, my agreement to give him quotes every now and then coming back to mind. *Gods give me strength.* Had the man never heard of making an appointment? I had promised to help Heath out, but damn it, his timing couldn't have been worse! Going home still seemed like the right thing to do considering my run-in with Gabriel and my argument with Tai.

Nevertheless, I typed in a reply to Erik, telling him to send Heath in. "Sorry," I said to Asher when I finished. "I'm going to have to cut our meeting short."

He shrugged. "That's all right," he said, standing up and slipping the tablet under his arm. "We're pretty much done here. I need to catch up with Maralis anyway."

My brows raised. *Ah yes, the fair Maralis.* I sat back, looking up at him. "I'd love to meet her," I said, a smile tugging the corner of my mouth at the bashful look that had come over Asher's face. "You should bring her by my office one day."

A grin split Asher's face. "I think she'd like that," he said then turned around at the sound of a soft rap.

I glanced over the top of my monitor to find Heath's tall, lanky figure hanging back at the threshold of my office door.

"Sorry for the short notice," he said with a shrug, one hand resting on the strap of his messenger bag.

I highly doubted that but gestured for Heath to enter all the same.

As Heath shuffled in, glancing about, Asher winked his goodbye to me then slipped out of the room. When Heath lowered himself into the chair Asher had just vacated, his gaze landed on my monitor.

His eyebrows shot up. "*You* read the Realm Anarchist?" he asked, focusing on me.

I stiffened. The article with the glaring headline was still displayed on my screen. "I try not to," I said, my cheeks starting to burn. "But it seems it can't be helped."

Heath pulled his tablet out of his bag, all the while considering me. "So what do you think?"

I blinked. "Of the Realm Anarchist?"

He nodded, unrolling his tablet on his lap.

I glanced at my screen again with a wry twist to my lips. "I suppose he's not half bad," I said then looked to Heath. "I just wish he'd tell the truth and use his platform for some greater good than spinning outlandish tales about people like me."

Heath considered that for a long moment. "I suppose not everyone can be as honorable as you," he remarked.

I raised my brows. "Honorable?"

"You're considered one of the most upstanding of our peers," he said, thrumming his fingers on the edge of his tablet. "You've done very well for yourself. A lot of subordinates are inspired by your quick rise here at the Judiciary."

I flushed and fidgeted in my chair, not certain what to say to that. Thankfully, he seemed to take pity on me. "I know you're probably really busy," he said, "so we should probably get started."

I nodded, grateful, and straightened in my seat.

He referred to his tablet. "I understand that you'll be advising Realm Council should they approve the special committee's recommendation and that you've established an advisory group to assist you should Realm Council approve exploration," Heath said, glancing up at me. "Do you find it challenging to lead a group of your peers?"

I pressed my lips together, wondering how to reply. It was challenging, yes, but I didn't want to give the worlds the impression I couldn't handle myself. "I believe everyone who knows me would say I love nothing more than a challenge."

"And that you're ambitious too."

I cocked my head. "I beg your pardon?"

He held my gaze. "Just look how far you've come at the Judiciary in less than a year," he said. "Based on what I've seen of you in action, I figure people who know you would say you're pretty driven to get ahead, wouldn't they?"

I frowned. The words *driven to get ahead* had a self-serving connotation, but if working hard and doing my best made me ambitious, then so be it. "Yes," I said with a lift of my chin. "I suppose people would."

Heath nodded, leaning forward to rest his elbows on his knees on either side of his tablet. "You know," he mused, considering me, "as popular as you are in the media, I don't think citizens know very much about you. In fact, any information I've managed to pull up about you is kind of limited. Can you fill in the blanks and tell me a little about your friends, family ... who you're involved with?"

I stiffened. *Involved with?* "What does who I'm involved with have to do with the advisory group or the special committee's recommendation?"

Heath shrugged, sending me a regretful smile. "You'd be surprised what people want to know."

That was all well and good, but from where I stood, people knew more than they needed to about who I was. "Let's just keep the focus on my professional life, Heath," I said, "not on my *personal* one."

"All right," he said, blue eyes sharpening. "Since you started at the Judiciary you've gained an impressive reputation by working on important projects with leadership, most notably our newly appointed high chancellor."

I nodded. Something about his change in disposition compelled me to do so even though he hadn't asked me for confirmation. "That's correct."

"Then tell me," he said. "Now that you're going to be advisor to Realm Council, do you look forward to staying involved with Gannon Consul?"

I blinked, certain I had heard wrong or maybe he had spoken in error. "You mean ... do I look forward to *supporting* him?"

"Of course," he said with a smirk. "What else could I mean?"

And there it was. That smug look on Heath's face reminded me of when I had first confronted him weeks ago about telling lies about me in his articles. I had expected him to be his usual coy and apologetic self at the time, but he had come across as unrepentant and almost taunting, as though he was the only one in on some sort of joke. And just like then, I didn't know now what in the worlds to make of his bizarre response.

My comm vibrated, breaking the silence. When I checked the device, the name Derek Lecturer faded in and out of its transparent screen. I jumped to my feet. There could only be one reason Sela's partner would be messaging me.

The legs of Heath's chair scraped against the tile as he stood up. "Is everything all right?" he asked, eyes wide, all signs of his cryptic self now gone.

"It's my best friend," I said, hurrying around my desk with a growing smile. "She's having a baby."

* * *

Please don't let me be too late.

I yanked open the double doors and rushed into the clinic. After a quick glance around the near empty lobby, I made a guess then a beeline toward a hallway to my right. I didn't bother checking for Talib. His heavy footfalls sounded on the tile behind me, telling me he was keeping up.

Eighteen thirty-five, thirty-six, thirty-seven ...

Voices and laughter bounced up the hall against the walls as I searched for Room 1838. Soon I rounded a corner and found a small waiting area packed with people, most familiar, some who weren't. I hurried to a woman with sleek auburn hair who opened her arms to me.

"There you are!" Sela's mother announced, drawing me into her arms for a tight, tear-filled embrace. After a moment, she released me and allowed me to exchange hellos with Sela's family and friends then nudged me toward a door behind me. "Go on," she said, squeezing my hand. "She's waiting for you."

I nodded then turned to locate Talib, wondering how, after my close encounter with Gabriel, I would convince him to give me some space. Fortunately, I didn't have to plead my case. I found him standing, on guard, at the end of the same hallway I had just walked through. I smiled at him, thankful that he had understood my desire for privacy without having to be told.

Excitement built as I entered Sela's room. It was a brightly lit, cheerful space made even more joyful by the scattered bouquets of bright red and purple flowers. The scene inside made me hang back, just inside the door. Sela was sitting up on a bed with Derek standing by her side, both of them beaming down the small bundle in her arms.

"I guess I wasn't fast enough," I said quietly, but loud enough for them to notice me.

Derek chuckled, his brown eyes bright. "I think you would've had to defy the laws of physics to get here in time," he said. "This baby came *fast*."

I chuckled.

"A week early, in fact," Sela noted, eyes awash with tears, smiling at me. "Come look what we made."

My own tears threatened as I approached the bed. Derek stepped aside to give me room to look, and when I did, I placed a hand over my heart.

"Oh my gods, Sela," I whispered, staring down at the baby sleeping in my best friend's arms. "She's so beautiful."

Sela beamed. "Just like her name," she whispered. "Lahra."

I sniffled, recalling the meaning of Gannon's endearment for me, the very reason I had recommended it to Sela.

"Hold her," she said, holding Lahra toward me.

Sela didn't need to ask me twice.

I quickly divested myself of my coat and bag then reached for the baby, cradling her close to my chest. She was so soft and warm, and so tiny

I could hardly see her within the thick layers of her cream-colored blankets. Thank gods for her crown of swirling dark hair, or I wouldn't have been able to locate the child within all the fabric.

I sat down gingerly on the edge of Sela's bed, careful not to jostle Lahra, then pulled back a corner of the swaddling to admire her more closely. Her brows were drawn together as though in deep thought, her fists curled into tight balls by her cheeks. My breath stuttered at the warmth that spread through my chest, uncoiling a knot, the strong and all too familiar unease I had been struggling with. It was a tension that had been building inside me over the past few months, formed by my conflict with Gabriel, my responsibilities at the Judiciary and, of course, my ongoing indecision about Gannon and Tai. My sight swam with tears at the realization that *this*, this moment sitting here, watching Lahra sleep, was the first in a long while that I had been able to simply be still, in a state somewhere near peace, and not worry about something or some*one* and how frustrated or angry they made me feel.

Only when Derek eased Lahra out of my arms did I realize that I had been crying. After he slipped the baby out of my hold, I dropped my face into my hands, giving over to wracking, heartrending sobs.

"Derek," Sela said quietly behind my noisy weeping. "Why don't you take Lahra out to see everyone again? I'm sure they're missing her by now."

I wiped at my tears with the back of my hands as Derek walked out of the room. "I'm so sorry," I choked out, alarmed at myself. "I'm just so happy for you."

Sela's gray eyes were round, wide, with worry. "Those aren't happy tears," she said, shaking her head. "What's wrong?"

I wanted to tell her, but damn it, I couldn't. This wasn't the time to lean on my best friend's shoulder and ask her to drown in my sorrows. She had just had a child. She should be focused entirely on Lahra and Derek, not on *me*, but Hallowed Halls, I was a dam about to break. I needed to relieve the pressure, confide in her, tell her *something!*

"It's Tai," I blurted out. "I asked him to be in a multiple with me."

Sela's mouth went slack. "You did *what?*"

I wiped my nose, not bothering to respond. She had heard me, of course. I could see it all over her blinking-like-an-owl face.

"Just to be clear," she said with a raised hand, "you asked *Tai* to be in a multiple with you and *Gannon?*"

I sent her a withering look through watery eyes. *I mean, truly, who else would I want to be in a multiple with?* I indulged her with a reply. "Yes. It was Gannon's idea."

Shock made her shoulders wilt. "*Gannon's idea,*" she breathed as though she needed to say it to believe it. She searched my face. "And what did Tai say?"

I sagged, staring down at my hands. What *didn't* he say? "He called me manipulative, spoiled and a liar all in the same breath."

I steeled myself for her response. No doubt, Sela was about to launch into some detailed explanation about how justified Tai was in his response ... And maybe he was. I mean, multiples could be as complicated as any other type of relationship. Even more complicated if you added in a mix of people from restricted castes and two men who barely tolerated each other. No wonder Tai had nearly kicked me out on my ass. All Above! Why *couldn't* I be happy with *either* man? Why did I want, *need*, to be with *both?!*

Selfish. There was one word Tai hadn't called me that maybe he should have. I bit down on my bottom lip to stop from crying all over again.

Sela shifted on the bed, and I glanced up to find her scowling, face red.

"How *dare* he throw names at you!" she spat, and I rocked back. "*He* was the one who waited *years* to tell you that he wanted to be with you, that he *loved* you, and when he did, what did he do?" She jabbed a finger at me as though I were the accused. "He still resisted, pushed you away for *months*, and only gave in when he was faced with competition from someone else!"

You could have knocked me over with a feather. *That* was the last thing I had expected her to say!

I looked her over. "What happened to you wanting me to be with Tai, that I should just give him time and he'll come around?"

Sela sighed, anger deflating as fast as a popped balloon. "I still want Tai for you," she said. "Because you love him. But, oh, I don't know. Maybe it was impending motherhood, but I've been very introspective over the last few days."

I inched closer to her, searching her face. "What do you mean?"

"I just want you to be happy, but since you left Gannon …" She shook her head. "Since then you just haven't been yourself."

I frowned, trying to recall my behavior. I hadn't been myself for a *multitude* of reasons, but the way she connected my mood to Gannon made me sit up.

"My focus has been on making sure that you didn't get hurt," she continued, staring at the bouquet sitting at the end of the bed, "but you've been so torn up over the last few weeks, crying all the time — hurting, anyway." She shrugged. "I just wonder whether I've made your being with Gannon a bigger, much *worse* thing than it needs to be."

I stared at her, speechless. Since I'd told Sela about the depth of my feelings for Gannon, she had been *entirely* against the idea of me being with him. Yet there she was now, seeming to relent, even if a little bit.

I couldn't help it. I leaned over and wrapped my arms around her, embracing her. She laughed, shifting into a comfortable position so she could do the same to me.

"Thank you," I said into the hair at her nape, tears welling in my eyes. "I don't know what's going to happen, where things will end up with Gannon, Tai and me, but it helps to know you'd be all right with all of it."

She snorted and pulled away. "Now don't get ahead of yourself," she said in a huff, crossing her arms. "It's not like I'm giving you my consent to be in your forbidden relationship or anything."

I rolled my eyes, a laugh spluttering through my lips. "Like I would need it."

Part II

CHAPTER 10

I strode toward the boardroom armed for the advisory group meeting with a surefire strategy. Maybe it was spending the evening with Sela and Lahra that had inspired me, but no ... That wasn't it, or rather, that wasn't the *only* reason.

When I had returned to my apartment the night before, Rhoan had been just sitting down at the kitchen table to eat. He had a bowl of what, by the scent wafting within the room, I knew was Ma's vegetable and meat stew. After I announced Lahra's arrival and gushed about the incomparable beauty that she was, I slipped into a chair beside him, eager to probe his mind for advice regarding my challenges at work.

"I need your help," I said.

Rhoan snorted, shoving a spoon into his bowl. "So, am I out of your bad books now?"

I frowned, recalling resentfully that he had tattled on me to Tai. "I shouldn't even be lowering myself to talk to you," I said, "but I've decided to overlook your stupidity if you make good on your promise."

His eyebrows climbed his forehead as he chewed. "And which promise is that?"

"To help me," I said, inching closer to him. "I need to know how to get the advisory group to take me seriously."

Rhoan swallowed then took another bite. "Well, first off," he said around a mouthful of stew, "you have to shut that down."

I blinked. "Shut *what* down?"

"How insecure you feel," he explained, shoveling into his food again. "You're letting the media get to you."

I went stiff as a board, staring at him. *Insecure?* "I don't care about the media," I said. "I just want to do a good job." *Is he trying to suggest I'm not?*

Rhoan shifted his focus from the bowl to me then chuckled, apparently finding amusement in my distress.

"Look," he began, resting his spoon on the edge of the bowl. "You and I both know you can lead this group with your eyes closed, but the advisory group? They haven't seen you working hard every day at the Judiciary, supporting both the task force *and* the special committee. Most of what they know about you is from the media. In the minds of your advisory group, you're just some pretty media personality with above-average brains."

I groaned. "You're not making me feel any better, Rhoan," I muttered. "I'm fully aware they view me as some sort of spectacle. My problem is getting them to see passed my reputation in the media and respecting me."

"No," he replied, "your *problem* is that you think of your reputation as something to be *overcome* when you should be using it to your advantage."

There were truly only rare moments when I considered my brother more than just an ass, and this was one of them.

I quirked a brow at just how astute he was. Rather than digging deep and taking the bull by the horns like I normally would have, I had been intimidated by the experience and knowledge within the advisory group. It had been one thing to support leadership and respond to their questions, but in a position leading a group of my peers, many of whom I looked up to, my confidence had flagged. I needed to stop apologizing for my reputation and own it — recognize it as part of what made me someone who deserved to be advisor from whom the group could take direction.

"So what you're saying is that I need get over myself," I had said to Rhoan, thinning my lips.

He tucked into his meal again with a grin. "Your words, not mine."

Outside the boardroom, I squared my shoulders then strode in, eager to reset the dial. But when I entered, instead of finding the group ready to start work, I found Wyatt looking on as Kate, Elias and Lenore huddled at one end of the table, staring down at a tablet.

"What's going on?" I asked Asher, meeting him where he stood by the table.

"The Realm Anarchist," he replied out of the side of his mouth, arms folded, taking in the group. "He just announced he's going to be breaking a big story later this morning."

Well, *that* was far from news. I placed my tablet on the table, glancing about. The Realm Anarchist broke "big stories" no less than ten times a day.

Lenore looked up and a flush came to her cheeks when her eyes met mine. "Forgive us," she said, moving away from Kate as Elias did the same. "We all got a bit carried away."

Wyatt frowned, the embodiment of disapproval. "Speak for yourself," he said, walking to his seat. "The Anarchist is simply stringing you along, the way he always does."

"His story is supposed to be about leadership," Elias said as he drew up a chair.

Wyatt sat down with a snort. "*Everything* he writes about has to do with leadership," he remarked. "Nothing new there."

"Oh, I don't know," Kate jumped in. "He's never promised news that —" She peeked at her tablet before continuing: "*will test the very integrity of Realm governance and law.*"

Lenore's eyes lit up with anticipation as she pressed a palm to her chest. "Oh, good gods, I wonder what the story's about."

Kate and Lenore fell into a conversation guessing what the news could possibly be with Elias facilitating their animated debate. Meanwhile, Wyatt began swiping through his tablet, seemingly trying to ignore us all.

I surveyed the group, sensing a familiar threat. Only a few minutes in and they were already more focused on gossip than on what I had assembled them to discuss.

Asher glanced at me over the rim of his glasses, a mildly anxious look on his face. He probably expected me to be paralyzed with worry about how I should handle this. His concern wasn't misplaced. I had subjected him to a minor pity party after the last meeting, complaining about not being able to manage the group. Well, this time I had a better hold of myself and knew exactly what I needed to do.

"Anything the Realm Anarchist has to say can certainly wait," I said in a loud, clear voice that brought silence to the room. "I'm sure you all agree we have much more pressing matters to attend to."

Kate grimaced as Lenore sent me a look of apology and Elias raised his brows in response to my remark. Even Wyatt was compelled to shift his focus to me, though with a mildly disgruntled frown.

A ghost of a smile flitted across Asher's face. Thankfully, he managed to rein it in — for now at least. He was bound to tease me relentlessly about my newfound assertiveness for days to come.

"Did you check that everyone has the report on safety measures?" I asked him, trying to get him focused on the meeting.

He nodded, all business now. "As soon as I arrived," he said before moving to his chair.

"Good," I said, then sat down, unrolling my tablet. "Then let's get star—"

Wyatt cleared his throat, cutting me off. "Before we begin, I wonder if I could ask a few questions."

"Of course." I checked in with my colleagues with a glance around the table. "I'm sure we'd be happy to answer them as best we can."

"Actually," he said, eyeing me and resting his elbows on the table, "these questions are from my superior. He asked that the responses come directly from you."

I studied him, careful not to react. Any question that came from Wyatt, much less Xavier Minister, was worth approaching with wariness. It seemed Wyatt had returned to the advisory group armed with ammunition from his combative superior. Very well. I had survived challenges from Xavier Minister directly before. I could certainly manage them from Wyatt too.

I nodded, sitting up in my chair. "All right," I said. "I'll do my best."

He dipped his head in thanks, but a smirk touched the corner of his mouth.

"At the last meeting," he said, referring briefly to his device, "you brought up the matter of security. How do you plan to prevent citizens from abusing arc travel technology?"

I frowned, cocking my head. Xavier — every member of the advisory group, for that matter — should have known the answer to that question. Rhoan had walked Xavier and the rest of the special committee through a process to address that potential obstacle. It was the very thing on which Realm Council approval hinged.

"By developing regulation for a multi-caste training program," I reminded Wyatt, wondering all the while what he had up his sleeve. "And providing citizens with clearance according to a system of graduated exploration zones."

"But what about the forbidden zones?" he asked.

I blinked then shot a quick look around the group before my gaze landed on Asher's. Had I missed some development he had yet to fill me in on? Asher shook his head with a shrug, reading my mind, and so I focused on Wyatt once again. "What *forbidden* zones?"

Wyatt raised a brow. "You can't expect leadership to simply allow citizens to go as far and wide as they please, exploring beyond the Realm."

As a matter of fact, I did. "According to the special committee's recommendation," I said, "citizens will be permitted to explore where they wish within parameters set out by Realm Council, but those *parameters* aren't meant to restrict how far they go, just outline how they can do so safely."

Wyatt sniffed. "According to my superior," he said, "no matter how much training we provide citizens, there will always be areas beyond our system that Realm Council will never allow exploration."

A prickle of unease jogged my memory. During the special committee process, Xavier Minister had inadvertently confirmed leadership's hidden ongoing exploration beyond the Realm. Had he told Wyatt too? I couldn't imagine why. Xavier had been so on edge about Asher and me knowing about Realm Council's deception that he had agreed to throw his support behind the special committee's recommendation just to keep it quiet. Was *this* how he planned to continue keeping the Realm's secret was safe? By blocking sections of the Outer Realm from citizens?

"Why are there forbidden zones?" I asked Wyatt, trying to find out.

He raised a brow. "You know your Realm history as well as we all do," he said, scanning the group to include them too. "We mentioned it at the last meeting. I'm sure I don't have to rehash the tale of how our citizens were killed because of exploration beyond the Realm."

I shook my head. "You're misunderstanding my question," I said. "Why is there such a thing as a 'forbidden zone'? You can only deem a zone forbidden if you know what's in it. Do you?"

Lenore, Kate, Elias and Asher swung their gaze from me to Wyatt, attention rapt, awaiting his reply.

Wyatt shifted in his seat. "The minister didn't go into that level of detail with me," he said. "He simply wanted me to ensure you're developing a policy that allows exploration within a restricted framework."

"I'm sure he does," I said, suspecting the reason for that. "But you can't prevent *and* allow something at the same time."

Kate smothered a light laugh, making Wyatt stiffen, and I suddenly regretted my response. I hadn't said that to be smart, just to make a point.

I sighed at the belligerent set to Wyatt's mouth. "My purpose as advisor, and so that of this group, is to help Realm Council develop policies for exploration that will keep citizens safe," I said, hoping to get him onside so we could move on. "Not to restrict how far they can go."

Wyatt's mouth turned down. "I look forward to you making that very argument to leadership."

"As do I," I said with a shrug. "I've handled leaders at every level of this system. I know how to get my point across."

A few chuckles from Lenore and Kate made me cut them a glance, silencing them. I didn't need Wyatt's back up any more than it was, but one look at the glint in Wyatt's eyes told me the damage had already been done.

I braced myself as he leaned in. "You think that because of your notoriety and legion of adoring fans you can take some sort of stand," he said. "You're a *subordinate* just like the rest of us, a token of diplomacy at best. I've been working at the Judiciary for a long time, *much* longer than you have, and leadership rarely listens to me, so there's no way they're going to listen to someone like *you*."

I studied Wyatt, taken aback. A bitter string of words meant to put Wyatt in his place was on the very tip of my tongue, but I held back from speaking them. What would that accomplish? It would have done a lot to stroke my ego and injure his, but I had to work with this blasted fool at the end of the day.

Gannon had told me once, early in our relationship, that what leadership despised the most was vulnerability; if I planned on being of any help to Realm Council, then I had better get used to handling mine. If I lashed out at Wyatt, he would know he had touched a nerve by suggesting that I was unqualified and would probably use that vulnerability against me for the rest of our time supporting me on the advisory group. So, I only had one option left: I had to set the right tone and ensure he and everyone else understood this was my group to lead whether they liked it or not.

"They might not listen to me," I said, "but I'll make my opinions heard. *All* of our opinions, as a matter of fact. The truth is when Realm Council approves the recommendation, they will look to *me* as their advisor. I was appointed to this position for a number of reasons, some of which have to do with the media but most of which have to do with the hard work I've put into this project from the very start. At the end of the day, the reason doesn't matter, only my commitment. I'm here, ready, willing and prepared to help Realm Council develop a policy for exploration that will advance our system." I took a breath. "The question is, are you?"

He considered me evenly, holding himself so stiff I wondered whether his joints had fused. I kept his gaze, chin raised, refusing to give in until he did, which to my distress didn't appear likely to be any time soon. I bit down on the inside of my cheek to stop from caving under his glare.

After a long, strained moment as Wyatt and I squared off and the group looked on, he sat back in his chair then said, "Where do we start?"

Oh, thank gods. I exhaled slowly, hoping no one could tell I had been holding my breath, before a buzzing sound made me jump.

Lenore gasped. "Oh! I'm so sorry," she said, glancing at her comm. "I should've silen—" She froze.

Kate peered at her from across the table. "What is it?"

Lenore raised wide eyes to me. "N-nothing," she said, her gaze dropping to her lap as color came to her cheeks.

Kate frowned, as did I, and then the sound of vibrating devices filled the room. Kate checked her comm, and everyone else did the same before slowly, one by one, they each looked at me with varying levels of disbelief blooming in their eyes.

Wyatt folded his arms, shaking his head. "I don't know whether to be impressed or outraged," he scoffed.

What? I looked to Asher and, when his gaze lifted to mine, a sliver of trepidation ran up my spine at the stricken expression on his usually jovial face. "What's wrong?"

Asher swallowed and opened his mouth, but the door to the boardroom slid open at the same time. I twisted around in my chair as Theo, our former receptionist, walked in.

"Subordinate Metallurgist," he said, standing by the door. Everything about him was as imperious as I remembered. "The minister would like to see you."

Something was wrong. *Very* wrong. It had to be. If Mila was summoning me away from the advisory group, then it had to be for a serious reason. My heart began thumping in my chest.

"I'll go with you," Asher said, his chair scraping on the floor as he pushed away from the table, ready to do just that.

I swallowed. "No," I said, eyeing Theo, trying to get a sense of what was going on. "I'm sure this won't take long."

"I suggest you adjourn the meeting," Theo remarked with a raised brow. "You won't be returning to the advisory group, at least not any time soon."

A gasp, probably from Lenore, burst out from somewhere behind me. Meanwhile, I stared at Theo, mind spinning. *What the fuck is this about?* It was Asher's hand on my shoulder that spurred me into action. I stood up, fumbling with my tablet as I tried to roll it up.

"Are you sure you don't want me to go with you?" he asked, and the worry in his voice urged me to meet his gaze.

"You should stay here," I said unsteadily. "Please. Just review the report and then adjourn the meeting. All right?"

Asher appeared reluctant, but he agreed with a nod, face grim.

I tried to summon a reassuring smile for him and the group, but my effort was useless. Dread and confusion kept my mouth in a tight line. After a final glance at Asher, I ducked my head and followed Theo out of the room.

* * *

By the time Theo ushered me into Mila's office, my heart was lodged firmly in my throat. Mila was standing behind her desk, hands on her hip, facing me with a deep scowl. "I guess the jig is up," she said. "Isn't it."

I stopped in the middle of the room, searching my mind for clues as to what she meant, but I soon gave up. "I don't understand."

Mila sighed and gestured to one of the chairs on the other side of the desk. I sat down on the edge of my seat, trying to steady my pulse, as she came around to my side.

"I tried to warn you once about pushing boundaries," she said, perching on the desk, staring down at me. "It's fine until you get caught. I can't imagine what your family must be thinking right now."

A fleeting moment of sheer panic stole my breath. "My family?"

Mila expelled a heavy sigh. "Everyone knows, Kira," she said, face grim. "It's all over the news. Your secret's out."

My family ... everyone knows ... secret's out ...

Then it clicked. She knew. They *all* did. All Above, this was about my parents! *That's* why the advisory group had been staring at me, stunned, after checking their devices. *This* must have been the "big story" the Realm Anarchist had promised to break! Fear made my hands tremble. My gods, but how did he find out? Was Gabriel behind this? And if so, *why?* He had yet to contact me for the files. Why would he expose me without first getting what he wanted?

Mila's expression became even more bleak as she continued staring at me, and I lowered my gaze to my lap, squeezing my eyelids shut. I couldn't look her in the eye. Gods, what she must think of me! My family's support of the factions, Khelan's hidden status and relationship with my mother — *none* of that could be overlooked by someone in her position. Still, I had to try to make her understand.

I lifted my chin. "My parents, they're really good people," I said, tears welling in my eyes. "They didn't want any of this."

"I'm sure they didn't," she said, folding her arms. "No parent would want to know their daughter's been having an affair with someone in a restricted caste — high chancellor or not."

The world seemed to tilt on its axis. One, two, no, it took me *three* attempts to reply. "What?!"

Mila grimaced. "I know. It's hard to believe this is happening," she said, twisting around to reach behind her. "I suppose you could deny the whole thing, but the images are pretty damning. You can always count on that asshole the Realm Anarchist to back his news up." She turned to me, tablet in hand, and showed the device to me. Every muscle in my body went slack.

Underneath the dazzling headline *Kira Metallurgist: Sleeping Her Way to the Top* were four photos of Gannon and me. The first image showed me walking with Gannon into Realm Council residences through the private entrance; the second was of me entering his townhouse; the third, of the two of us standing under a glass pergola, which must have been in Commune after his father's ash ceremony; and the fourth — oh holy mother of gods — the fourth was the most damaging of all. It was a photo of Gannon and me wrapped in passionate embrace, kissing as though we were alone, oblivious to the many people around us!

I covered my mouth with both of my shaking hands as my thoughts splintered, trying to figure that one out.

How could anyone have possibly been able to take a picture of us in such a compromising position? And in a public place? Gannon and I had always been so careful. We were *never* intimate in public except — *oh no.* I fell back against the chair, remembering. Except that one time after the attack on Septima. Gannon and I had been put into quarantine and had been forced to wear plain clothes since our uniforms had become too dirty and tattered to put on after we had cleaned up. Gannon and I had taken advantage of the common attire, thinking it and all the upheaval following the attack would give us anonymity. Looking back now, how could we have been so foolish? Gannon was a member of *leadership*, easily identifiable — uniform or not!

Mila pulled the tablet out of my sight with a worried look. "I can see these images have shocked you as much as they have everyone else."

My hands fell to my lap. Shocked? How about floored! My mind continued spinning, going a mile a minute, wondering whether Gannon had heard the news, what he was thinking, where he was. And what about Tai? Oh gods. My comm hadn't vibrated or chimed to signal a message from either of them. What did that mean?

Mila was studying me closely, so I swallowed and sat up. "I'm so sorry, Mila," I felt compelled to say.

She scowled and stood up. "Don't apologize," she said, walking back around to her chair. "I take some responsibility for what's happened. I willfully overlooked your relationship with a member of Realm leadership."

My thoughts collided, coming to a stop. "You knew?" I asked. But then, hadn't I already suspected as much?

Mila nodded, frowning. "I did know," she said as she sat down. "And I didn't push back."

"You tried." A few times, if I remembered correctly.

"But not hard enough," she replied. "Maybe if I had, none of this would have happened and I wouldn't have to do what I'm about to do."

I stilled. "What do you mean?"

A rueful twist came to Mila's mouth. "I had just returned from my meeting with the election candidates when the ambassador called to tell me the news about you," she said. "I've never heard the man so riled up."

"About *me?*" Yes, my relationship with Gannon was scandalous and would put a mark on my character, but this was gossip, trivial, nothing that should have spurred the leader of our dominion to become so distressed. "Why?"

"You've been working alongside the high chancellor on two high-profile projects," Mila said, "and the ambassador knows that I've tapped you to be advisor to Realm Council, which means you'd be reporting directly to Gannon. He's worried about conflict of interest. He even mentioned something about dismissing you."

I froze. *What? No!* All Above, such a consequence had never even entered my mind. I could handle public scrutiny and media smears, even being part of the gossip mill for a few painstaking weeks, but I couldn't, *wouldn't* lose my job.

I rose quickly to my feet, hands clasped. "Please, Mila," I begged. "*Don't* dismiss me. I *love* working at the Judiciary."

She waved me back into my seat. "Relax," she said. "I'm not going to dismiss you. The ambassador will have to dismiss me himself if that's what he wants me to do. My gods, if leadership got rid of every subordinate or protector fooling around beyond their permitted castes, they probably wouldn't have anyone left to lead!"

I sat down, eyeing her, still wary. All right. So I wouldn't be dismissed, but then that raised the question … "What *are* you going to do?"

Her mouth flattened into a hard line. "First off," she said, "I'm going to do some damage control, save face a bit about this love affair that was going on under my nose."

I continued to study her, sensing worse was yet to come. "And then?"

She faltered, her shoulders drooping as she leaned on her forearms, on her desk. "I'm going to have to make an example out of you, Kira," she said, and I tensed. There really was only one action left that she could take. "I'm suspending you until further notice."

My eyelids slid shut. *Damn it.* Even though I had anticipated what she had been about to say, it still stung to hear it. Tears made my throat ache.

"Is there anything I can do to change your mind?" I asked, opening my eyes.

Mila shook her head. "I'm sorry," she said. "This is the best I can do."

And of course, it was. Because it was either be suspended or dismissed. This price to pay was the better of the two.

"Don't worry," Mila said, a deeply apologetic look in her eyes. "When things die down, I'll have you come back, but …" She winced, shaking her head.

She didn't need to finish her sentence. I understood. It went without saying that when I returned to the Judiciary, whenever that was, I would be returning without my rank.

CHAPTER 11

I ignored my comm when it vibrated again, continuing to tug on the coiled strands of my hair. The device had been alerting me nonstop to incoming requests from the media who wanted to "hear my side of the story."

I snorted, dropping my hand to my thighs with a sputtering sigh. As though there could *be* any other side! The photos of Gannon and me were as incriminating as they were true.

After leaving Mila's office in a daze and collecting my things, I had found Talib waiting for me in the reception area wearing a solemn expression. With a frown, he had wasted little time escorting me downstairs, and, like the protector he was, shielded me from the prying eyes of ogling citizens as he had led me through the lobby. Only once I was in the safe confines of Gannon's hover, waiting outside the Judiciary, had Talib informed me that he had been ordered to take me to home, which meant Gannon must have heard the news.

Tears rushed in, welling in my eyes. How could Gannon *not* have heard?

By the time I had arrived at my apartment, the story was all over the newsfeed and I had been forced to put my comm on vibrate to avoid its incessant pinging and chiming. Amidst all the requests from the media were messages from my friends and family asking me what was going on, whether I was all right, where I was. I had responded with a quick message to Sela, Asher and Rhoan, but had yet to reply to any communication from Nara or my parents. I just couldn't bring myself to admit the truth to Nara, fearing her disappointment in me.

As for my parents, well, a brief "I'm okay" just wouldn't suffice. I would need to speak with them face to face ... especially considering the assumption they had made.

My parents, in their unwavering trust in me, didn't believe a word of the media story. They had determined, instead, that I had been caught in the middle of some rumor mill manufactured by the media and fueled by lies.

I groaned, imagining Tai, arms crossed, looming over me with the words "I told you so" spouting from his mouth. He was right, of course. I should have told my parents about Gannon and me when Tai had told me to. Instead I now had to confess everything to them under a cloud of public disgrace.

A shudder moved through me at the thought.

My comm vibrated again and I glanced at it this time, expecting a message from Tai but finding one from Gannon glowing on the transparent screen.

I'm on my way up.

I blinked away tears, convinced I was seeing things. Gannon was *here?* In my building?

Certainly, I had expected Gannon to contact me after Talib had brought me home, but by *comm*, not *in person*. Him being seen with me *before* the story broke was already a bad idea; being seen with me at my apartment would only make matters worse.

I got up from the couch and hurried to the front door. When I disengaged it, Talib was there, standing watch just as he said he would, shortly after we had arrived.

He moved to me, a question on his face, but I stopped him with a raised hand. "It's Gannon," I said. "He's here."

The protector nodded, stepping back, not appearing particularly surprised, which made sense. He would have known about his superior's imminent arrival, probably before me.

Just then the elevator at the end of the hallway opened and Gannon appeared with Jonah behind him.

As usual, despite my efforts and the commotion surrounding me, every part of me lit up, hummed, at the sight of Gannon. As he strode to me, he looked every inch the high chancellor in his crisp Senate uniform, gleaming crests and all, cladding his tall athletic build. I held onto the doorframe, gripping it to stop from embarrassing myself by running into his arms the way I had done in the past. The taut lines of his face were a cold reminder of the media storm that had us in the middle of it.

"Should you be here?" I asked when he stood in front of me. "Everyone will know you came to see me."

His brows met, eyes flinty. "What difference does it make now?"

Oh.

I frowned and stepped back to allow him to enter, but before he did, he turned to Jonah and Talib. "Wait for me in the lobby," he ordered and, as the protectors moved off down the hall, stepped passed me and into the apartment.

After disengaging the door, I found him standing behind me, tension seeming to radiate from his very core.

"Gabriel did this," he announced.

My eyebrows shot up. "You think *Gabriel* sent the photos to the Realm Anarchist?"

His face tightened as though arguing with himself. "I don't know," he said finally, turning to walk into the sitting area as he raked a hand through his hair. "But what better way for Gabriel to hurt you, *us*, than to use the media to make our relationship public."

He had a point, but I was shaking my head. "It *can't* be Gabriel," I said, following him into the room. "Why would he reveal one of the secrets he's holding over my head without even attempting to contact me first? Why would I bother to help him now?"

Gannon turned to me, eyes glittering. "Maybe so we understand his threats are serious and to make sure you comply to his demands," he said. "It's not as if he doesn't have other, more damaging secrets to manipulate you with."

My family.

I expelled a deep breath, suddenly more weary than I had ever been. "Well, if it *was* Gabriel, his plans to ruin my life are right on track," I said, dragging myself to the couch while averting his eyes. "I've been suspended."

It was a few moments before he replied. "What?" he asked so quietly I knew just how angry he was about to be, which was why I didn't bother to look at him.

Still avoiding his gaze, I sat down and wrapped my arms about my waist. "Conflict of interest," I said. "Apparently, my being involved with you during the task force and special committee has been deemed a colossal breach of ethics, worthy of my immediate suspension until further notice."

The air seemed to shift, becoming cool, in the room. I risked a look at Gannon and found him staring steadily, unmoving, at me. "Did Mila do this?"

I considered him. "Yes," I said. "Why?"

"When is she announcing your suspension?"

I hesitated at the familiar glint in his eye. "I'm not sure," I said slowly. "She said something about doing some damage control first."

"Good," he said, looking away, seeming to drift into his "That will give me time."

Oh no. I searched deep inside for patience. "To do what, Gannon?"

"To call a meeting with both Mila and the ambassador," he said, eyes clearing as he looked at me. "You'll be back at the Judiciary within the week."

I stared up at him, shaking my head. Predictably, Gannon wanted to *fix* everything for me.

"And what will you say?" I said with a small, bitter laugh. "That you love Kira Metallurgist so very much that her suspension should be lifted?"

He sent me a quelling look that had probably worked on many a subordinate, but I held his gaze.

"I believe I'd take a less bleeding-heart approach than that," Gannon said, "but the outcome would be the same."

I slumped. That wasn't the point. "You jumping in like that will only confirm the conflict of interest they're accusing us of," I said. "The best thing for me to do is to just ride this out. Mila said she'll call me back in to the Judiciary as soon as the news dies down."

"But you'll lose your rank," he countered, looking me over with a scowl. "You don't deserve that. This is above and beyond what anyone's ever had to face for something like this."

It probably was, but recalling the dismissal I had just narrowly escaped, I mumbled, "It could have been worse."

Gannon didn't appear in the least bit mollified. With a curse, he prowled the room, his overpowering desire to do something, *take control*, making his moves stiff. While his anger was warranted, I couldn't help but wonder if he was outraged over something else as well.

I sat up with a gasp. "Is the Corona taking action against you for this too?" He had said that leadership wouldn't demote him over something like this now that he had been appointed high chancellor, but after everything I had been through with our sovereign, I had little faith in that.

Gannon stopped in the middle of the room, turning to me with a glint in his eye. "She's welcome to try, but I highly doubt it," he said. "The fact that she hasn't contacted me yet is a pretty good indication she doesn't see this as a matter she needs or wants to address."

I relaxed even as the unfair irony of that sank in, making me frown. Both Gannon and I had been involved in this relationship, yet it was *me*, the lowly subordinate, who would take the brunt of this whole godsforsaken mess. I clenched my fists.

Gannon looked me over and the challenge in his gaze softened into worry. He came over and sat down in front of me, on the edge of the small table, his knees bracketing mine. "I'm so sorry," he said so earnestly it took me off-guard. "About all of this."

I wilted. "Gannon, this isn't your fault."

"Isn't it?" he challenged, his eyes dimming with unnecessary guilt. "I should have anticipated this, what being with me could have done to you."

What? "I didn't become involved with you with blinders on," I countered. Thanks to Tai, Sela and of course Rhoan's well-meaning but unwelcome advice, I had gone in knowing what I could face. "I knew what I was getting into."

"But not *this*," he said, reaching for my hands, his palms hot on my skin. "This whole time you've been concerned about what being with me would do to *my* future while disregarding what it would do to your own." He shook his head, face pale. "What does that say about me that I barely gave any of this a thought?"

That gave me pause. I had never looked at it that way. My mind started wading through the confusing puddle of emotions that now bubbled up inside me.

I had told Gannon repeatedly that I didn't care what anyone thought about us being together, but he had never believed me, not truly. He had once said that I seemed to always be waiting for the shoe to drop when it came to our relationship. Well, there it was. The shoe had dropped. Our relationship was out and in the open. With nothing left to hide, here was my chance to demonstrate how little I cared about the opinion of others by thumbing my nose at everyone who was judging Gannon and me. And I would be doing just that right now if I hadn't been burned by a consequence so unexpected and unjust that I wanted to pull my hair out by the roots.

Gannon had hit the nail on the head. I had expected to be shunned, ostracized for a while for being involved with him, but never to be *suspended*, something that would negate all the hard work I had done so far. The harsh reality of my being with Gannon stung — *stung* just as much as the blasted tears that were returning to my eyes.

I lowered my gaze to our clasped hands so he couldn't see the hurt.

Gannon released my hands and cupped my face, lifting it to stare into my eyes. "You'll be back where you were meant to be," he vowed, thumbing the tears from my cheeks. "I promise you that."

I didn't see how that was possible, but I nodded jerkily between his hands, hoping to smooth away the sharp edge of worry that had hardened his face.

The front door buzzed, a harsh sound, cutting into the moment.

Gannon glanced behind me, toward the door, his hands slipping from my face. "Are you expecting someone?"

I wiped away my remaining tears and stood up to approach the monitor. "No," I said, activating the screen with a touch. It lit up with a view into the hallway where two familiar people — an imposing man and an elegant woman — stood outside my door.

"Oh holy mother of gods," I whispered, my knees nearly buckling at the sight. *Not here! Not now!*

Gannon came up beside me. "What's wrong?" he asked then glanced at the screen. "Who are they?"

I closed my eyes briefly. "My parents." *Shit.*

A flicker of surprise flew across Gannon's face before he straightened his jacket and pivoted toward the door.

I lunged after him, grasping him by the wrist, stopping him just in time. "Where do you think you're going?" I asked, eyes wide.

He looked at me over his shoulder, confusion knitting his brow. "To open the door," he stated as though it were the most logical thing in the worlds. And of course, it was, but I couldn't let him do it. Dear gods, I couldn't do it myself!

"When they see you here ..." I couldn't finish my sentence. The moment Khelan and Ma laid eyes on Gannon they would know the media story was true. Good gods, I had dreaded telling my parents by myself, but now, *now*, with Gannon present, the act of my confession would only be so much worse. "They'll wonder what you're doing here."

He cocked his head, body still turned away from me. "Why? They know the truth."

I winced, glancing away, before he narrowed his eyes.

"Don't they?" he asked.

I forced myself to meet his gaze. "They think this was all some mistake," I explained. "That the media made up the story about us."

He stilled. "You *lied* to them?" he asked but it sounded very much like an accusation.

"No," I rushed out then I exhaled a harsh breath. "I wouldn't lie to them about *this*. They drew their own conclusions."

Gannon considered me carefully as the door buzzed again. Finally, he turned his body to me, coming back into my space.

"I won't force you to let them in," he said with a mild expression, "but if you do, you should know I'm not going to hide or cower in a corner or leave you here alone to fend for yourself. I *will* speak with your parents. I won't allow your mother and father to leave this apartment without knowing just how much you mean to me."

My breath caught as Gannon stared down at me, waiting on my next move. I didn't know what to do. There was just too much in what he had said for me to digest.

Should I let my parents into the apartment or not?

If I didn't, I'd simply be delaying the inevitable, and if I *did*, I would be bringing together the two worlds I had tried so hard to keep apart. And in the middle of all the inevitable tumult would be Gannon declaring his feelings for me in a move that demonstrated such complete devotion I wanted to weep.

Oh gods.

I glanced at the door when it buzzed again, much longer, insistently this time.

Maybe I'm overthinking this. My parents would be disappointed and angry, but they would be understanding too. Wouldn't they? Khelan and Ma were in a similar position as Gannon and me. Truly, they were the only two people in *all* the Realm who could even remotely find compassion for us. After the way my parents had taken the news about Gabriel and Maxim, I had to assume that their love for me would trump their immediate anger and any of their concerns.

"What do you want to do, Kira?" Gannon asked, breaking into my stream of thought.

I looked at him, assessing, but his expression was still guarded. I couldn't get a sense of which way he preferred me to go. Yet, I figured by the unwavering focus he had on me, that whatever I did next would be significant to him in some way. The truth was, it would be significant for *both* of us.

"All right," I said, swallowing and squaring my shoulders. "I'm going to let them in."

* * *

"Kira Grace Metallurgist!" Ma cried the moment I opened the door. "Where in the worlds have you been?"

"We've been trying to contact you for the past two hours," Khelan stated with a glare that was tempered by the sudden relief in his eyes. "Rhoan, Sela — *no one* knows where you were. We had to leave your Da, stricken with worry, at home with Addy so we could come here to find you. My gods, we almost called the authorities!"

I looked over my parents with a frown, guilt crowning the top of my pile of warring emotions. If their words of distress hadn't made their worry evident, the tight hold they had on each other would have. Khelan and my mother had been careful over the years to hide their relationship from everyone, but it seemed their concern for my welfare had thrown caution to the wind. My mother was huddled against Khelan's side, her hand at his chest, while his arm was wound firmly about her waist. After what I had told them about being abducted by Maxim, their worry was justified. I should have done better. I should have contacted my parents as soon as I had returned to my apartment, if only to tell them that I was safe.

I swallowed. "I'm sorry," I said, gesturing to my comm and coming up with an excuse. "I had it on silent." I didn't bother noting that the device had also been on vibrate.

Khelan blew out a tight breath. "To avoid the media, of course," he said, the incorrect assumption clearing his brow as he looked down at Ma. "They've probably been hounding her, seeking more fuel for their lies."

Ma nodded, agreeing with him.

I shrank, leaning against the doorframe.

"Come on," Khelan said, placing a hand at my mother's back, urging her to enter the apartment. "Let's figure out how we're going to clean up this mess."

I inhaled sharply and shifted, blocking their path. They both startled and stopped, staring back at me.

Khelan searched my face. "Is there a particular reason you're not letting us in?"

I pressed my lips together then glanced over my shoulder, into the sitting area where Gannon stood. He watched me silently, an expression on his face that, while blank, was easily understood: the time had come.

I sighed and faced my parents. "No." I stepped aside. "There isn't. Come in."

With a curious eye directed at me, Khelan ushered Ma in. I disengaged the door and followed.

It was like watching a video in slow motion. Ma steps faltered first then Khelan's as they neared the sitting area. My mother's lips parted as her gaze landed on Gannon, and Khelan froze by her side. I watched, dread rising, as they stood stock still, their surprised expressions sliding into confusion then diving into stunned disbelief.

"What is this?" Khelan demanded, focus still on Gannon, but I sensed his question was meant for me. I shared a look with Gannon then skirted around my parents to stand next to him.

I cleared my throat unnecessarily. "This is Gannon Consul," I said, looking between them clutching my hands tight at my waist. "High Chancellor of the Realm."

Khelan's gaze cut to me. "We *know* who he is," he said, spelling out every word as though speaking to a simpleton. "What is *he* doing in *your* apartment?"

I swallowed at the storm gathering on Khelan's face. "The media …" I began on a shaky note. "They didn't make up the story. Everything the Realm Anarchist reported is true."

There was a beat of silence before my mother said, "What?"

I frowned at the unsteady way my mother held herself. "Gannon and I are … We used to be …" I bit down on my bottom lip. What fucking difference did it make? "We're involved. Have been for some time now."

My parents resumed their staring, this time at me, appearing etched in stone all over again.

Meanwhile, Gannon shifted closer, offering me much-needed strength. He eyed the tongue-tied forms of my parents with a frown. "I wish we could have met under different, better circumstances," he said carefully. "This isn't how I would have wanted to introduce myself."

"*Introduce* yourself," Khelan repeated as though Gannon had spoken some foreign language, then his gaze swept over to me, pinning me to the floor. Lightning, thunder, an ominous sign from the gods — *anything* would have been better than the rage and disappointment that gripped his face. "So *this* is what you've been doing at the Judiciary all this time!" He jabbed a finger in Gannon's direction. "*Him!*"

I flinched, and Gannon's lips thinned.

"I understand this comes as a surprise," Gannon stated. "You have every right to be angry, b—"

"You're damn right I have every right to be angry!" Khelan cut in, face mottled with rage as he clenched his fists. "Who the fuck do you think you are!"

A tic came to Gannon's jaw, but he kept silent. He appeared reluctantly resigned to allowing Khelan's anger froth and ride itself out, at least for a bit.

Khelan stormed across the room, scrubbing a hand over his mouth.

"My gods, Kira, what are you thinking?" Ma said, shaking her head, then looked to Khelan, who had stopped in front of the monitor, facing her. "Wait until Hugo hears about this."

Khelan scowled, glaring at me. "To think your Da was just boasting to everyone who would hear it about you getting the chance to work directly with the high chancellor," he said. "He's going to be crushed when he learns just how you got the position."

I stood there, Khelan's remark and Da's certain disappointment rendering me speechless.

Gannon inhaled deeply as though trying to keep a rein on his temper. "Kira was appointed to that position for no other reason than because she was qualified and deserving," he said evenly. "Whether we were involved or not had nothing to do with it."

Khelan raised a hand as though finding his way through a fog as he approached me. "Hold on," he said, disregarding Gannon altogether. "You *must* have been called in by your superior for something like this, maybe even the ambassador, since it involves *him*." He blanched, searching my face. "What happened?"

Holy gods. I wanted to hide, but hadn't hiding been the cause of all my problems so far? I exchanged a glance with Gannon, gaining strength in the resolve sitting in his eyes, and braced myself. "I've been suspended, until further notice."

Ma covered her mouth with a hand as Khelan's shoulders slumped.

"You'll never gain rank after this," he said, wonder in his eyes as though only now realizing the true reason for his anger. "I helped to get you into the Judiciary because it was what you wanted, because I *knew* it was where you were meant to be. And what have you done with that opportunity?" His voice rose with each word. "You've tossed it, and all your hard work away — for *him!*"

I wobbled on my feet, and Gannon placed a hand on my back, steadying me. Khelan noticed the interaction and his blue eyes darkened as he looked Gannon over with a cool gaze.

"I'm familiar with men like you," he said, eyes narrowing as he moved toward him. "You prey on young, vulnerable women in lower castes, luring them in with your rank before you cast them aside."

I inhaled a sharp breath, staring at Khelan, my mouth slack. How could Khelan, a man who helped *raise me*, think I could be so naive as to let Gannon's position turn my eye! "That's not true," I bit out, but Khelan didn't spare me a look. He glowered at Gannon whose hand fisted at the small of my back.

"I'm not some philanderer deceiving women from world to world," Gannon said through clenched teeth, his gaze never wavering from the older man's.

Khelan scoffed, exchanging a bitter look of disbelief with Ma, over his shoulder. She drew closer, considering Gannon out of the corner of her eye.

"I *chose* to be with Gannon," I stated firmly, disgusted by the picture Khelan was painting of him and Ma's apparent willingness to believe it. "He didn't *trick* me. Being with him was always my choice."

"I'm sure that's *exactly* what he would want you to think," Khelan said.

Gannon thinned his lips. "I would never deceive Kira, especially not the way you're implying," he countered, his own anger bringing a flush to the top of his cheeks.

"Yet you would put her in a position where the media would drag her name through the mud," Ma remarked, standing beside Khelan now, with her arms folded. "Where everyone would view her as less than she is."

A shadow moved across Gannon's face. "I would have done anything to protect her from what happened."

"Except leave her alone," she replied.

Gannon paled.

There was a beat of silence where no one spoke, but words weren't necessary when the tension spoke volumes about the strain within the room. Gannon's gaze moved from my mother to me where it rested for a searching moment before descending on Khelan.

"I'm in love with your daughter," he said to him.

My lips parted, surprise making me go slack. Gannon had said he would tell my parents what I meant to him, but I hadn't realized he would go so far as to tell them he *loved* me. Unfortunately, Khelan wasn't as moved by the declaration as I was.

He snorted, giving Gannon his back. "Of *course* you are," he spat as he stalked across the room. "What else would you say?"

I clenched my fists, forcing myself not to cry. Through watery eyes, I looked for help from Ma, a woman who was usually the voice of reason, but instead of getting her support, I found her staring at Gannon, face ashen, mouth agape.

She staggered to him. "You know," she whispered, staring up into his face.

Gannon looked down at my mother, but didn't reply.

She gripped his wrist and shook it. "You looked straight at Khelan and called Kira *his* daughter," she said, the light brown of her eyes glistening. "You *know*."

My heart dipped.

Khelan spun around to look at Gannon at the same time I did. I would have expected the same surprise that was surely on my face to be mirrored on his, but Gannon didn't appear anything remotely close to being shocked. In fact, he appeared remorseful, wary, *resigned* even, as he looked at me.

Because it wasn't an accident. Gannon had *meant* to disclose that he knew Khelan was my birth father.

Looking back at the now stricken faces of my parents, it occurred to me why. They had stood there, doubting him, lambasting him, making him out to be some womanizer laying waste to the female subordinate population across the Realm. Meanwhile, they knew nothing about what Gannon had done for me, for *our family*. When I had told my family about Gabriel and Maxim, I had begged Tai to leave Gannon out, worried that my parents would discover his connection to me. Well, I no longer had a need to worry about that.

I straightened my spine. "Gannon knows everything," I confirmed.

Ma's face crumbled as she released her hold on Gannon and took a step back. "Kira … no," she gasped. "Why?"

Khelan pulled Ma into his side. "What do you mean by *everything?*" he demanded, looking to Gannon with a wary eye.

Gannon frowned. "I know about your status as a senator, your relationship with Kira's mother and your connection to Maxim," he said, considering them evenly. "I know it all, but I want you to know your secrets are safe with me."

Khelan's eyes narrowed. "Are they now."

Gannon nodded, but I could tell by the stiffness in my parents' postures that they didn't believe him. They probably expected Gannon to send for the authorities and betray whatever confidence I had put into him at that very moment.

"Gannon was the one who located Aunt Marah after she and Uncle Paol ran off," I said, trying to soothe their concerns with more proof of Gannon's love and commitment to me. "He provided for them while they were in hiding in Husk."

Ma shook her head, leaning heavily into Khelan. "My gods, Kira," she gasped. "Do you want to be with this man so much that you would tell us lies, give *him* credit for something *Tai* did?"

I blinked, struggling for words through my shock. "N-no," I managed. "Tai said he found out where they were so you wouldn't know Gannon was involved with me, but it was *Gannon* who first located them."

Khelan tightened his hold on Ma. "Are you trying to say that Tai, a protector of the highest regard among his caste," Khelan said, eyeing me, "is aware of your relationship with the Realm high chancellor and has been covering it up, ignoring his *duty*, at your request?"

I winced at the disbelief in his voice. "Something like that."

Ma frowned. "Tai has certainly proven time and again that he would go above and beyond for you, Kira, but *this* ... protecting such a relationship considering his feelings for you ... I just can't believe that."

I gritted my teeth. "Whether you believe Tai was aware about Gannon and me or not isn't the point," I said. "The *point* is Gannon's been protecting our family. He's been working with Tai all this time to track down Uncle Paol and keep him safe. And after I was abducted, he's been working with Tai nonstop to find Maxim and Gabriel."

Silence.

I fisted my hands, looking between my parents. What was wrong with them?! "*Gannon* was the one who had Gabriel dismissed after he abused and threatened me," I said. "After Tai beat Gabriel to a pulp, *Gannon* was the one who had Gabriel removed from the Judiciary." There. If that didn't move them, I didn't know what would.

I took satisfaction in watching their stupor of disbelief flag, become unsteady.

Gannon must have seen the same crack in their wall, because he stepped forward. "Kira's welfare, and so that of her family, is my utmost concern," he said. "I can help you stop Maxim and Gabriel."

Khelan seized on that. "We don't need your help," he bit out. "Look what your *help* has done so far."

Gannon stiffened, but ignored the jab. "I wouldn't do anything to put Kira, you or the rest of your family at risk."

"And when the going gets tough," Khelan countered, "what happens then?"

Gannon hesitated. "What do you mean?"

"It's a matter of priority, *High Chancellor*," Khelan said, releasing Ma. "What happens when you have to make a decision that goes against Kira's wishes or her welfare? What if Paol is taken in among a group of rebels and they ask you to oversee his ruling? Will you rule against the interest of the Realm and let him go?"

"If protecting the Realm means jeopardizing Kira or your family, then I'd step down from my position," he said. "At the very least, I'd remove myself from the role of overseeing the decision."

Khelan raised an eyebrow. "Just like that," he said with a lift of his chin. "You'd give up everything, your father's legacy, yours, the faith of the citizens of your caste … for Kira?"

"Yes," Gannon said evenly. "Just as you would, and *have done*, for her mother."

Khelan faltered at that, drawing back as his gaze met Ma's. My mother's mouth twisted, pinched with anger.

"You should be ashamed of yourself," she said, scowling at Gannon. "Using my relationship with Khelan to charm yourself into Kira's life, telling her you love her and making promises you can't keep, knowing full well nothing could come of your relationship with her." She walked up to him, eyes narrowed. "You say you love her, but tell me, during this entire affair, did you ever think about her and what being with you would mean?"

Gannon recoiled, face becoming drawn. I had never seen Gannon speechless before. Stricken with grief, beside himself with worry, incensed — yes. But *never* had I been witness to him rendered silent.

I had had enough.

"How can you two be such *hypocrites!*" I fumed, tears pricking the back of my eyes and clogging my throat. "How can the two of you stand here, judging him, *us*, when you did the same thing yourself?"

Ma's shoulders wilted so severely, she drooped. "My gods, is *that* what this is about?" she cried, eyes wild, searching. "Are you trying to get back at us? Is this some *act of rebellion* where you follow in our steps to hurt us the way you think we did you?"

I shut my eyelids briefly. Gods give me strength. "No," I muttered, wishing now I hadn't brought their relationship up. "This has *nothing* to do with you."

Khelan shook his head, looking between Gannon and me. "Where in the Realm do you think this is going to go?" he demanded. "With both of you defying the odds and building a life together in illegitimate harmony."

Ma let out a mocking laugh, infuriating me even more.

"Why not?" I muttered, glaring pointedly at her. "It's been done before."

She raised a brow. "It's never been done with a *high chancellor*, Kira," she said, catching my snide remark before tossing it back with one of her own. "You would have done better in plotting your revenge against your parents by soiling your good name with a citizen from a much *lower* caste."

I curled my fists so tight they shook.

Ma shared a look of satisfaction with Khelan before sliding a look at Gannon. "If you were half the man she thinks you are," she said to him, drawing herself up, "you would leave her and forget anything and everything you've ever learned about her and her family."

Khelan came close, studying Gannon as he folded his arms. "And since you love her so much," he said, "doing what's best for her shouldn't be a difficulty for you."

Gannon held their gaze steadily, appearing unaffected until his fists clenched at his sides.

My gods, they were *challenging* him. It was like my parents had intuitively come up with some coordinated attack, knowing exactly how best to deliver it directly at Gannon's weakest spot.

How could I have been so wrong? I had anticipated their concern and anger, but this malicious assault was like nothing I had seen from them before, *nothing* I could have expected.

I peered up at Gannon, and my mind grappled for a word to describe the wretched look on his face. He appeared … *defeated*.

I reached for him. "Gann—"

"I should go," he said, cutting me off as his gaze lowered to mine.

My gut wrenched. *No*. "Please, don't." I didn't know what I was begging him *not* to do. He had to leave, of course. There was nothing left for him or me to say. But I didn't want him to go. Not like this. Not with that shattered look in his eyes.

At every point along the way, Gannon had shown that he would do anything to be with me, that he loved me. He had even been willing to give everything up if that's what it came to, and what had I done? I had pushed him away, fighting against something I couldn't prevent. As Sela had said and I had come to realize, I wasn't willing to give Gannon up. I couldn't. I wanted to be with him. And now, even after all this, I wouldn't let him slip away.

Fear and heartache made me bold.

I reached up, cupping his face, and pulled him down to me before kissing him. I poured every ounce of the desire, hope and love I had buried for him into the kiss, giving my emotions free rein. Gannon stiffened, but thank gods he didn't stop me. He held steady as I molded my lips over his, searching with a thumping heart for some sign of the man I had fallen in love with, the one who said that he wouldn't give me up, that we were inevitable. After a hesitant moment, he gripped my sides, his unsteady fingers flexing against my waist as though he wondered whether to hold me tight or let me go. I rolled up onto my toes, deepening our connection, unwilling to give him the choice. I needed to show him, show my parents, exactly what he meant to me.

All too soon, the weight of my parents' stares crept through my focus on Gannon despite my effort to block them out. I broke our kiss reluctantly and stared up at Gannon, tears pooling at the corners of my eyes, wondering what next, whether he had understood the love I was trying to convey.

Expelling a deep breath, Gannon gently moved my hands from his face. He turned to my parents, who stood stiff, frozen by anger and dismay, looking on.

Gannon cleared his throat. "I'm sorry for how this turned out," he said, his voice hoarse. "But not for loving your daughter. I'll never apologize for that."

Ma pressed her lips together as though trying to keep her emotions in check. Khelan, on the other hand, didn't bother with restraint.

"High Chancellor," he said, eyes glinting with spite, "I fear for the future of our worlds with a man like *you* at its helm."

CHAPTER 12

"Holy shit, woman!" Nara exclaimed, grabbing me by my upper arms as a broad smile bloomed across her face. "When you mess up, you don't fucking hold back!"

I yelped as she swept me into a full-body embrace. After strangling me with a hug, she shoved me aside and strode into my apartment. As I staggered, trying to steady myself, I caught Ben's frown at Nara and Cade's wink at me as they followed her in.

"I hope you don't mind they're here," Sela said in a quiet voice, shuffling up behind them with Derek, who was holding a sleeping Lahra, packed tight in her baby carrier. At least, it *looked* like a baby carrier. With all the bells and whistles on the thing, the sleek contraption seemed like something that would even make Tai, a high-tech gadget aficionado, impressed.

Sela urged Derek to enter the apartment, ahead of her. "Nara said you haven't answered any of her messages," she said to me. "She sounded so worried, I told her Derek and I were coming to your apartment to check on you. I figured you wouldn't mind if she and the guys showed up since ..." She shrugged with a frown.

Since the secret's already out.

I sighed then glimpsed into the sitting area where Nara and her partners were now making themselves comfortable and digging into the bowl of *kimea* berries I had been forcing myself to eat. I studied Nara and found no sign of judgment or contempt. In fact, she appeared her usual buoyant self. *Huh.* I hadn't wanted Nara to know about my relationship with Gannon, but it seemed I should have afforded *her* more credit than my parents for understanding.

Sela tugged the cuff of my sweater, drawing my attention back to her. Her face was still long as she waited on my reply.

"No. I don't mind they're here," I said, giving her a small smile to smooth the worry line between her brows. "In fact, I could use the company." Because truly, there was only so long I could stare blindly at my apartment walls.

Two days after my parents had left my apartment, riding off on their high horses of righteous indignation, I had yet to come to terms with their unbelievable hypocrisy. I still bristled at the memory of their sanctimonious behavior and the way they had laid guilt and blame at Gannon's feet. I had spent the better part of the days either sinking into despondence or devising vindictive ways to disown my family. Well, to disown my *parents*. Rhoan, well, he had wisely chosen to give me a different response than my parents. After he had arrived at our apartment later that night, I had waited in my bedroom, girding myself for another verbal attack, but instead of beating down my door to scold me, my brother had sent me a simple message via comm:

I'm here when you're ready to talk.

And just like that, I forgave my brother for every annoying and meddlesome thing he had ever done to me up to that point in my life.

Sela hooked my arm with hers and dragged me into the sitting area. There, Cade shouldered her out of the way and wrapped an arm loosely around my waist.

"Well, well," he drawled with mischief in his brown eyes. "Here I thought you were just a girl with clever methods to get good grades. Little did I know you were willing to sleep with the teacher to rise to the top of the class."

I slid him a quelling look that served only to make him laugh. I didn't need him using my questionable acts at the age of *fifteen*, for gods' sake, to make jokes at a time like this.

Still chuckling, Cade gave me an affectionate squeeze then released me to go to Nara, who was giggling at his smart remark. She sat down on the floor beside Ben's chair and patted a space on her other side to indicate where Cade should join her. Sela and her family, meanwhile, sat on the couch.

Nara popped a berry into her mouth and slanted a devious look at me. "Scandal has made you even more of a force to be reckoned with, Kira Metallurgist."

I sent her a questioning look, lowering myself into the remaining armchair and curling my feet underneath me.

"The Realm seems to have a thing for high chancellor–seeking harlots," she replied, her blue eyes twinkling. "Your ratings have improved."

Sela made a face at Nara as she helped Derek release their child from the grips of her infant apparatus. "I don't think Kira's too interested in her *popularity* right now."

Nara shrugged, but didn't seem the least bit remorseful.

I sat, mystified, wondering what they were talking about, then it clicked into place.

Oh, good gods. "Are you trying to tell me that my … *following* has grown?"

Nara nodded, her blond bob brushing her chin. "It certainly has," she said. "An impressive number of citizens seem to think your whole ordeal *incredibly* romantic." She held a hand to her chest and sighed.

I rolled my eyes at her theatrical swoon. "That's because they aren't *living* said ordeal," I said, yanking a cushion from behind me and onto my lap. "If they had to endure a suspension and the wrath of my parents, they would be much less spellbound by it all."

Nara frowned, losing quite a bit of her cheek. "Yes," she said. "That would certainly remove the tint from anyone's rose-colored glasses."

I slunk deeper into the chair.

"And Tai?" Sela asked, tucking Lahra into Derek's arms. "How does he feel about all this?"

Good question.

Among the many messages I had received since the news broke, I hadn't received even one from Tai. Finally, I had reached out to him an hour or so before Sela and everyone else had arrived, but had yet to receive his reply. I didn't know what the make of that. All Above, was Tai truly still so angry with me since our last conversation — well, *argument* — that he wouldn't contact me at a time like this?

I sighed, wrapping my arms around the cushion. "I haven't spoken with Tai yet."

Sela cocked her head, brows knitting. "That's odd."

It was, but I didn't bother agreeing with her. It would just make me more glum.

"Who's Tai?" Ben asked, looking around the room.

"Tai's a protector Kira's been pining over for the past five years," she explained for the men's behalf while holding an inquisitive eye on me.

Cade guffawed. "The plot thickens," he said before scooping up a mound of berries.

Nara leaned forward, resting her elbows on her thighs. "So, are you in love with Tai too?"

I frowned. *Too?* "Why do you think I'm in love with either of them?"

She laughed. "I've know you for years, Kira Metallurgist," she said. "You've been daydreaming about Tai since you were sixteen, and no matter how ambitious you are, *you* wouldn't go against protocol and become involved with the *high chancellor of the Realm* unless you were completely head over heels in love with him."

Heat crawled up my neck. I truly had to stop underestimating Nara. The woman had me all figured out.

Nara grinned. "So, are you in love with Tai or not?"

I sighed. "Yes."

She scooched forward and folded her arms on the coffee table, peering up at me. "We already know the high chancellor's willing to flout convention to be with you, and I would bet my right arm that Tai's in love with you too," she stated. "Therefore, the question is whether to be with one or *both* men."

"Or neither of them," Cade added with a snicker, earning him a hard swat on the shoulder from Nara. He rubbed at the spot on his arm with a downtrodden frown.

"Neither is *not* an option," Nara declared. "That would mean giving them both up."

"And take it from me," Sela commented under her breath with a roll of her eyes, "Kira's *not* about to do that."

I tossed an evil eye and the cushion at my best friend, making her laugh out loud.

"Hold on," Ben said, raising a hand. "*Both* men? The high chancellor may want to be with her, but what makes you think he'd want to be in a multiple or that the protector would want that too?"

The room quieted. Nara seemed at a loss as to how to respond to that. Fortunately, I had an answer, at least to *part* of that question.

"Gannon offered to be in a multiple," I said. "And told me to ask Tai."

Everyone but Sela appeared taken aback by that. I couldn't blame them. I knew Gannon intimately, had been involved with him for *months*, and had never expected him to show such willingness to compromise.

"Did Tai agree?" Nara asked.

I fidgeted, staring at some spot on my sleeve. "As I said, I haven't had a chance to talk to Tai yet."

No one said anything for a moment, and I refused to look up to gauge their responses. I could just imagine the sympathy on their faces. They, like my parents, probably couldn't see Tai subscribing to being part of a relationship like this. Maybe they were right. Gannon had said that he had barely given thought to how our relationship would impact me, but I had done the same thing to Tai. He had a successful career. Being in a relationship like this could be a mark on him.

Nara slapped her hand on the coffee table, making the bowl of berries shake. "Well, it's a good thing I'm here then," she announced and squared her shoulders. "I know how to help you figure this whole mess out."

Ben and Cade groaned, and I looked at them with a frown.

"What's wrong?" Derek asked, rubbing a soothing hand up and down Lahra's back.

Ben hooked an ankle over his knee, sitting back. "Nara's zodiac of sexual compatibility is what's wrong," he said. "She made it up on the way over here."

Nara favored Ben with a dazzling smile. "So you *do* listen when I speak."

He shrugged. "I do when it's about sex," he said, earning a chuckle from Cade.

Nara sent him them a peevish look that immediately lost impact when she rolled her eyes.

Wait a minute. "What does *sex* have to do with anything?" I asked.

"Indulge me," Nara said, turning a sharp eye on me. "In *one* word, how would you describe sex with Gannon Consul, the high chancellor of this, our much-divided Realm?"

I crossed my arms. "This is silly," I said. "My life is falling apart and *this* is what you want to do. Analyze my *sex life?*"

Nara held up a finger. "Answer the question," she ordered.

I scowled, shaking my head. "No."

Nara raised a brow as the rest of the group looked at me, waiting for me to reply with an embarrassing amount of interest.

I groaned. All right. It seemed I would have to relent if I wanted to get Nara and everyone else off my back. Looking off to the side, I recollected the times when Gannon and I had made love. My mind wandered from the first time at his residences when I had asked him to fuck me to when he had done that very thing on my desk at the Judiciary to when we had fallen all over each other just before he had given me the promise ring.

I licked my lips. *Sex with Gannon is … moving … breathtaking … all-consuming …* "Powerful," I decided.

Cade hummed. "Good word."

By their thoughtful nods, it seemed the other two men agreed.

Nara considered that with a finger tapped at her chin. "*Powerful* is a really good descriptor," she said then prompted me with a rolling wave of her hand. "Now Tai. Give me one word to describe sex with him so I can evaluate your response."

Evaluate? Good grief, you would think her theory to be scientifically sound!

I took a deep breath, skin warming as my mind receded, surfacing memories of when Tai had made love to me with only his mouth after I had seduced him then my striptease and wanton masturbation at his request, and then more recently, when I had controlled him, telling him I would be the one to fuck him instead of allowing him to do it to me.

I rubbed my lips together, thinking hard. *Sex with Tai is ... exhilarating ... arousing ... intriguing.* "Challenging," I offered up.

Cade snickered while Sela, Derek and Ben appeared perplexed. Even Lahra seemed baffled by my reply. She whimpered and Derek murmured soothing words in her ear.

"What?" I asked.

Nara scrunched her face as though she had tasted something bitter. "*Challenging?*"

"Yes." I squirmed. "Like in a ... *fun* way."

Nara nearly choked. "*Fun* does not a lasting romance make."

"What does *that* mean?" I asked, affronted for some bizarre reason.

"It *means* you've just put lovemaking with Tai in the same category as two friends getting it on," Nara said. "If you and *I* had sex, *that* would be fun."

Cade perked up, spine ramrod straight. "Please dear gods, yes," he said, shooting a shamelessly hopeful look between Nara and me.

Sela clapped her hands, eyes wide. "Ooh, Derek," she crooned to her partner, "can we *please* watch Nara and Kira make love?"

He hesitated with a frown, but then after a moment of seeming deliberation, threw a considering glance my way.

I threw my hands up in the air as I came to my feet. "I don't want to have sex with Nara!" I yelled.

Nara gasped, hand to her chest, appearing hurt by my outburst.

Cade moved closer to Nara, so he could pull her to his side. "Kira doesn't mean it that way, babe," Cade soothed. "She's under a lot of stress right now. She would *definitely* have sex with you if she were in her right mind."

Ben chuckled and Sela giggled. Even the usually quiet Derek managed a throaty laugh.

I jammed my hands on my hips, staring them all down. My worlds were falling apart and my friends — if I could call the *hedonists* who sat in front of me that — were making a *mockery* of my life!

"Why aren't you all taking this more seriously?" I demanded, barely holding myself together. I wanted to be consoled not … *ridiculed!*

Sela's eyes widened, sobering as she stood up to approach me. "We *are*," she replied, shooting a sharp glance over her shoulder and silencing everyone. "We're just trying to lighten your mood."

Nara got up and came over as well, a solemn look on her face. "It was just for fun," she said. "Something to take your mind off your troubles."

The two women stared at me, their expressions full of apology. I wrapped my arms around my waist, now filled with regret. My friends had just been trying to help. I supposed if they had been aware of the balance of my troubles, the ones that had to do with Gabriel and Maxim, they probably wouldn't have been so cavalier about my crisis.

"I'm sorry," I said. "Everything just feels out of control. I don't know what to do."

Sela shrugged. "Look on the bright side," she said. "It's not like you were dismissed or anything. You'll be returning to the Judiciary soon. Won't you?"

I hoped so. "Mila asked me to meet her tomorrow," I said, and the fact that I had forgotten about the message my superior had sent me earlier that day revealed just how out of sorts I had been since the fallout from the Realm Anarchist's story.

In all truth, I hadn't given Mila's request much thought, figuring she probably just wanted to check in with me and get a rundown on where things with the advisory group had left off, but now that Sela mentioned it, perhaps she wanted to meet me for another, more hopeful, reason. Maybe to tell me when I could return to work. Hope grew inside me.

"Well, there you go," Nara declared, holding her arms out wide as though she had just solved a crime. "It's only a matter of time before you're back to telling leadership what to do."

I snorted and sent them a wobbly smile.

"*And*," Sela continued, "your parents *will* get over their anger. They have to. They love you, so they really have no choice."

I nodded, sighing. "But what should I do about Gannon and Tai?" I couldn't be sure that either one of them would want anything to do with me now.

A slow smile spread across Nara's face. "Well, isn't that the best part?" she said. "You don't have to *do* anything. You've already made your decision. Now it's up to them."

* * *

Realm whore or not, I'm happy to call you my friend.

I smiled down at Nara's message on my comm as I sat on my bed.

Rain had been falling steadily throughout the evening but had only begun to pour in earnest an hour ago, just after my friends had left. Worried about their travel home in the torrential squall-season weather, I had asked Nara and Sela to message me as soon as they had arrived home. Sela already messaged me with a straightforward "We made it," while Nara's message, of course, had an approach as brazen as she was.

Despite my irritation by the silliness of their methods, my friends *had*, in fact, lifted my mood, but the change was short-lived. Rhoan had yet to come home and the quietness following my friends' departure had left a vacuum, ample space for all my worries to rush back in.

Gabriel did this.

I tightened my blanket around me as a shiver skittered up my spine. Gannon's declaration had sounded more like a fact than a guess. He had said he wasn't certain, but at this point, I wouldn't be surprised by anything.

If Gabriel *had* in fact done this, then Tai had been right. Gabriel didn't care about anything except ruining my life — not even accessing the information he had seemed so eager to get.

And then there was the matter of Gannon and Tai.

Are you in love with Tai? Or do you just love him? Because I don't think you know the difference.

Gannon's challenging questions still twisted my insides into a knot. I had dismissed his queries, unwilling to patronize them with even the barest thought, much less a response, but I forced myself now to consider them for the very first time.

All Above, I couldn't imagine *not* being in love with Tai. I had spent the last five years loving him from a distance and then finally up close. He had my love even before I had even known what love meant! And now that I did, it couldn't be denied that I loved him, was *in* love with Tai. I knew it as surely as I knew he loved me ... which begged the question: if Tai loved me, then wouldn't he agree to be in a multiple with me?

I cringed, stung by how self-centered and ironic that question seemed to me now. Gannon had expressed guilt for only barely considering how our relationship would impact my life, and there I was, doing the same thing to Tai. He too had a family, friends, a *career* — a full life of his own to consider. Being part of a multiple, especially like the one I was hoping for, would bring challenges that would unsettle everything. But it wouldn't be the end of the worlds. Wouldn't Tai even want to at least give it all a chance before rejecting the idea?

I groaned, yanking on my hair with both hands. Evening had flowed into night with me still going around in circles. What to do about Gabriel? What about my job? Who should I be with? Did they still want to be with me?

Fuck it.

My hands fell to my lap in clenched fists. At some point, I was going to have to realize that *I* was the common denominator in all this. Maybe Cade was on to something. I should just cut ties with everyone and call it a day!

The idea of running off and finding some remote little town untouched by rebel activity where no one would be able to find me — not the Quad, media, my parents, Gannon or even Tai, with all his tracking gadgetry — sounded like pure bliss. Good gods, I had been out of the Academy less than a year. If *this* was only the beginning of my life, then I had no desire to see what came next!

I jolted at a flash of lightning, and through the illumination my gaze caught on something small, round and unspeakably valuable lying just underneath my chest of drawers.

I gasped, lunging off the bed, and released a breath of relief when I picked up the pouch. The delicate weight of the ring Gannon had given me slid around, safe and sound, inside it. The bag must have fallen out of my chest of drawers at some point. Maybe when I had been rummaging through it, looking for the lapse kit.

After a moment of indecision, I opened the pouch, turning it over to allow the jewelry to drop into my palm. The luminous diamonds sparkled and glowed, and in the flickering arcs of lightning I could just make out the intricate pattern decorating the rose gold band.

My heart throbbed as a roll of thunder reverberated throughout my room.

Gannon had given me the promise ring as a token of his love, but it had become more than that: it had become a catalyst forcing me to make a decision, one Tai had demanded from me. Unfortunately, my decision hadn't been the one he had been hoping for.

Nara had been trying to be comforting when she had said whatever happened between Gannon, Tai and me was now up to them, that the decision was no longer mine. But that's what was so fucking frustrating. My hands were tied!

I curled my fingers around the ring, holding it tight. Enough was enough. I couldn't stand it anymore. Tai's silence was killing me. I needed to know where his head was at, get some answers. I didn't care that I had arguably more dire matters to deal with right now. There wasn't going to be a perfect time to speak with Tai. At the end of the day, if Tai wanted to be with me, it was a simple answer — yes or no.

I went to my side table and picked up a slim gold chain. After threading the ring with the necklace, I fastened the chain around my neck then tapped out a message to Tai, hoping that this time he would respond.

Are you awake?

After a few moments without a response, I winced. If I had to ask Tai whether he was awake, he probably wasn't. But then, as a protector, Tai was used to being up at odd hours.

The merry jingle from my monitor filled the room, and I squinted at the screen when it lit up with a notification of Tai's incoming call. Relief bloomed. I quickly voice-activated his call and returned to sitting on the edge of my bed to face the monitor.

Tai was sitting in a gray-walled room with very little light. The space was bare except for a printed map of some region I couldn't make out, hanging on the wall behind him. He certainly wasn't at home, but thankfully, wherever he was, he appeared wide awake. His hazel eyes were bright and alert, and his gray and black uniform was crisp and unrumpled as though he had just put it on. The only sign of the late hour in his appearance was the slight disarray of the short strands of his hair and some stubble around his jaw.

He considered me quietly, seeming to have decided based on some unspoken rule that I should be the one to speak first. I gave him a tight, awkward smile, uncertain where to begin.

I sighed, giving in. "Aren't you going to say 'I told you so'?" I asked.

He shrugged. "Why bother?" he said, his chair creaking as he sat back. His badges caught some of the overhead light as he did. "I heard you've been reprimanded enough to last you a lifetime."

My brows rose. "You did?"

"I called Rhoan," he explained while folding his arms. "He told me you were suspended."

So Tai had time to call my *brother*, but hadn't done the courtesy of reaching out to *me*. I frowned. "Did he tell you about the argument with my parents?"

He frowned. "No," he said, "he didn't, but I suspect they were mad."

I sniffed. "*That* among many other things." Like hypocritical, mean, imperious and viciously cruel.

Tai's mouth turned down as he studied me, still appearing committed to allowing me to direct the conversation, which would have been a good thing if I wasn't now at a complete loss for words. With a sigh, I glanced at the map behind him and, thankfully, found some inspiration there.

"Where are you?" I asked.

"Port," he said, surprising me.

Port was a town over two hours away, just outside of Helios, where Maxim had taken me to meet Gabriel.

"Has Port been taken over by the Quad too?" I asked, fretting that rebels had spread into the town Nara's family was from.

"Not yet, but they're trying to," he said with a frown. "There was a violent raid nearby, which can only mean they're planning to establish a command center in the town. The good news is, since my request to increase the Corona's security was approved, I now have all the Protectorate's resources at my disposal to hunt Gabriel, Maxim and the rest of the Quad down."

I blinked. *Oh.*

Guilt rode me hard. There I was wondering why Tai hadn't contacted me, thinking me the center of his universe, when he had simply been occupied trying to protect the Realm *and* me.

I frowned. "When will you be back?" I asked.

"Soon enough," he said. "There's someone I need to have few words with back in Merit."

Tai reverted to assessing me with a pensive gaze. Once again, he was leaving it up to me to decide where our conversation would go next.

I drew in a fortifying breath, hating that, despite what he had just told me, I still couldn't fight the compulsion to ask, "Why didn't you call me?"

"I just did."

I thinned my lips. So *that's* how he wanted to play it? Tai was quicker than that. "I sent you a message earlier today," I pressed. "Why didn't you reply?"

His expression darkened. "I wanted you to give you time."

I searched his face. "Time for what?"

"Time for you to digest the fallout and hopefully realize this fantasy relationship Gannon's put in your head could never really work."

I stared at him, rocking back. So he thought that my suspension and the tension with my parents would make me think twice about Gannon? Poor Tai. He had no clue. "I haven't changed my mind."

Tai's face pinched, as he leaned forward to brace both hands on his thighs. "So he still has you firmly in his grip."

Hallowed Halls! Why was it that everyone believed that my wanting to be with Gannon was a result of some impenetrable power the man held over me! "You talk as though Gannon's some sort of *criminal mastermind!*"

"He may not be criminal," he countered, "but he's definitely made a masterful play."

My shoulders fell. *Oh gods, what now?* "What are you talking about?"

"Don't you see?" he said, shaking his head as though pitying the poor state of my mental health. "He's pit you against me."

I recoiled. "What?" I asked, bewildered. "How?"

"Tell me," he said, eyes glinting. "If *I* had been the one to offer you the option of being in a multiple, would you have asked Gannon?"

Of course not. The response flew into my head so quickly I almost wasn't able to keep it on the tip of my tongue.

Tai sniffed. "Exactly," he said, having correctly read my thoughts. "You wouldn't have asked Gannon because you know he wouldn't have agreed. Despite everything he's telling you the man doesn't want to be in a multiple any fucking more than I do."

I balked. "You think he's *lying* to me," I said. "Why would he do that?" What would be the point?

"To make *me* the bad guy," Tai said through thin lips. "*I* say no to being a multiple, which he knows full well I will, and *he* ends up looking like the selfless hero willing to do *anything* to be with you."

I stared at Tai, amazed by the alternate universe he had created. My gods, no one could ever accuse Tai of suffering lack of imagination. If I had any hope of getting anywhere with him, I needed to disprove this diabolical myth Tai was determined to wrap Gannon up in.

"Gannon met my parents," I stated, letting that fact speak for itself.

Tai's eyebrows flew up his forehead, his expression shifting at once from contempt to surprise.

"I suppose *met* isn't the right word," I allowed. "It certainly wasn't a pleasant affair. Gannon refused to let me face my parents alone. He wanted them to know how much I meant to him, that our relationship wasn't some trivial thing, so he stood by my side, right in the middle of my apartment, and told them that he loved me."

Tai sat back with a noncommittal twist to his lips. "He's no coward," he muttered. "I'll give him that."

I clenched my fists. He was missing the point! "In the face of my fuming high and mighty parents, Gannon told them that he would be willing to step down from his position if he had to," I said, trying to get him to understand. "Just to be with me."

Tai stiffened, eyes going hard. "I believe I've proven to you time and again how much I care for you."

"Yes, you have," I said, hope rising as I latched onto that. "But I want to know if that means you're willing to be with me?"

"Holy fuck, Kira," he blurted out. "You've been suspended from your position, your family and you are at odds and your name's been tainted — *all* because of your relationship with Gannon Consul — and you're pressing me *now* for my decision on whether to be a relationship where I share *you* with *him!*"

I flinched. Any sane person would have backed off at Tai's tone. Instead, I held his gaze, refusing to give in. I had become very familiar with Tai's tactic of trying to push me away when challenged hard enough. "Yes," I said. "As a matter of fact, I am."

Tai narrowed his eyes. "Forgive me," he said, voice dripping with sarcasm, "but I've been a little busy."

"And I appreciate everything you've done and *are* doing for my family and me," I said, hating how self-centered our conversation was making me feel, but I just couldn't let this go. "But this *must* have crossed your mind."

Tai scowled as he glanced away briefly. "Damn it, Kira," he cursed. "Of *course* it's crossed my mind!"

My heart thumped so hard the beats pounded in my ear drums. I swallowed. "And?"

He stared at me for a long while, disbelief, frustration and anger wrinkling his brow. Finally, he shook his head, a sharp, terse move. "I haven't come to a decision," he said. "Not yet."

CHAPTER 13

All was not lost. At least I *had* to believe that.

The following morning, I waited outside Mila's office, fanning the quivering flames of hope that she had called me in to the Judiciary for no other reason than to tell me that I could return. Because, truly, why else would she have asked to see me so soon?

I sighed, glancing about the hallway and fiddling with my promise ring, then stiffened at the sight of a small group of subordinates who were staring at me as they walked by. Fighting the impulse to look away, I considered them with a steady eye until they averted their gazes and scurried off.

Good. I had received enough of those looks of curiosity, and now judgment, over the past few weeks to serve me well for the rest of my life.

Mila's voice captured my attention and I turned to peer into her office. She tapped at her monitor, ending the call she had been on, and when she gestured for me to enter, I smoothed down the pleats of my black silk dress before walking inside.

"We finally have something to thank those bloody rebels for, don't we," Mila remarked, sitting back and grinning at me.

I came to a slow stop in front of her desk. "I beg your pardon?"

She quirked her lips. "Yes," she drawled, "I imagine you've been avoiding the newsfeed as much as possible over the last few days, but you *must* have heard about the unrest in Port. If not for this latest outburst in rebel activity, the media would still have those photos of you and our high chancellor on a loop." She laughed, but I managed only a small smile as I sat down.

As much as I admired Mila for her many qualities, her dark humor was one I had yet to get used to. Rather than going into a debate about the *benefits* of Realm-wide unrest, I encouraged Mila to get to the reason why she had called me in to see her.

"I expected to have to wait at least a few more days before hearing from you," I prompted, sitting forward on the edge of the chair with my hands clasped in my lap.

Mila's laughter waned as she sobered. She steepled her fingers and rested her elbows on the arms of her chair. "So did I," she said, quite serious now. "But plans have a way of changing when the Corona drops by."

My eyebrows rose. "The Corona?" I said. "She's here, on *Prospect Eight?*" After what Tai had told me about increasing her protection, her being *anywhere* but on Dignitas One seemed unlikely.

Mila nodded. "Our sovereign, as usual, refuses to be cowed no matter the circumstances plaguing the Realm," she said. "She's in town to hold a series of meetings with leadership who were part of the special committee on exploration, to determine next steps for the advisory group." Mila winced. "Unfortunately, yours truly had the *displeasure* of being the first on her list to be summoned."

I frowned, empathizing with her wholeheartedly. When I had been called in to meet with the Corona, I usually ended up leaving her in tears and with a much dimmer view of our worlds.

"And how did your meeting go?" I asked cautiously, not quite certain I truly wanted to know.

"To be frank, I don't know," she said, her gaze focusing inward as her eyebrows drew closer. "I had gone in expecting her to chew me out for what not handling the situation between you and Gannon better. Instead, she showed up with the high marshal and inquired at length about the importance of Judiciary protocol and security measures."

Odd, yes, but the Corona was as unpredictable as squall-season weather, so her erratic behavior held no surprise for me there. What baffled me was trying to understand what *that* meeting had to do with *me*.

Mila refocused on me. "Anyway, that's neither here nor there," she said with a wave of her hand. "The reason I called you in is that the Corona wants to speak with you. Right now, in fact."

Any hope I had held on to that I would be returning sooner than expected began a slow and painful death. If the Corona wanted to meet with me, and *right now*, it couldn't be for anything good. My shoulders drooped. No matter how far I dug this time around, I didn't think I could summon the strength to endure another round of her verbal and emotional abuse.

I sighed. "Do you know why?"

Mila snorted. "Of course not," she said. "But I can make a good guess. You were supporting the task force *and* the special committee, two very important projects for the Realm. She probably wants to describe, in no uncertain terms, just how ... *disappointed* she is about your breach of ethics."

My jaw went slack. "She wants to *scold* me?" *About a breach of ethics? Good gods, that was rich!*

Mila grimaced, not denying my remark, while I seethed.

Who did the Corona think she was! The woman was the keeper of so many secrets, my own paled in comparison, yet *she* wanted to upbraid me — *me!* She had expelled an entire dominion for conducting exploration, an act she had been secretly permitting for reasons unknown, and *she* wanted to take *me* to task about a breach of ethics! *She* was the one who sent the Realm into a state of turmoil and unrest, destroying citizens' lives. All *I* had done was fall in love! My gods, the last time we had met she had said she hoped Gannon and I would "find our way back together." And *now* she wanted to berate me about the very relationship she had advocated? I couldn't believe her audacity.

My reluctance to meet with the Corona again dissipated on the spot. I wanted — no, *looked fucking forward* — to meeting with that woman! If she thought to call me out on *my* illicit behavior, then I would gladly bring her own into the light!

I came to my feet. "Where does she want to see me?" I said then made a guess. "At Realm Council residences?"

Mila tilted her head back to meet my gaze. When she nodded, I turned on my heel and started a message to Talib on my comm telling him I was ready to leave.

"Kira," Mila called out sharply, stopping me by the door.

I faced her, waiting though impatiently.

She considered me with a speculative eye. "Don't do anything brash," she advised. "This meeting just might mean the difference between you returning to the Judiciary *with* or *without* your rank."

* * *

The meandering corridors of Realm Council residences seemed to have no end. Luckily, they were so familiar to me by now that when the Corona's protector, who was leading my way, turned down one hall, I could already anticipate the next.

And it was a good thing too. Despite Mila's efforts to calm the riot of bitter emotions, she must have witnessed, in both my body language and on my face, the anger that continued to surge through me, blotting out everything in my sight.

After another turn, the female protector stopped in front of a tall open doorway. The warm, flickering light coming through it signaled a fireplace burning in the room beyond. "I'll let the Corona know you've arrived," she said, then, after a nod, walked off.

I entered the intimate, library-like meeting room that was as familiar to me as the path I'd just taken. This was where the Corona and I had first met privately, the place where she had speculated about my commitment to the Realm while idly sipping her tea. To imagine she had thought *my* motives questionable when all along *hers* had to be the most dubious of them all!

I approached the hearth and glowered at the crackling flames within, more than willing to stand there and draw more fuel for my anger until the leader of our worlds deigned to make her entrance. By the time the soft rustle of fabric and a flurry of footfalls alerted me to her arrival, I was wound up and ready to launch into battle, but I didn't have the chance.

The Corona sailed over to where I stood, skirts fluttering around her ankles. "Don't you want to succeed?" she snapped, brown eyes hard, glittering, as she glared up at me.

I recoiled, staggering back at the pure vehemence in her stance. "What?"

"You had the worlds at your feet," she spat, curling the fingers of one hand into a fist and shaking it in front of my face. "My gods, I was *handing* them to you!"

Heat warmed my back as I took another step away from her, toward the fireplace.

All Above, I had never seen the woman so agitated! The most profound emotion she had ever displayed, as far as I could remember, was her despondence at Gannon's father's ash ceremony. And even *that* had been more a *lack* of emotion than anything else. I had expected her to be 1 usual cool, detached self, but she had proven her unpredictability again by sweeping in to meet me with an anger that rivaled my own.

I steadied my footing, gathering my wits about me. "I don't know what you're talking about."

She sniffed and lowered her hand to her hip. "How could you be so careless?" she muttered, looking me over with a look of pure distaste. "If you have no care for yourself, then at the very least consider the interests of those who've been overseeing you."

Careless? Overseeing me? My shock morphed right back into the anger I had arrived with. So she *had* called me in to scold me like some errant child!

I drew myself up, staring her down. "The last thing I would have wanted was for anyone, *especially* the media, to have found out about Gannon and me."

"I'm not talking about you and Gannon," she snapped. "At this point, the two of you could make love in the streets of Capita for all I care. The truth about your relationship has only served to increase both *your* popularity and *his*."

I ground my teeth and clenched my fists. Then what the fuck was all *this* about? If Gannon was being viewed favorably, then so too was the rest of leadership on Realm Council — no matter the cause. As usual, trying to understand the Corona's circuitous verbal attacks was an exercise in futility.

"So why am I here?" I demanded, having no interest in walking through the maze of her mind to get to the point. "What do you want?"

The Corona raised her brows, apparently having picked up the deliberately caustic bite to my tone.

She straightened her shoulders and gave me her back. As she went to stand by one of two deep-seated leather armchairs, the light from the fireplace made a dazzling display of the bejeweled combs holding up her ash-blond hair.

"Someone at your Judiciary," she began, facing me now and clasping her hands at her waist, "a loyal citizen of the Realm, no less, notified the Protectorate about a possible breach in database protocol. Apparently, after your affair with Gannon became public, this individual felt obligated to report an unusual file request you recently made."

I prayed for the ground to crack open and swallow me whole. *Erik!* He had to be the person she was talking about. But why would he report me to the Protectorate? I searched through my mind, and the memory of my last two interactions with the wide-eyed receptionist surfaced. *Of course he reported me! How couldn't he?* I had been frazzled, completely unlike myself, when I had asked Erik about Gabriel's note and then for access to the Arc Meridius and Zenith dockets. After the news about my relationship with Gannon had come out, my behavior had probably come across to him as incredibly suspicious.

"What were you looking for?" the Corona asked. "Proof?"

My mind went blank. "Proof of what?" The dockets, at least the one Erik had been able to access for me, had contained information about leadership arc travel — nothing that would be considered *evidence* of any kind.

The Corona eyed me. "Proof of Realm exploration, of course," she said. "It's the only reason you would have tried to access the Zenith docket."

My lips parted and the room swam as I made the connection. "*Zenith* contains proof of *exploration?*" I breathed.

All Above, Gannon's unwillingness to tell Tai and me what the docket contained started to make sense. Something as significant as that couldn't be discussed over comm.

The Corona's gaze hardened as she pinned me with a glare. "Come now," she said, "Don't play me for a fool. Obviously, Gannon told you. The man seems to lack willpower and good sense when it comes to you."

I shook my head, stepping up to her. "He didn't say a word," I said quickly, grateful to be able to tell her the truth. "I promise you."

She continued staring at me for an uncomfortable amount of time, seeming to try to determine my authenticity. Meanwhile, my indignation rose. There she was, admitting that proof existed of her support of a violation of *Realm law* while assessing *me* for honesty!

"You're a liar," I stated, surprising her enough to make her flinch.

"I beg your pardon."

"As well you should," I replied, stepping toward her and enjoying with unholy satisfaction the way her hauteur started to wane. "You expelled Argon for an act that you've been supporting all along on the quiet. Why?"

She paled, holding an unsteady hand to her chest, but I had no pity for her. I wanted answers.

"Why did you do it?" I demanded again, realization and dismay making my voice harsh. My gods, what she had done had led to the death of my aunt, to the *murder* of Gannon's father! "Why are you playing with people's lives?"

Her gaze darkened though her complexion remained blanched. "I don't owe you an explanation."

"Yes, you do," I snapped quick on the heels of her reply, and she stepped back, her thigh hitting the arm of the chair. "I was on the arc craft the rebels attacked on Septima Two in retaliation for your *unjustified* expulsion of Argon." I shuddered at the memory of twisted metal and bloodied bodies that had been surrounding me when I had emerged from the rubble with Gannon's and Tai's help. "I was almost *killed* because of you."

The Corona considered me for a good while before shifting her gaze from mine to the blazing fireplace, but did not reply.

I glared at her so hard my vision blurred.

If the woman thought she could ignore me, that I would leave Realm Council residences without an answer, then she was in for a surprise!

I opened my mouth, about to repeat my demand when she said, still staring into the flames, "Exploration is vital to our system's advancement."

That stopped me cold. *What?!* "Then why was it banned?"

For a few pregnant moments, she remained silent, staring at me. Finally, she gestured to the chair beside me. "Would you like to sit?"

I hesitated. The Corona didn't make *requests* — she issued *orders*. I wondered what to do, what it would mean if I refused.

"It's not a trick question," she said impassively. "Whether you sit or stand is up to you. I simply think you'd prefer to be comfortable for a story as long as this."

I frowned, looking her over, searching for what … sincerity? deception? I supposed both, but I had never been able to read the Corona accurately; I had yet to acquire that skill.

After an indecisive moment, I moved away from her and sat down uneasily into the proffered chair.

A derisive smile touched her mouth lightly as she moved to her own seat. "As you know," the Corona said, sitting down and arranging the folds of her skirt, "the Realm was formed because our founding guardians believed our worlds were stronger together than they were apart. They realized that if people wanted to explore and discover new worlds at a faster, more coordinated rate, it was best to pool our knowledge and technological resources."

She paused, and I stifled my impatience. Every citizen learned at Primary Academy, in Early Realm History, why the Realm was formed. Nothing the Corona had shared so far justified her duplicity!

The Corona fiddled with one her gold bracelets as she continued. "It soon became evident, however, that not *everyone* wanted to federate under the Realm and adhere to its communal approach to technological advancement," she said. "After much debate, in-fighting and, at times, violence between dominions, four worlds seceded, *left* the Realm, believing the system too rigid. They went off on their own and formed an independent dominion, which they called Zenith."

My breath caught. That was the name of the docket, which meant it contained information about the Zenith dominion. I had learned by now, of course, about numerous rogue worlds in the Outer Realm, but I had never considered that they would be structured in any organized way, much less as a *dominion*. We called them *rogue*, after all! Like everyone else, I had been told that the Outer Realm was fractured and lawless, a cruel place where no citizen should go.

The Corona shifted in her chair to cross her legs. "Zenith started to outpace the Realm in terms of exploration, and it was no wonder," she said. "Realm leadership was too busy establishing our system, taking stock of our resources and creating governance and law for its citizens. We had little time to invest in exploration, but that was fine with us. Our founding guardians figured our two systems had found individual paths to advancement: the Realm by focusing on social and political order, and Zenith by focusing on the discovery of new worlds. But we were wrong; Zenith soon felt threatened by our progress."

"Threatened?" I frowned. "Why?" Zenith, it seemed from what she said, had been making leaps and bounds in terms of exploration. They should have been pleased to not be held back by the Realm and its inherent need to regulate and create order.

The Corona's eyes glittered in the firelight. "Despite calling themselves a *dominion*, Zenith functioned nothing like any of our own," she said. "The Realm excelled in its creation of a stable societies where intellect and technology could thrive. Unfortunately, Zenith had no appreciation of such noble pursuits. Their leadership treated its citizens poorly, leaving them to fend for themselves and, in many instances, not providing for even their most basic needs." A smirk curved to her lips. "As rigid as Zenith believed the Realm to be, the dominion soon realized just how catastrophic lack of order could be to their own system. As you can imagine, such chaotic conditions led to violent civil unrest."

I considered her as she paused and looked off into the fireplace, the smirk slipping from her face. I clenched my fists in frustration. The tale the Corona was telling was enthralling, truly, but I couldn't help but wonder what it had to do with why she expelled the dominion.

I tamped down another wave of impatience and sat forward. The fact of the matter was, learning as much as I could about Realm exploration could only help me in the end. Perhaps her story would reveal why the Quad was interested in the Zenith docket in the first place.

The Corona's gaze shifted to mine. "Instead of listening to their people and answering their demands," she said, "Zenith chose to cast blame, accusing the Realm of invading their system and stealing resources, both natural and technological, from their worlds. The result was a growing animosity between Zenith and the Realm that culminated in an act of violence our system will never forget."

There was only one such act. "The attack on the Old World," I said.

She nodded, face grim as firelight flickered across her face. "Zenith used our very own technology to kill everyone on Septima One," she said, a blush of anger coming to her cheeks. "Realm Council banned exploration from that point on to prevent our citizens from going into Zenith and being harmed or inviting more violence. It's the reason I have demanded that leadership monitor the dominion, from afar, to this very day."

I gasped as pieces of the puzzle started to click into place.

When I had first heard about Realm exploration from Liandra, she had said her father had been mandated by the Corona and Realm Council to gather intelligence about the Outer Realm. *This* must have been what she had been talking about.

"Zenith is why there's talk about *forbidden zones*," I said as another puzzle piece suddenly slid into alignment. "Forbidden zones are how leadership plans on preventing citizens from going to the rogue dominion if exploration is approved." This was why Wyatt had brought them up during the last advisory group meeting.

"*Once* it's approved," she said with a rueful curve of her cheek. "Certainly, I would prefer to reject the recommendation for exploration, but as you know, I have no choice. The factions have whipped citizens into such a frenzy, I must appease them and everyone else by giving in to something that goes against Realm interests."

I swallowed, trying to wrap my mind around it all. Now more than ever I appreciated the Realm's ban on exploration — it was meant to protect us — but her story hadn't answered one of two niggling questions lurking at the back of my mind.

"But why hide the truth?" I asked, inching forward in my seat. "Why not tell everyone about Zenith and what they did? I'm sure they would have appreciated the need for the ban in light of all that happened."

"True," she said, conceding to my logic with a tilt of her head. "But I cannot risk my citizens wanting to learn about worlds that used to be some of our own and so becoming tempted to break the law to explore them. I keep the knowledge of Zenith's existence secret to keep us *all* safe. As Corona, I'm expected to maintain balance, not encourage *upheaval*."

I nearly laughed. What pure and utter bullshit! Did she mean the *upheaval* she had caused by her expulsion of Argon?

My mind went full circle, seeking an answer to my initial question, the one I had asked before she began unraveling the mystery behind the Realm's secret support of exploration.

"Are you saying then that Zenith is why you expelled Argon?" I asked, attempting to connect the dots. Based on everything she had said, the only defensible reason for her to expel the dominion was because its leadership must have gone to Zenith and reopened old wounds, thereby jeopardizing the Realm's safety.

The Corona stilled, but only after a lift to her chin. "That's a private matter that I hope to never discuss again," she said tightly. "Doing so could have dire consequences."

Dire consequences! I gaped at her. She *couldn't* be serious. The woman had just spent the last half hour confiding in me about what had to be the largest scandal in Realm history, one which had already resulted in unthinkable *dire consequences*, and she wanted to draw the line *now?*

My thoughts ground to a halt. *Wait a minute.* I had been so caught up, grappling with the significance of the story, that it hadn't occurred to me to wonder why she was divulging everything. "Why are you telling me all this?" I asked, heart skipping a beat.

The Corona met my gaze. "Like you said," she said, "I owe you the truth."

"This is some sort of an *apology?*" Was she trying to clear her conscience by confessing to me?

She folded her hands on her lap, making her bracelets clink. "I suppose it's an apology of sorts," she murmured with a sigh. "But I'm telling you this for another reason altogether. You deserve to know the reason you're no longer at the Judiciary."

I cocked my head, still confused. I *knew* why I was no longer at the Judiciary. What did my *suspension* have to do with Realm exploration? "I don't understand."

"I had high hopes for you, Kira Metallurgist," she said, disregarding my remark with a rueful shake of her head. "I admit, we've had our ups and downs, you and I, but I happen to like you. I find you … *tenacious*. It's an admirable quality, one that would have taken you far in governance and law."

What was I supposed to say to that? She had given me a compliment, such as it was, but was speaking as though the same quality she had praised I would never use again … at least not at the Judiciary.

I froze. No. This *couldn't* be happening. The word "Please" slipped out of my mouth. My stunned brain couldn't manage a response more articulate than that.

The Corona frowned. "If this were simply a matter between you and me," she said with an undercurrent of regret and disdain, "then I could work something out, but since the high marshal is aware of your request for the Zenith docket, he's obligated to inform the rest of Realm Council. You're now considered a threat. None of the councillors, except Gannon, of course, will allow someone — a *subordinate* — who could hold the truth about Realm exploration over their heads work in Realm governance and law."

Time stood still as my mind came to terms with exactly what she was saying. I curled my fingers into a fist on my thighs, crushing the fabric of my dress. "You're ..." *Oh my gods.* "You're *dismissing* me."

The Corona's expression cooled, what little emotion she had displayed, now entirely gone. "I have no choice," she said, her voice sharp and defensive. "Leadership would question your motivations and commitment to the Realm."

I stared at her, the irony of what she just said eating me alive. I had known the truth about exploration for a good while now, never once thinking to reveal it to anyone or use it in some way for my gain. Instead, I had continued to work for the Realm the entire time, with fierce dedication!

Maybe I should tell her about how Gabriel — her very own minister and member of leadership — had attacked, hunted and *threatened* me for weeks, that *he* was the reason that I had attempted to access the files. All of that was on the tip of my tongue, but I held back. I just had too much at stake. If I told her about Gabriel's hatred for me, the next step would be her discovery of my family's dissidence. Bearing that mind, a *dismissal* was welcome if it meant preventing the detainment of my entire family.

Still, I still had to try.

"You're not thinking this through," I argued. "Dismissing me won't prevent me from telling anyone the truth."

She smiled thinly, appear unimpressed. "You wouldn't do that," she said, "because revealing the truth would only create even more unrest and still leave you out in the cold. Moreover, because of your carelessness, you've ruined your reputation, and no one would believe you. After your public disgrace, everyone would simply think you spiteful against leadership — not some credible truthseeker."

I faltered. Gods help me, but she was right. I had no leg to stand on when it came to exposing the truth.

Panic made me desperate. I leaned over and reached for her hand, making her flinch. She stared, with a startled expression, from my hold on her wrist to my face.

"Don't do this," I begged. "Please."

"I have to," she said, extracting her wrist out of my hold with a look of distaste on her face. "You're lucky I haven't had you detained."

Ice coursed through my veins. The threat of a greater punishment making me go cold.

This was it, then. Tears brimmed in my eyes as reality sank in. There was nothing for it; I was being dismissed.

I sank back into my chair as the impact of what was happening rushed in. My gods, if Khelan had been angered by my suspension, he was bound to be *infuriated* when he learned about this! All my life the one thing I had wanted was to work at the Judiciary, to be like him, and within less than a year there I had lost all chance of such a possibility. I had just realized how much I wanted to be at the Judiciary, how much of a difference I could make, and now, because of a whirlwind of circumstances *all* out of my control, my future was being taken away.

I covered my mouth with a shaking hand to hold back a sob, but I couldn't stop the tears that ran down my face. The injustice of it all made them hot on my cheeks.

"Tell me," the Corona said quietly, peering at me. "Does anyone else know about the Zenith docket?"

I brushed the tears away with an angry swipe. "No," I lied, pleased to no end when my gaze never wavered from hers. There was no way I would tell her that Tai knew the truth too. Who knew what she would do?

She raised a brow. "What about your brother?" she asked. "Surely, you must have discussed this with him or some other member of your family."

"No," I said truthfully, holding her gaze.

She assessed me for a long, untenable moment, her brown eyes dark, probing and sharp. "Lucky for them."

CHAPTER 14

"Need a drink?"

I glanced over my shoulder and found Rhoan walking in from the kitchen, holding up two glasses and a bottle of moss-colored liquid that glittered as it sloshed around.

"*Quix*?" I asked, eyeing the alcoholic beverage.

Good gods, I must look even worse than I feel.

A stiff drink was one thing, but liquid fire was another. *Quix* was a tart and spicy ale that was best consumed in small doses. The taste was so pungent, people usually used it sparingly in their recipes for flavor to rather than drink the foul thing straight.

I scooched over on the couch just before Rhoan fell into it beside me. "Desperate times call for desperate measures," he said, filling the glasses with the brew.

And he doesn't even know the half of it.

Hours after I left Realm Council residences in an astounded haze, the shock of what the Corona had revealed and done still hadn't sunk in. I hadn't told anyone about my meeting with the Corona yet — not even Gannon and Tai. There was just too much to wrap my head around. And, if I were to be honest with myself, a large part of me dreaded everyone's responses.

A thick wave of nausea moved through me.

Rhoan plunked his feet on the coffee table then hooked one ankle over the other. He held out a glass to me, now filled to the rim. I stared at it for a brief, ambivalent moment.

Should I be sober in my misery or endure it in complete intoxication?

I took the drink.

After downing a mouthful of the brew, I nearly threw it up, gagging at the ale's revolting scent and scorching heat.

Rhoan chuckled before tilting his head back and downing half of his in one go. He winced against the taste of his drink then eyed me.

"So," he began hoarsely, "how'd it go with Mila? Will your banishment from the Judiciary be ending any time soon?"

I grimaced, my gaze dropping finding the bottom of my glass now cradled between my palms on my lap. I had told Rhoan as I was heading out the door that morning that I was going to see Mila. Now I wished I hadn't. My brother had apparently read into my meeting with her the same way I had — as a hopeful sign of the end to my suspension.

I took another sip of drink, biding my time, and said when feeling returned to my tongue, "Not quite."

Rhoan frowned. "What does *that* mean?"

I shifted, staring down at my drink. "Let's just say my *banishment's* going to last much longer than expected."

"Khelan's mood isn't going to get any better when he hears that," he said. "Or Ma's."

I tightened the hold on my glass, lifting my gaze to his. So they were still mad, were they? Good. Served them right. Having a willful child like me would just have to be their cross to bear.

"You'd think they'd be more reluctant about throwing stones," I remarked, anger simmering just below my surface, "considering that *glass house* they're living in."

Rhoan made a noncommittal sounded that almost passed for agreement but replied, "Ma said you told the high chancellor everything. She said he's known about our family for a long time." His light green eyes went dark. "What were you thinking? Why would you put all of us — *Addy* — at risk like that?"

My anger rose to the top. How could Rhoan think, even for a *moment*, that I'd take a reckless chance with our family?

"*Gannon*, just like your beloved Tai, has been helping our family from the beginning," I spelled out. "The furthest thing from Gannon's mind is turning any of us in."

Rhoan considered that for a full minute then regarded the bottle in his hand. He jostled it, making the drink light up. "Look," he said, still considering the *Quix*. "I don't want to argue. It really doesn't make any sense at this point."

I blinked, the wind taken out of my sail by the lack of his resistance. "Well ... good," I said, with an unnecessary but thoroughly satisfying nod for emphasis.

I took another swig of drink. The stuff must have been growing on me. It was much less putrid this time around.

Rhoan chuckled suddenly with a shake of his head then clinked the corner of my glass with his own. "You win, hands down," he declared as our drinks sparkled. "No matter how fucked up things have been for me over the last couple of weeks, they've been a hundred times worse for you." He tossed back the dregs of his ale.

I frowned as he struggled to recover from the *Quix*. *Worse for me.* "Why?" I asked. "What happened to *you?*"

Rhoan plunked his glass on the coffee table. "Beth and I aren't together anymore," he announced, leaning back and interlacing his fingers behind his head.

My eyes widened. I twisted around on the couch to face him. "What? When?"

"She broke things off just after Realm Council meeting."

I cocked my head, attempting to compute that. "*She* left *you?*"

He nodded, and my jaw dropped. I could now count on one hand—no, on one *finger*—the number of times a woman had ended a relationship with my brother. It was usually *him* who did the leaving.

I looked him over, searching for signs of anguish, but found resignation instead. *Huh.* If I were him, I'd be an inconsolable mess, but by the looks of my brother, he appeared thoroughly indifferent.

Maybe *that* was the problem — his disregard. Rhoan had mentioned that Beth had been feeling ignored, and if she was anything like his past girlfriends, which she seemed to be in *every* respect, then she could simply be trying to *manage* him somehow.

"Maybe this is just some ploy for attention," I suggested, eyeing him.

He scoffed. "Well, if it *was* a ploy, it failed," he said, glancing at his comm when it buzzed. Rhoan's eyes flared wide as he stared at his device. "Holy shit."

"What?" I asked, but he probably didn't hear me. He had already jumped to his feet and rushed to the front door.

Frowning, I rested my glass on the table as my brother disengaged the door. When Rhoan stepped back a moment later, he revealed the haggard figure of Uncle Paol standing in the hallway.

I gasped and lunged to my feet, about to go to him, but Rhoan glanced at me sharply and shook his head, telling me to stay where I was.

Rhoan and I stood silent as uncle slunk into the apartment, scanning the space around him with wandering blue eyes. His gaze landed on me. "I've been trying to reach you," he stated with a surprising accusatory note.

He has?

Reflexively, I glanced at my comm. "I have a new code," I murmured, realizing why he hadn't been able to contact me, but I may as well have been speaking to the walls. He had already walked off and into the kitchen.

Rhoan and I exchanged an uneasy look. By the knot between my brother's brows, I could tell he was just as concerned as me by both Uncle Paol's sudden arrival and his disheveled appearance.

The last time anyone in our family had seen Uncle had been when he left Adria in our family's care. Back then, he was distraught and broken over the loss of his wife, but he also had a thirst for revenge. Now, Uncle Paol appeared haunted and hollow, a ghost of himself. He no longer looked anything like the man Rhoan and I had grown up with and had come to love.

Rhoan dipped his head toward the kitchen, and I followed my brother there, where Uncle was glancing about.

"Fortunately," he continued as though he hadn't just left us staring after him in the sitting area, "your brother answered my message, or I would have had to wait on some goodly neighbor of yours to grant me access to your floor." He turned to face us. "Are we alone?"

I glanced at Rhoan who hesitated before saying, "Yes."

"Good." Uncle Paol shoved the hood of his coat back, off his head, then drew out a chair. He sat down, scrubbing a hand across his mouth. "Do you have anything to drink?"

I nodded and went to the cooler. For a second, I considered giving him *Quix* — he certainly looked like he could use it — but then I thought better. He appeared frazzled enough as it was. And he had obviously come for a purpose. I would have rather he had his wits about him when he told Rhoan and me what it was.

I pulled out a bottle of water and handed it to him. He had drunk half of it by the time I sat down in a chair beside him.

My heart ached as I took him in with a closer view: grief and revenge had ravaged him. He was in his mid-forties, but after just a few short months, he now appeared much older. The gray hair around his temples had spread throughout his crown, and wrinkles had sunk deep around his eyes.

He lowered the bottle to table with a heavy hand, shaking the table, and sent an anxious look between Rhoan and me. "How's Addy?"

"She's fine," Rhoan said, standing by my chair now.

Uncle closed his eyes briefly. "Thank the gods," he said, and hope lit up inside me.

"You've come for her," I blurted out, but realized my mistake as soon as the words left my mouth. Had he come for my cousin, he would have gone to our family home, not come here.

"No," he said, confirming my error. "I've come for information."

I sat there, baffled, as he eyed me.

Rhoan frowned. "What do you mean?" he asked.

Uncle Paol thinned his lips. "Your sister knows what I'm talking about."

I searched his face as a memory slipped into my mind.

Don't worry, Metallurgist ... Next time, I'll send a much friendlier face.

My stomach flipped. He hadn't come for Adria. He had come to carry out Gabriel's demands.

"You," I breathed. "*You're* how he planned on getting the dockets?"

His gaze slipped from mine, but I caught the flicker of guilt that moved through his eyes. I slumped, staring at him aghast. *My gods.*

"Someone needs to tell me what's going on," Rhoan demanded, looking between Uncle Paol and me.

"Uncle Paol's come to collect the confidential information Gabriel and Maxim are threatening us for," I explained, looking up at my brother now.

My brother's face cleared. "You're *still* working for the rebels?" he asked, voice rising as he loomed over him. "And now against your own family!"

Uncle held up a hand, warding Rhoan off. "You don't understand," he said. "I went to Helios weeks ago to try to locate Gabriel and Maxim so I could tell them I wanted out, but instead they were the ones to find *me*. They wanted to enlist me in some group they're organizing — said it would be wise for me to be on the right side of history."

"Oh gods, the Quad," I whispered. "Please don't tell me you agreed."

My brother tensed, eyes narrowing into slits as he glowered at the older man. "Do you have any fucking idea what kind of trouble you'd be bringing down on yourself, on *Addy*, if you joined a group like that?" he spat. "Supporting a rebel is one thing, but becoming part of an organized, widespread faction is another!"

Uncle Paol clenched a fist on the table. "I'm *fully* aware of the risks," he replied. "That's why I told them no. I'm tired of being on the run, hiding, being away from my daughter. I went to them out hoping to break things off with no bad blood, so I could return to Addy without any fear of retaliation, but I should have known better." He grunted, making a disgusted sound. "Instead they made me an offer. They told me to collect two dockets from you. Once I deliver them, they said they'll let me off clean — no harm, no foul."

Rhoan snorted. "The fuck they will."

I couldn't have agreed with my brother more. Khelan had broken things off with Maxim, but the renegade had simply turned right around and threatened me for support, with Gabriel's help.

"Maybe they won't," Uncle Paol conceded to Rhoan, the little color that had remained in his face disappearing. "But this is the only hope I have of getting out of the shit I've gotten myself into, and being with my daughter again." He turned to me. "You *have* to give me the files."

I swallowed, shaking my head. "I don't have them," I said.

Uncle Paol's shoulders drooped as Rhoan scowled.

"You couldn't really have expected Kira would have tried to obtain the information, much less be *willing* to hand them over to Maxim and Gabriel," my brother said.

"Of course not," Uncle said, and holding my gaze. He leaned forward to grip one of my hands tight in his. "I'm hoping now that I've told you what they said … that maybe you'd try to access them now."

Rhoan made a bitter sound. "You've got to be kidding me," he muttered, starting to pace the kitchen. Meanwhile, I stared at Uncle Paol, devastated by the hopeful tremor in his hold.

I had adamantly refused to give in to Maxim and Gabriel's threats so far, but now, looking into my Uncle's anguished gaze and imagining Adria without her father, I experienced a strong urge to comply. But even if I wanted to …

"I can't," I said.

His face fell. "I understand how much I'm asking of you," he said, shadows darkening the skin under his eyes, "but I *beg* of you, do this one thing for me."

"No, you don't understand," I said. "I've been dismiss—" I caught myself with a quick look at Rhoan, who was standing directly across from me. "I mean, I'm no longer at the Judiciary. I can't access the database."

"Yes, I heard about that," Uncle said with a slight frown. "Gabriel appeared somewhat discouraged when I reminded them of your suspension, but he didn't care. He's of the belief that you and the high chancellor are still involved and so you still have the means to get the information he wants."

That took me aback. If Gabriel had been "discouraged" by my suspension, then it *couldn't* have been him who sent the photos of Gannon and me to the Realm Anarchist. If he had done so, he should have pleased. The article must have had nothing to do with him. Even so, the fact didn't change my response.

"I'm sorry," I said. "I can't obtain those files." Even if Gannon were to agree to obtaining the dockets on my behalf, giving them to Uncle Paol, and so to the Quad, was the last thing I would do.

All vitality in my uncle's body melted away, leaving a hollow shell. "Then there's no hope," he said, releasing my hand and sitting back. "You were the only hope I had of getting out of this alive."

My breath caught, heart thumping now. *Alive? Holy gods, would Gabriel and Maxim actually* kill *him for cutting his ties with them?*

I exchanged a worried glance with Rhoan. My brother appeared just as stricken by the thought, which wasn't a farfetched one at all. Gabriel and Maxim had already proven themselves to be murderers. Killing a member of my family would mean nothing to them.

Rhoan shoved a hand into his hair. "Holy fuck, man," he cursed, glaring at Uncle Paol. "What's so blasted important in these files that they're threatening to *kill* you?"

Uncle scrubbed a palm over his face. "I don't know," he muttered, sounding tired, then looked to me. "I figured you would know."

I did, but I wasn't about to fill him or Rhoan in. I needed to do something else first.

My chair scraped on the floor as I pushed myself to my feet and started tapping out a message to Talib on my comm, asking him to pick me up.

"When do Maxim and Gabriel expect to hear from you?" I asked Uncle.

He glanced briefly at Rhoan, a crease between his brow. "They gave me two days."

I frowned. That wasn't much time.

"What are you doing?" Rhoan asked.

I shook my head, dismissing both his question and the suspicion glittering in his eyes. I considered Uncle Paol. "How can I get in touch with you again?" I asked him.

He hesitated, his gaze skittering away from mine, then said, "I'll be around."

His reply was a non-answer, but it would have to be enough. I hurried out of the kitchen and into the entryway, where Rhoan caught me by the arm.

"Where are you going?" he demanded in a low hiss.

"To get help," I replied, yanking my arm out of his hold. I reached for my leather jacket and started putting it on.

Rhoan glanced over his shoulder to where our uncle still sat in the kitchen, out of earshot, holding his bowed head between both hands.

"You're going to *him*, aren't you?" my brother asked, cutting a look at me now.

I didn't have to ask who *him* was. "Yes, I'm going to Gannon," I said, tightening the belt around my waist with a hard yank. "And then I'm going to speak with *Tai*, if that makes you feel any better."

"Don't involve the high chancellor in this any longer, Kira," Rhoan bit out, anger pinching his face. "He already knows too much. Let *Tai* handle this."

I blew out a tight breath, tamping down anger and frustration. Even now, after knowing all Gannon had done and *was still doing*, my brother

249

doubted his sincerity. I wondered whether Rhoan would ever come around. I supposed I could only hope he would, because if he didn't, he would be putting a wedge between us that didn't need to be there.

"Whether you like it or not, Rhoan," I said after disengaging the door, "Gannon's going to be a part of my life, so you may as well get used to it."

* * *

When Talib led me into his Gannon's townhouse a short while later, the low, muffled sound of two voices filtered into the foyer from the sitting area. Puzzled, I looked to the protector as I removed my jacket.

"Is the high chancellor holding a meeting?" I asked, hoping for Gannon's sake he wasn't, because I was fully prepared to break up any discussions he was having with leadership if I had to. I needed to talk to him now — they would have to wait.

"Yes," Talib confirmed. "With Tai Commander."

I blinked. *Tai?* "He's *here?*"

The protector nodded then gestured toward the sitting area, urging me to follow him in.

I had assumed Tai was still in Port, preoccupied by his mission. It was why I hadn't thought to message him before leaving my apartment. If he had returned and gone straight to Gannon, he must have learned something about the Quad … but then, why hadn't he contacted me? As frustrated as Tai was with me, I couldn't see him withholding information that could impact my family just because of any hard feelings, no matter how awful things had become between us.

"How much fucking longer do you think you can keep this up!"

I flinched at Tai's outburst, which boomed throughout the sitting area at the exact moment I walked in. He glowered, hands on his hips, at Gannon, who stood on the opposite side of the room. I must have made a sound because both men swiveled their heads to look at me, a mix of surprise and displeasure all over their faces.

Talib, who was standing by me just inside the threshold, cleared his throat. "I'll be in the study," he said in a low voice, and the receding sound of his footsteps told me he was walking off, in the direction of said room, I supposed, but I couldn't be sure — my eyes were still focused on Gannon and Tai, and theirs firmly on me.

When neither man ventured to speak, I eased into the room, though uncertain whether I should. The tension was suffocating.

"I didn't expect to see you here," I said, eyeing Tai.

His uniform jacket stretched across his shoulders as he folded his arms. "I told you there was someone here, in Merit, I needed to speak to."

He did? Then I remembered my last conversation with Tai, via monitor, while he had been in Port. *Gannon.* He's who Tai had been talking about. Then Tai *must* have learned something about the Quad!

"Is this about Maxim and Gabriel?" I asked, stepping farther into the room. "Did you find out what they're forcing Uncle Paol to do?"

Tai's arms fell to his side. "Paol?" he asked, surprise blotting out the belligerence in his gaze.

Gannon approached me, eyes wide. "What happened?"

I looked between the two men, taking in their stunned expressions. So they *hadn't* been discussing Maxim and Gabriel, or at least not this. They had met for some other reason. Unfortunately, I didn't have the liberty of time to get to the bottom of it.

"Maxim and Gabriel sent my uncle to see me," I said and, when their expressions went from shocked to confused, quickly recounted everything about my uncle's surprise visit — from the fact that he wanted out to the reason Maxim and Gabriel had sent him to me.

Tai frowned. "You *do* realize they sent Paol to ask for the dockets because you'd probably be more willing to give in to him than to anyone else."

I hadn't thought about that, but it *did* make sense. "I suppose so."

Gannon studied me. "How certain are you that we can trust your uncle?" he asked. "He's been on the run for months now. He could very well be *working* for Maxim and Gabriel — not trying to free himself."

I hesitated. He had a point. They *both* did. Uncle Paol had aligned with rebels out of revenge over my aunt's death. Wouldn't supporting the Quad would be the next obvious step in his crusade? Possibly ... but I shook my head.

"No," I said, glancing between Gannon and Tai. "You didn't see him. My uncle's been completely destroyed, *shattered*, by what he's done. He's desperate to get out. It's the only reason he agreed to come and ask me for the dockets. His *only* motivation is to be free of them so he can be with his daughter, nothing else."

Tai exchanged a look with Gannon before he replied, "And so he pops up all of a sudden asking you to become a rebel informant."

I understood their distrust, but it was misplaced. "He said Maxim and Gabriel would kill him if he didn't come through," I insisted. "He had no other choice but to ask me for help."

The two of them considered that for a moment during an uneasy silence.

Tai firmed his jaw. "How much time did Paol say he had?"

"Two days."

"Damn it," Gannon muttered, running a hand around the back of his neck. "That's not a lot of time to come up with a plan."

"I know," I said with a sigh, relieved to see their skepticism fading into action. "What are we going to do?"

"There's only one thing we *can* do at this point," Tai stated. "We have to give them the files."

I stared at him, shock nearly making me knees nearly buckle. "What?"

I wanted to get to the bottom of this too, probably more than anyone else, but handing over the information was *entirely* out of the question! Doing that would only keep Maxim and Gabriel coming back for more. My family and I would never be rid of them!

"Are you out of your ever-loving mind?" Gannon demanded, echoing my thoughts.

Tai leveled Gannon a cool look. "I don't mean the *real* files," he said. "I mean versions filled with doctored information."

But Gannon had already been shaking his head. "It would be a waste of time," he said, folding his arms. "You might be able to trick Gabriel, but not Maxim. As an elite, he'll know at once that the files are fake."

"It wouldn't be the first time I've falsified records," Tai replied icily. "I'm certain I can come up with documents that could fool the high marshal himself."

Gannon thinned his lips. "I'm not challenging the quality of your work, Commander," he replied in just as cool a tone. "There's just coding in the Zenith docket that even the highest levels of the Protectorate wouldn't be able to decipher, much less hide."

Tai drew back. "All right, Consul," he said, jamming his hands on his hips. "It's time to talk. What the fuck is in the Zenith docket that's so important to the Quad?"

The answer was on the tip of my tongue, and I was eager now to reveal all I had just learned, but Gannon beat me to it.

"Zenith is proof of Realm exploration," he said simply.

Tai's eyes went wide, his earlier skepticism returning with a darkening of his gaze.

I tensed. Tai had barely believed it when Gannon and I had told him about exploration weeks ago. It had only been when I had disclosed hearing the very same thing come out Xavier Minister's own mouth that he had appeared to believe me. If it was more confirmation he needed, then I had the ultimate kind.

"It's true," I insisted. "The Corona told me so herself."

Two pairs of eyes became fixed on me.

"The *Corona*," Gannon said, confusion making his brows crease. "When?"

I winced, considering for an anxious moment about holding back the news about my dismissal. I needed them focused on Maxim and Gabriel, not sidetracked by yet another of my disgraces. But I couldn't do it. The Corona had probably already started putting the wheels in motion to announce my dismissal, which meant Gannon, Tai and everyone else in the Realm would soon find out. And hadn't hiding truths been the cause of the most disastrous aspects of my life?

I sighed, fiddling with the belt around my waist. "The Corona told me everything moments before she dismissed me from the Judiciary."

Stunned silence reigned.

Tai shot Gannon a foul look. "And you thought the news about you two would blow over," he sneered. "That everything would all work out. How much more fucking proof do you need before you call an end to all this?"

I blinked between the two men, wondering what was going on.

Gannon paled, but his eyes snapped bright with anger. "Tell me that woman didn't dismiss you because of our relationship," he demanded, and suddenly the tension that had been flooding the room when I had just arrived started to make sense.

Gannon and Tai had been discussing — or rather *arguing* about — *me*, and from what I could gather, Tai had been making every effort to show Gannon the error of his ways.

Deep despair welled up inside me as I stared at Tai. I had believed there was hope when in fact there was none. Tai had said that he had been considering whether to be in a multiple with me, but it must have been a lie. Why else would he have gone around me and met with Gannon to strong-arm him into giving me up? My gods, who was the *manipulative* and *lying* one now?

"I wasn't dismissed because I was involved with Gannon," I said, glaring at Tai. "The receptionist I asked to call up the dockets reported me to the Protectorate. Apparently, the Corona believes me untrustworthy and a threat to the system."

Tai's mouth went into a hard line. "Damn it, Kira," he said. "I told you that type of request could be traced back to you!"

He had, but that warning wasn't worth rehashing now. My dismissal as well as his manipulative ways would have to wait until we had taken care of more urgent matters.

I looked to Gannon, hoping he could see passed his anger at the Corona to focus on Maxim and Gabriel. He studied me quietly, his mind clearly working. I prayed he was calculating a way to help Uncle Paol and not some retaliation against his superior.

Thankfully, after a moment of deliberation, he turned to Tai. "Now you understand why the Zenith docket is so important to the Quad," he said.

Tai nodded with a scowl, planting his hands on his hips. "They want it to destabilize the system and create new Realm order."

I stilled, remembering Gannon had suspected just that about the Quad's ulterior motives.

Gannon nodded. "If Maxim and Gabriel reveal the truth, they would be heralded as the ones who unearthed evidence of the very hypocrisy the rebels have been accusing leadership of. It would lead to a coup — exactly the thing they want, so they could rise to the top."

It took us all a minute to absorb that.

I chewed on my lip then started cutting a path across the room. Damn it, we had to think! Figure this out, and *now!*

"Gabriel said *Maxim's* the one who's desperate for the Zenith docket," I said, calling on my memory. "*He's* the one we need to focus on. If we find him, then we can stop the Quad."

Tai sniffed. "Believe me," he said, folding his arms. "There's been no lack of trying. The Protectorate's been working full tilt at locating Maxim or *any* members of the Quad. The only person who seems to be able to get to Maxim these days is Liandra Ambassador."

He had a point. Maxim had been a ghost since he had abducted me and had been even more elusive before then. Still, Liandra had managed to be in contact with the man with little difficulty.

I froze. That was the answer! Or rather, *she* was the answer. "Liandra," I said, stopping in the middle of the room facing them.

Tai frowned. "What about her?"

"Don't you see?" I asked, looking between them. "We need to ask for Liandra's help. *She's* the only one who could possibly know where Maxim is."

Tai scoffed. "First off, you'd have to be permitted to *speak* with Liandra to ask for her help," he said. "She's in detainment, so how in the worlds do you plan on arranging that?"

"We won't speak with her — the *Corona* will," Gannon interjected, and it was a good thing too because I hadn't had a response. His eyes glittered with growing interest as he considered me.

Tai balked. "You two can't be serious," he said, glaring between us. "Have either of you *met* the Realm sovereign? She's not going to lower herself to ask a dissident for *anything*, much less help."

I couldn't argue with that. The Corona would sooner abdicate her position as leader of the Realm than appear vulnerable, and asking Liandra, the person she had publicly denounced, for help would cause *exactly* that.

Gannon met Tai's gaze. "She will when I tell her about the Quad's plans to create a new Realm order," he said. "The Corona will agree to negotiate with just about anyone, even an exiled leader, to prevent a threat to the system."

I looked to Tai, wondering what he thought as hope knotted my insides.

"Liandra's not simply going to agree out of the goodness of her heart," Tai countered, appearing more curious now than doubtful. "What's in it for her?"

That was easy. "Argon's exemption," I said, gaining Tai's focus. "It's the one thing we all know Liandra wants."

He regarded me, thinking, then finally raised his gaze to Gannon's. "It could work."

"It had better," Gannon said, stepping away before calling out for Talib. When the protector arrived a moment later, he said to him, "Find out if the Corona's still in Merit. Tell her support we need to meet with her as soon as possible."

My eyebrows raised as Talib exited the room. "We?" I asked Gannon.

"You're coming with me," he said.

I am? "Why?"

Gannon's eyes glinted. "The Corona needs to know that the person she's deemed a threat to our system is the same one who's trying to protect the Realm."

I admired his indignation, but couldn't help but note one important thing. "If I go with you, she'll make the connection between Gabriel, Maxim and me," I said. "She'll know about my family." My gods, if she discovered that, she'd kick me out of the *Realm*, not just the Judiciary!

He took my hand, eyes softening. "She doesn't need to know anything more than that Gabriel and Maxim are working together and threatening you for information," he said, drawing me to him. "That's it."

I supposed he was right, but to be honest, I didn't know whether I could handle *two* face-to-face meetings with the Corona in *one* day.

Talib suddenly entered the room at swift stride, drawing our attention. "The Corona's still here, at Realm Council residences," he said. "She'll meet with you, but we'll have to leave now. She's scheduled to leave to meet with the ambassador within the hour."

Gannon squeezed my hand. "Are you ready?" he asked, looking at me expectantly.

I frowned, indecision making me hesitate. Was going with him a good idea? I still didn't know, but every moment I stood there wondering was a moment lost trying to stop the Quad.

"All right," I said before hurrying to the front door. When Tai didn't move, simply stood in the middle of the room, watching us, I stopped to face him.

"Aren't you coming?" I asked.

Gannon came up beside me and glanced Tai's way, awaiting his reply.

A flicker of indecision moved across Tai's face before his expression went blank. "My superior's expecting a report from me about my mission to Port," he said, rolling back his shoulders. "You two can manage on your own."

CHAPTER 15

Maybe this isn't such a good idea.

As Gannon and I followed Talib into the building, a pair of protectors strode by then slowed, watching us from a distance with the same abject fascination as did a handful of senators who were standing nearby. Since Gannon had probably walked the halls of Realm Council residences more times than I could count, I had to assume it was the fact that *I* was there and *with him* that they found us so enthralling.

"Perhaps I should have stayed behind," I said to Gannon under my breath, eyeing more gaping citizens as we walked across the rotunda. "I think my being here might just make things worse."

Gannon glanced down at me, by his shoulder. "I don't think things could actually get *worse*," he muttered. "Do you?"

I winced. *Good point.*

Talib led us down a hall, and I realized as we passed the various meeting chambers that we were headed to the same meeting room where the Corona had just dismissed me earlier that day. On second thought, yes, maybe things *could* get worse.

A protector stepped out of the room and we slowed to a stop in front of the door. The woman cut a quick look at me before addressing Gannon.

"The Corona is waiting for you and your guest, High Chancellor," she said, stepping back. "Please come in."

Gannon acknowledged that with a short nod then told Talib to wait for us in the hall. A moment later, Gannon and I walked in and found the Corona standing by the still blazing fireplace, with her mouth set.

"So you've come to plead her case," she stated as soon as the door closed behind us, glaring at Gannon.

Gannon's eyes narrowed. "I beg your pardon," he said.

She thinned her lips, her glower shifting to me now. "Do you really think you can get your position back by asking *him* to beg for it on your behalf?"

My eyes widened at the accusation. My gods, the woman had complimented me on my tenacity, but just how relentless did she think I was? "That's not why we're here," I insisted.

"Though we'll get to the matter of her dismissal soon enough," Gannon remarked. I sent him a questioning look, but he ignored me, watching as the Corona with a wary eye.

"Then tell me," she said, walking toward us with her chin raised. "What's so terribly important that both of you need to meet me so urgently and at this hour?"

"What do you know about the Quad?" Gannon asked, startling her.

She came to a stop in front of him. "The *Quad*," she repeated, looking him over as she lowered her hand to her side. "I believe I know as much as you on that matter."

He considered that. "You're aware then that Gabriel Minister has aligned with its founding leader, Maxim Noble?"

"*Gabriel?*" she said. "I haven't heard a word about him since your father dismissed him from the Judiciary."

"After *I* asked my father to dismiss him," Gannon said.

She drew back. "*You* did that?"

Gannon nodded.

"But why?"

Gannon's face tightened. "He physically assaulted Kira, struck her, in his office," he replied through thin lips. "A man like that shouldn't have the privilege of representing the Judiciary, much less acting as the leader of a world."

The Corona arched a brow. "Is that so?"

"Unfortunately, it is," he said. "Since then, to avenge his demotion, Gabriel's been threatening Kira, demanding that she give him classified information to prove Realm exploration."

"Oh my," she said then slid a look over to me, placing a hand at her heart. "And I suppose the information Gabriel's interested in is the Zenith docket?"

I nodded. "That's right," I replied, eager to explain. "I only attempted to access the files to find out what Gabriel and Maxim were up to, so that I could try to stop the Quad."

"I see," she remarked, considering me.

I glanced at Gannon, trying to understand her pause. She should have been alarmed, or at the very least greatly disturbed to know that another member of leadership, one who had been once been charged with overseeing a world, was now plotting against the Realm.

"You don't believe us," Gannon said, studying her.

She sniffed, shaking her head. "Is *this* the best you could come up with?" she said to him. "Do you think such an over-the-top story about a disgraced leader would put your darling here back in my good graces?"

I clenched my fists, glaring at her. "We're telling the truth!"

She snorted, brown eyes snapping. "You're fortunate I admired your father as much as I did," she said to Gannon, "or I would report your actions this very evening to Realm Council."

Gannon's nostrils flared. "I swear on his legacy and mine that everything we're telling you is the truth," he said in a low voice.

The Corona's smug air evaporated. She opened her mouth then closed it, eyes losing their heat as she appeared to search for words.

A few seconds passed before she turned away, wringing her hands as she crossed the room. Suddenly, she turned to me, her skirts swishing around her legs.

"Why now?" she demanded. "You could have told me all this when I dismissed you."

I balked. "What difference would it have made?" I said. "You wouldn't have believed me then any more than you do now. The only reason I'm telling you now is because I need your help to protect my family. Gabriel and Maxim are threatening to kill a member of my family if I don't give them the information."

She searched my face, then looked to Gannon, who nodded.

"They've given us two days or else they'll kill her uncle," he said.

She paled. "My gods," she said, holding her chest as she walked with an unsteady step to an armchair to sit down. "There's only one reason the Quad would want the Zenith docket: to expose it and create chaos, possibly lead a coup. We can't let that happen."

Gannon expelled a deep breath. "I'm glad you understand the gravity of the situation for Kira *and* the Realm," he said. "We need to stop them."

She stared up at him. "What do think we've been trying to do?" she said. "The Protectorate has been focused on nothing *but* trying to stop the Quad and other rebel groups for months now. If there was a way to capture Maxim, Gabriel or any other dissident for that matter, we would have done so by now."

"That's why we're here," I said, stepping forward. "We have an idea."

She eyed me then said, "I'm listening."

I exchanged a quick look with Gannon and sat down in the armchair beside her. "Liandra Ambassador is the only one who's been able to contact Maxim since all the unrest began," I said as Gannon came to stand next to me. "We think you should offer her Argon's exemption in exchange for her telling us where to find Maxim, and possibly Gabriel too."

The Corona laughed, surprising me, and by the way he stiffened, taking Gannon aback too.

"You think I haven't already made that offer?" she said. "I had to. It only made political sense. Realm Council is on the cusp of approving exploration. I *have* to retract Argon's expulsion or leadership would look like hypocrites and the Realm would face even more acts of violence."

Gannon frowned. "Why have I heard nothing of this before now?"

"Believe it or not, Gannon," she replied smoothly, "the position of high chancellor means you're involved in *some* decision making — not all."

Gannon firmed his jaw, appearing to try to rein in his temper. "Are you saying that Argon's expulsion is no longer in place?" he asked, and worry made me hold my breath.

If she had already accepted the dominion back into the Realm, then we had no leverage, nothing to offer Liandra in exchange for her help in finding Maxim, and so Gabriel.

The Corona sighed. "Unfortunately, no," she said. "I met with Liandra, offering her an olive branch, but she accused me of presenting a Trojan horse instead. She says she no longer trusts me and is putting her faith in those who are fighting for her cause."

"My gods," Gannon said, stalking across the room, his frustration evident in his stiff moves. The flames from the hearth crackled as he passed it by. "Is the woman so filled with spite that she would put the future of her people in the hands of rebels?"

I clenched my fists at the defeat in his voice, refusing to believe that we had run out of options. There had to still be a way to use Liandra's relationship with Maxim to our advantage. We had to break this incredible bond they had. It was understandable for not to trust the Corona, but to give her faith to Maxim, the man who had killed her father, was unbelievable!

I inhaled sharply, realizing how Liandra's connection to Maxim could be broken, and looked to the Corona. "She doesn't know," I said. "The only reason Liandra would put so much trust in Maxim is because she doesn't know he was responsible for her father's death."

Gannon considered me from where he now stood, in front of the fireplace. "That's right," he murmured, catching on. He glanced at the Corona. "Maxim coordinated the attack on Septima, the one that nearly killed you, and murdered her father instead. If you tell Liandra about this, you'll shake her faith in Maxim. You'll be able to convince her to help us stop the Quad."

Her gaze turned inward as she thought that through. "I suppose," she said. "But as I've just said, Liandra doesn't trust me. If I go to her with this, she'll merely think me a liar."

Gannon stepped toward her. "Then let me speak with her," he said. "If she won't listen to you, she just might listen to me."

"I admire your infinite confidence, Gannon," she said, "but might I remind you that as high chancellor, you're a member of leadership too. Liandra will view you as responsible as me for the situation she's in. She won't trust you."

"But she would trust *me*," I said, the truth of my words dawning on me as I spoke.

The Corona and Gannon focused on me, surprise and question in their wide eyes.

"*I* was the only one willing to believe Liandra when she said her father wasn't responsible for the attack on Septima," I said. "I helped her find her father's body in the wreckage and consoled her as she cried."

The Corona sent an uneasy look at Gannon who was staring at me as though I had grown two heads. "She'd know the Corona sent you," he countered. "Liandra would just view you in the same light as she does the rest of leadership now."

I shook my head. "Not with everything the media's been saying about me," I insisted. "To her, I've fallen low in the public eye the same way she has."

The Corona eyed me. "You would go to *Argon*, a rebel hotbed, on my behalf?"

I faltered. "Argon?"

She nodded. "After increasing my security, the Protectorate decided to transfer Liandra back to her residence in Virtue, sooner than scheduled. She's being monitored there by a team of my protectors."

The bottom fell out of my belly. *Virtue?* It was one thing to try to reason with an exiled leader in Capita, the Realm's capital of governance and law, but it was something entirely different to do that on her own familiar ground, ground which, to my despair, had become a location of increasing rebel activity.

As the capital of Argon, Virtue was where the mounting frustration and dissatisfaction with leadership were being experienced the most. The idea of going there, where outbursts of violence would be commonplace, made me go cold.

"Kira's not going to Virtue," Gannon pronounced as though it were the law. "She can speak with Liandra via monitor, or maybe prepare a video message asking for her help."

I looked to the Corona, hopeful that one of those plans would work.

She thought about that for a moment before the corners of her mouth turned down. "All communication to and from the dominion is limited and being monitored," she said. "I'm not risking a negotiation as delicate as this being picked up and spread by the media. She will have to go to Argon."

Shit. I tensed and glanced at Gannon, prepared to go against his wishes if I had to. We didn't have time or any better ideas at this point!

He searched my face, the internal battle he was waging twisting the lines of his face. Finally, he turned to the Corona, mouth pinched with frustration. "A team of my protectors and I will accompany her in and out of Virtue," he said, and I exhaled in relief. "I'll be with her every step of the way."

The Corona appeared ambivalent, but soon relented. "Very well," she said with a light shrug. "But she will need to speak with Liandra on her own. If Liandra sees you with her, she will refuse to help before Kira utters a word."

By the responding scowl on Gannon's face, I could tell he was about to argue. I stood up and went to him, cutting him off.

"She's right," I said, taking his hand in my own. "You can stay close, but we can't risk giving Liandra any reason not to hear what I have to say."

He vacillated, but after a moment, gave me a reluctant nod.

The Corona looked between us then rested back in her chair. "Good. Now that that's all sorted out," she said, focusing on me, "what do you want?"

I blinked, releasing Gannon's hand to move closer to her. "I beg your pardon?"

"Come now," she said, running a finger along her jaw. "You can't tell me that you'd be willing to do this, put yourself at risk, simply for the protection of the Realm."

I stared at her, speechless. She thought I wanted to *negotiate*, that I would use this crisis to gain something for my personal benefit. My gods, hadn't she heard a word I had just said!

"I'm doing this to protect my *family*," I said, glaring at her hard.

"Don't insult me," she said, dropping her hand to her lap. "I'm sending you into rebel territory to negotiate with an exiled leader on my behalf. What. Do. You. Want?"

I clenched my fists, fighting back rage. She thought everyone was as manipulative as her! I glanced over my shoulder, at Gannon, but he was studying the Corona with a speculative eye, offering me no insight on how to respond.

"Nothing," I said, confused now. "I don't want anything else."

She thinned her lips. "Very well," she said, coming to her feet and walking toward the door. "I'm sure you'll come up with something soon."

"There is one thing," Gannon said from behind me.

I startled and turned to him. *There is?* I searched his face, trying to figure out what he was about, but he was still focused on the Corona, giving nothing away.

She sniffed. "As I thought," she drawled, squaring her shoulders as she faced. "What is it?"

"In exchange for having Kira act as your representative," he said, "you'll appoint her to the subordinate position on Realm Council."

The floor fell out from beneath my feet. "What?!" I gasped, gaping at him.

The Corona's face fell. "You can't be serious."

"I most certainly am serious," he said, still ignoring me. "Kira has done nothing but work in the interest of the Realm only to be raked over the coals by you, the rest of leadership and now the media. In exchange for her negotiation with Liandra, you'll give her the position she's due, the position you intended to give her all along."

Intended to give me? What was going on?

As Gannon and the Corona regarded one another steadily, the air in the room went cool despite the fire blazing in the hearth.

"You *did* come to plead her case, after all," she said, glaring up at him.

Gannon smirked. "I'm not pleading," he responded. "I'm *demanding*."

Her mouth tightened while a look of deep displeasure swept across her face. "You ask for too much, Gannon," she said before gesturing at me with a dismissive wave of her hand. "Her reputation is in tatters. It would be political suicide if I appointed her. She's of no benefit to Realm Council. No one would respect, much less *follow*, her now."

"One look at the newsfeed will debunk that myth," he remarked, eyes going dark. "I'm sure you'll think of something. You know as well as I do that *any* reputation can be fixed."

* * *

"*Handing the worlds to me*," I murmured when Gannon slid into the hover, on the seat beside me.

He sent me a questioning look, fastening his safety belt.

"Before the Corona dismissed me, the first words out of her mouth were that she was *handing the worlds to me*," I said, recalling how overwrought she had been. "I didn't understand what she meant, but I do now. She was going to appoint *me* to Realm Council."

Gannon's gaze roved across my face before shifting toward the front seat of the vehicle, where Talib sat. "How long before we arrive at the arc station?" he asked the protector.

He glanced at Gannon in the rear-view mirror. "Twenty minutes."

"Good," Gannon said. "We're not to be disturbed until we arrive."

The protector nodded as he maneuvered the hover away from Realm Council residences and onto its route. At the same time, Gannon pushed a button on his right and tinted glass slid up between the front and back seats. He turned to me when the privacy window was in place.

"Shortly after you were abducted, the Corona called me in for a meeting," he said. "She told me she wanted to appoint you to Realm Council."

I stared at him. "But why?" No matter how convincing Asher was and how much I would want the role, I'd never believed that the Realm sovereign would actually give me the position. "My gods, the woman barely tolerates me."

Gannon scowled. "Isn't it obvious?" he said with a bitter twist to his mouth. "By the end of the special committee process, you had subordinates in the palm of your hand. The Corona wanted to take advantage of that type of influence. By appointing you to Realm Council, she would improve her own reputation and the rest of leadership's as well."

I shook my head, appalled by the calculated moves the Corona had been making for *my* life.

"When she told me about her plans for you," Gannon continued, "I pushed back at first, telling her to find someone else to use as her political pawn. But as she spoke, I gave the position more thought and realized it was one that's long overdue for the Realm and …" — he regarded me steadily — "one you would want."

My lips parted, primed to deny it, to say I hadn't considered the position once, but I didn't form the words. I would have been telling him a blatant lie.

A small smile came to Gannon's mouth, a knowing look to his eyes. "I told the Corona giving you the position was a good idea — not that she was asking my opinion," he said. "She merely told me, and Mila too, in order to ensure that we were on board before moving forward."

"Mila?" I blinked. "*She* knows about this too?"

He nodded. "Mila got approval from the Corona to appoint you as advisor and recommended that you lead an advisory group," he said. "She said it would help prepare you for leadership."

I stared at him speechless that all this had been going on behind my back. "Why didn't you tell me?"

Gannon winced, glancing through the window. Night had fallen some time ago and the lights from passing hovers and towering buildings filled the sky.

"I thought about telling you," he said, looking back at me. "But you had enough to worry about with your family and then Maxim and Gabriel. I didn't want you to feel pressured to prove yourself for a role that, to be frank, I didn't think you were ready to take on."

I stiffened. "You don't think I can do it?" I asked, surprised by the defensiveness in my voice. *Then why in the Realm did he just try to persuade the Corona to give it to me?!*

"That's not what I said," he replied, holding my gaze firmly. "I *know* you can do it. I just wasn't sure *you* knew that. The last time we talked about the role, you mentioned your brother, not yourself."

Oh, yes. I *had* had a tendency to do that, but that was no longer the case. "I *did* want the position … not that it matters anymore," I added, shoulders drooping as I sank into the seat. "The opportunity's lost to me now."

Gannon frowned. "We'll see about that."

I studied the determined lines of his face, and an overwhelming wave of guilt and pity for him nearly drowned me. Gannon was in love with a woman who had brought him every trouble known to man, and yet there he was, continuing to look out for me. There was no way the Corona was going to allow me back into the Judiciary, much less appoint me to Realm Council, but the fact that he would try made me want to weep.

"Thank you," I whispered, my voice threadbare from emotion.

Gannon fisted a hand on his thigh. "You shouldn't be thanking me," he bit out, glancing away. "It's the least I could do. I've been single-minded, selfishly focused on my wants with little thought about yours."

I searched his profile, wondering where this was coming from. Then I stilled, recalling Tai's harsh words. My anger at him came back in a rush. "What did Tai say to you?" I demanded.

Gannon shook his head, still looking away from me. "Nothing your parents didn't say," he murmured. "That I should have left you alone. That I was thinking only of myself." He released a weary sigh. "When this shit with the Quad's all over, we're going to have to figure out what comes next for us."

The air left my body in a gust. *What comes next?* "We're going to be together," I said, heart leaping to my throat. "*That's* what comes next."

He sent me a sidelong look, eyes a cloudy blue in the dim light. "Even without Tai?"

I blinked. "What?"

He hesitated then shifted his body toward me as much as his safety belt would allow. "If Tai tells you he doesn't want to be in a multiple, would you still want to be with me?" he asked. "Because after my conversation with him today, I don't think he does."

My heart ached. Dear gods, Gannon thought that my wanting to be with him was conditional on Tai's response. But then, why wouldn't he? I had acted willing to be with Gannon only *after* he had put a multiple relationship on the table. Before that, I had pushed him away at every turn, even using Tai to hide my feelings for him. I had become so good at putting walls between Gannon and me that I had given him the impression he wasn't enough.

"I love you, Gannon," I said fiercely, holding his gaze. "Nothing will change that."

He studied me, quiet and unmoving, and I searched his face, growing more alarmed each second by his lack of response. After telling him the three words I had held back for so long, I expected him to be overjoyed, thrilled or at the very least compelled to tell me he loved me too. Instead, Gannon sat there, simply watching me. Fear made my breathing short.

"*Say* something," I begged when I couldn't take his silence anymore.

He expelled a long, ragged breath. "I love you too."

I had never heard words so meaningful sound so bleak. Tears burned my eyes. This couldn't be happening!

I had sensed him slipping away, but had I already lost him? I had wanted to tell him I loved him so many times. Had I waited too long? My heart lurched as I unfastened my safety belt then slid over to him.

"Kira …" He glanced off, closing his eyes briefly.

I ignored the warning note in his voice and straddled his lap before shoving my hands into his hair. "I just told you I love you," I said, turning his face to mine. "Do you need me to prove it to you?"

He scowled. "Why?" he demanded, gripping my wrists and pinning them to my thighs. "Are you planning on fucking me in a hover to convince me you do?"

I stilled at the bite in his tone. He was … *angry?* Why? My gaze roamed his face, searching for answers, but found none. "Why are you mad?"

His fingers dug into my skin. "Because you're telling me what I've wanted to hear, *now*, after I've just come to realize why I shouldn't be with you!"

I wilted. "What?"

"I'm so fucking frustrated," he bit out. "I don't know how to make *us* work without *you* getting hurt."

"Weren't you the one who said a relationship didn't have to be perfect for it to work?"

He winced, shaking his head. "That was before everything came down on your head."

Anger, white hot and blinding, rushed through my veins. I shook his hands off my wrists and curled my fingers into his coat, yanking him toward me. "Don't you *fucking* dare," I seethed.

Gannon recoiled so abruptly, he might as well have hit a wall.

I shook him, tears blurring my vision. "After everything we've been through, you're not going to give me — *us* — up!" I cried. "Not now!"

His eyes widened. "You think I'm giving you up?"

I froze, struck dumb by the question. "You just said …" I released him, wondering if I had imagined the last part of our conversation. "You just said you shouldn't be with me."

"Not that I *won't*," he said, almost angrily. "My gods, I'm riddled with guilt, not madness."

Thank gods. I squeezed my eyes shut and slumped forward, against his chest.

After a silent moment during which my emotions settled, Gannon ran his hands up my back. "Is it safe for me to assume then, from your ardent response, that you're not giving *me* up?"

I sighed, sitting back to look at him. "I tried giving you up before," I said with a frown. "It didn't sit very well with me."

A small smile flittered across his mouth before disappearing just as fast. "Are you sure about this? About *us*?" he asked, eyes dimming. "I'll try my best, but I won't be able to protect you from all the adversity you're going to face."

I scoffed, lifting a brow. "You think I can't handle being with you, High Chancellor?"

He frowned, apparently not finding any humor in my quip. "I just want to prepare you," he said. "It's bound to get worse before it gets any

A relationship between restricted castes and involving someone / position has never been done before as far as I know, at least not publicly."

I sobered, but never wavered from his gaze. "I can handle it, Gannon," I said. "I'm not leaving you again. This time, you have my word."

He studied me for a few moments until a corner of his mouth curved. "Say it again," he said, running his hands down my back to grip my hips. The heat in his eyes told me exactly what he wanted to hear.

I grinned and leaned against him to wrap my arms around his shoulders. "I love you."

He smiled. "I know," he said. "I always did."

I laughed, realizing that this was true, then met his lips with my own.

Our kiss started out soft, searching and sweet, but soon turned into something else altogether. It became urgent and desperate, underscored by so much need that my arms shook as I tightened our embrace. Tears sprang to my eyes, and only when I tasted the salt between our lips did I realize they had fallen down my cheeks.

Gannon pulled away and cupped my jaw, thumbing away my tears with an expression so tender, it said more than any combination of words just how deeply he felt for me. I stared down at him, wanting to show him the same depth of my feelings right then and there. At that point, I would have shown him in the hover just as he had challenged, but a dip in our altitude signaled that the vehicle had begun its descent.

Gannon's hands slipped from my face as he glanced out of the window. I followed his line of sight, noticing the strobe lights of the arc station in the near distance. Suddenly, the love I had been basking in was replaced by dread.

Holy shit, am I really doing this? Am I going to an expelled dominion to meet with a exiled leader? I frowned, sagging under the weight of the decision I had made. What had I been thinking?

"We can think of some other way," Gannon said, breaking into my thoughts, his hands tightening around my waist as the hover got closer to the ground. "You don't have to do this."

I could tell by the determined set of his jaw and worry in his eyes that if I said the word, he would put a stop to this harebrained plan of ours, but I couldn't do that. He knew that just as well as I did.

"Yes, I do," I replied, starting to ease off his lap. "Come on. Liandra Ambassador awaits."

CHAPTER 16

Argon wasn't anything like I remembered. While the warm climate, wide expanses of seas and wild exotic foliage remained the same, a somber mood now permeated the air, dulling the impact the dominion had once had on me. Of course, when I had first visited Argon so many years ago, I had gone with enthusiasm and glee, eager to finally set foot in Khelan's birthplace. This time around, anxious determination was the only emotion that coursed through my veins.

As per protocol, Talib led the way, but in addition to him, three other protectors escorted Gannon and me into Liandra's residence. Actually, *residence* was inadequate for the place Liandra called home. The estate was a sprawling two-story building of glittering glass and steel that sat, imposing, in the middle of a maze of rambling gardens and lakes.

"You ready?" Gannon asked as we strode through an entryway filled with protectors and into a cavernous anteroom that was cool despite the heat outside.

"I don't know." I frowned, standing in front of a pair of gold-paneled doors. "I hope so."

Gannon's gaze skimmed my face before he gave Talib the go-ahead to open the doors. And then, right there, in front of his protectors and everyone else, Gannon cupped my face and planted a solid kiss on my mouth.

I gasped against his lips, and clung to his waist to steady myself. A second later, he pulled away with a small smile as heat burned a path up my neck and to my cheeks.

"I'll be standing out here if you need me," he said, gesturing to where his protectors had positioned themselves a few feet away, along the opposing wall. "Good luck."

My body was still humming, trying to recover from Gannon's very deliberate public kiss, so I simply responded with a jerky nod. I moved to the doors as he watched, marveling at the lovesick delight with which Gannon had successfully replaced my anxiety.

I entered a large meeting room and soon spotted a blond woman sitting in an armchair, facing a wall of windows that overlooked a lush garden.

"Hello?" I said, venturing farther into the space, searching it. I'd expected to find Liandra waiting for me.

"I didn't think I was allowed visitors," the woman muttered then twisted around to look at me with flat gray eyes. "To what do I owe the honor?"

My breath caught as I recognized who the woman was. *Liandra.*

I struggled not to show my surprise — not because of what she said, but because of her appearance. Liandra's fair complexion now had a drab pallor, and it seemed to have leached into her hair. The brilliant red that she had when I first met her was gone, leaving her locks a dull, muddy blond.

She looked me over before frowning and turning to face the windows again. "Why are you here?" she murmured, folding her arms.

Where to start? I drew in my lips and walked toward her, glancing about for somewhere to sit. I opted for the chair between her and a large wooden desk covered with an assortment of small trinkets and an intricate large metal box.

"Thank you for agreeing to meet me," I said, lowering myself in a seat.

She chuckled lightly as though amused by my remark. "You've made quite a name for yourself since we first met, haven't you," she said, then glanced at me from the corner of her eye.

I stilled. "So you remember me then," I commented, relieved. After all, I was depending on our brief, but significant, interaction to get her on my side.

"How could I forget?" Her accent, a cultured one known to many in the Elite caste, made the words sound fluid on her tongue. "You helped me find my father, dead, under a heap of rubble after the attack on Septima Two. And then, before I was placed into this glorified prison, I heard quite a bit about you from the newsfeed. It seems you, like me, have run into quite a bit of misfortune."

I thinned my lips, reading into the sarcasm in her voice. "Unfortunately, I have," I said. "But I'll get back on my feet."

She smirked. "I'm sure you will," she said. "We should all be so lucky to be involved with the high chancellor of the Realm. Shouldn't we?"

I stiffened at that, but let it go. I was there to get her help, not her respect. But before I could open my mouth, she asked, eyeing me, "So what happened to the other one?"

I blinked. "Who?"

"The self-important protector who stalked off when I told him the truth about Realm exploration," she said with a lift of her brow.

I winced. *Tai.* "You have a long memory," I said, recalling her conversation with Tai, Gannon and me while we were all in quarantine on Septima Two.

"Yes, well," she said, glimpsing out the window. "I've made it a point to commit to memory everyone who's called me a liar since Argon was expelled."

I appreciated her resentment. She had been adamant that the Realm had been exploring for a long time and that her dominion had been unjustly expelled, but no one had believed her.

"I've learned a lot since the attack," I said, eager to tell her I wasn't one of those disbelievers. "You aren't a liar. The Corona told me everything."

Liandra's eyebrows climbed her forehead. "Is that so?"

I nodded.

"Is this the Corona's new strategy then?" she asked. "Sending negotiators of ill repute to bargain on her behalf?"

My eyes widened at the quick and accurate conclusion she had drawn. Liandra Ambassador didn't suffer fools easily.

She snorted, taking in my expression. "You may as well leave now," she said, standing up and walking to the window. "I already told that woman I'm no longer interested in Argon's exemption."

Unfortunately, leaving wasn't an option — not when my uncle's life hung in the balance.

I ground my teeth, staring at her back. "I understand that the Corona lied about Realm exploration and expelled Argon unfairly," I said, "but isn't *exemption* the very thing you want for your people, what you've been demanding?"

"It is," she replied, still looking outside. "But how can I trust someone who expelled an entire dominion simply for revenge?"

I stilled. "Revenge?"

She glanced at me over her shoulder, eyes narrowed. "I thought you said the Corona told you everything."

she told me about Zenith," I said, searching her face. "What else is know?"

Liandra snorted, turning her body to me. "So the Corona sent a negotiator armed with only *part* of the truth."

I frowned. "I don't understand."

"Yes," she said, walking to the desk beside me. "I can see that you don't."

I stared at her, confused, as she picked up the metal box from the desk then pressed the pad of one thumb against the lock until it clicked and removed a crumpled sheet of paper.

"Everyone wondered why my father and I were on Septima Two at the time of the attack," she said, returning the box to the desk. "The Protectorate believed my father was responsible, but as I told you and anyone who would listen, the only reason we were there was because the Corona had invited my father."

I nodded, thinking back. "You said the print invitation she sent you had been lost in the attack."

"And it was, but not *this*," Liandra said, coming to me with the paper in hand. "This is a letter from the Corona that I found among my father's belongings after his death." She stood in front of me and held the tattered sheet out to me. "Read it."

After only a moment's hesitation, I took the piece of paper. When I straightened it out, rows of swirling handwritten text became visible.

Donal, my love,
I am mindless in my despair, completely undone.
The hours pass like years and the days like months as I pray for your return to me. Like a child, I lashed out, trying to hurt you the way you did me, but I fear I've gone too far.
I beg of you, forgive me. Come and meet me, so that I can set things right.

Yours always and forevermore,
Layla

I lifted my gaze to Liandra, words escaping me.

"I know," she drawled. "Who would have thought a woman as cold-hearted as her could express such ardor?"

The Corona's moving words weren't the reason for my shock. "Why haven't you shown this to the Protectorate?" I asked, coming to my feet, eyes wide. "This explains why you and Donal were on Septima Two, that you had a *valid* reason for being there."

While the letter may not be enough to exempt her dominion from expulsion for exploration, it would have been enough to clear her father's name *and hers* of any culpability in the attack.

"Showing it to the authorities was one of the first things I did," Liandra muttered with a scowl. "But they were of no help. They said the letter proves nothing except that the Corona and Donal had an intimate relationship, one that was none of their business or anyone else's."

My gaze fell to the letter again, reading the words over with new eyes. There actually wasn't anything in the letter that proved Donal and Liandra were invited to Septima Two. The note only revealed the Corona had been filled with regret and yearning for someone she loved.

"They were in love with each other," I murmured, meeting Liandra's gaze.

"Well, she certainly was in love with *him*," she said. "My father never mentioned the Corona as a love interest. Not even once. As far as I knew he was heavily involved with a woman from Septima. He told me he was thinking of partnering with her but needed to end a relationship with someone else first."

I easily made a guess. "The Corona."

She nodded, smoothing her palms down her beige dress. "From her letter, it seems my father had, in fact, broken things off with her," she said. "And if you know anything about Layla Sovereign, then you know my father's rejection wouldn't go over very well."

I studied her. "My gods, you think the Corona expelled Argon to get back at your father," I said, searching her face. "That's what you meant by 'revenge.'"

Liandra's eyes hardened. "Isn't it obvious?" she said, gesturing to the letter still in my hand. "The woman was beside herself, enough to have wanted to hurt my father. Expelling his dominion would be the most effective way to get back at him."

I shook my head, having a hard time believing it. The Corona was a cunning woman who plotted actions far in advance. I couldn't imagine her acting so recklessly. But then ... hadn't she said something along these lines just weeks ago, before my abduction?

I made a rash decision to spite someone I loved but who didn't love me back ... People are dead and the Realm is fractured and torn apart because of me ... I hope you and Gannon find your way back to each other ... I don't want Gannon to do what I did.

"My gods," I breathed.

Liandra frowned and took the letter from my hands. "Now you understand why I'm no longer interested in exemption and why I will never trust that woman," she said, replacing the sheet in the box. "There's only one person I can trust from now on."

Yes, I understood, but she was misguided if she thought turning to rebels was the answer. "Are you sure you can trust Maxim Noble?" I asked.

Liandra's gaze sharpened. "How do you know that name?"

I exhaled a tight breath. "He and his partner Gabriel Minister are threatening to kill a member of my family if I don't help them," I said. "That's why I'm here. If you tell us where to find Maxim in exchange for

Argon's exemption, then maybe we can stop him before he hurts my uncle or anyone else."

Her expression went cold, but her eyes blazed with defiance. "Maxim would *never* kill anyone, especially someone who has nothing to do with the cause."

The cause? Was Liandra so far gone, needing to trust someone, that she was willing to romanticize Maxim's crimes?

"Maxim's not some virtuous savior fighting against a system that has done you and your citizens wrong," I said, scowling at her. "Maxim's *cause*, his primary motivation, is a new Realm order."

"Well, maybe that's just what we need," she tossed back. "Because the system we have is ruled by a woman who makes decisions on a whim and out of spite!"

I narrowed my gaze. "Would you want the Realm to be ruled by the man responsible for your father's death instead?"

She shrank, paling. "What?"

I stepped toward her. "Maxim coordinated the attack on the Corona's arc craft on Septima Two," I said. "He didn't know you or your father would be there, but it's because of *Maxim* that your father and so many others are dead."

For a long time Liandra said nothing, just stared at me as a combination of misery and contempt spread all over her face. "Get out," she said through clenched teeth.

"I'm not leaving," I said, holding my ground. "I'm telling you the truth."

She shook her head. "You don't know what you're t-talking about," she stammered, emotion breaking her speech. "Maxim could never have p-planned something like that."

"Yet he did," I insisted. "He told me so himself after taking me hostage in an alley behind my Judiciary on Prospect Eight."

"You're a liar," she spat, clenching her fists so hard they shook by her side. "I said get out!"

A movement beyond Liandra's shoulder caught my attention. I shifted my gaze to the door and found Gannon standing there, body tense with concern, appearing ready to intervene. He must have heard Liandra's shout. I raised my hand, staying him, and was grateful when he remained where he stood.

I took a breath and met Liandra's wary gaze. "Your father's gone, but your citizens still depend on you," I said, attempting to tackle her resistance from a different angle. "Think about them. Will you make your people suffer under some rebel regime just to spite the Corona? Look at all the upheaval acts of revenge have caused so far."

Her gaze shuttered, anger flagging a bit, but she shook her head. "That won't happen," he replied. "Maxim only wants what's best for me and the people of Argon."

My shoulders fell, failure crushing me. In my desperation to save my uncle, I had hoped to convince Liandra to give Maxim up, but her connection to the man was too strong. If she wouldn't give him up to save her own people, there was no chance she would do so to help my family.

I looked to Gannon, encroaching helplessness making me wilt.

He clenched his fists as he stepped farther into the room. "Maxim doesn't *care* about *your people*, Liandra," he bit out, and she turned to face him. "He coordinated an attack in Tork to try to kill me, but my father and others were killed instead. If your father was anything like my own, he'd want you to lead, not to become a follower, taking direction from the rebel who ended his life."

Liandra stilled and took an unsteady step toward him. "Tork?" she said, searching his face. "On Hale Three?"

Gannon frowned. "Yes." He exchanged a look with me, and I went to stand by his side. "Why?"

Liandra sagged. "Weeks ago, while I was still in holding in Capita, a subordinate working for the Corona came to me late one night," she said. "I found it odd that he had arrived unaccompanied, without the official entourage, until he handed me a note. It was from Maxim. He said he had failed to get justice from leadership on Septima Two, but that he would try again … on Hale Three."

Gannon nodded, searching her stricken face. "He was talking about both attacks," he said. "The one that nearly killed the Corona and the one that murdered my father. How much more proof do you need?"

"Maxim isn't the answer, Liandra," I said, heart aching at the torture in her gray eyes. "Accept the Corona's offer of exemption and tell us where Maxim is before he hurts anyone else."

Liandra's face crumbled as she glanced away, a palm pressed to her mouth. For a long moment, she struggled with her emotions, appearing torn between falling apart and railing against the worlds. Then she swallowed, seeming to gather herself, and raised eyes glittering with tears to mine.

"All right," she said in a hollow voice. "I'll tell you where he is."

The relief that came over me nearly knocked me out cold.

"But it won't be enough."

Gannon's worried gaze mine before he asked her, "What do you mean?"

"You said Maxim wants to hurt a member of her family," she said to him. "Unfortunately, if you do manage to capture Maxim, his partner will simply pick up where he left off."

My recent relief receded, becoming a distant memory. "We're hoping that finding Maxim will lead us to Gabriel too," I said.

She shook her head. "It won't be quite that easy," she said, looking to me now. "They make sure to stay in different towns, changing locations every few days. I know Maxim's movements, but not Gabriel's. You'll have to find some other way to draw him out."

*　*　*

I walked at a clip, matching Gannon's pace as we headed for the front doors of Liandra's residence. "We have to think of another plan," I said as we approached the row of glittering hovers that had been waiting for our return.

"I know," he replied tightly, squinting against the sun when we stepped outside, into the hot, humid air. "But first things first."

He turned to Talib. "Tell the high marshal that Maxim Noble and possibly other members of the Quad are in Summit, on Prospect Eight."

The protector nodded then addressed his team, giving them orders in a clipped voice.

Before disclosing Maxim's location, Liandra had provided Gannon with a long list of demands she expected to be met in exchange. Within less than a week, she expected her father to be publicly absolved from all allegations related to exploration and the attack on Septima Two. She also demanded that her dominion be compensated through funding for her citizens' months of hardship and grief.

I expected the Corona to have no problem with those demands, but I couldn't imagine her agreeing to some of Liandra's others, including her own immediate appointment to her father's position as ambassador of Argon on Realm Council. Still, I didn't argue the point. I was too anxious to leave her residence and use the information she shared to track down Maxim.

The door to our hover slid shut after I sat down, inside it. "What are we going to do?" I sent Gannon a fretful glance as he settled into the vehicle beside me.

Gannon took my hand. "We're going to do exactly what Liandra said, Kira," he said with a determined set to his mouth. "We'll draw him out."

But how?

Talib slid into the front seat of the vehicle then addressed his superior, looking back in the rear-view mirror. "The high marshal's coordinating a team heading for Summit," he reported. "Would you like to go to Summit to meet him or return to Merit?"

"Merit," Gannon said, face grim. "The Corona will want to hear what Liandra had to say as soon as possible."

Talib nodded then started navigating the vehicle as what Gannon said sunk in. Liandra had had *plenty* to say — more than Gannon or I had banked on.

I glanced at Gannon, a knot tightening in my belly.

If what Liandra had said was true, the Corona had expelled Argon and sent the Realm into turmoil for selfish and unforgiveable reasons. What she had done out of spite had led to many deaths, including Gannon's father's.

I considered Gannon with a knot in my belly, wondering how to tell him. I couldn't let him speak with the Corona without knowing the full story, at least the story according to Liandra.

Gannon must have sensed my gaze on him because he glanced down at me. When his eyes went wide, I knew my expression looked as anguished as I felt.

"What's wrong?"

I squeezed his hand. "I have to tell you something."

He watched me closely as I fumbled through an account of what Liandra told me, about the reason she believed the Corona had expelled the dominion. Tears blurred my eyes as I described the sovereign's handwritten letter and how she had expressed guilt to me for having taken some drastic action. It was all just a speculation, of course, but one that offered a fitting explanation for what she had done.

When I finished, Gannon sat quietly, fingers still wrapped around mine, but now his palm was as cool as his expression. I couldn't imagine what he was thinking. In some perverse way, it would have been easier for me to accept that rebels, foes of the Realm, were responsible for my father's death instead of the leader of our system and someone he and his family had known for years. I mourned his loss all over again.

"I'm so sorry," I whispered, wishing he'd respond in some way.

He sat back against his seat and stared through the window. I didn't release him. Instead, I kept hold of his hand, warming it between my palms.

By the formidable slant to his mouth, I assumed his thoughts had turned to the Corona or his father, so it took me aback when he said, "What's Gabriel's weakness?"

I blinked a couple times. "What?"

He turned his head to look at me, eyes still remote, but thankfully now with a flicker of his usual determination. "You worked with Gabriel for some time," he began. "You probably know him better than anyone in the know at this point. The only way to draw Gabriel out is to use his weakness against him. What's his?"

I balked. *Weakness?* Gabriel *had* no weakness. The man was as vindictive and manipulative as the sovereign, but the surprising vulnerability she had shown in her note to Donal Ambassador just wasn't something Gabriel Minister was capable of.

"I-I don't know that he has one."

Gannon scowled. "Everyone has a weakness, Kira," he said. "*Think.*"

I hunted my brain for clues. What in the Realm would drive Gabriel to risk making himself vulnerable and possibly captured! *Vulnerable* just wasn't part of Gabriel's genetic composition ... Then again, I hadn't thought vulnerable was a part of the Corona's makeup, either. Hadn't her impassioned letter proven otherwise? There was another side to the Corona. *Was* there another side to Gabriel as well?

No one thought Gabriel would amount to much, but he did. Well ... until he was dismissed from the Judiciary.

When Asher had told me about Gabriel's past, I hadn't been willing to give it much thought. The woeful tale had only explained the strength of Gabriel's hatred toward me. If Gabriel had *any* weakness at all, it had to be his unrelenting need for power and revenge. It was those personality traits that had probably driven him to join the Quad after his dismissal from the Judiciary. To Gabriel, being at the helm of a new Realm order was probably the *only* opportunity for leadership and retribution he had left. He would fight tooth and nail, and maybe do something foolish like come out of the woodwork, to keep it.

My eyes widened. *That's it!*

Gannon's eyes roamed my face. "You have an idea," he guessed, his grip tightening around my hand.

"I think so," I said, hope making the idea grow. "But for it to work, I'll need to call in a favor that's *long* overdue."

* * *

I craned my neck and squinted, trying to make out the face of a passerby through the windows. But from where I sat, at a table at the back of Drunk Dominion, I had no luck.

I sighed and checked my comm for the fourth time. *Where is he?*

I had expected Heath to have arrived already. Despite his odd hesitation when I had called him, telling him I wanted to meet, I figured he would have greeted me at the bar with a full media crew in tow. Yet half an hour after the time we had agreed upon, he had yet to show.

Hopefully, he wasn't *actually* trying to round up a media crew. I would rather make my plea for his help *without* an audience. Well, an audience besides Talib, who stood patiently behind me.

After talking my idea through with Gannon and contacting Heath, Gannon had ordered Talib to accompany me to Drunk, while he went on, escorted by his other protectors, to meet with the Corona. By the time the protector and I had walked into the Old World pub–style bar, hours later, the sun had sunk low enough that the chandeliers had been illuminated inside. As I had hoped, the crowd was meager since the work day hadn't quite ended.

My comm vibrated, and I glanced down at its screen, anticipating an update from Gannon. Instead, the amber glow bloomed then faded as Mila's name appeared.

Come to the Judiciary tomorrow morning.

My hearted stopped. Why did Mila want to see me? Despite how much Gannon believed in his ability to make the Corona do what he wanted, I didn't believe for a second she had any intention of welcoming me back to the Judiciary ... *Which can only mean Mila wants to discuss the terms of my dismissal.*

I scowled at my comm. All Above, had the Corona no loyalty to anyone but herself? I had just helped her locate a member of a major rebel group! I hadn't for a moment expected her to give in to Gannon's demands, but could she not have given me a few days, put on some *pretense* of complying, before giving me the boot?!

Talib shifted behind me, and I glanced up as the door to Drunk opened. The noisy sounds from outside wandered in, and so did someone I couldn't remember ever being so happy to lay my eyes on.

Heath!

Like everything else in my life, my worries about the Judiciary would have to wait and take a back seat to dealing with Gabriel.

I stood up and waited, fidgeting with my hands, for him to see me. When he did, he shuffled forward, hands shoved deep inside the pockets of a knee-length jacket that swamped his narrow build. He approached, skirting tables and chairs as he glanced about from under his lashes. He was only a few steps away when he came to a sudden stop, his hands raised.

"Whoa," he said, eyes flaring wide as they took in Talib. "What's with all the brute force?"

I frowned. Certainly, it was unexpected to see a protector with me, but Heath was more taken aback than he should have been. While he didn't know yet about the threat hanging over my head, Heath *was* part of the media. He *had* to know just how much attention I had attracted after my relationship with Gannon had been revealed. Having protection of some sort shouldn't have been too difficult for him to understand.

I sighed, folding my arms. "After everything the Realm Anarchist said about me," I replied, "I should probably have my own *team* of protectors, don't you think?"

Heath had a fair complexion, but as soon as I said that, he went sheet white. "No matter how things turned out for you," he said, gaze skittering to Talib then back to me, "you *have* to admit your reputation grew because of that story."

My gods, had Heath become so blinded as part of the media, he couldn't see what *that* kind of popularity had cost me?

"Yes, my reputation grew, Heath," I said, frown deepening. "But I would never have wanted to be suspended from my position in exchange for that."

Heath's shoulders caved, making his slight build appear even more thin within the folds of his coat.

"Holy shit," he breathed, holding onto the back of the chair closest to him. Its leg scraped the floor, shifting under his weight. "How'd you find out?"

My eyebrows climbed. "Find out about what?"

"You *have* to believe me," he said, tossing another uneasy look at Talib. "I *never* expected all this to happen to you."

I tilted my head, trying to understand. "What are you talking about?" I asked as something teased the edges of my mind.

For a few moments, Heath stared at me, mouth working as though he were trying to figure out how to speak. "Nothing," he said finally, drawing up the chair.

He sat down and glanced up at me, clapping his hands together, all business-like, before resting them on the table. "So what can I do for you?"

I frowned, looking him over and wondering what all that was about. It would take me more than a lifetime to figure out all of Heath Reporter's quirks. Unfortunately, I didn't have the luxury of that time.

I sat down. "I need your help."

A smile crept across his mouth. "This should be interesting."

Over the next few minutes, I told Heath about Gabriel, the reason for his despise for me and how it led him to align with Maxim Noble to establish the Quad. I ended on a shaky breath, hoping beyond hope that this was the last time I would have to recap my ordeal.

"So … let me get this straight," Heath said, sitting back and hooking an arm over the back of his chair. "Two defected members of leadership abused and abducted you, and are now threatening to kill a member of your family if you don't give them some highly classified information that would, *should it get out*, rock the Realm to its core."

"Yes," I breathed, relieved he had understood the quick and dirty rundown of my life.

He grinned, dark blue eyes gleaming now. "Now *that's* the kind of story that'll grant me seniority!" he declared. "Halls, I'll have my superior eating out of the palm of my hand for *years* to come."

The glee on his face made me grit my teeth. "I'm not telling you this to help you *gain rank*, Heath."

His grin fell and he shifted forward, placing both his elbows back on the table. "Then I don't get it," he said. "If you don't want me to tell your story, why are we here? Shouldn't you be off embedded somewhere with the high chancellor and the full force of the Protectorate, trying to dig up the Quad's whereabouts, as we speak?"

I sighed. "That's the thing," I said. "We know where Maxim is. It's *Gabriel's* location we're not sure about. Our best bet right now is to lure him out of hiding by using his weakness against him, and the only way I can think to do that is by threatening the one thing he has left: his standing among the Quad."

Heath nodded slowly. "All right. Got it," he said. "Now, what does all of *that* have to do with me?"

I leaned forward with my elbows on the table. "I want you to run a story about Gabriel, telling everyone what he's been up to," I said. "That he's been working with the factions against the Realm."

Heath's brows knitted. "But how will giving Gabriel a bad rap hurt him or help you?" he asked. "He has nothing to lose. He's been demoted, and on the fringe. All you'll do is push him further into hiding."

This was where it got sticky. "Not if your story reports that Gabriel double-crossed Maxim and told the authorities where to find him," I said. "If word gets out that Gabriel's an informer, the Quad won't trust him. Actually, *none* of the factions will. They'll all kick him out for throwing their own to the wolves. Gabriel's last hope for power will be taken away."

It took Heath a minute, but soon clarity brightened his eyes. He rocked back in his chair. "You want me to frame Gabriel Minister as a *traitor* to the Quad."

I fidgeted, gaze sliding away from his for a split second before retuning to his. "Well, not outright," I said. "If you simply report Gabriel's support for the Quad and note that the Protectorate has learned about one of Maxim's hideouts, it shouldn't be a hard sell."

Heath tilted his head, eyeing me. "But Gabriel *isn't* responsible for Maxim's capture," he remarked. "Is he."

I stiffened at the unnerving smirk that bloomed across Heath's face. He folded his arms, looking me over. "Who would have thought that you, *Kira Metallurgist*, would be asking *me* to make a story up."

I didn't blame him for throwing that in my face, but considering how had played with words before, he was in no position to act like some champion of integrity. "I'm sure you realize then just how desperate my situation is that I would ask you for a favor like this."

"I do," he said readily. "But it doesn't change the fact you want me to twist the truth for your own self-interests."

I frowned at Heath's self-satisfied expression as a boisterous group of subordinates spilled into the bar. They spoke animatedly, making a beeline for an empty table not too far from three other subordinates who had been sitting there since Talib and I had arrived.

Damn it. The after-work crowd was starting to show up. I needed to get Heath onside before the bar became too crowded and we could be overheard. The only way to do that was to speak his language.

"This is about just about my family and me," I said, holding Heath's gaze. "It's about protecting the Realm as well."

Heath's gaze narrowed, smirk slipping from his face. "I'm listening."

"The Quad isn't just some struggling grassroots faction," I replied. "It's probably the largest organized rebel group in our history, and its sole purpose is to create a new Realm order. Do you want to live in a system with rogues at the top? What significance will *your career* have when men like Gabriel Minister lead our worlds?"

He considered that, eyes flickering from me to Talib, who still stood silently nearby. "I don't know, Kira …"

I staved off panic. "*Please*, Heath," I pleaded, gripping the edge of the table. "This time use your storytelling for something more than just getting ahead."

He flinched then studied me for an agonizing length of time before releasing a deep sigh.

"Look, I wish I could, but I can't," he said, shaking his head. "It's one thing to tell a story about a subordinate and her love interest, but to tell a story like *this*, about a member of leadership and without evidence? Holy shit, if my superior found out, I'd be lucky if I ever held a position in the media again!"

Any hope I had remaining took a sharp nosedive. I hung my head, squeezing my eyelids shut. All Above, I didn't have any cards left to play! If Gabriel wasn't in Summit, there just wasn't any way Gannon and I could come up with a plan to stop him in time. He had won. Gabriel would kill Uncle Paol and reveal everything about my family. We would be torn apart and Adria left fatherless, all because of the hatred of a man I had tried my best to support.

For the first time in my life, I resented having worked at the Judiciary. If I hadn't been there, then I wouldn't have met Gabriel and *none* of this would be happening. Then again, I wouldn't have met and fallen in love with Gannon, which was an alternate reality I'd never accept.

Love interest?

I opened my eyelids, staring down at my hands. Had I heard Heath correctly or had I made those words up? No, he had said them. But why? He had never written a story that reported on any *love interest* of mine. He didn't know about my relationship with either Gannon or Tai.

How'd you find out? I never expected all this to happen to you. Heath's confusing question and remarks suddenly became clear.

I gasped, lifting my head. "*You*," I whispered.

Heath stilled. "Me what?"

"You did this," I accused, and a flush of color came to his cheeks as his eyes went wide. "You told everyone about my relationship with Gannon. *You're* the Realm Anarchist!"

Heath's face twisted as he leaned across the table to grip my wrist and pulled me hard toward him. "Would you keep your voice down!" he hissed, eyes glittering as he glanced over my shoulder at Talib.

To his credit, the protector kept his gaze on our surroundings, acting as though he hadn't heard a word, which was impossible since he was standing so close.

I yanked my wrist out of Heath's hold. "This whole time ...," I said hoarsely, looking at him anew. "That's why you've been so interested in me. You've been collecting material for your anonymous tabloid. My gods, you got me suspended!"

Heath wilted, but there was a scowl on his face. "I didn't expect that," he said tightly. "I figured you'd just get a slap on the wrist. Who would've thought the Judiciary would punish its rising star?"

Fool. "How did you get the photos of Gannon and me?" I demanded, wanting to shake him by the collar.

"It's not as hard as you think," he muttered. "There are cameras in most governance and law buildings. It was just a matter of sifting through a few hours of video footage and connecting the dots."

I stared at him. Halls, *Heath Reporter* was the *Realm Anarchist?!* I couldn't imagine two more *different* personalities. Heath was so focused on his career, driven to get ahead by any means. Whereas the Realm Anarchist, he was all about attracting attention by spreading rumors and bending the truth ... well, kind of like Heath.

I glared at him. "You cost me my position," I said. "You *owe* me."

Heath balked. "What?"

"You're going to run the story about Gabriel," I said. "You can't sit there, on your high horse, and tell me you're worried about the *integrity of your career* when you're leading a double life."

He frowned, searching my face. "Are you going to blow my cover?"

I considered that a moment. "No," I said. "I'm not interested in bringing the authorities or the hundreds of people who probably have a bone to pick with you down on your head. I just want protect my family." My shoulders drooped. "So, *please.* Help me."

Heath shoved a hand through his hair, leaving it in a disarray. "All right. All right," he ground out. "I'll do it. But under a different name."

CHAPTER 17

Where was everyone?

I peeked into the kitchen, but no one was there, so I leaned against the doorframe, looking around. My parents' house was unusually quiet considering a rambunctious two-year-old lived there. Could they have gone out?

Somewhere deep inside, I hoped that was the case. My parents' absence would give me the excuse to turn tail and head home instead of having to face them and their shameless judgment all over again. But Rhoan had probably told them about Uncle Paol's visit and that I had gone to Gannon for help. I may not have wanted to speak with my parents since our argument, but I couldn't bring myself to leave them, or Da, worried and in the dark about my whereabouts all over again.

A ripple of my cousin's laughter trickled down the hall out of Da's study. Taking a deep breath to ease the sudden tightness in my chest, I pushed away from the door and followed the sound. As soon as I reached the threshold of the room, Adria spotted me.

"Kira!" she squealed, launching herself toward me and wrapping her arms around my legs. I scooped her up, smiling then burrowed my face into her neck. The little girl giggled and squirmed out of my arms to pick up where she must have left off, playing with her assortment of toys. With no other choice, I steeled myself and met my parents' gazes.

Da was sitting on the chair closest to his desk close to Addy, while Khelan and Ma were together on the couch. Their expressions were drawn and cheerless, but the underlying relief on their faces was hard to miss.

"We were wondering how long you'd leave us to suffer, wondering what happened to you," Khelan said, eyes sunken and dark.

I hung back by the door. "I came as soon as I could."

Da sighed, thinning his lips. "Rhoan said you spoke with the high chancellor," he said.

I nodded, stepping farther into the room. "And Tai too," I said. "The three of us came up with a plan and now we know where Maxim is. It's just a matter of time before we capture Maxim and hopefully Gabriel too."

I didn't utter a word about meeting with the Corona, going to Argon or my conversation with Heath. The same went for my looming dismissal. Telling my parents would only send them into another fit of worry. We needed to focus on stopping Maxim and Gabriel, not arguing about actions that were irreversible, completely beyond their control.

Khelan scowled up at me. "I told him we didn't need his help."

I stiffened. I knew who *him* was. "And yet you have Gannon's help all the same."

Khelan's eyes were snapping when his lips parted, about to speak, but Ma cut in, stopping him by placing her hand on his.

"*He's* the James you were talking about, isn't he," she asked me.

"Who?"

"The high chancellor," she explained, and I remembered at once. "Your father showed me an article about his appointment. It had his full name."

Oh. I shifted my weight on my feet, looking from one parent to the other.

The three of them stared at me, an expectant look on their faces.

What did they expect? Some word of praise for the amateur sleuthing they had done behind my back?

Khelan clenched a fist. "So, you haven't changed your mind then," he said. "You *still* plan on throwing everything away so you can be with him?"

I shook my head. My gods, were they still dwelling on that? "I'm not *throwing* anything away," I stated. "I'm more than capable of rebuilding my career, having a *happy* life, no matter who I'm with."

Khelan didn't reply. In fact, no one did. They simply considered me quietly, eyes dimming with equal parts of displeasure and dismay. Meanwhile, Adria made a little sing-song noise, as oblivious as she should be to the drama unfolding around her.

My lungs seized up, chest aching at my parents' silent refusal to give an inch. I took a step back, toward the door.

Why had I even bothered to come? I should have listened to my gut feelings and left, to give them more time. Maybe once Maxim was captured, they would believe Gannon had my best interest at heart, just as much as Tai.

"I … I should go," I mumbled, bumping into the doorframe in my haste to leave. "I just wanted you to know I was all right and that everything might be working out."

I considered Adria, wanting to hug her goodbye, but didn't. She'd just become alarmed by the tears coming to my eyes.

Inhaling a sputtering breath, I hurried out of the room and ignored Ma when she called out to me, rushing back to the kitchen instead. I managed to make it to the table and collapsed, wheezing now, into a chair. Of course! After everything I had gone through over the past few weeks — an abduction, multiple threats, the loss of my rank, venturing into rebel territory — *now* was when I decided to have another panic attack!

I glanced about the room, dragging in mouthfuls of air. I needed *solumen*. Ma usually kept a bottle of the treatment somewhere in the kitchen. I just needed to calm down enough so I could find it.

After a few more gulps, I flattened my palms on the table and tried to push up to stand, but couldn't. The room tilted, and I became light-headed before falling right back in my seat.

Damn it! *Deep breath in. Deep breath out.* I closed my eyelids and rested my head between my shaking hands.

A moment later, the sound of cabinets opening and closing made me glance up. I found Da walking to me with a bottle of clear liquid in one hand and a glass in the other. He stood by my chair and filled the glass with the *solumen*.

"Here," he said, holding it out to me.

With a trembling hand, I took it and drank. Da sat down beside me and waited, as did I, for my attack to subside.

"I guess you didn't outgrow your panic attacks," he murmured minutes later.

I glanced at him and found a shadow of a smile on his face. I couldn't help it. I laughed, then Da joined me. Soon, both of us were laughing hard as though it had been a long while, which I supposed it *had* been. I couldn't remember when we had had something worth laughing about.

Moments later, our laughter waned, and we considered one another, me wondering what to say and him appearing to ponder the same thing.

Da placed the bottle of *solumen* on the table then braced his hands on his thighs, staring down between his legs at the floor. "We just want more for your life than what we had," he said, still not meeting my eyes. "It's what every parent wants."

I sighed, resting my now empty glass on the table. "I know," I said, my breath coming much easier now. "But shouldn't my life be based on what *I* want, not you?"

He glimpsed at me from the corner of his eye. "What you want is an uphill battle, Kira," he said, frowning. "We want you to have *every* opportunity. Khelan, your mother and I made a lot of compromises so you wouldn't become the outsider you're so willing to be."

My face fell. Ma's parents had almost disowned her and Khelan had had to hide, leaving everything he knew behind just to be with Ma and me. Da, too, had to make compromises and set aside his differences. Looking back, it was a testament to the strength of their relationship and their love for Rhoan and me that they had remained together and maintained a family.

I swallowed. "Are you saying you regret everything you did?" The idea of it nearly brought tears back to my eyes.

Da made a face, his shoulders falling as he sat back in the chair. "No. *Never*," he said firmly. "What I'm saying is being with Gannon Consul isn't going to be as romantic as everyone in the newsfeed is making it out to be. His position will probably keep a few doors open, but there are going to be many others that slam in your face."

I appreciated his concerns — they were valid, after all — but he didn't have a chance in the Realm of convincing me to stay away from Gannon. "I can handle it," I said, echoing the very words I had spoken to Gannon just hours earlier.

Da studied me then scrubbed a hand over his face. "All right," he said, dropping his hand to his lap. "What about Tai? Where does he fit into all this?"

I glanced away, staring down at the neat crisscross pattern of Ma's tablecloth. Da's question was a logical one, but I couldn't find the right words to reply. My emotions and thoughts were all jumbled around inside my head. Tai had been evasive, combative and flat-out resistant to the idea of being in a multiple with me from the start. And now, after the way he had gone around me and confronted Gannon, I truly couldn't say I knew where he stood.

"He can't handle it," Da said.

My gaze moved to his, a question on my face.

"Tai, that is," he clarified, expression grim. "He can't handle the idea of sharing his love for you with someone else."

My lips parted as I stared at Da in wonder. How he always managed to do that, I didn't know. In just a few words, he had hit the nail on the head, summarizing my fears and making me face the truth I had been unwilling to accept.

I pressed my lips together, trying to hold it together. "No," I whispered. "I don't think he can."

* * *

"Should I tell the high chancellor you'll be delayed?" Talib asked, as we exited the elevator and entered the dimly lit hallway.

I shook my head, leading the way to Tai's apartment. "Actually, I won't be seeing Gannon tonight."

The protector's usually blank expression slipped, and he grimaced. "He won't be pleased to hear about this," he replied. "The high chancellor sent strict orders that you were to return you to his residence after your meeting with the reporter."

"I know." I recalled the message Gannon had sent me ten minutes earlier, demanding that I do that very thing. "Can you please tell him I'll see him tomorrow, right after my meeting with Mila?"

Talib's jaw tightened but, thankfully, he didn't push. I had a strong feeling I would need a moment by myself after the conversation I was about to have with Tai.

When we stopped in front of Tai's door, I pressed the call button and held my breath until it slid open moments later.

As expected, even at the late hour, Tai was fully dressed in a uniform that never seemed to crease. He rested a hand against the doorjamb as his gaze moved impassively from me to Talib. He gave the other protector a short nod of recognition before stepping back and looking to me. "Come in."

I swallowed and stepped through the door.

Tai's apartment was as orderly as usual, except for a noticeable disarray centered in the middle of his sitting area. His duffel bag rested on the floor by the couch and sheaves of paper were scattered on the coffee table among an assortment of tablets. By the way everything was strewn about, Tai seemed to have been readying himself for something, and with a great urgency.

I frowned, confused and worried. When I had sent a message to Tai asking to meet, he hadn't mentioned anything about being in a rush or on the way out. He had simply said I should come to his apartment within the hour.

"Are you going somewhere?" I asked him as he walked toward the couch.

He bent over to collect his bag. "I'm heading to Summit."

My eyes widened. There was only one reason Tai would be headed there. "You heard from Gannon then?" I asked, stepping closer to him. "He told you we found out where Maxim is."

He shook his head, picking up a tablet and dropping it in his bag. "It was the high marshal who told me, actually." He glanced at me. "I guess this means your meeting with the Corona was successful."

I nodded slowly, wondering at the firm set to his jaw. "I ended up having to meet with Liandra myself."

Tai's face fell, and his shoulders went slack. "You went to *Argon Four?*"

I winced. "With Gannon," I rushed to add. "Liandra told the two of us where Maxim is."

He studied me, brows knitted, as though trying to piece together everything I had said. "And Gabriel?" he asked. "Did she tell you where to find him?"

I sighed, shaking my head and wrapping my arms about my waist.

Tai's lips thinned. "All right," he muttered before scrubbing his free hand across his mouth. "We still need to come up with a plan to stop Gabriel, then."

"We already did," I said before wincing. "At least, I *hope* we did. You see, I met with a reporter. Gannon and I are hoping that, by framing Gabriel for Maxim's capture, we'll force him out of hiding."

"So you're using the media to your own advantage now," Tai said, eyes going flat.

I stiffened, struck by the irony and a sudden attack of conscience. Heath certainly owed me an apology after the story he had written as the Realm Anarchist about Gannon and me, but did he owe me *this*? Although I'd had a good reason for asking, I had essentially demanded that Heath use his alter ego, one that could ruin his career should it be revealed, to serve my own interests.

I sighed. "I take it you think that was a bad idea."

Tai snorted. "Would it matter to you if I did?"

I frowned at his tone and overall detachment. "What's wrong?"

He tossed his bag on the couch then pinched the bridge of his nose. "Why are you here?" he asked, looking at me now with his hands on his hips. "You and Gannon obviously have everything taken care of."

"I'm here because we have a lot to talk about, Tai," I said then sighed, dropping my hands to my sides. "You went behind my back. After telling you what I wanted, that I wanted to be with both you *and Gannon*, you tried to convince him to give me up." I searched his face. "How could you *do* something like that?"

"What did you expect me to do, Kira?" he said through tight lips. "Relationships like that … they don't work for everyone, especially when it involves someone from a restricted caste."

What was he *talking* about? He should have known better. "My *parents* are in a relationship like that," I said. "And they're doing just fine."

"Are they?" he scoffed, making me draw back. "It may seem so on the surface, but someone *always* plays second fiddle in that kind of arrangement."

It took me a few tries to recover from the shock. *Second fiddle? Is that* what he thought? "You think I would put my love for Gannon *above* my love for you?"

A flicker of uncertainty skipped across his face. "I'm not saying that it would be your intention, but …" He shrugged.

Tai's unwillingness to complete his sentence said more than enough. "If *that's* how little you think I care about you, *love* you," I said, "then it's a wonder you were even willing to *consider* being in a multiple with me."

"I was willing to *consider* it because I didn't have choice," he stated, eyes glinting. "I was losing you."

"*Losing* me?" I shook my head, wondering who this man was. "You were *never* losing me. I've *always* been here, willing to do anything to be with you."

"Except let him go."

I flinched. "What?" I whispered, hurt he was trying to make this about me.

"You made your decision to be with Gannon a long time ago," he ground out, his body rigid as he stared me down. "The moment you took *that*," he gestured to my chest where the promise ring still rested, "it was *him* over me."

Reflexively, I touched the jewelry, staring up at him, *shocked* at the lengths he would go to push me away. First he had tried to make Gannon into some diabolical mastermind, and now he was trying to suggest I would play favorites — both of which were untrue. Now more than ever I knew Da was right. Tai was smarter than this. His resistance *had* to be tied to some unexplained reason he didn't think he could handle a relationship like the one I wanted with him.

I moved to him, reaching for his hand. "Are you worried about your rank?" Like my position, his own would come under scrutiny if he agreed to be part of this kind of multiple. "It would be awkward at first, but your superior has a lot of respect for you, and I'm certain your reputation would ensure you maintained your position."

Tai cringed as he pulled his hand from mine. "I don't care about that," he said, stepping back and running a palm around his nape. "It hadn't even entered my mind."

My hand fell to my side. Then what *had* entered his mind?

I gave what he had said earlier some deeper thought. "Very well. You're right," I admitted. "My parents *aren't* fine. They've had a difficult time and have gone through a lot to be together, but they're making it work. You have to believe I would do *everything* in my power to do the same."

"I'm sure you'd try," he said, eyes glittering with some pent-up emotion. "But not everything works out just because you want it to."

I searched his face, clenching my fists. "Why are you making this so much harder than it has to be?" I demanded, giving up trying to figure out the reason for his uncompromising attitude. "If you love me, then why won't you just *be* with me?!"

His nostrils flared. "You act as if not wanting to share you with someone else makes me some selfish fuck," he cursed, glaring at me. "I want to be with you, Kira, but not like this!"

My body went cold, heart sinking low, nearly into my gut. There it was: the answer I was looking for, the reason I had come.

"So you've made up your mind then," I said, sagging. "About us, that is."

A tic came to Tai's jaw as he glanced away. "Damn it, Kira," he said in a strained voice before his gaze returned to mine. "I don't have the time to get into this. I'm supposed to leave in ten minutes to report to my superior. We'll talk about it when I get back from Summit."

"Why wait?" I shrugged, but it was only a pretense of nonchalance. My heart beat heavily behind my ribs. "Let's just get this over with. Now."

His face tightened, expression shuttering. "No."

I looked Tai over, truly took him in. *A cowardly lion.* That's what he reminded me of. The timeless storybook character who talked a big game, but when it came down to it, couldn't — or rather, *wouldn't* — put words into action because of fear. Tai was a protector, brave enough to fight off all my enemies, but not strong enough to tell me the truth: that he was scared, that he couldn't manage not being the only love in my life.

Why am I forcing this? I had already *begged* Tai to be with me. I wasn't about to do it again. I was tired of fighting for a man who didn't want me — at least, not enough.

My nose burned with unshed tears. "One day you're going to have to allow yourself to be vulnerable for someone you care about," I said quietly. "Nothing's perfect, Tai. Love's no exception to that."

He stared down at me for a long, painful moment, face locked in misery.

I swallowed back a sob, resenting his refusal to respond. "I just want you to know it didn't have to end this way," I said, heartache making my voice shake. "You didn't have to give me up."

He grimaced, eyes flashing with pain and remorse as he studied me. Finally, he said, "I can't give up someone I never had."

CHAPTER 18

"I want to introduce you to someone."

At the sound of Asher's voice, I pasted a smile on my face then turned to find him poking his head in through my office door. Well, *the* office door. The space was no longer mine, so I was going to have to get used to referring it that way. And the sooner the better. I was probably only minutes away from having the office taken away.

Just as Mila had ordered, I had turned up at the Judiciary the following morning, numb after a restless night's sleep yet prepared to hear what she had to say. *So* prepared, in fact, that I had already started packing my few belongings away. I placed the framed photo of my family inside a packing container I had discovered in a meeting room down the hall and inhaled a fortifying breath.

Asher's grin was broad as he stepped aside and revealed a young woman with candy-colored hair and a bright smile. She rushed forward.

"I'm *so* excited to meet you!" she squealed, grabbing hold of my hand with her pink bangs bobbing. "When Asher told me you were here, I just *had* to stop by and say hello!"

My eyes widened as the woman shook my hand so earnestly, my entire body shook.

Asher peered at me from around her shoulder. "*This* is Maralis Clerk," he said with a waggle of his brows.

I chuckled. "I figured as much," I said, reclaiming my hand from her grip before introducing myself. "I'm Kira Metallurgist."

"Oh, I know," she gushed, smoothing her hands down the front of her black knit cardigan and skirt. "It's such an honor. My friends couldn't believe it when I told them I worked in the same branch of the Judiciary as *the* Kira Metallurgist!"

Asher beamed, but my smile shook.

Everyone at the Judiciary was under the impression I had returned to the Judiciary to reclaim my position after enduring a high-profile punishment, one which had only left me more popular than disgraced. The first thing I should have said to Asher when he had met me in the reception area that morning was that I had come to face an even more dismal fate. But I hadn't, too emotionally spent after the tumult I had been embroiled in over the last few days to do anything but allow him to usher me to the office and sit quietly as he updated me on Judiciary affairs.

"So." Maralis clapped her hands together and leaned toward me, a conspiratorial glimmer in her hazel eyes. "Were you *truly* in a relationship with the high chancellor?"

I blinked at the blunt question, and Asher groaned.

"Oh my gods, I'm so sorry," Maralis gasped, hands flying to her chest. "I have this *awful* tendency to say the very first thing that comes to mind!"

A smile grew on my mouth. I was going to have to get used to responding to questions like this. Moreover, it was refreshing to be asked *directly* about my relationship with Gannon rather than be subjected to whispers about it behind my back.

"Yes," I said, rolling my shoulders back. "I *was* with the high chancellor, and I *am* with him still."

Maralis fairly swooned. "How romantic!" she declared, making Asher roll his eyes.

I laughed. Asher couldn't fool me. Despite his apparent exasperation, I knew just how much of a romantic he was too!

A light rap at the door called my attention. Simeon Administrator, a colleague I had the fortune of calling a friend, poked his red head inside the office. "Good to see you back," he said with a wink.

I smiled, ignoring the pang of guilt that came from not telling my colleagues, my *friends*, the true reason I had returned.

I should tell them now. No, that wasn't a good idea. Asher and I had been through a lot. He was going to be crushed to learn we were no longer going to be working together. I needed to tell him *first*, one on one.

After speaking with Mila, I would take Asher aside and give him the bad news.

Simeon dipped his head toward Maralis. "Meeting's starting up again," he said. "You coming?"

"Oh yes, I have to go," she announced, glancing at me. "My superior's probably wondering where I am by now. Lucky for me, everyone's been so busy talking about the Anarchist's upcoming announcement or I wouldn't have been able to sneak out to meet you."

I leaned against the desk, pondering Maralis' remark as she waved a goodbye to Asher and hurried out of the office with Simeon.

The Anarchist's upcoming announcement?

Heath had promised to run the story about Gabriel and Maxim under a different name. Unless Heath had *other* shameless alter egos I wasn't aware of, I took his promise to mean he would publish the article as the Realm Anarchist. Was *that* the announcement Maralis was talking about? I hoped so. I didn't have any more cards to play if Heath lost courage and backed out.

Asher perched on the desk, beside me, and flicked a glance my way. "So, you and the high chancellor have worked things out, huh?" he asked. "Are you really involved again, even after all that happened?"

I nodded and leaning against his side. "Yes."

Asher sighed, shifting to wrap an arm around my shoulder. "Good," he said with a bob of his head. "Now the two of us can be weak in the knees *together* for someone we work with at the Judiciary."

I chuckled for a fleeting moment before remembering that wasn't true. I *wasn't* working at the Judiciary. Damn it, I really needed to tell Asher the truth. I had procrastinated long enough.

"Asher, I have something to tell you," I began, staring down at my feet. "I —"

Another rap at the door, this one sharp and quick, made me look up. I straightened, and Asher did too.

Mila swept a frigid gaze from Asher before focusing it on me. "Come along," she said, and without waiting for a response, stalked off.

My stomach turned.

"Whoa," Asher said, looking me over with wide eyes. "Is there some *other* misdemeanor you've committed that you haven't filled me in on? Mila usually reserves the foul attitude for the rest of *us* — not *you*."

I sighed, stepping away from my desk on unsteady legs. "I'll look for you after I talk to Mila," I said. "All right?"

He nodded, but curiosity burned bright in his eyes. "You know where to find me."

By the time I caught up to Mila, she was striding across the main work area and nearly at her office.

She glanced at me out of the corner of her eyes. "Do you know why I called you in this morning?" she asked, our path clearing as people caught sight of us.

I pressed my lips into a thin, tight line, yet still managed to say, "I have a good idea."

Mila sniffed. "Good," she said, walking through her office door, ahead of me. "This should be a very brief meeting, then."

I nodded. Yes, I supposed issuing a dismissal wouldn't require much of small talk or lengthy conversation.

She gestured to the chair as the door slid shut, closing out the din from the buzzing work area. I sat down heavily and waited patiently as Mila moved to stand behind her desk.

"The last time I saw you," she said, considering me with a steely eye, "I sent you off to meet the Corona, expecting I'd be welcoming you back to the Judiciary within a few days, but that wasn't to be the case, was it."

I shook my head, my gaze slipping from her and to my hands.

"Instead," she said, "hours after your meeting, the Protectorate issued a memo to select leadership, including me, about a breach in database protocol. You can imagine my surprise when I learned someone used *my* issuer ID to access highly classified files, and that *that* someone was *you*."

Despite a twinge of guilt that burned my cheeks, I lifted my chin to meet her eyes. "I had a good reason."

Mila scowled. "Oh, I'm certain you did," she said. "Which only pisses me off all the fucking more that you didn't think to simply come to me. I would've given you any file you needed, Kira, within reason."

The guilt eating away at me took a deeper bite. *Would* Mila have helped me if I had gone to her? Probably not, but I would never know because, no matter what, I couldn't have asked her. Doing so would have only resulted in *her* being dismissed as well as me. I couldn't do that to her. Not after all she had done for me.

Mila had been more than just my superior. She'd been a mentor. She had helped me through the special committee process, had appointed me to the position of advisor and had even supported the Corona's plans to appoint me to Realm Council — all clear signs of the confidence, respect and *trust* she had had in me. All Above, the woman had even overlooked my relationship with Gannon! Mila wasn't the type of person who would do all that for just *anyone*. And what had I done? I had used her name to commit a felony. In her mind, she probably believed I had taken all her good intentions for granted and thrown them in her face.

I couldn't leave the Judiciary with her thinking I would be so callous and ungrateful.

"Mila," I began, ready to spill everything out, to tell her about Gabriel and Maxim, why she wouldn't have been able to help me, why I *had* to do what I had done. She would probably dismiss me anyway, but at least I would go having earned back even a *little* bit of her respect. "I can expl—"

"The time for *explanations* has passed, don't you think?" She unbuttoned her jacket before lowering herself into her chair. "And truly, what difference would it make? It's not as though you'll be suffering any lasting consequences. I can only assume you managed to negotiate your way back into our sovereign's good graces."

I frowned. Mila's humor could be harsh, but I didn't think she could be so cruel as to *joke* about something as important as my career, or lack thereof. "Good graces?"

Mila nodded. "The Corona told me to return you to the Judiciary, with rank, immediately."

My mouth fell open. "She did what?"

Her eyes narrowed. "This shouldn't come as a surprise," she said. "You just said you knew why you were here. Didn't the Corona tell you all this?"

I stared at her, snapping my mouth closed and scouring for a way to cover up my slip. My gods, I wasn't being dismissed! The Corona, a woman who had no compunction to lie, manipulate, or deceive had kept her word. But why? And what did this mean?

To get answers, the best thing to do was keep my mouth shut and listen to what Mila had to say.

"Um, y-yes," I hedged, sitting up straight. "The Realm sovereign and I might have had a conversation or two about my future here at the Judiciary." That wasn't a total lie.

Mila nodded, eyeing me. "That's what I thought," she said, leaning to one side and resting an elbow on an arm of her chair. "You see, she told me there was a misunderstanding, or rather a *mistake*, on the Protectorate's part. She said you never tried to access those confidential files and ordered me to bring you back. She also ordered me to have a very thorough conversation with the receptionist who reported you to ensure he understands this error has all been sorted out."

Oh. "I see."

Mila snorted, smirking. "Kira, you know as well as I do that the Protectorate doesn't make *mistakes*," she said. "I don't know what the arrangement is between you and the Corona, why exactly she's letting you off the hook, but I have a strong feeling the weight of the high chancellor has something to do with it."

I remained quiet on that point. It really was the best thing to do.

Mila shrugged. "You don't have to tell me the reason," she said. "I don't really give a shit. All I have to say is: Well played, Kira Metallurgist."

I stared, dazed by her unexpected pat on the back. "So …" I cleared my throat. "Are you saying I'll be able to lead the advisory group again?" I couldn't keep the disbelief and hope out of my voice.

"Maybe."

I blinked. Did Mila mean to invite me back to the Judiciary with rank while limiting my responsibilities at the same time? "I don't understand."

She contemplated me for a moment. "The Corona told me to bring you back," she said, "but I'm going to need some assurances if I'm going to allow you to actually *lead* the advisory group again."

So, I had been given another chance but had lost Mila's trust nevertheless. *Damn it.*

"You have my word, Mila," I vowed. "I'll *never* to try to access confidential files, or misuse your ID, again."

She snorted. "You're smarter than to commit the same felonious act again," she said with a hint of warning that was both fair and unmistakable. "*That's* not my concern. What I want to know is what you hope to accomplish."

I frowned. "Accomplish?"

"Yes," she said. "Here at the Judiciary, leading the advisory group."

I shifted in my seat, wondering whether that was a question, then said, "I want to help Realm Council implement safe exploration across our system."

"Yes," Mila replied. "But what's your end goal, your ambition?"

It clicked. My motivation: *that's* what she wanted to know.

Mila had asked me that question just after appointing me advisor, and I had said something about upholding the law and advancing my dominion and the system because it was the right thing to do, but she had found my answer lacking. Reflecting on my earlier reply now, I had to agree.

I had given Mila a textbook response, something probably inspired from my time at the Academy. After my public disgrace and breach of database protocol, I couldn't give her such a shallow answer again. Mila deserved a response worthy of someone she could respect and that better reflected who I had become.

"I have to be honest," I began, fiddling with the cuff of my sleeve. "When I started at the Judiciary, I didn't know what I wanted to do with my career. I just wanted to travel beyond my own world, to visit others our system like someone who was, and *is*, like a father to me."

I reflected on how much I had looked up to Khelan and his own career at the Judiciary. He had had such high hopes for me at the Judiciary, and had always encouraged me to go after my dreams. While Da had always shown support for my career, Khelan was the one who had always believed I was meant for more. What that *more* was, I had never considered. I had taken Khelan's unwavering encouragement simply as a sign of his love for me, something one loved one said to another. But now, looking back at all I had accomplished at the Judiciary, maybe he had seen something in me I had only recently started to recognize in myself.

I wet my lips, sitting up. "It didn't take long for me to find my own path, though," I continued. "I formed relationships with citizens of every caste as I supported the task force and special committee, gaining their trust and respect. It's because of those relationships and my work ethic that, even with all that's happened to me and my reputation over the last few weeks, I've *still* managed to hold so many people's confidence." I held Mila's steady gaze. "I know now, without any doubt, that I'm meant to advise Realm Council on exploration because I'm a leader, and there's no one better prepared or driven to a better job than me."

Mila nodded. "I agree," she said. "But think *beyond* all that. Being advisor on exploration is an opportunity that could lead to even greater opportunities, perhaps representing your caste's interests in broader areas. So, as a *leader* of your caste, what is it you'd hope to achieve?"

I stilled. My gods, could it be? I had doubted every step of the way that the Corona would appoint me to Realm Council, but there Mila was, talking as though it was a very *real* possibility.

I blew out a shaky breath, the import of her question weighing even heavier on me now. *My motivation.* I had to remember: *that* was what Mila wanted to know.

My gaze dropped to my lap where one hand was now wringing the other. The tracking device Tai had given moved loosely around my wrist, reminding me of the threat waiting for me beyond the walls of the Judiciary. At the same time, the ring Gannon had given me, resting in plain sight on my chest, reminded me of the heartache he and I had experienced, all because of the restrictions between our castes.

Most, if not all, of the problems I had faced in my life so far had been triggered by some decision, lie or act of revenge that had been carried out by leadership. My uncle had been driven by grief to rebels after my aunt's death during the early fallout from Argon's unjust expulsion. My parents had hidden their relationship and the truth about who my birth father was for *years* because of Realm restrictions on intercaste relationships. Those same restrictions had turned my love for Gannon into a scandal that had jeopardized my career. And now Maxim and Gabriel, two former members of Realm leadership, were threatening to take even more away from me.

Everything in my life had been determined by leadership. Once, not too long ago, I would have adhered to leadership's decisions without question, viewing leadership as wise and well intentioned as they worked toward the advancement of the Realm. But now, after understanding what they were capable of, what they had done and how much of an impact they had had on my life and others', my view had changed. It had *had* to. Leadership were fallible, had their weaknesses, just like every other citizen — no matter the caste.

I met Mila's gaze. "For years, subordinates have wanted their interests to be heard at the highest level of our system," I said. "As leader of my caste, I would voice our interests and ensure that leadership include them in their every decision. My goal, my *motivation* would be to balance the scales by removing all boundaries between our castes that encourage acts of dissension and prevent the advancement of the Realm."

Mila raised a brow. "*All* of them?"

I frowned. "Pardon me?"

She shifted forward in her seat and rested her elbows on the desk, in front of her. "You said you would remove 'all boundaries between our castes,'" she said, gaze narrowing. "What does that mean?"

I studied her, catching the shrewd glint in her eyes, and instantly realized what she was getting at.

Mila was no fool, and never would be. She liked me, maybe even respected me, yet she wondered now whether my *personal* interest — that is, my relationship with Gannon — was underlying my motivation. I certainly had every personal reason to be motivated to remove intercaste restrictions, but that wasn't the foremost matter on my mind. Perhaps it was because I had already flouted that convention, and my parents had too, that I didn't see taking on intercaste restrictions as an immediate burning need. Frankly, it probably wouldn't be too difficult to petition for a change in the restrictions. Gannon had threatened to do it in the past, before he had become high chancellor, but I had told him not to, that he had too much to lose. Though everything had changed now, I still didn't like the idea. Should the Corona actually appoint me to Realm Council, I couldn't make the removal of intercaste restrictions one of my first proposals. Leadership would view it a self-serving to both Gannon and me. Moreover, the Realm had much greater, more critical, issues to tackle right now.

"Maybe one day those boundaries will be removed," I said to Mila, who was still considering me with a steady gaze. "But right now, my focus would be on giving my caste a voice and ensuring their welfare. And with the factions gaining members every day and becoming more of a threat to the Realm, I would see protecting subordinates and the future of *all* our citizens as my number one concern."

Mila studied me, brows knitted, the lines of her face drawn tight in apparent dep contemplation. She assessed me for so long, I soon started to doubt my answer. I had given her the best response I could, one that meant something to me, that I could stand behind, that would drive my work whether it was to support her *or* Realm Council. If *that* wasn't enough to assure her that I had enough motivation, then nothing would be.

I tipped up my chin, staring her down. "Is that the answer you were looking for?"

Mila considered me for another long moment before eased. She nodded with a faint smile. "It'll do."

* * *

Gannon wrapped his arms around my waist and held me against him, in a tight embrace.

"I was expecting you last night," he said quietly against my ear.

I stiffened at the accusation in his voice. I had asked Talib to tell Gannon I wouldn't be able to go to him the night before, but I hadn't explicitly told the protector to tell him why. I had simply assumed he would have told his superior my whereabouts.

"I went to see Tai," I explained, wishing I had told Gannon earlier. Now it could only look as though I were trying to hide something from him. "We had a lot to discuss."

A pause. "Such as?"

I sighed and eased out his hold to look up at him. "I don't think we should get into this now," I said, frowning. "We have a lot of more important things to talk about first. Don't you think?"

A flash of impatience sped across Gannon's face. Apparently, he was prepared to discuss those *more important things* later, not now.

Before I could react, he glanced over my head, and said, "What is it?"

I turned to see Talib standing behind me.

"Perhaps I should contact Jonah," he said. "There's still time for him to come here before I'm required to leave."

I frowned, surprised by the rare unease in the protector's tone. On the trip over to Gannon's residence, Talib had mentioned something about being called by the high marshal to an urgent meeting and having to leave immediately after we arrived. He hadn't appeared too concerned about anything at that time, or even before he had left Gannon and me in the entryway and had announced that he wanted to conduct a security check of the townhouse before heading out.

Gannon pulled me into his side, seeming to sense my disquiet. "Is something wrong?" he asked.

"When I arrived with Subordinate Metallurgist," he said before gesturing to the front door, "I had to enter the entry code three times before we were able to enter."

Gannon frowned. "Isn't the system working?"

Talib hesitated. "I didn't find any malfunctions in the program during my security check," he said. "Every now and then, the security system resets and requires reauthorization. This is probably one of those times."

Gannon studied him, his hold on me tightening. "I see."

The two men then engaged in a silent communication that I didn't understand. I would probably need *years* of having Talib as my confidant and guard to do that.

Gannon's gaze fell to me briefly before returning to the protector. "Go on to your meeting," he ordered. "It's too important for you to be late. On your way, tell Jonah to get here as soon as he can."

Talib covered a brief display of dissatisfaction with a deferential nod. As he exchanged a few parting words with Gannon, I wandered into the sitting area.

The monitor was on but the volume low; images of different members of leadership moved onscreen. Every now and then a reporter would be displayed, speaking animatedly. I walked farther into the room, tugging on the sleeve of my jacket to remove it as I went. Heath had said that he would run the story, but he had yet to do so. Could I trust him to follow through? Who knew? The fact was, I had put a lot of my faith in a man whose alter ego was an untrustworthy shit-disturber. *Damn it.*

I sighed, dropping my jacket on the couch, and my worried thoughts fell to the wayside when my gaze landed on the veritable feast spread out on the coffee table in front of me.

In another life, Gannon would have been a chef, but I couldn't imagine he felt the compulsion to create a *banquet* like this after the whirlwind we had just been through. "My gods, did you *make* all this?" I asked him when he entered the room.

He snorted, approaching me. "When would I have done that?" he drawled. "During my free time between helping you try to save your family and the Realm?"

I sent him a quelling look, which he answered with a smirk.

He stood by my side, hands on his hips, and joined me in surveying the dishes filled high with fruits, pastries and meats. "I may have gone overboard," he admitted, "but I figured the consumption of copious amounts of food was the best way to celebrate."

I cocked my head. "Celebrate what?"

A smile spread across Gannon's face as he turned his head to look at me. "We got him," he said, smile deepening. "We captured Maxim."

I stilled. "What?"

He searched my face as though trying to gauge my response and reached for my hand. "I received a report from the high marshal an hour ago," he said, excitement making his blue eyes gleam. "It's why Talib is going to meet with him now. The high marshal wants to debrief him on what happened and the next steps."

Eyes wide, I staggered to him when he pulled me against him. "Where?" I breathed, crushing his shirt between my fingers. "Where did you find him?"

"Just where Liandra said he would be," he said, still smiling down at me. "In Summit, in some abandoned storage building he was using as a base. The high marshal says Maxim's on his way to Capita right now, to a facility where he'll be detained until the rest of Realm Council has been informed."

I stared up at him, tremors of shock moving through my body. I couldn't believe it.

"Why didn't Talib tell me?" I demanded. The protector had been quiet, saying nothing on the way to Gannon's townhouse except that he had to leave for a meeting with the high marshal. I wasn't Talib's superior, but my gods, we had history! He must know how much this news would mean to me!

"I told him not to," he said with a laugh, cupping my jaw. "I wanted to tell you myself. And the news hasn't been made public yet. It was best to wait until you were here."

My gods. It was over. Or *was* it? "What about Gabriel?" I asked, eyes tearing up with hope.

The light in Gannon's eyes faded a bit. "He wasn't there."

I squeezed my eyelids shut and rested my forehead against his chest. Of *course* not. That would have been too easy. A few tears slipped down my cheeks.

"We'll get him," Gannon vowed, rubbing my back. "We've got Maxim in holding. I told the high marshal to interrogate Gabriel's whereabouts out of him any way he can. It's just a matter of time."

It *was* a matter of time — time that was running out fast. Any moment now, I could expect to either hear that my uncle had been killed or that my family secrets had been revealed.

A few tears escaped through my closed eyes, and I held onto Gannon, trying to draw strength. Suddenly, his body went stiff, and I raised my head.

"What is it?" I asked, wiping at my cheeks, but Gannon didn't reply.

Instead, he stepped toward the monitor and issued a command to increase the volume. A reporter's voice filled the room.

"News from the Realm Anarchist continues to grip the attention of citizens across the Realm — this time, with an announcement the anonymous reporter just made about senator Gabriel Minister, former leader of Prospect Eight. The Anarchist alleges that since his suspicious demotion months ago, the minister has been supporting the factions, going so far as aligning with an unidentified rebel elite and establishing the Quad, the largest rebel group in Realm history.

"Unfortunately, it seems the minister's loyalty to the Quad was short-lived. The Anarchist suggests that, in an effort to regain his rank, Gabriel Minister informed the Protectorate of where to find the elite and possibly other members of the growing rebel group."

My shoulders went slack. My gods, he did it. Heath, as the Realm Anarchist, had come through after all!

"Didn't you say you were going to meet a reporter, someone named Heath?" Gannon asked with a frown, gaze focused on the monitor.

I grimaced. "I did."

Gannon eyed me, over his shoulder, raising a brow. "Either *Heath* has friends in low places, or he's got a disturbing secret."

I figured I didn't need to answer. I mean, Gannon hadn't actually asked me a question.

"Holy gods, Kira," he said, turning to glare at me. "Tell me you didn't spill *our* secrets to the *Realm Anarchist* — the man who exposed our relationship and got you suspended."

I scowled, jamming my hands on my hips. "Of course, I didn't *know* Heath was the Anarchist when I went to meet him," I replied. "But it worked out in the end. Because of what he'd done, he felt obligated to help to me."

Gannon continued glowering, and I responded with a lift of my chin. He could get as angry as he wanted. As he had said, my situation couldn't really get any worse than it already was. I'd had no other options, and the horse was already out of the gate.

Gannon ground his teeth before turning the monitor off with another verbal command. "I don't care who published the bloody story, as long as it's out," he said, running a hand through his hair. "Hopefully, between that story and the Maxim's interrogation, we can ferret Gabriel out."

Thank gods he understood. I didn't want to argue with him about my methods when so much was on the line. I sighed, dropping my hands to my sides.

He looked me over. "Come on," he said, gesturing to the couch. I moved toward it, but instead of sitting on the furniture, I lowered myself to the floor and sat cross-legged. I patted the spot beside me, and smiled when he joined me with an indulgent grin.

"How'd your meeting with Mila go?" he asked, reaching for a plate then filling it with food. After handing it to me, he picked up a small quidberry and a carving knife then stretched his legs out beside mine.

"My meeting with Mila was …" I searched for the word as I fussed with the hem of my dress around my thighs. "… *unexpected.*"

He raised a brow in inquiry as he handled the knife with deft fingers, slicing into the fruit.

I bent a knee, shifting on the floor to face him, a ribbon of excitement winding through me. "You're not going to believe it." I couldn't help the wonder in my voice. "Mila told me I could return me to the Judiciary with my rank, effective immediately. I think … maybe … that the Corona's planning to appoint me to Realm Council after all."

He frowned. "Why wouldn't I believe that?" he asked. "I demanded that the Corona do that very thing."

I rolled my eyes. As usual, Gannon believed once he commanded something, it *must* happen. "The woman's not exactly the most trustworthy individual."

He nodded. "Let's just say she had a little *extra* motivation to comply with my demands," he said before placing a bite-sized piece of fruit in his mouth.

I took in the hard, determined glint to his eyes. *Oh no.* "What did you do?"

"While you were off meeting with the *Realm Anarchist* ..." — he snorted, shaking his head as though in disbelief — "I was meeting with the Realm sovereign. I told her if she didn't meet Liandra's or my demands, I would issue a notice to leadership in short order telling them the *real* reason she expelled Argon and sent the Realm into a tailspin of civil unrest and death." He glanced at me, and my eyes went wide.

I sat up straight. "You threatened the *Corona?*" Senator or not, Gannon could have been detained for committing an offense like that.

"I did." He slid another piece into his mouth and chewed.

I stared at him, at a loss for words, until it dawned on me. The Corona wouldn't have allowed Gannon to make that type of threat if it didn't carry weight.

"Are you trying to tell me the Corona *admitted* she was in a relationship with Donal Ambassador and that she falsely accused Argon of exploration?"

Gannon laughed. "The Corona rarely, if ever, admits to guilt," he said, "but her silence when I confronted her with Liandra's claims spoke louder than words."

Ah, now *that* made sense. I couldn't imagine the Corona confessing anything. I had never met someone so unwilling to take responsibility for their own actions.

"Now that I think about it," I said, staring down at the food on the plate, now cradled on my lap. "I don't know that I should want that position on Realm Council as much I do anymore. I'm not sure I could stomach working with a woman like that."

"That's all right," Gannon said easily, placing the knife and remainder of his fruit on the table, in front of us. "She won't be on Realm Council for long."

My gaze snapped to his. "What?"

His gaze darkened in the unseasonably bright afternoon sunlight that was filtering in through the windows. "Did you think I was going to simply allow her to continue to lead the Realm after what she's done to citizens across our systems, to *your* family, to *mine?*" he said, fisting a hand on his thigh. "I won't rest until the Corona is removed from her position."

A sliver of apprehension slid up my spine. "But how?" I asked. "Only the Elite caste can vote to remove a Corona from position, and they've never done anything like that before."

"There's a first time for everything," he said, gaze focusing inward. "It'll take a while, but I've already put the wheels in motion. Believe me, there are more than enough elite citizens willing to take the Corona's place. It's just a matter of identifying the right one."

Revenge. I stared at Gannon, instantly recognizing the emotion burning in his eyes, and it made me sick to my stomach. My discomfort wasn't born out of any sense of morality — the Corona *should* be made to pay for her manipulation and lies. I just didn't want vengeance, something that had claimed so many people in my life, to consume Gannon, or *me*, any more than it already had.

Gannon shifted, folding his arms. "Now tell me about Tai."

I jarred, lips parting in surprise at the shift in conversation. "About Tai?" He nodded. "There's really nothing to say."

"Does he want to be in a multiple?"

I swallowed, my gaze finding my plate of food again. "No," I said. "He doesn't."

"And how does that make you feel?"

I took my time before responding, searching for the right word. "Sad."

"Why?"

I released a wobbly breath. "Because he's too scared to give us a try," I said. "Instead he gave me up."

Gannon seemed to give that some thought then asked, "If Tai turned around and said he wanted a second chance. What then? What would you do?"

I gave the question the consideration it deserved then raised my head. "Then it would be too bad," I said. "He had his chance." He wouldn't be getting another.

Gannon's eyes didn't shift from mine. "Good."

I blinked. *Good?*

"Now that *that's* out of the way, there's something I've wanted to tell you," he said. "It's been burning a hole in my chest."

My breath caught at the worry lines forming around his mouth. "What is it?"

He continued holding my gaze. "I only offered to be in a multiple because I knew Tai would say no," he admitted.

I rocked back. *Oh my gods.* "You *lied* to me." Was it just like Tai had said? Had Gannon simply been using strategy to get what he wanted?

Gannon grimaced, taking my hand and squeezing it hard. "I wasn't lying," he insisted. "I was trying to prevent you from having to choose, to make a decision you weren't willing to make. You love Tai *and* me, and you weren't going to let either of us go. I wasn't about to let you go either, so it came down to Tai. *He* had to be the one to make the decision, and he made the one I suspected he would."

I searched his face, trying to make sense of what he was saying. On one hand, Gannon said he wasn't lying, that he had been trying to bring an end to the limbo we had all been in. But on the other hand, he admitted to betting against Tai's willingness to be with me, which sounded at the very least like manipulation, if not a lie. There was only one way to get to figure it all out.

I eyed him. "What would you have done if Tai had called your bluff and said he wanted to be in a multiple?"

"Then I would have swallowed my pride and followed through," he said quickly. "I would agree to a multiple because all I want is to be with you, Kira, no matter what it takes. After you left my office in Capita, I immediately started rethinking what I'd done, but then the shit hit the fan about us in the newsfeed and your uncle reappeared." He released a deep breath, deep grooves forming around his mouth and eyes. "I wish I could say I regret forcing Tai's hand and pushing him to finally let you go, but … I *love* you, Kira. I wasn't going to let you go, especially without a fight."

I swallowed, trying to ignore the shameful wave of delight and yearning his words sent rolling through me. Holy gods, why that aroused me, I didn't know.

I should have been spitting mad, but I couldn't summon anything even *remotely* close to such a justifiable emotion. Instead, my traitorous body warmed, lighting up, my nipples stiffening. I licked my lips as my gaze fell to his.

Gannon's gaze swept over my face and chest. "You're turned on," he observed, a slight tinge of awe in his voice.

Rather than lying through my teeth to deny it, I remained silent.

He cocked his head, studying me like I was some puzzle to be solved. Slowly, a wicked gleam filled to his eyes. "Where do you want to do this, *Lahra?*" he asked. "Here, on the floor, or upstairs, in my bed?"

I shuddered, nearly coming on the spot.

I swallowed and closed my eyes, trying to pull my thoughts together to form a response.

I liked the idea of quick and dirty sex on the floor, but it had been too long since we'd last made love. What I needed, what *we* needed from each other now, was going to be long and hard. I wanted to be in Gannon's bedroom, somewhere Jonah or some other protector Talib might send wouldn't walk in and catch us, mid-fuck.

I looked up at him. "Upstairs," I whispered, and Gannon grinned.

"Good choice."

CHAPTER 19

My sex was wet, tight and throbbing by the time we made it to Gannon's room. I headed for the bed, but Gannon had other plans. Grabbing me by my waist, he stopped me and pressed my back against the wall, just inside the door, before capturing my mouth with his. I sighed, releasing a ragged breath, as I wound my arms around his shoulders and tipped up on my toes to deepen our kiss.

"I think you misunderstood me," I said with a smile as his lips moved to my jaw. "I wanted to be taken mercilessly in your *bed*, not against the wall."

"It's too far," he complained, making a trail of damp kisses toward my neck. "I want you here."

I laughed. "We're less than two feet away," I said, catching sight of his bed beyond his shoulder, just behind him. Its crisp white sheets beckoned under the soft glow of the late-afternoon sunlight.

I placed my hands on his chest with a laugh, trying to urge him toward the bed, but he caught my wrists and pinned them to the wall next to my thighs.

"I said," he stated in a quiet voice, "I want you *here*."

Oh. I sagged, a puff of air escaping between my lips. There it was. The control, the dominance I had always craved from him. It had been so long since we had made love, *fucked*, that I had forgotten myself, forgotten how it was between us.

I wet my lips, staring up at him, nodding. "All right."

A smile tugged at the corner of his mouth. "Keep your hands here," he instructed.

When I nodded again, he chuckled. "I must say," he remarked, bracing his forearm against the wall, beside my head, "I've been going about this all wrong. To try to keep you with me, I should have simply made every one of my demands in the bedroom. It's the only place I've ever seen you so compliant."

My head lolled back against the wall as his free hand moved down my leg. "I don't think it has anything to do with *where* we are," I mumbled, distracted by his searching caresses under the hem of my dress. "It has everything to do with *you*."

He leaned in, his mouth a breath away from mine as his hand eased between my thighs. "Are you saying no one else has never made you feel this way?"

I raised my head, frowning at his question, sensing where it was coming from. "That's right," I replied. "No one, including Tai, has ever made me feel this way."

His hand stilled, close to the heat of my sex, as he stared down at me. Shadows came to his eyes, darkening them. "I hated every second being apart from you, wondering if you would come back to me," he said, gaze roaming my face. "After you left me, I had never felt so at a loss, confused. First I lost my father and then you … I didn't know which was worse."

Remorse pierced my heart, making my breath catch. The words "I'm sorry" came to my mind, but they never reached my lips. Gannon knew why I had left him, why I had *had* to. I wanted to protect him, but in the

332

end it had been no use, an act of futility. We were inevitable, just like he had said.

I have no future without you.

What Gannon had said to me weeks ago, after I had left him, or had *tried* to leave him, shattered me now as much as it did then. I had disregarded the declaration at the time, dismissing it as simply a final attempt to keep me with him. But I should have known better. Gannon didn't say anything he didn't mean, at least when it came to me.

When he had said he had no future without me, he had meant it. It was why he had given me the promise ring. It was a symbol of our future together, that we were *meant* to be together. And I couldn't think of anywhere else I would rather be.

I smiled up at him, tears clogging my throat. "I love you," I said, and marveled at the way those three words chased away the darkness in his eyes.

A smile came to his lips before he leaned forward and kissed me. I matched him lick for lick as he devoured my mouth. When he grazed his teeth along my bottom lip, I did the same to him, drawing out a hoarse groan from deep inside his chest. My fingers flexed, nails clawing the wall, as I willed my hands to stay where they were.

But when his fingers moved under the thin edge of my panties and slid into my throbbing sex, I reached for him reflexively, pulling him close. His fingers stilled at once and he pulled back to look down at me, brows knitted by a look of disapproval.

Oh, right. I flattened my palms against the wall.

His forbidding expression lightened. "Thank you," he said with grin, then leaned closer to me to capture my lips again.

The buttons at the back of my dress scratched the wall as I moaned, body arching toward him, growing more desperate to have him inside me, to have him own my body the way he always did.

His fingers started pumping inside me as we kissed. I writhed, parting my legs more to give him better access, but still it wasn't enough. I needed more than just his hand and tongue.

"Please," I panted, grinding down on his fingers, showing him just how hard I badly I wanted to be fucked.

He pulled back, eyes at half mast with desire, and pulled his hand away from me. I had just opened my mouth, about to protest the absence of his fingers inside my heat, when he pressed them to my lips.

"Taste it," he said with an air of challenge and expectation.

I stilled as my arousal scented the air between us. I nearly laughed that he considered what he was asking for to be a challenge. I would have done anything to keep that savage look of desire glinting in his eyes.

Holding Gannon's gaze, I lapped at his fingers and my body thrummed with delight as he watched me with his hooded eyes. The salty, tangy flavor of my sex coated my tongue, and he licked his lips as though tasting it with me. He must have wanted to do just that because, after watching me a moment, he pulled his fingers from my mouth and slid them into his own.

Holy shit. I swallowed, body quivering, as he sucked away whatever flavor I had left behind.

Gannon's eyes had gone a dark shade of blue that mesmerized me as he licked his lips. He looked me over and I squirmed, pressing my thighs together to alleviate the ache. He may as well have bound me with chains to the wall for how easily he controlled me, kept me in place, with barely a touch and without removing a stitch of either our clothes.

Thankfully, he took pity on me. He made quick work of undoing his pants and releasing himself, revealing an erection as hard and long as it was mouthwatering. I licked my lips, wanting to touch him, and almost did, not caring if Gannon disapproved, but he was reaching for me before I could get my brain to work and coordinate my limbs. He gripped me by my thighs and pressed me up against the wall, splaying my legs around his waist before thrusting into me in one hard motion.

I cried out, relief and need making my voice hoarse as I curled my fingers into his shirt at his back, trying to hold on. My sex grasped at his cock greedily, hungry to be filled, desperate for release. Gannon crushed me between him and the wall and drove into me, relentless, straining against his own rising need to climax.

I angled my head as he took my mouth, holding me firmly against the wall. Sighing, I allowed my eyelids to fall closed and him to fuck me whichever way he wanted. I didn't care. He could do no wrong at that point. As long as he was inside me, loving me, I would be satisfied with however he chose to make me come.

His teeth nipped at the soft skin of my bottom lip, sending a mind-numbing shiver up my spine.

"Gannon!" I cried as he pounded into me, the sound of our lovemaking loud within the silence of the room.

He grunted, the sound rumbling from in his chest and filling my ears as he widened his stance so that he could reach higher, deeper.

I couldn't take much more. It had been too long. Tears pricked the back of my eyes as I grasped desperately as his shirt, my body tightening so much, I feared I would snap.

My skin lit up, burning under Gannon's relentless thrusts as they sped up and took on a more urgent pace. I bore down on him, clenching around him so hard, stars filled my sight and he gasped between my lips.

"*Lahra*," he breathed against my mouth, and my body prepared, readying for what he would say next. "Come for me."

I quivered and came hard, climaxing on a long cry as he slammed me against the wall. His cock flexed, hardening almost painfully inside me as he joined me in his orgasm with a harsh groan.

For a long time, I rested my forehead against his shoulder, panting, while he recovered from his own exertion. When he finally stepped back and pulled out of me, leaving a delicious trail of moisture between my thighs. The lack of support made me lose my footing, and I slid with a laugh to the floor.

"Good gods," I said, laughing and leaning back against the wall.

He stared down at me with a satisfied smile that made my hunger for him stir inside me all over again. He adjusted his clothing and glanced over his shoulder. When he met my gaze, all trace sign of amusement was gone.

"*Now* the bed," he stated, and my pulse leapt.

He held a hand out to me, and I took it promptly, rising to my feet with his help. I followed him on weak limbs as he led me to the bed.

"Turn around," he said after facing me.

Without hesitation, I did as he instructed. His fingers moved along my spine as he started to undo the long row of buttons that ran down my back.

"How did you get this dress on by yourself?" he questioned, amusement in his tone.

I closed my eyes, enjoying his touch as his hands grazed my skin. "I asked Rhoan to do up the buttons at the top," I murmured.

"You know," he said with a thoughtful note, "if you lived with me, then you wouldn't have to ask your brother for that type of help."

I stilled, my eye lids flying open. *All Above!* "You want me to *live* with you?" I blurted out, spinning around.

He snorted. "Forget I mentioned it," he drawled, eyes gleaming with mirth. "I've never seen anyone freeze in fear as quickly as you just did."

"No, it's not that." I frowned, holding my dress up with one hand. "You just took me by surprise, and …"

He studied me, curious. "And what?"

I chewed my bottom lip, working through my thoughts. I had considered moving out of the apartment I shared with Rhoan quite a few times, mostly after his nosiness got in the way, but … "I think I'd like to live on my own at least *once* in my life before living with anyone else."

He searched my face then nodded but didn't appear particularly satisfied by my reply, so I added a point he would easily understand. "Do you really think it's a good idea to give leadership any more reason to resent us?" I asked, resting my free hand on my hip.

He arched a brow. "Fuck them."

I stared at him then burst out laughing at how perfectly *right* his response was.

I went to him, wrapping my arms around his shoulder, and he held me close, grinning down at me. He had wanted to make me laugh. I could tell by how thoroughly pleased and self-satisfied he appeared now.

Still laughing, I pulled him down to me then and kissed him, hard and fast, startling him into stillness. I took advantage of his surprise and controlled the kiss, urging him to part his lips. When he did, I tasted his love for me on his tongue and felt it in the shuddering of his breath.

When we parted, he smiled down at me with heat in his eyes, but with an expression so open and yearning I nearly fell apart. His usual, unfettered arrogance was absent, replaced now by emotions that appeared to be as brittle as mine. I barely breathed as he touched my cheek, brushing his fingers against it, looking at each feature of my face, my lips, my eyes, my nose, even the hair curling around above my brows. When his touch moved to the promise ring hanging around my neck, he met my gaze with his pride and satisfaction, but above all else his *love*. I swallowed back tears.

Finally, he smoothed my dress down my shoulders with a gentle caress before helping me out of my bra and panties. When he gestured to the bed, I kicked off my shoes and crawled onto it before falling back onto the pillows and seeking him out. He wasted little time removing his own clothing and coming to me.

My gaze ran over him, drinking in the sight of his athletic build and graceful moves. He prowled my body, kissing every inch of my skin from my thighs to my belly up to my breasts, where he nipped and sucked my nipples into hard, wet peaks.

Gasping, I held him close with my fingers in his hair, relishing his touch, ready to be ravished by him again, but a moment later he raised his head and came to my eye level. I stared up at him, helpless, moved by the breathtaking emotion still brimming in his eyes. A second later, he pressed into me slowly, tenderly, sweetly. I stilled, devastated by his sensuous assault and how different, *overpowering*, it was to be loved by him such a way. A dull, yearning ache spread through my chest, nearly stopping my heart.

His gaze moved to the ring, now resting between us on my chest, and he bent his head to press his lips just beside it, caressing my skin.

"I promise to make every day you love me worth all the hurt and pain," he said, moving inside me.

I swallowed, mouth trembling as I fought back a wave of tears, but it was no use; they began to slip down the sides of my face and into my hair.

"I promise to hold you above everything and everyone."

My breath caught as he kissed my cheek and slid out and back inside of me with a gentle thrust.

"I promise to love you until I take my last breath."

He then brushed his mouth at the damp spot at the corner of one of my eyes. When he was done, he shifted his weight onto one elbow and used his free hand to brush a thumb along my cheek. "Do you understand what I'm saying?"

I nodded, cradling his face with my shaking hands, the importance of the vows he had just made not lost on me. We would never be married or partnered, not as long as the Realm's intercaste restrictions remained in place, but it didn't matter. What he had just said, everything he had done, meant more than any official ceremony or arrangement ever could.

No words could capture just how much I loved him in that moment. Even the words that I had given him readily now — "I love you" — seemed insufficient, lacking the required depth and meaning. So I didn't bother responding with words. Instead, I gave myself, my body, my heart, my *very* soul over to him as we made love.

* * *

I startled, my eyelids opening at the sound of a click.

Staring up at the ceiling now dappled with fading sunlight, I tried to recall my surroundings. An arm curled around my waist, reminding me at once. I turned my head and found Gannon lying beside me in bed, eyes closed, breathing steadily through his parted lips. I smiled. We must have dozed off, which wasn't a surprise. We had made love, fucked, then made love all over again before throwing in the towel. We had talked, touching and grinning like lovesick fools, until we had both apparently fallen asleep.

I reached over and slid my fingers through his hair. It was a terrible mess, as though someone had had their way with it, tugging and raking the blond locks ruthlessly. I sighed, still smiling, pleased that that someone had been me.

A slow creak by the door made me still. I lowered my hand and shifted, trying to push up into a seated position to look, but Gannon's arm tightened, keeping me down. I laughed. Apparently, his slumber wasn't very deep.

My body stirred as he rolled atop me with a grin, promising another round of hard and fast sex. I parted my legs, allowing him to wedge himself between my thighs, but froze, gasping, when something dark — *maybe a shadow?* — moved in my periphery, past the door.

Gannon stopped moving, staring down at me. "What is it?"

I glanced briefly at the door, doubting myself. "I thought I saw something," I said, trying to replay the image in my mind.

The bed dipped as he looked over his shoulder. When his gaze met mine again, he said, "Are you sure?"

"I think so," I said. "I heard something too."

His gaze flitted across my face before he pushed up and off me and reached for his clothing on the floor.

"It's probably Jonah," he said, pulling on his pants then walking to the door. He sent me a meaningful look. "Stay here."

I frowned, sitting up as he exited the room. *But if it's Jonah, why would he be lurking around?*

I sat, staring at the door, wondering what to do, whether I had overreacted. It more than likely *was* Jonah, which meant the protector had probably come upstairs to speak with Gannon and had seen his superior with me, both naked, in bed. I cringed, embarrassed by the thought. But when a faint sound of breaking glass filtered through the door, my embarrassment turned to worry.

I scrabbled out of bed, about to head for the door, but stopped when a vibrating sound filled the room.

Gannon's comm. It was on the side table, where he had left it just before we had fallen asleep. When it vibrated again, I glanced at the door and rubbing my lips together, trying to decide whether I should stop to check his device or go searching for Gannon. *It could be an important message about Gabriel.* With all that was going on in Summit and at the Protectorate, the Corona or some other member of leadership might have been trying to contact him.

I hurried to the side table, and Gannon's comm lit up with a message from Talib as soon as I picked it up.

Jonah delayed due to recent activity following the news coming out of Summit. Now on his way.

I stilled. *Now on his way? That means Jonah isn't here.*

So who *was*?

Pulse racing, I tossed the comm on the table and searched the room. I picked up the first piece of clothing my gaze landed on. I had slipped my arms into Gannon's shirt and buttoned it by the time I stepped into the hallway.

"Gannon?" I called out, cocking an ear to catch his reply.

None came.

I swallowed, peering down the stairs, but from where I now stood, at the top of the staircase, I couldn't see clearly into the foyer below. Holding the balustrade, I started slowly down the stairs, trying to steady my shaking hands.

Partway down, the front door came into view. It stood open slightly ajar, allowing in a sliver of light that sliced across the white tiles of the entryway.

Why is the door open?

"Gannon!" I called out more loudly this time, stepping off the last stair. My voice shook, the effect from my thumping heart.

Still no reply.

I looked around, wondering whether I should close the door, then noticed drops of what looked like blood splattered on one wall, to my right, and bits of broken glass scattered below, on the floor.

I gasped, covering my cry with both hands as I staggered back, nearly toppling onto the stairs. I screwed my eyes shut, blocking out the path of blood and glass that led to a space just behind the staircase. *Oh gods.* Heart jackhammering and every part of my body shaking, I forced my eyelid to open and hesitated a fraction of a horrific second before following the trail.

Please dear gods. No. Please no.

I didn't know what I was praying for until I rounded the staircase and my worst fear came into view.

"Gannon!"

I rushed to him, landing hard on my knees beside his motionless form. I cried his name again, skimming his body with trembling hands. There was so much blood! It was everywhere — on his chest, on the floor, on shards of glass.

I didn't how where to look, what to do! Panic filled my eyes with tears, but I blinked them back. I didn't have time for them. *I have to stop the blood!*

I ran my hands over every inch of his body, wondering why he didn't seem to be breathing or have a pulse, praying with every fiber of my being the cause wasn't the obvious one. I choked back a sob as my fingers skated across his forehead, and found the wound. Blood flowed lazily from a spot at his temple, oozing into his hair and onto the floor.

Please!

Sobbing now, I pressed my palm against the deep cut to try to stanch the blood. I wept, looking around, trying to understand what had happened. A large curved piece of glass lying on the floor nearby glittered in the sliver of sunlight. It looked like the top of one of the wine bottles that had been delivered as part of the feast Gannon had ordered.

Someone had used the bottle as a weapon. I stilled, going numb. *Oh gods. Someone who could still be here.*

"I didn't kill him, if that's what you're bawling about," he said, from behind me.

My eyelids slid closed at the vile and familiar voice. I didn't have to look to know who it was.

"At least I don't think I did," he continued. "But then, who knows? Men of his rank tend to be much weaker than they appear."

My eyelids flew open as I turned my head to glare at him. "How did you get in here?" I demanded.

Gabriel stood at the threshold between the entryway and the sitting area. He appeared as he had the last time I saw him, wearing all black and using optics that had made his skin and hair darker and his eyes green. He sent me a baleful smile.

"How do you think you got all this food?" he said, gesturing into the sitting area where the table in front of the couch was still covered in food and drink. "I came in with the help, of course. It took a little maneuvering to slip in with them unnoticed. Fortunately, Gannon Consul is a man who trusts his team to do their work and check everyone who enters his place of work or leisure. Your high chancellor probably assumed I had been vetted and didn't bat an eye when I came in." He grinned, glancing at his clothing. "And of course, I look a little different from the last time he saw me."

I recoiled. "How long have you been here?" *My gods.* What had he heard? What had he *seen*?

Gabriel smiled. "Long enough to hear you in the deepest throes of your passion," he said. "No wonder he kept you, Metallurgist. By the sounds of it, you're a really good fuck."

I gagged, sickened at the thought of him overhearing Gannon and me, maybe watching us, while we had been making love. "So that's what you've been doing?" I choked out. "Lurking around Gannon's residence house, like some depraved coward?"

"Of course not," he said, approaching me. I curled my body around Gannon, holding him close. Gabriel sniffed, seeming to find humor in my protective response. "As per security protocol, Gannon's protectors had to account for all the delivery staff to ensure everyone had left the premises. I returned just before you arrived." He frowned. "Though, now that I think of it, I should have stayed here after the delivery, after all. When I tried to use the entry code I had memorized from one of the help's tablets, it didn't work. It took me a few tries to get it right."

My body wilted. That must have been why the security system had reset, as Talib had reported.

Our plan to draw Gabriel's out of the woods had worked, but what good had that been? There was only one reason Gabriel would be here, boldly in Gannon's residence, and it couldn't be to demand any files as he had done in the past. His opportunity to use *any* information, whether from me or anyone else, was lost to him now that Heath — or rather, the Realm Anarchist — had run the story.

I searched my cramped surroundings, palm still pressed to Gannon's wound. My fingers had become slick with his blood, and so had most of the hair around his temple. Dear gods, I had to do something! Jonah wasn't going to arrive for some time yet, and I couldn't activate a call on my comm without Gabriel noticing.

Maybe I could use my tracking device! I grimaced. What good would *that* do? It wasn't that I had been abducted and taken away without a trace. Jonah and Talib knew where I was. I didn't need to be found — I needed help!

Fear raised goosebumps on my skin, then my heart lurched with a spark of hope when Gannon twitched, a barely imperceptible move that I wouldn't have noticed had I not been wrapped around him. *Thank gods!* Steadying my breath, I made sure not to react, wanting Gabriel to keep his attention on me, and not on Gannon. One way to do that was to keep him talking.

I glared up at Gabriel. "What do you want, Gabriel?"

He sniffed, approaching me. "There's no need for me to spell it out," he said. "I'm sure you have an idea."

A shudder moved through me at the menace in his voice. I tried to draw back as he stood over me, but couldn't move with Gannon's weight. I gritted my teeth, filled with rising frustration and despair.

"Gannon's protectors will be here any second," I threatened.

"Oh, I'm sure they will." He crouched down to my level, and the sight of blood on his hand made me hold Gannon even firmer against me. "That's why I'm going to make this quick. You know, Metallurgist, you and I are more alike than you think."

My gaze was watery as I glowered at him. "You and I are *nothing* alike," I hissed.

"I beg to differ," he said, looking me over.

He reached up to touch my cheek. I flinched, turning my face away, out of his reach.

He smiled, green eyes glittering. "I saw the Realm Anarchist's story about me," he remarked. "Very clever. Like me, you don't have a problem aligning with rabble-rousers to get what you want."

I narrowed my eyes. "I don't know what you're talking about," I lied through clenched teeth.

"I find that very hard to believe," he sneered. "First, Maxim's been captured, and then I've been framed as an informer, effectively driving me out of the inner circle of the Quad. What a fortunate ... coincidence that *both* your adversaries have been taken care of so tidily, and in one fell swoop."

I glowered at him, refusing to take the bait. I wasn't about to confess and take responsibility for anything that was happening to him or Maxim. They had brought their ruin down on their own heads.

"Your day of reckoning has been a long time coming, Gabriel," I said in a cool voice. "I'm just glad to be able to watch you suffer for everything you've done to try to destroy me and my family. I can't wait to see you punished for every one of your crimes."

Gabriel's gaze went hard as his hand curled into a fist at his knee. "Maybe you're not as smart as I thought you were," he said. "Even in the face of imminent death, you're as naively bold as ever."

Gods, I wanted him dead. Truly, I did. How could I not? Because of his fucked-up insecurities, Gabriel had tried to take everything away from me, and now he wanted to take my life. I was tired of living a nightmare with him lurking in the shadows, tired of his threats and having to plot ways to stop him before he could hurt someone I loved. Most of all, I was tired of his unjustified hatred for me. I didn't deserve it. If anyone deserved such contempt, it was *him*, and from *me*.

"You won't kill me, Gabriel," I said. "You're too much of a fucking coward to do that with your own hands."

Gabriel's eyes went hard, glittering with pure malice, before he backhanded me across my face. I lost my breath from blinding pain, toppling backward, away from Gannon, almost onto my side. Before I could regain my wits, Gabriel caught me by the back of my head and yanked on my hair, hauling me to my feet.

"You never did know your place," he bit out as he dragged me by the hair away from Gannon and into the sitting area. My bare feet slipped on blood and slid on broken glass as Gabriel propelled me into the other room. I staggered, nearly tripping over my feet when he suddenly released me. I spun around in the middle of the room and immediately tried to dart out of his reach, but he caught me at the waist and shoved me, with his fingers wrapped around my throat, back against a wall.

My hands flew to his wrists, trying to stop him as he tightened his hold.

"If only you had been less of a pretentious bitch," he said, leaning into me. "You and I could have been such a great team. The Quad could have used someone like you."

Team? My gods, the man was mad if he believed even for a *second* I would have ever sided with him and his renegade group!

I clawed at his hands, trying to dislodge his fingers, fighting for air. I tried to scream, beg, say *something* to make him stop, but couldn't get any air past his grip, so I shoved against his chest. It was then that I noticed how much blood was on my hands. My gods, it was everywhere! As I tried to fight Gabriel off, I left streaks of red on his jaw, neck and arms. He either didn't notice or didn't care.

I kicked out, intending to shove him away from with my feet, but Gabriel easily avoided my attempts by pressing his body against mine, pinning my legs against the wall.

I gasped, trying to inhale, but it was like breathing through a straw; I couldn't get enough. *Oh gods, I couldn't die! Not yet! Not like this!*

Gabriel's eyes gleamed with venomous intent, and tears ran down my cheeks as darkness closed in on the edges of my sight. My thoughts turned to Gannon. If Gabriel didn't kill him, he was going to waken and find me dead. What was it going to do to him to lose me so soon after we had finally committed to one another? My gods, Gannon would have to be the one to tell my family and friends that I had been killed! My parents would never recover from the loss! Tears choked the last bit of air out of my lungs.

My hands fell from Gabriel's wrists and my arms went limp at my sides. I had no fight left. That was it. He had won.

Gabriel jerked and his eyes suddenly flared wide. In a daze, gasping for air, I watched as he stumbled back, appearing confused before a fist collided into his jaw.

Gannon!

He grabbed Gabriel by the shirt collar and shoved him, sending him crashing into the table in the middle of the room. Food, cutlery and bottles scattered in every direction across the floor as the table shattered under Gabriel's weight.

I slumped against the wall as relief and fear flowed through me as Gannon rushed toward Gabriel. I tried to call out to Gannon's name but couldn't. My voice was hoarse and my throat sore from Gabriel's assault.

Gannon fell on top of Gabriel and started pummeling him with blow after blow. Blood still oozed from Gannon's wound at his temple, but he appeared unaware of it. He was driven, focused wholly on fighting Gabriel. For a second, it seemed he had the upper hand, then the balance of power started to shift. Gannon slowed. When he started to list to his side, it dawned on me that he was weakening, probably from the loss of so much blood. A moment later, Gabriel managed to shove Gannon off him and onto his back. He started to punch him, striking him in the face and chest.

I needed to do something!

I shook off the shock and fright and searched the room, looking for a weapon of some sort, something to take Gabriel out with, but my eyes found something better. A knife! The one Gannon had used just that afternoon lay now on the floor, by the fireplace. I hurried over to it as fast as I could on wobbly legs. Gabriel glimpsed me from the corner of his eye just before I reached the hearth. He must have spotted the knife as well and put two and two together, because a moment later, he lunged away from Gannon and toward me.

I cried out when Gabriel grabbed me by the waist and brought me down to the floor with a snarl.

"Kira!" Gannon called out, eyes going wild with rage.

He went after Gabriel and struck him in the chin, sending the other man reeling back. Gannon didn't allow him to regain his footing. He sank his fists into Gabriel's face so solidly, I expected him to pass out, but once again Gabriel proved me wrong. He gave as good as he got and didn't seem anywhere close to giving up.

I winced against the pain that shot through me when I tried to sit up. I had to help Gannon. He could only fight for so long before losing steam again. I searched for the knife, but it was nowhere to be found. It must have been knocked away when Gabriel took me down. I couldn't give up. Already Gannon appeared to be weakening. His breath was coming out in short, harsh spurts, and his punches were heavier, less quick.

A metal object glinted just beyond the two men, in the corner, within their reach, but out of mine.

"Gannon!" I yelled out in a brittle voice. "The knife!"

He paused his attack, hearing me, then searched the room. He quickly caught sight of the knife and lunged for it. Unfortunately, Gabriel saw the weapon too, and did the same, trying to reach the knife before Gannon, but it was too late.

Gannon dived for the knife, grabbing it, then flipped over onto his back at the same time Gabriel advanced. The knife sunk deep into Gabriel's chest.

The room went silent.

I covered my mouth with both hands, staring in stunned horror as Gabriel's body slumped and collapsed onto the floor at Gannon's side.

Oh gods. Oh gods. Oh gods.

Gannon sat up, and I crawled over to him, uncaring about the streaks of blood I was leaving on the floor beneath my hands and knees.

Gannon sat hunched over now, chest heaving, looking between his upturned hands, coated with blood, and Gabriel's body. I captured his shaking hands and drew them to my chest, just to get them out of his sight.

"Gannon," I whispered, then said it again, praying he would focus on me and not on his hands or the body laying deathly still, in front of us. "Gannon, look at me."

Slowly, his gaze shifted to mine and his eyes roamed my face blankly before awareness snapped back into place. He blinked, twisting his hands out of mine to capture my face. "Are you all right?" he asked urgently, bringing me close.

My breath came out as a shudder. I swallowed, forcing my mouth to work. "Yes," I said. "I am now." It was all over. The nightmare had come to an end.

EPILOGUE

Eight months later

I bounced onto my bed, sat down, cross-legged, and poked him right between the ribs. Gannon flinched and mumbled something indecipherable before dragging a pillow over his head. I promptly yanked it off, grinning.

"Wake up," I demanded.

With a groan worthy of the most gruesome torture, he scrubbed the sleep from his eyes. "Tell me you have a good reason to be up this early," he said, voice deep from sleep, blinking against the sun that streamed through the windows.

"I couldn't sleep any longer," I confessed and stretched out alongside him. My body was warmed instantly by his. "I'm too excited."

He rolled onto his side to look down at me, with his chin rested on a fist. "That's understandable," he said, smiling. "It's not every day a subordinate gets appointed to Realm Council."

I tried to suppress the tremor of delight that shuttled through me, but it was no use. After so many months and a lot of hard work, the day had finally come!

It had taken some time for me to regain the advisory group's focus and, to be frank, earn back some of their respect, but I had eventually managed to achieve both goals. Thankfully, I did, because supporting Realm Council throughout its review of the special committee's recommendation had resulted in the group working many a late night at the Judiciary — late nights that had paid off though when leadership finally approved exploration.

Gannon, armed with information from me and my group, had to make concessions, however.

Realm Council had refused to pass the recommendation if it didn't support the implementation of forbidden zones. Knowing there was much to be learned about the Outer Realm, Gannon had consented, and as uncomfortable as I had been with the idea of protecting leadership's deception about the worlds beyond the Realm, I understood that the compromise was the best option, at least for now. Realm citizens *needed* to know the truth about Zenith dominion, but there was much else to be learned before simply allowing them access to a potentially dangerous unknown.

In the end, the compromise didn't dilute the impact of Realm Council's decision. The approval of exploration was unprecedented, and gave the Corona the platform she had been waiting on to announce my appointment to Realm Council. Despite the string of events that had led me there, I bubbled with excitement now at the challenge that laid before me and that would start that very day.

I hope Asher likes Capita, I thought, *because I plan on finding him a role supporting me as soon as I settle in!*

My comm vibrated on my side table. I shimmied, trying to get out from under Gannon to reach it, but he beat me to it. He picked up the device with a grin that soon disappeared as he read the message.

"The cavalry's coming," he muttered, his face becoming drawn.

My family. I cringed.

"They've just boarded an arc craft in Merit," he reported, still focused on my device. "They should be here by early afternoon."

I studied his troubled profile, brushing his hair away from his temple. "You're not used to this, are you," I said. "Having the family of the woman you're involved with dislike you."

He made a face. "I'm more familiar with it than you think," he said, gaze shifting to mine as he returned my comm to the table. "I know it's too much to ask your fathers to like me, and to be frank, I don't need their friendship. But I'd like their respect, especially Khelan's."

I stopped playing with his hair. "Because you and Khelan are in similar positions," I guessed.

He nodded. "And because the life he's made with your mother is proof that everything between us will be all right."

My heart squeezed. Was it possible for me to love this man any more than I did in that moment? I touched his jaw.

"Khelan'll come around," I promised. "He's already begun to. After what happened with Gabriel, you saw how differently he started acting around you."

He snorted, shifting into a better position atop me. "Is that all it takes to get in his favor," he drawled, "killing a man to save your life?"

I scowled. "You mean *almost* killing a man," I said quickly.

He made a half-hearted, noncommittal shrug then looked off, staring at one of the many *Gallah* plants in the room. Apparently, Gannon didn't have as much of an appreciation for the difference. But I did.

Jonah had arrived shortly after Gannon had stabbed Jonah. After checking on his superior and me, the protector had contacted the authorities, who spilled into the townhouse minutes later. It was they who confirmed that Gabriel wasn't, in fact, dead, but holding on for dear life with the barest of breaths. Gannon and Jonah had immediately started arranging for Gabriel to be sent to a clinic monitored by the Protectorate. Days later, he was charged and sentenced to spend the rest of his days in detainment in the company of Maxim and other rebels who had been captured during the raid on Summit.

As much as I had despised Gabriel, and had even at times wanted him dead, I thanked the gods every day Gannon didn't have to live with someone's murder resting on his conscience *or* marring his reputation. His family already had enough to resent me for.

"Hopefully, *your* family will come around with regards to me as well," I said, moving my hand to his cheek.

Gannon drew back. "Of course they will," he said. "They already *are*. Why do you think Gillian invited your family to dinner after your appointment ceremony?"

That was encouraging; however, his sister's show of support only made the absence of another member of his family stand out. "But your mother's not going to be there."

He made a dismissive sound. "My mother's *always* been resistant to change," he declared. "When she realizes you're not some passing fancy, she'll come around."

I nodded, but silently wondered whether that was true. Maybe. If Gillian could have an about-face regarding my relationship with her brother, then maybe his mother could too. I hoped so for Gannon's sake. While I had never had much a problem ignoring the opinions of others about our relationship, Gannon continued to struggle with it. He would have preferred everyone focus on more important matters, like the fact that the Quad, with its remaining leaders, still ran rampant across the Realm. He had vowed to bring anyone aligned with rebels to justice and he had kept his word — to a point.

After completing the process to secure Gabriel and Maxim's detainment, Gannon had pardoned Uncle Paol for his connection to the rebels, citing him as a *victim* of the factions and not an *instigator*. By placing the pardon on my uncle's public records, Gannon had said he was ensuring no else in the Quad or in any other faction who knew about my uncle's dissident past could use it to threaten him or *me* for information again. The rebels would no longer have any leverage. When I had told Uncle Paol about the pardon and that he would be able to be with his daughter again, he had sobbed outright, nearly falling to his knees.

I sighed. I didn't like talking about our families. I just ended up sad. It was for that reason too that I had stopped asking Rhoan for updates about Tai.

I had only heard from Tai on two occasions since I had left his apartment in tears. The first time was after Gannon and my altercation with Gabriel. Tai had called from Summit to confirm that Maxim had, in fact, been captured and to find out how I was. The second time he reached out to me was after the Corona had announced my appointment to Realm Council, but then, he had only sent a brief message to my comm:

You're where you were meant to be.

I couldn't be sure whether Tai was saying I belonged on Realm Council or with Gannon or *both*, but it didn't matter. I had just been too relieved to hear from him again, if only through a brief and obscure message.

"Let's talk about something else," I suggested, not liking the morose energy that was crowding out my excitement.

"Very well." Gannon glanced about the room as though it were the first time. "I like your new apartment."

I snorted at his gall. "Of course you do," I said. "You're the one who ensured that I got approved for it."

His blue eyes widened with an admirable amount of innocence. "Me?"

I laughed. "There's no way I could have gotten approval for a property like this — in the middle of Capita and *five* minutes away from you — without your help, Gannon James Consul."

"What can I say?" he said with a grin. "It was the power of *your* influence, Kira Grace Metallurgist. Not *mine*."

I didn't buy that for a second, but tackled him on something else instead. "You mean Kira Grace *Advisor*, High Arbitrator to the Realm, don't you?"

He raised a brow. "My, my," he drawled. "How quickly we pull rank."

I chuckled. "You may as well get used to it, High Chancellor."

He brushed a thumb along my cheek with a grin. "It's fortunate for you that you have two allies on Realm Council who'll support you," he said, "because not everyone is going to stand by silently as you throw your weight around."

I cringed. "I wouldn't exactly count Liandra Ambassador as an *ally*," I said. "She could barely look at me when I met with all the councillors yesterday."

He shrugged. "She's still smarting — resentful, really — about everything that's happened," he said. "But she's back where she belongs on Realm Council and has a job to do leading her people. She'll figure it out."

For her sake, I hoped so. Because I had a lot I wanted to get done.

"Well, if I have to issue a few orders to get things done around here, then I will," I said, smiling cheekily now.

Gannon raked his gaze across my face, making my skin heat under his. "Oh, believe me, *Lahra*," he drawled. "I'll have no problem taking orders from you, just as long as you submit to me, and *only* me, in bed."

I rolled my eyes then pulled him down toward me for a long, exquisite kiss to show him I would *never* need or want anyone but him.

~

AUTHOR'S NOTE

I have a secret.

You see, Kira's story was only supposed to be one book — a stand-alone novel that would span her falling in love, rise to leadership, discovering her identity and choosing between the two men of her dreams. I was halfway through writing *Awakening*, the first book in Kira's trilogy, when I figured out that I had a lot more to tell about the Realm and the characters who filled it.

It's certainly bittersweet to see Kira's trilogy come to an end, but hers is just the first of many Realm stories. After everything Liandra Ambassador has been through, I think she's due for some happily ever after, don't you? You can read what's in store for Liandra on the following page. And, of course, there's Tai. How could I ever leave *him* out? He still needs to find that special someone who'll do absolutely anything for. I've got plans for him, so stay tuned. You're in for a treat!

With love,

Rebel

COMING SOON

Liandra's Story

~

Liandra Ambassador was once among the elite of all the Realm's castes, but a year after her life falls apart, she's still picking up the pieces, trying to fill the role her late father left behind.

When **Rhoan Advocator,** a disdainful leader from the lowest caste, is assigned to help Liandra regain her status, she struggles to keep her distance from the gorgeous subordinate. While unable to see eye to eye at every turn, Liandra and Rhoan must work together for the good of her people even as passion burns hot and bright between them.

~

The title of this standalone novel coming soon.
Check www.rebelmillerbooks.com for book release news!

INTRODUCING

The Hot Pursuit Series

Sera's Story

~

Seraphina Calloway is on cloud nine. After *way* too many years studying abroad, she's finally landed the job of her dreams — never mind that it's located at the same Ivy League university where her estranged father has just been appointed president.

It doesn't take long for Sera's excitement to wane when **Jackson Hunt**, a sexy, rough-around-the-edges professor, tells her a secret about the university's past that leads them on a whirlwind pursuit and into each other's arms.

~

The title of this standalone novel coming soon.
Check www.rebelmillerbooks.com for book release news!

ABOUT REBEL MILLER

Rebel Miller is a contemporary and futuristic romance author who over-indulges in Pinot Grigio, caramel popcorn and an eclectic mix of movies, music and angst-filled romance novels.

Rebel earned a graduate degree in Communications and Culture from Ryerson University and an undergraduate degree from the University of the West Indies in Jamaica.

Rebel lives in the outskirts of Toronto, Canada with her husband and two sons.

~

Follow her on [Facebook](), [Twitter]() and [Instagram]().